WINTER LOSSES

WINTER LOSSES

Mark Probst

FARRAR STRAUS GIROUX

NEW YORK

Published simultaneously in Canada by
Collins Publishers, Toronto
First printing, 1989

Library of Congress Cataloging-in-Publication Data
Probst, Mark.
Winter losses.
I. Title.
PS3566.R586W56 1989 813'.54 88-24335

for Maureen, who by example and by love . . .

... of all the possible paths to disorder, nature favors just a few.

JAMES GLEICK, "Solving the Mathematical Riddle of Chaos," *The New York Times Magazine,* June 10, 1984

WINTER LOSSES

But it took whole seconds for Kreg's mind to follow his body. Then he realized that he was standing and holding the telephone. He heard his own voice. At first it was a bark. It was hoarse, remote. . . . He began to place himself to get used to it being evening and to the fact that he was at home. That he was home from the office and had been sleeping in a chair.

He had said *yes* into the phone. Sleep still dragged at him. Now, in a different voice, he spoke again. *Yes.*

Adam, the man said. *Was Adam there? Was Kreg in touch with Adam?* The man said he was Adam's boss. His employer. He apologized for tracking Kreg down at home but didn't give an impression of sincere regret. . . . The thing was that Adam hadn't been in the office lately and he didn't answer at home.

A pleasant strong voice. Somewhat rough. Not loud.

"Lately?"

"A couple of days. But it's important, you know. He's very central to what I need him for right now."

No, Kreg said. He hadn't heard from Adam. But if he did, then who should Adam call? . . . There was his immediate apprehension of his son's damaged existence coming out of damage that he himself had caused, of Adam as a product of Kreg's own failed past. He had the sense of a turning point. And of his own inability to do anything. He remembered back fifteen years to when Adam was at boarding school.

Kreg had been out of the country, negotiating a contract in Milan. A rare foreign trip . . . a rare treat. He didn't have that kind of practice. So naturally the call came to Iris Minto, Kreg's friend, once his mistress . . . Adam's friend.

"Where are you now?" Iris had said to the scared boy. One in the morning and she was shaking herself awake.

"New Haven. The railroad station."

She was there at three. And she found a hotel that would take them in. She seemed hardly to listen to Adam's explanation of what had happened.

"Although later," Kreg said to her when he got back from Italy, "you went on the offensive." He meant the compromise she'd forced which got Adam back into a school from which, after all, he'd never actually been expelled but only left. Even his punishment for taking off was mitigated by an allowance for panic.

"I couldn't let them throw him out. Stupid headmaster. It was only circumstantial."

"Weak, you mean," Kreg said. "The money," he said. "Do you think he took it?"

"Probably. Maybe he didn't. I never asked him. Tell me about Italy. . . . Besides," she said, "I didn't attack. I persuaded the man. I do that for a living, you know. I persuade people."

Kreg ignored that. "You discussed with Adam, didn't you," he said, "what he'd tell them at school?" He was thinking of Iris *persuading* as she'd said. She held a job on a middle level in a large public relations firm, and public relations was of course an occupation having to do with persuasion. But Kreg always questioned whether Iris was suited to her job . . . whether she was sufficiently flexible. He was sure she would hold in the iciest contempt anyone who conducted her business by any but the most exacting standards of professionalism . . . but also that she maintained always a cool and unforgiving independence as the central standard of her life. How did such views accord with a business of persuasion?

"Of course," Iris said, "we discussed what he'd tell them. I never asked him if it was true." She met Kreg's eye. No apology in her tone or in the way she looked at him.

"But you discussed with him what he'd tell the school?"

"We didn't talk about it being true."

"Here," Kreg said, disapproving, "I brought you a scarf." He was thinking that circumstantial evidence was usually the most reliable kind. And wondering about going wrong. Wrong as a father.

More than a decade and a half later, through his office window, there was a bare stirring that brought with it the thick smell of a sour day in the early fall. . . . And with it an awareness of loss that Kreg sometimes got when he woke before light. Even when he was able to fall straight back into a full sleep, a sense of having had the feeling would stay with him. He'd decided this had to do with age. . . . And he'd had the feeling when this man called. It was a new thing for it to happen in the evening. Of course sleeping then, as he'd taken to doing, was a new thing too.

Well, the man said, it wasn't the end of the world if Adam had taken off for a few days. They sometimes did that. Adam would turn up. "So just tell him his office. Tell him Karl Van Atta. Or if I'm not here, he can leave a message with Mr. Frankel. With Ish."

"Do they?" Kreg asked. *This isn't right, he was thinking. He doesn't sound right.*

"What's that?"

"Take off that way? For a few days?" CALL CALIFORNIA, he wrote in block letters on a pad next to the phone.

"It's *are they ever here?*" Van Atta said. "That's the question."

After the telephone went dead, Kreg placed a question mark next to CALIFORNIA. He considered before he began to dial that Van Atta would already have tried this number.

Five rings. He was about to hang up. . . . It was a young woman's voice that came on. He wanted Adam? she repeated after him.

Yes. Could he speak to Adam? . . . No answer and he said that this was Adam's father.

After some short wait the woman said, "You see, Adam is away for a while. I kind of have the place while they're gone." She introduced herself. Tuke. She spelled it for him. *Tuk-ee,* it was pronounced. She was a friend of Debbie's. "Both of them but Debbie especially."

"Debbie?"

"Who lives here with Adam."

There had been a message, Kreg said. Adam was supposed to get in touch with his office. And he could also call home.

"This is his home."

"He could call me. His father."

"Well," Tuke said. "Then he'll probably be calling. I mean, wouldn't he do that?" Because she didn't know exactly what she could do. She didn't have a number or anything. But if she did hear, she'd pass it on that Kreg had called. . . . Of course Adam wasn't always so reliable about communicating. Kreg would know about that side of his character, wouldn't he?

Yes, Kreg thought, I would. That's something I'd know quite well. "Yes," he said. "I know that side."

"Debbie too. She's pretty much the same."

The sound of a nice uncomplicated Western girl.

Kreg asked if she had even some general idea where Adam had gone. And how long he had been away. Could she tell him that?

"I've been here a week." Tuke said it as if she were unsure about the distribution of valuable information.

"He had friends in San Miguel. San Miguel de Allende. Would he be in Mexico?"

"Mexico. Who said anything about Mexico? Look. *How do I know who you are?*"

Then there was no one at the other end and no point in calling back. He was sure of that. He went into the bathroom and heard the briefly comforting splash of his stream. Afterward he looked in the mirror and contemplated dumbly a reflected image that was never a source of pleasure to him. Those thick Rembrandt faces, as in the self-portraits, hardly sculpted by feature (his own face heavier, more punishing than the Dutchman's), could only be illuminated by something from within. But he saw nothing like that, no such light. Only a big somber powerful man in his middle fifties, not athletic, who often had it in mind that he should take off thirty pounds.

And with something of a tendency to melancholy, which Kreg accepted as he would a chronic physical weakness or any incapacity. He accepted his temperament as he did events and conditions. A quarter of a century ago, the failure of his marriage, now the weak character of his son, who, three thousand miles away, was as he was. Was a disappointment. Kreg accepted his own inability to laugh easily, to touch easily.

He was a practicing attorney and a writer on constitutional issues. A writer who for some years had not been writing. He was known in his field and was always satisfied that his reputation was deserved. Whether the work represented a significant achievement was another matter.

It was increasingly Kreg's view that it did not.

Significance in his view had to do with the release of force into human affairs. He did not see constitutional scholarship as performing that function. Not anymore. Or so he often told himself. But he remembered the work itself as something, not trivial or merely compelling . . . or rather that it had been when he was doing it.

Once he had been spurred by the idea of a system that permitted civilized conduct among men. He still did a certain amount of research. He was a horse for work and the notes piled up. But they were only notes. This issue and that. No focus toward a completed product. No *throughput,* as they said.

He began to think again about Van Atta. Did they really do that? Take off once in a while for a few days? *They.* Kreg had no basis for an opinion. And as to Adam specifically, he wouldn't particularly know. There wasn't usually so very much communication between them. And mostly whatever calls there were would have to come from him . . . so that Adam could hold to some necessary illusion of independence.

But there were exceptions. Sometimes Adam would call. For instance, there had occasionally been a quick need for Kreg to invest in some barely sketched-out project . . . Adam's entrepreneurial side . . . although actually these activities might have come to an end. Over a year ago Adam had made a connection with a real-estate group that operated for its own account, private investors with also an affiliated import-export business. Machinery and instruments, Adam had said, and he said it was all very profitable. He did seem to be making a truly solid living and his requests for money tailed off.

Van Atta, then, would be the head of that business. But what kind of business was it . . . really? Because, after talking to him, wouldn't you have to wonder?

Kreg went to the kitchen to make the first of the two drinks he allowed himself most evenings. This time, somewhat more whisky than usual. Then soda and the spread of fizz and the brown liquor going paler. Satisfying to watch. And the moment's anticipation before the first swallow. Also, he was trying to clear his mind, to stop thinking about Adam.

Which he was able to do by forcing the thought of another name. Marcu. He made himself think about Marcu and the shares Marcu had been buying.

They were the shares of a company Kreg still thought of as a valve company, although over the years there had been expansion into other areas. He had a long history with the company, which had been started by a client, Brandt, now dead, and he took a somewhat proprietary view of its affairs. Brandt had also left as much of the stock as made sense to a foundation which Kreg administered. He had a sudden recollection of himself explaining to Brandt (who hadn't wanted to be constrained) the rational limits set for such dispositions by the Internal Revenue Code.

There hadn't been a friendship between the two men. Not in any usual sense. They were two loners and they didn't socialize. But still the involvement and the tie . . . everything growing out of Brandt's unhurried and inexorable will to do his work. So that merely by being with him you were drawn into the calm terrific field of his expectations.

Now the conglomerate Marcu controlled had begun to buy Brandt Systems shares.

From the reports he'd drawn, Kreg knew that Marcu often took positions in what he'd been quoted as calling *value situations* and stayed with them. He had a portfolio of such holdings. But a history, too, of SEC filings, tenders, takeovers, allegations of greenmail.

Marcu's picture appeared in fashion magazines. He was a figure out of Europe after World War II. And had been nothing then. Now he did business on a grand scale and made regular appearances at benefits for major charities. . . . A connection, too, to Kreg's own recent experience. A dinner Iris Minto had given. Perhaps six months ago. A man named Cotton there. Recently divorced. Cool about that, generally cool. Cotton worked for Marcu and had immediately known that Kreg was counsel to Brandt Systems and a director. *She was attracted. You could see her watching him. The two of them watching each other. . . . There's a voracity when she wants something. And she doesn't hide it.*

Which wasn't really Kreg's business. At one time what Iris did and what she thought had been very much his business. But not anymore. Not in that same urgent sense. Now they were old friends, merely that.

Marcu, though. As to Marcu, where was the threat to a company whose stock was held twenty percent by the Foundation with Kreg in full control and almost as much more by management and employees, mostly old-timers, Brandt's people? But he would tell the other directors about Marcu. And about Cotton arranging to see him to tell him about this small position Marcu had taken in Brandt Systems stock. Probably a minor flap when they heard this. Jarvis Dalton especially. Jarvis was president, a hearty salesman. Timid under the bluster, Kreg always thought.

Kreg usually brought work from the office and there was a brief on appeal he could go over. He read and made notes on a yellow pad. Opposing counsel was relying essentially on a decision of a federal agency. This was a state matter but the court would be influenced. *Distinguish,* he wrote. *Dicta. . . . Matter outside area of competence. Also just wrong. Show why.* He began to sketch the lines of his own argument. After a while he made his second drink.

He thought again about Marcu. What if Marcu did go after Brandt Systems? What then? What effect on the parties at interest? Kreg thought about the Company . . . and the Foundation . . . and himself. The Company had no losing operations, no reason for layoffs, no operations to be chopped. What it had were assets and cash and earning power. And he thought about the Foundation, which didn't get from its Brandt Systems dividends the return any child could generate out of the proceeds from the sale of its stock . . . if it ever sold that stock.

There remained the question of the attorney for the Company, the controlling trustee of the Foundation. A man of somewhat abrasive manner or anyway not ingratiating. That man and the major portion of his income that derived from his position as counsel to the Company. What about that man? What future might he have under new ownership? If it should ever come to that.

Kreg refused to take into account any possible disadvantage to himself. But what would Brandt have made of this situation? . . . assuming there was in fact a *situation* in that sense. Certainly Brandt would have handled it. And would have felt no need for the support of others. *Dear God, I am fifty-six years old and still longing for someone to carry my burdens for me. . . . Another child of this weak age.* There was a sense of exposure, an almost physical crawl of shame over the skin of his back and shoulders.

At first you wouldn't have known Brandt's views. Because his considerations were private, kept to himself. Once in a while he might make some brief comment that had tangentially to do with the problem at hand. And when he was ready, he would call you in. You and Henry Juszczyk and Mouse Kelly. By that time he was only listening. He already knew what he wanted to do.

Brandt Valve, the Company had been called in those days.

Brandt had been a user of small notebooks. Pens in his breast pocket and usually some tool or gadget to handle. Silences in his conversations when he would look at you and maybe blink. Often at least some trace of a smile. A small man, fair-skinned. Spare. A moderate eater. He came out of a tradition of garage tinkerers, cellar developers, boys who spread disassembled mechanisms over whatever surface was available to them and later held briefly some factory job before starting their own shops. As Brandt did. He began to supply his small exquisitely milled valves to manufacturers of scientific instruments. Later he added lines of other delicate parts and expanded his customer base. He began to bid on military contracts. Before he died, he brought into the Company a microchip division. "Take us right into the middle of the computer age," he said.

He was without family, it seemed. Which later was confirmed. He had no apparent connection to his past except the slight accent, the occasional swing of his voice or weight on a modifier out of his Scandinavian heritage.

He gave the impression of a consistent good temper. The easy amiability of the naturally mild man. . . . Which he was not. Sometimes he made a point of holding your glance and he would be saying, possibly, that it was a shame this or that person had not worked out . . . or that he was a touch disappointed in him.

Of course the voice wasn't raised and there was no explicit show of anger. But changes would be made.

Brandt was a toucher. He would walk into his factory and run his hand over a workbench or the shaft of a lathe and rub machine oil between his thumb and first finger. He would put a hand briefly on a worker's shoulder when he stopped to look through the first run of a new line of valves. Small bright objects, parts for some most precise control or measuring instrument. . . . And at the spring outing (which was always held, which he started when the Company was a company of less than twelve) or at the Christmas party, he moved from group to group, almost in the hesitant way of someone who wasn't fully a member of the gathering. But there was his light hand here or there on an arm or back.

At one time, Kreg began a period of joyless heavy drinking. He was having his first difficulties writing and had come to believe that his estrangement from his son was irrevocable. The loneliness seemed intolerable. Adam was still at home then, a twelve-year-old picador of words (place this one only to prick you a little. But watch out for the jabber). Kreg drank at night when he came home from work. He always had a book by him but he wasn't reading. He drank until it was time to get himself out of his clothes and into bed. Sometimes he would realize that he'd been talking.

One night Brandt came to his apartment. With no warning and carrying a bottle of whisky. "Son-of-a-bitch," he said. "You want to drink. I'll show you drink."

Kreg eventually fell and Brandt was not there in the morning. What resulted was a cure through shame.

Kreg now began to think about his dinner. There was an Indian restaurant on Broadway. Maybe a lamb curry. Beer with it.

But his son's name began to sweep his consciousness. And he tried to consider just how it was that he'd failed him.

It was when Adam was eight that Kreg had divorced and the two of them began to live together, or rather alone. In the country on weekends, families with children asked Adam for an afternoon or a sleepover. Or for a cookout, with Kreg also invited. Iris had a place nearby and a different way of doing things. She took the boy shopping sometimes on a rainy day and had him with Kreg to dinner parties. At those affairs there were no other children. . . . She saw Adam also in the city. She took him once in a while to a museum or the movies. Adam liked it, being a little man, an escort. He was quick to put aside childish ways.

And it was a connection that lasted. It lasted when Adam went to boarding school. And when he got into trouble there and made the call to Iris. Who else, with his father away? Not Susan, his mother, a shopper and a taker of courses now in Marin County. A devotee, there in the West, of the extended cocktail hour.

Time together in the evenings and on weekends. He watched to see that Adam did his homework and they went to Forest Hills for the tennis. Movies, museums. But by the time the boy was twelve or thirteen, Kreg had known he was out of reach. Only a little contact would be enough. That message came through out of an ironic politeness that Kreg could never breach.

Except sometimes there were brief staccato exchanges that flared into warfare. And then the quick triumphant smile that crossed the wronged boy's face, the winner in some losing calculus of family conflicts. And so often a bright dig to close the exchange and feed the image of the clever wastrel with his twisted smile.

Objectively, Kreg always considered that he had done as much as a single father could (although he found, too, that objectivity was a quality of limited utility in such matters, a quality that didn't meet his needs).

"He wants to see you," Iris had said. He says Adam is 'very intelligent, but.' "

"The headmaster, you mean?"

"Of course, the headmaster. . . . You know," she said. "He's not like you." Adam, she meant.

"Then who is he like?"

"Maybe you're too moral for him. You try to lead a different kind of life."

That wasn't a response and not even a logical sequence but Kreg didn't push his question.

At the interview, the young headmaster of course had reaffirmed what he had already told Mrs. Minto about Adam being readmitted to school. And he suggested, not explicitly but clearly enough, that it might be better if some other place were found for him. *Possibly a kind of care we're not equipped to give.*

Kreg then had begun to turn over in his mind the idea that the world was recognizing Adam as bad goods. *Yes,* he said to the headmaster, *he would think about another school.* But he didn't really believe that to be a solution for Adam (if you were going to think in terms of solutions) and never did anything about finding one.

So Adam finished at that school and then was away at college and then he moved to California. He'd suddenly announced his intention to get into the motion-picture business. That didn't happen and there was never any reason to think the interest was serious.

In Los Angeles he seemed to fall in with an almost intellectual crowd. These people were oriented toward serious film but not on the commercial side. Kreg's impression was of light wills and of a set in which commerce, popular culture and the more easily accessible aspects of the arts touched gently against each other with no danger of significant penetration.

Since Adam had taken the job with the operation Kreg now knew to be run by a man called Van Atta, there had been no mention of his earlier friends. Kreg supposed that his son's connections were now with a different kind of person. More conventional business types.

He had supposed that until this evening, until this evening's conversation with a man who didn't sound like such a type at all.

He was sometimes made uneasy by his own quick willingness to accept the idea of Adam making his life on the other side of the continent. To prefer that, really. . . . In that connection he would think of Susan. The mild willingness (which had angered him) to relinquish custody of her son. *Probably that's right, she'd said. Probably it's better for him with you.* She had wanted it understood though that sometimes she could send for Adam. Would Kreg agree to that?

Alcohol heaven, Adam said pleasantly when he was eleven and he said he didn't think he'd go out there again. He was very jolly describing elaborate meals that never quite got served. The extra hour that carbonized the fillets and caked the creamed onions in the pan, a fairly high incidence of spills and dropped plates.

Adam told Kreg that it seemed to be a happy marriage that Susan had with her new husband, Ted. Handsome Ted, who nightly assisted his gently protesting, not quite with it, bride to bed. "Clean this stuff up in the morning," he always said to Adam about whatever mess there might be in the kitchen. "Find something in the refrigerator. Get yourself some dinner."

Although it wasn't usually Adam's way to talk at length with his father, he did so about his experiences in Marin County. About those, he was most informative. Forthcoming.

Kreg had his own memories of Susan but no comprehensive view of how she had got from then to now, from here to there. He listened to what Adam said about her life but didn't really reply to what he heard . . . which seemed right to him. He tried to show a polite appropriate interest and spoke pleasantly of Susan or not at all. But in his mind he picked over the news.

He thought of Susan's life in terms not so much of waste as of breakage. She had several times accused him of breaking her. How had he done that? Of course he would take whatever responsibility was loaded on but that brought him no closer to understanding what had happened between himself and the dark-haired professor's daughter.

In the beginning, as he knew it, there'd been a Wellesley girl who embraced with great enthusiasm the life he offered her.

She joked about what she wanted. "Marriage, motherhood, mind," she said. "My three m's." She wanted to pop babies and to take care of them and to read with Kreg through the long evenings of their lives.

Everything was nice. She met his friends and they were enchanted by this gentle witty girl who so often had a close observer's snap to what she said.

At first they did read together. Or Kreg had work from the office or he wrote. After Adam was born, she began to talk about going to work part-time. When Adam was older, she meant. Some kind of editorial work. She could do that, couldn't she? When she was ready, Kreg said, they'd set it up. They'd get an *au pair* for Adam. But he had noticed already the immediate fade of her energy against the strong demanding presence of their infant child.

Her disintegration came on in stages. Kreg didn't know what was happening. The TV was always on and it now seemed to take three hours to make their dinner. Nine o'clock and he would hear the sweet slur of Susan. Was he ready to eat? Would he come inside?

The apartment began to be filled with magazines. And it seemed to Kreg an unmade place, not overtly untidy but with the air of having been pulled together at the end of a sluggish and indolent day. Pulled together, perhaps, specifically against the occasion of his own anticipated return from the office. In that way there was the implication of something secret about the late afternoons of Susan.

It began too to be assumed that Kreg would take care of Adam in the evenings. Sometimes he took care of Susan also. He remembered himself (as he sometimes recalled himself) in the kitchen of the apartment, watching Susan, with Adam watching both of them. Susan, nearly through perhaps only her second Wild Turkey, moved with the unsteady dignity of the drunk toward the stove. Kreg thought he remembered a stew. Water left running in the sink behind her. She turned from the stove, the flame now so low that it flickered like a bet against the idea of chance. Lose out to any faint breeze that might blow through the room. Adam watching. That was the important thing. *I have to do something. For myself too. . . . No more of this.* She went to the refrigerator for ice. Always touching something to steady herself. She went out toward the bar. *And I went after her. I took the glass from her hand and led her into the bedroom. What are you doing? she said. But I knew she'd sleep.* Turned then to face in the doorway the blazing silent glare of the five- or six-year-old Adam, his fury directed, not at his now sleeping mother in her bed, but at Kreg who'd placed her there.

Why? What did I do? What else could I do?

Do something.

"Talk to me," Susan always said when they came back from a party or an evening out. "You never talk to me." Thick-voiced, she would say that . . . unsteady, swaying against his arm or the back of a chair. Falling asleep, she would be saying it.

Kreg might go to his desk or into the kitchen, usually into the kitchen, where he would sit with his arms flat against the hard flat table there and where he would endure the unfocused cycles of rage that came over him. Marriage, motherhood, mind, he thought. That had been a mere aphorism. Only that. A phrase going around the dorm. Where was the marriage? Where was the mind? And what kind of motherhood?

After the divorce he mentioned once to his friend Etkind Rossoff what Susan has said about breaking her. Rossoff, a diminutive chain-smoker who held his cigarettes in the European way between thumb and forefinger and wore a beret, was out of Germany in 1938 and knew about hard times.

"Yes," he said. "Maybe you were too much for her. Maybe with some nice soft man who would joke with her about two drinks and that's it, maybe she would be better. I don't think so, but maybe. So either way it's not your fault. You didn't do anything bad. It's just a talent for guilt you have. You let that take over."

Even so, an image recurred of the girl, Susan, in an old house through the unending winter of northwestern New York. Kreg thought of her there, alone with her father, the depressed widower, the taxonomist of spiders who had a laboratory in the basement and worked when he was home by the light of an overhead lamp. Kreg thought of those things and also of the winds that swept and bucked down from Canada and across Lake Erie and Lake Ontario. He saw himself hunched over his desk and Susan across the room, each facing the prospect of the evening and mildly desiring to achieve the condition of being *a couple together.*

"Of course" (Rossoff had also said to him) "I'm not sure she was a person to you. You know, the way they say it, a real person. Charm. It isn't enough you thought one time she was a charming girl."

Which was something else Kreg remembered when he thought about the long winters of northern New York. And he thought too that Susan would have known what he felt about her or didn't. She would probably have known before he did.

At the restaurant, Kreg allowed himself another drink and then ordered a curry as he'd planned. He'd brought with him *The Dialogues of Alfred North Whitehead.* After a while, he began to be dissatisfied with the book. Whitehead was thoughtful but a gentle tone was of absolutely no use to him at all.

The next time, just fifty hours (Kreg later reckoned) after the first call, there was no special attempt to be pleasant. Not hostile either but the insistent note was more dominant. There was more *demand* in Van Atta's voice.

Adam's boss, he had said. *His employer.*

Yes, Kreg thought. Van Atta no doubt was that. He was no doubt in charge of any operation he might be affiliated with. "Nothing," he said. "And you neither?"

"Or I wouldn't be calling. Isn't that right? . . . I take it you mean no postcard, no letter? No kind of message at all?"

Slow here. Kreg usually made it a point not to allow himself to be pressed. But not now. Not with Adam in whatever situation he was in. Because, yes, this did seem to be a *situation.* He thought about the man who had come to the building today. "No," he said. "No communication."

The doorman had mentioned the man. "Big guy, dressed nice," he'd said when Kreg was coming in. "He asked for Adam. 'No,' I told him. 'You're five, seven years late, you know. Adam doesn't live here anymore.' He tries to tell me Adam's here. He's on a visit home. Hard to discourage. I tell him anybody's in this house, I know it. 'So why would he tell me he's comin home?' he says."

". . . of any kind," Van Atta said, picking up on Kreg's mention of communications. "So it's a failure to communicate. . . . Listen," he said. "You know he'll surface. He'll be in touch."

"I'd expect."

"You tell him to call me. That way it's better all around. You tell him I said that? Tell him it's better he makes the call."

"When I hear from him," Kreg said. He said nothing at all about a big man here in New York who was inquiring after Adam. He assumed Van Atta would already know about that.

Then there was Van Atta ringing off and only, at Kreg's end, himself sitting foolishly in his kitchen, at the table there, still holding the receiver of the black rotary dial telephone that he had had for at least twenty years. The phone began to beep to tell him that it was off the hook and he reached to the receiver to cradle it. ADAM? he wrote on the pad next to the telephone. This was next to the message of the other day that was still telling him to CALL CALIFORNIA. Fly out there? There was no point to it. Where would he look?

A Friday evening. Friday in the middle of October. Usually by now he would be in his car driving north to his place in Connecticut, often accompanied during the last two years by the pretty woman he had been seeing. The woman had a rent-controlled apartment and a poorly paid job as librarian of a suburban college. She existed in a whirl of impossible parking situations and commuting crises. Naturally she wanted stability in her life but Kreg felt himself unable to provide it.

Continuing with her had begun to seem a pretense to a mild life he wasn't leading. He wanted something denser, more acute.

He had told the woman he had work that would keep him in

town over the weekend. But they were to see each other on Saturday for a while during the afternoon.

Adam's name or the idea of Adam began to run in his mind. Just that and a feeling of dread. He hadn't even the beginning of a plan. He had no ability to think.

Not a spectacular autumn. Hardly any of the leaves were flaming and dying. Kreg, with the woman on his arm, walked into Central Park.

It had turned warm and he could feel the sweat beginning under the scratchy wool of his jacket. And he felt the pressure of the woman's hand on his arm. It seemed duplicitous to let her hold him that way. Kreg's face puffed with the difficulty of what he had begun to say. He stopped and looked through a light haze across the landscape, the Great Lawn. Mostly touch football and soccer. One late baseball game. Vendors, pedestrians, dogs being walked. To the side of the pond, next to King Jagiello's statue, there was a circle of folk dancers. The amplified Greek music they danced to carried across the lawn.

Kreg heard himself speaking. He was saying to this nice pleasant woman that they ought, each of them, to look elsewhere. That this was to be a final break between them. The woman was still holding him and inadvertently he pressed her arm. She pulled against him. He watched the arc of a football. The perfect free loft of a long spiral.

They began to walk.

"Why?" the woman said.

Kreg had no answer that wasn't hurtful. *Why?* He remembered Susan. That one moment of anger. *Why, she wanted to know. And I had nothing to tell her.*

You have to tell me, Susan said. You have to give me a reason.

"Our relationship," the woman said, when he didn't answer her question.

She tended to speak mostly in ironies which was partly why Kreg had begun to think of her as light. *But what else could she do? What room did I leave her?* He began to consider that he had lived more or less alone for almost the last half of his life. He had in theory no preference for solitary ways. In fact, he wanted a partner. Warmth. So he often told himself. But he had failed with Susan and then with Iris and now with this woman. Others too. *Bastard, Iris had screamed at him. Blocked ungiving bastard. Will you please, just once, allow just one inch? Don't you know how to do that? Relax and give yourself some room? Give us both some room.*

Room for what? He no longer remembered.

"You want to be different," the woman said. She disengaged her arm.

"Different from what?"

"From what you are."

"All of us," Kreg started to say. Others, he was thinking, no doubt had ways of easing the pain they caused through conversations like this. *My point is that we were together and she cooked and we were at the theater and in bed.* There were ways of softening bad news. Certain ways of speaking. *So why can't I talk to her?* . . . Hard rock from a giant box marched over the Greek folk tune. . . . Surely there were ways. Techniques.

". . . are different," the woman said. She chewed at the inside of her cheek and said that Kreg was a holdover. A self-directed type that had gone out with the nineteenth century. "You operate from ideal views about the way things ought to be. And watch out for whoever doesn't measure up. But who can measure up?" Kreg was as hard, she thought, on himself as on anyone else. But that didn't really help now, did it? Actually a troubled man. "You would admit that, wouldn't you? That you're a troubled man?"

In the Ramble, there was no music. It was woody there but the light was held by the leaves. Only one stand of trees had turned. Yellow, yellowred, red, orange. All yellow on the ground though from the dead maple leaves. A boy in a black vest over a tee shirt sat on the backrest of a bench with his feet on the seat. A black wristband with studs around one thin wrist. A sour look for the wrong people.

"Nothing you want is going to work for you."

"Not if I'm on an evolutionary byway," Kreg said.

The woman said, "The perfect freedom of the divorced man." Then she said, "But it was only an arrangement. Isn't that so?"

Only. Everything was an arrangement. But not *only.* "No," Kreg said. "That's not correct." She wasn't actually crying. In these circumstances, it was impossible to take her arm. Or to hold her.

They began, as if they'd agreed on it, to walk to the Eighty-first Street exit.

Kreg was wondering if there was any chance Adam had called while he was out. Or if anyone had been to the building asking about Adam. . . . Adam might have tried him in the country, which was where he'd normally expect to find his father on a weekend. . . . He wanted to do something for Adam. He wanted to do something for this woman.

One week later, in the country, Kreg made a big breakfast of fried eggs with toast and bacon. Then two cups of coffee and he went into the barn and hitched a sickle bar to his baby tractor. There was a patch of brush he wanted to cut. Later he could work on the leaves. A light sharp wind came up. He found himself enjoying the moderate sting of it against his face and hands. But he also began to think about the woman's remark of the week before, the remark that nothing he wanted would work for him . . . and why that might be so. Pride, she meant, habits of intransigence. They were shields against nothing.

But there were no shields. *Vide* Job. And some things did work out. Adam, for instance, seemed to be all right.

During the week, he had heard from Adam. Kreg had been coming back from dinner. He had been unlocking his front door, not immediately without his glasses finding the right key. Then he did and he left the door open behind him.

No reply at first when he began to speak. "Hello," he said again.

"I see," Adam said, "you don't exactly rush to answer that thing."

"I answered it," Kreg said, "as soon as I could."

"That's all right. Take your time but I guess you miss a lot of calls."

So he felt the relief of hearing from Adam. A major anxiety allayed by this communication from the field. But the conversation itself began to be unsuccessful in the particular way of certain family talks. An intimate dynamic of missed connections, cross-purposes. "Your office," Kreg eventually said.

"I know about that. I talked to him." It hadn't been anything, Adam said. A big nothing. He'd decided to take a few days off and there'd been this humongous misunderstanding about whether he'd left a message. He got across his thought that somebody in his office was pretty fucking dumb for not knowing where he was. Also his less than high opinion of Tuke who was terrific about borrowing your apartment but less than that about telling you what was going on. "And not the greatest housekeeper in the world. We got back, we didn't exactly love the way it looked."

He'd spoken to her, Kreg said. He conceded that it hadn't been an enlightening talk. But now, he said, he understood. Everything was all cleared up.

Adam didn't know about *cleared up.* "It never is," he said. "Is it?" He coughed and then yipped like a puppy. "Excuse," he said.

"Excuse?"

"A little pain there. My ribs. I cracked a couple of ribs. *Alles* okay though. Ten days, the doctor tells me, and I'm new again. Healthy young man."

"This was while you were away?"

Adam didn't answer immediately. Then he said, "Windsurfing. I was Windsurfing and it got a little complicated."

"In Mexico?"

"Mexico," Adam said. "Yes, I was in Mexico." Then he asked about Kreg. Was Kreg going to take any time off?

"Weekends."

"Vacation? A week or two?"

"Possibly."

"That true?"

It was possible, Kreg said. He admitted there were no actual plans along those lines.

"And there won't be either. You won't do it. You should but you won't."

"I may not be able to."

"About living . . ."

"About giving advice."

"You don't think I should do that? I mean, I'm not qualified, am I?"

Kreg heard the immediate build of confrontational hoarseness in his son's voice. *Don't,* he told himself. *Don't respond to that.* But he wasn't able to hold back. "On the record?" he said. "It isn't the best record in the world, is it?"

So he heard the clunk of the receiver. Adam ringing off. . . . Kreg would have liked to have been able to bend. Be a bamboo in the wind, he thought. He would have liked to be able to explain, qualify, occasionally give in. Those things could be done. You didn't have to be abject. Just work with others. And wouldn't a kind of grace imply an ability to rest at critical moments?

When the tractor was put away, Kreg walked to the fence that divided his place from the one next to it. On the other side of the fence, Nathan Thatcher Hobart was pruning the scraggy ramblers that covered it. Chopping at the dead canes actually. Every summer they got out of hand.

The two houses had more or less a hundred yards between them, but nothing beyond on either side for quite some distance.

Nate Hobart, in his seventies, wore a denim shirt buttoned to the neck like an old-fashioned foreman. He was six-four, although now somewhat bent. Scraggy like the dead roses. Rich. Thirty years ago he'd abandoned his family and the advertising agency he'd built and had come up here to live. His reasons weren't something he discussed but Kreg over a period of time had formed the opinion that Nate's decision had had to do with a revulsion from lying as an integral part of his daily activities.

Nate straightened himself. Rubbed with his left hand against the small of his back. "Why I bother with this," he said.

"Why do you?" Kreg said.

"I tell you, lawyer. To keep it shipshape."

"I don't think so," Kreg said. Because he doubted that Nate cared about shipshape. Nate seemed in fact to let things go a touch. There was always a wash of careless disorder over his place.

Nate looked slightly away and commented that Kreg was alone that weekend.

"Yes, I am," Kreg said. "And I will be after this." He didn't explain but he said about the woman that things hadn't worked out.

"You see," Nate said. "I can't tell you she wasn't good-looking. But she was too nervous to have around so much. Not my business, though. You liked her was all I knew."

"Yes, I did," Kreg said. "I still do."

Nate scratched at his cheek with the point of the pruning shears. This evening, he said, they could have some drinks and put a steak on the grill. He had a clear, upper-class, Eastern seaboard voice that was only slightly reedy with age.

"Seven," Kreg said, thinking of the carnivorous rip of Nate at meat.

"Seven," Nate said. "Whenever you want, I'm here. I'm taking the bastard out of the freezer right now. So whenever you want."

Every evening Nate in a fresh work shirt had his two martinis. And tonight a bottle of burgundy with the steak. Kreg could see advantages to that style, to living well and not dressing up to do it. The isolation was another matter. A special taste. Nate poured brandy and scraped the plates. This wasn't an attempt at cleaning up. There was no need. A woman came in to do that. It was only so he could toss the leavings to the heavy-boned black shepherd he kept for company.

Afterward they moved out of the big kitchen and sat on Nate's back porch, somewhat cold, even in the heavy clothes they'd put on.

Nate pointed along the fence with the wild roses and down the slope of his property to where the fence dipped into swampy thicket. "What we'll do," he said. "There's a fair. Harvest fair. Whatever. Some damn name. . . . Tonight we'll go over there. Tomorrow, though, I'm going to sit here with a rifle. Aim it right down there."

They were slightly drunk.

Kreg said, "Why would you do that? I mean with the rifle."

"Lawyer, I want you to tell me something."

Why not? Kreg had no reason not to tell . . . whatever Nate wanted.

"How old are you, lawyer?"

Fifty-six. Kreg thought about it and then said it. "Fifty-six."

"Then you better get another woman."

"Maybe I should." Although, Kreg thought, he hadn't actually asked for advice. Not from Nate or from anyone else.

Nate got a bored growl because he was pulling the fur at the back of the shepherd's neck. "I'm not talking about pussy," he said.

"Then what?"

"Living alone."

"Although that's the way I always live."

"All the time I mean."

"Like you?"

"That's different. It's a special temperament I have. Which is what it takes."

"Probably. Probably you do. No doubt. . . . About the rifle?"

"Woodchucks. The son-of-a-bitches are all over the place." So tomorrow, Nate said, would be a day for sitting right here and popping the motherfuckers whenever they showed themselves. Nate did, a little bit, affect a country manner.

"You do want to go to that fair?"

"We're going."

"Then I'd better take a leak."

In Nate's living room there was a weight of books that someday, Kreg imagined, might collapse the slightly bowed walls of that old structure. Nate was a closet reader, as it were. Perhaps a secret thinker. . . . Kreg imagined a fall of shelves. One moment of shock and then an implosion. . . . But why would he think that? Why would he imagine that scene? The passing fancy of an *isolato.* Not at all what he wanted.

Kreg passed through that room.

Nate had a 1972 white El Dorado convertible with red leather upholstery. "Bought it off a pimp," he'd said when he got the car. Although of course that wasn't true. Now he said, "They're so goddamned refined around here."

"It's not a slum."

"They have their nice Mercedeses and their Volvos or some nice practical U.S.-made station wagon."

"That's what I have. A U.S.-made station wagon."

"And you're no disco delight," the old man said. "That's my point."

"Exactly. Two by two," Kreg said, thinking again about *alone.*

"Numbers aren't talk."

"Noah's way."

There was no room in the parking lot nearest the fair. Even so, Nate, trading on his age, swore at the cop who sent him farther down the road. But it was only his way of handling himself. You could see that he was having a good time. He was enjoying the stir and movement, the crowd.

When he'd parked the white Cadillac, he'd kicked a tire in the way a football player would slap a teammate's ass. He walked with Kreg to the fairground and talked to strangers and patted at their children. He maneuvered to follow just behind a firm butt in a cotton print skirt. He jabbed Kreg's ribs. "No pants under that," he said.

What was the point of that? Why the persistence of lecherousness in oldsters?

"No pants, goddammit."

Even with his dinner still high in his stomach, Nate bought barbecued chicken thighs and drank two beers. Then shot at marching ducks in one booth and threw quoits at bottles in another. Amiable. Civil to whoever came by. But that mood passed and he started to stand straight with a killer glare coming over his eyes. He started to say things about the ways people were dressed. Fat-assed girls in too tight pants. He said he was in a sea of leisure jackets . . . with *epaulets.* Which wasn't so. Those clothes had gone to the attic ten years earlier. And he said there would always be some horse's patoot who, if he was over thirty-five, would be carrying one of those One-Step cameras because he was too dumb for two steps, and if he was younger than that would have a box the size of a house that would be playing monkey music loud enough so it could be heard where they really had the monkeys. The idea was that he didn't think well of the culture as it had evolved around him. "Take that stretch," he said, "from Danbury to New Milford. Drive it some Sunday around noon."

"Noon particularly?"

"About noon. When they're all out there buying. Family time together." Nate, an old structuralist, said that shopping was the most potent ritual of the age. One that bonded families and reinforced certain systems of belief and practice. "Take a look at those stores," he said. "You see what they're selling and who's in there buying it. *How* they're buying it."

"Their style?"

"Style is pretty much what this conversation is about."

Kreg agreed that consumerism *en fleur* wasn't edifying to watch. He noted, though, that Nate had organized his life so that such scenes didn't have to be a part of his regular experience.

"The whole thing," Nate said, "it's everywhere. It gets so everything in the whole fucking country was designed by a woman gynecologist and Johnson & Johnson. It's all got two wide adhesive strips and it comes on a sesame-seed bun."

They moved into a tent with livestock. Mostly rams there. You smelled the sharp rich odor of the animals and of their shit tamped into the straw and dirt they stood on and of the raw wood of the pens.

Nate was smiling at a pretty woman of thirty. One advantage of his age: he could smile at them and they'd almost always smile back . . . as this one did now. Nate led the pretty woman's glance, as if a hand held by his hand, into the stall he was leaning against and directly to the pumpkin-sized testicles of the ram there. Nate, our old grandfather, old mischief maker. Whipcord body, wrinkles.

The woman threw her head back. Turned and moved fast to the other end of the tent. Hard angry athletic movements.

Nate was naturally, Kreg thought, a little cruel. Seigneurial too, no doubt, in his relations with attractive women casually met. Formerly seigneurial.

Nate was watching in the direction the young woman had

gone. "Nice high tits like those," he said. "Time was." He focused directly on Kreg. He had to turn his whole body to turn his head, an arthritic limitation that certainly galled. But all that showed in his eyes was a flare.

Whatever it is he's remembering about *time was,* Kreg thought, he isn't regretting it. He doesn't regret anything. Resentment, though, was something else and something Nate might have.

Nate looked into the pen. "Animals," he said. If he was explaining anything, it wasn't clear what.

"Yes," Kreg said. "Of course."

In the next tent there were cattle. Black Angus. A bull, some cows, mostly calves. And in the tent after that, there were Charolais. Placid, the color of dirty cream. The cattle of the gentleman farmer. Where were the Holsteins? Then an exhibit of light farm machinery. The salesmen had little desks and tables with advertising literature, which had probably at first been arranged in neat stacks but wasn't that way anymore. Now there was a loose spill of pamphlets and folders, some of them on the floor. Clots of men, not weekenders, were talking to the salesmen and had an air of having been there for some time. There were paper cups on the tables with the marketing debris. This was a gathering of insiders. Old buddies. Decorous enough. Just private.

Nate knew the John Deere man and talked tractors for a while with him and with the other local men. "Give all my business to Harvester," he said when he and Kreg were leaving.

He put an arm around Kreg's neck and, with one of the salesmen's cigars angled up in the corner of his mouth, led him outside. He was like a tall old sailor let loose for Saturday night.

A six-footer with knotty shoulders, no waist, jeans that had been washed to the intimate softness of a second skin over the blocky curves of his upper legs and buttocks, had stripped to a tee shirt. And he dropped a sledgehammer now onto its flat target, as if with no special effort at all. The indicator shot its twenty-five-foot height and a bell rang.

A middle-aged woman with a silk bandanna around her head and flannel slacks and a light turtleneck was watching the strongman. Possibly to see him ring the bell. Or possibly to watch the bunch and shift of muscle under his tee shirt. *B,* Kreg guessed. Maybe *a* and *b* but not *a* alone. It was Iris Minto.

Iris put her hand on Kreg's cheek. Held it there for a moment. He was immediately conscious of his own bulk. Because he was always aware of Iris as long-boned and graceful. A type to be preferred to his type. Nate also had that build and, even past seventy, had, like Iris, the air of racy, aesthetic superiority that Kreg associated with it.

"Very nice," Iris said. She moved her hand from his cheek.

She wasn't beautiful. Long, bony face. Kreg tried to decide whether objectively she could be considered handsome.

Like him she had divorced early and not married again. But she had a little family money and also, like Kreg, an apartment in town and a house here in the country. She had a reckless manner which Kreg admired in some ways. Iris was usually with a man. Years before it had been Kreg for a while. She'd thought she'd be fine with a burly lawyer who tended to get abstracted when one thought crowded too closely on another. Later she told him she'd had a need then to be with someone easy.

Kreg never completely believed that. Because Iris might go through a wintering period but she wasn't dependent. Set her off, which wasn't hard, and it was cut and slash. She'd screamed that he was a stone. *Just answer me. Say something.* But he hadn't been able to. He hadn't even tried to hold her wrist or evade the blow when she slapped at him. . . . *Very nice,* she'd just now said. Kreg decided to assume she meant the evening. The fair. Yes, he said. It was. It was very nice. Although more organized than it used to be. And he wasn't sure he liked the change.

"Not that," Iris said. She stared blankly at him as if confronted by a kind of primal obtuseness that couldn't politely be dealt with.

There were characteristics, Kreg decided, that Iris had in common with Nate Hobart. A predisposition to arrogance, for instance. *You will know what's in my mind.*

Nate had the expression of a referee who saw things getting out of control and had decided just to let them go. Just watch what happened and enjoy the sight.

She'd spoken to Adam, Iris said.

Kreg said that, yes, Adam had been on vacation and was now back. Presumably he was touching base with old friends and family. Which was fine. Exactly what he should be doing. *Communication from the field, he'd thought when Adam called.* He asked if Adam had mentioned money.

"I might lend him money," Iris said.

"Some?"

"Some. If he asked."

"If he needed it?"

"No. If he asked."

"He probably knows that."

Iris said, "It wasn't money. He wanted to talk to you and you weren't home."

"When was this?"

Dinnertime, Iris said. "A couple of days ago. It was in the city." She remembered that she'd been holding a chicken leg while she talked to Adam.

"He thought I'd be at your place?"

"You sometimes were."

"He was remembering back," Kreg said, "to when he was a boy." Because it was when Adam was eight that Kreg had divorced and his affair with Iris had started.

"Actually," he said to Iris, "I spoke to him yesterday."

"And all went well?"

"It wasn't a completely successful conversation."

"That's too bad," Iris said. "It's too bad for both of you."

Now Kreg asked Iris how had Adam sounded. Had he mentioned anything that might be bothering him? Anything at the office?

"Nothing like that."

"Did he say where he was?"

"That didn't come up either. Should I have asked him that?" Iris showed a level gaze that she got when something was bothering her.

Kreg suddenly recalled an episode from the time of his affair with her. One whole afternoon they'd spent in the small upstairs bedroom of her house that was maybe four miles from where they were standing now. It was July or August in the kind of heat that stunned the countryside. A small fan going, old-fashioned window shades, green fabric on one side, cream on the other. No sound from outside. But his sense of lazy dangerous wasps there. Their potential for arousal and swift attack. "Say my name," she said when she was ready, but angry that she'd said it. Angry with him for hearing her say it. . . . His recollection was intense, essential. Complete. *Why would that come to me now?*

Nate, a little out of line, was rolling his eyes at her. Red eyes of a wolf at night.

"No," Kreg said to Iris. "No reason you should have asked him that."

They walked out of the fair to where Iris had her car. The ground wasn't perfectly level and somebody bumped into Nate and he tripped. Kreg caught his arm so he didn't fall. But he was old and he'd had a full evening and more to drink than he should. His fatigue began to show like a burden. Even so, he tried to get Iris to come back with them. One drink, he said. A nightcap. Then they'd send her home. He promised.

But it was too late, she said. She didn't think she could. Not this time.

When they got to Iris' car, Nate let Kreg help him in so she could drive them the quarter mile farther to where the El Dorado was parked. Kreg said maybe it would be better if he drove from there.

"No you don't," Nate said with no force but with conviction. "What I'll do for you though, I'll keep it under forty. . . . Come by some time," he said to Iris.

"I know the way."

"Well, you do," Nate said. "So don't be remote about it. Just come by some time." He closed his eyes.

Iris put her head against the wheel. Briefly she looked sideways to watch the old man next to her. Kreg was still outside the car on Nate's side. Iris looked up and caught his eye and then straightened up.

It was fairly complicated getting out of the parking lot. Cops were waving their arms and pointing. Cars flashed their lights and honked and got themselves into bull-headed arrangements with no room to back away from them. But eventually there took place a slow actual clearing of these bottlenecks, which might have been thought to represent in some larger sense a hopeful sign.

With that much confusion, it was ten or twelve minutes before Iris pulled up next to Nate's white chariot. By then Nate looked in charge of himself again and he got himself from one car to the other on his own. Kreg came around to Iris' side to say good night and she reached for him and kissed his cheek. "Do it," she said. "Give him a call. You'll feel better."

"Trust you?"

"Trust me."

Of course Nate wouldn't let Kreg drive but he did hold to his promise about speed and he slowed even more for curves and at crossroads.

Mostly when he was in the country Kreg used the kitchen for his sitting room and the big table there as a desk. He took an apple and some grapes and made a cup of tea and got out the papers he'd brought with him from the city. He always had work, his weekend burden.

He looked at the telephone. In California it would be early evening. Why not? he thought. He would do as Iris had suggested. And there was a reason for the call. He could ask Adam how he was coming along. His ribs. *Adam's ribs.* He dialed and held on for quite a while but got no answer so he went back to his papers. Grant applications for the Foundation. These days it was the Company and the Foundation, Brandt's creatures, that took most of his time.

Not a large foundation. Kreg and Etkind Rossoff between them read and screened and passed on whatever there was. Rossoff, a professor of international law at a poorly paying New Jersey law school, needed the money the Foundation paid.

The two lawyers stayed reasonably close to what they knew. Mostly they funded legal studies, although not always. Kreg tended to accept anything he thought intelligent. On principle, he told himself, he didn't want to be too pure. The application before him now had to do with linguistic patterns and political structures. Not a fresh approach but the applicant seemed smart.

Kreg was predisposed to approve it. He knew he could expect an argument from Rossoff. Rossoff would accuse him of trying to be an intelligent amateur in an eighteenth-century way.

More or less weekly, they dined together. Usually on goulash or boiled beef at a Czech restaurant that Rossoff had found. A middle-aged crowd there, many ethnics, and no music while you ate.

When Kreg went silent, Rossoff rolled on. A conversation with himself as it were. But *at* Kreg. *And sooner or later he gets me talking. And there's never afterward a sense of an evening badly spent.*

Rossoff always wanted to know why Kreg wasn't writing. *Because you don't know if the work will be useful? I don't believe that. Nobody knows if his work will be useful.*

What do people know about their work . . . in that sense?

They know they do it.

And why?

Sometime you'll start again.

Not an answer, is it?

It will be.

Two hours later he had three applications completed and he went upstairs to bed. Before sleep he thought of course about Adam . . . and about Iris. Fifteen years ago had she really not cared if Adam had taken that money? Preferred not to know (perhaps because knowing whether Adam had or had not stolen was unimportant, because she'd already known what Adam was and with or without conscious reflection had, however far back, decided that she was on his side)? It had been just after that spring, with Adam back in school, that his affair with her had ended.

Ten weeks earlier, at the beginning of August, Marcu worked every night until ten or eleven o'clock. Nobody could keep up with him, a man of almost seventy. On Friday his desk was clear. For lunch he had a minute steak and a glass of apple juice at his desk and he called Cotton into his office. "Now we can talk," he said. He told Cotton to ride to LaGuardia with him, but Claire was in the car and Marcu would only joke with her about her packages, the things she'd bought. His seventy-year-old, never married secretary was in the front seat next to the chauffeur. Her ears went red when Marcu asked Claire in detail about the cut of this year's bikinis. Marcu wondered what did she think of Claire? What did she think of a woman in her early forties with that free laugh and the evident sexuality that brought her silk, jewels . . . whatever she wanted to have, keep or crumple and put aside (that brought her him, Marcu).

The Beechcraft was already tuned up, waiting for them. Marcu and Claire fussed to make sure the secretary got comfortably aboard. Marcu told the chauffeur they wouldn't need him tonight. He could drive out in the morning. Marcu passed money to the man and suggested an evening out. "But with your wife," he said. "Listen," he said to Cotton. "Brandt Systems. Maybe that's interesting. Think about it."

In the country Marcu wore light cotton and espadrilles and went into Southampton every morning. In Job's Lane he bought wicker tables and cast-iron lawn chairs and three-foot porcelain animals. Claire would come back from tennis and look over what he'd got. She said they'd need a larger house. She hated clutter. She wanted fish for lunch.

"You'd like that?" Marcu said. "A larger house?"

"You'd fill that too."

Sometimes he played gin on the lawn with a fat man, Bronheim, to whom he'd sold some television stations. Bronheim had persuaded Marcu to stay on as a director. He was new out here. Worth forty million and impressed by eastern Long Island. Marcu didn't mind it when Bronheim got nervous and started making calls to the city. Bronheim's passion for his business covered him like a sweat. Marcu enjoyed the thought that he had more money than Bronheim and that he made everything he did look easy. All month he went into New York only three times. But those trips were nothing. He was gone and in a few hours he was back.

The fat man knew nobody and Marcu took charge of that. He arranged for Bronheim to give a clambake one Saturday night. Fifty guests: a crew came in to do it. Bronheim enjoyed himself and did it again two weeks later. He was convinced that he was making friends. By then he was able to talk knowledgeably to his children's tennis instructor. Marcu, observing, thought the man was thrilled in some obscure way because a blond square-featured boy was speaking to him with no particular show of respect.

The next afternoon he made a suggestion in a business matter. Bronheim said he was a genius. "Only a good analytical mind," Marcu said. Genius, he said, required an ability to brood, which he didn't have, a way of placing the unconscious at the service of the will. He said any hippie child would understand what he meant. The ironic tone came through. Bronheim was dimly aware he was being teased, decided that Marcu was talking nonsense, didn't answer. "What I do is nothing," Marcu said, smiling. He said qualities were to be judged by their effects. He might have been serious.

Bronheim spread his hand. "Go down with two," he said.

Marcu was able to lay off a king. He had two melds. Threes and eights. He added the other cards. "Seventeen," he said.

"In spades."

"Tomorrow," Marcu said. There was a new place for seafood. Dinner, he thought.

Bronheim flushed slightly and tucked his chin into his shoulder the way he did when he was going to lie in a negotiation. Not the kids, he said. They had other plans.

Marcu understood. The man in some ways was old-fashioned and didn't want his children exposed too closely to a mistress, and Claire was always with Marcu. What did he think they were exposed to in the homes and discos and pubs of this area? Or in the city? "The four of us," Marcu said. "That's what I'd assumed." He began to think about disentanglement. Bronheim wasn't pleasant. He didn't like the man. And there had been something in his background. A union matter. Men had been indicted and gone to jail. An association like that, someday, could be troublesome. *But plan it.* Marcu didn't have to remind himself. Caution was a habit.

The restaurant offered stewed fruit for dessert, compote. Not often available these days and Marcu ordered it. Bronheim pointed to his wife. "At our place sometime," he said, "you have that. It's something she does herself. She don't leave it to the cook."

Marcu took a spoonful of the fruit. His own mother, he said to Bronheim's wife, had made a compote every week. A similar receipe. Very much like this. He was charmed by the thought that what he said was true.

Mostly when he spoke to this woman there was social panic. She waited for her chance to look away. She had on a dove-gray dress with padded buttons in the same fabric as the dress. She was heavy, awkward. Marcus decided that she was not a modern wife. Both she and her husband seemed uneasy in a place where lean tanned people overpaid for small portions on oversized plates. Bronheim, though, did have a focus for his attention. Claire's breasts.

Before dinner he'd put a hand on Marcu's shoulder and rocked his body. "You bring your credit cards?" he'd said. "Because I forgot my wallet and I'm so hungry." Marcu hadn't tensed against the weight of that meaty burden. But he decided that Bronheim was too close . . . and not only then.

Where? Bronheim's wife was asking. Where was it that his mother had made the compote?

"Budapest," Marcu said, remembering journeys but not Rumania before them. A piece of apricot was trapped between two molars. He ran his tongue into the gap, dislodged the morsel, swallowed. His recollection was of a dining room in a pale brown color (that he'd later seen in one of the large rooms of the Assembly Halls in Bath) and fairly sparsely furnished. Not usual for Central Europe in the twenties. He remembered french windows and a view into the back garden and himself in a sailor suit.

After Labor Day he came into the little gym that was used by his senior executives. Cotton was on his back, lifting weights. They talked for a little about Southampton. This was his own favorite time, Cotton said. Late summer, early fall. Marcu should try it. Just for a weekend once in a while. Why let the place sit empty because the calendar said September? He sat up and wiped sweat with a towel from his face and shoulders.

"You like it when it's not so crowded," Marcus said. And then he said, "Brandt Systems," as if that followed from the other.

Cotton said he'd been thinking about that too. Give him five minutes, he said.

Later in his office Marcu talked about other matters. But he took the dossier Cotton gave him. It came back to Cotton after a few days with a note that read, *Hold for your files.*

Toward the end of the month Marcu commented abruptly that Brandt had had to take a large inventory write-off a few years back. A week later he said, at a time when it wasn't relevant, that those people didn't know how to *market* their stuff. They left the office together. Cotton's apartment was the first stop. Marcu leaned out of the limousine. "Why don't you get me a rundown on that foundation?" he said. Cotton knew which one he meant. It was the one that held twenty percent of Brandt Systems' stock. Marcu's request wasn't a surprise. There had been signs, Cotton thought.

Sales and revenues, fiscal years ended April 30:

1985	1984	1983
$128,637,421	$104,581,374	$89,701,938

Brandt Systems Annual Report
page 11

In the evening the company limousine, with a different driver now, came back to Cotton's apartment. Cotton had changed to a darker suit and had changed his blue shirt for a white one. He gave the driver an address in the east seventies. A woman he'd met some months ago and who always until now had declined when he asked her out. He was slightly intimidated by an air of disinterested contempt, although that also kept her in his mind.

The doorman rang up and started to speak but Cotton took the house phone. "I'm early," he said to Iris.

"But you don't have to come up," she said. She didn't say how long she'd be.

It was only, as it turned out, a few minutes. And while Cotton was waiting he was careful not to pace the lobby.

He took Iris to a very expensive restaurant and after that to a club. Not one of those places that catered to the kids, he said. "So it isn't that bad. Not too noisy."

Halfway through her forties, Iris was more angular than once, but Cotton thought she made a fine entrance. Good clothes and a long sure stride. Before they got to their table, he stopped twice with her to talk to people there.

"Everybody knows you," Iris said. "Do you come here a lot?"

Cotton made his living at game playing in the service of an unpredictable master. He was always in training and liked to think he could handle whatever might come along. It was a small thing Iris had said but his mind rocked with his sense of power here. He had a new conception of his short-term future. It seemed impossible that he'd been apprehensive about her.

At the table, she said he seemed to manage very nicely for himself.

What did she mean? he asked her. *Manage?*

"Having it all your way. Just the way you want it."

"I've always done that."

Then there was a quick carved smile that bothered him. He should have guessed she had a cutting edge she sometimes held back for a while. Hadn't that been evident when he'd met her before? . . . But he didn't mind. What he couldn't take suddenly, he could maneuver around. In fact, that might be the more natural way. "Why do you use Mrs. Minto?" he said. Because that was her maiden name.

"I didn't enjoy the marriage that much. Do you want me to commemorate it?" The lights dropped except for random plays of blue-white from the spots and an electric guitar kicked into a screech opening, but modified, toned down for a place like this. "If we're here," Iris said, "we might as well dance."

She blinked like a cat. Cotton followed her onto the floor. She danced without touching him and managed in that crowd to appear as if she had whatever room she needed. She had hard graceful movements. A young man in a tuxedo cut in and she danced with him. She was no closer to him than she had been to Cotton but there was no doubt he was her partner in the dance and not just with her the way Cotton had been. The young man brought her back to the table and when he left Cotton said it wasn't usually done like that.

"How isn't it done?"

"Cutting in. This isn't a country club."

"I've always done that," Iris said. "Just the way I want to. *If* I want to."

Cotton was excited by a quick careless punitive glint.

"You could get me another drink," Iris said, "and then you could take me home." At her door she said, not asking what he wanted, that he could come up for ten minutes. "You could use a brandy, couldn't you?"

Cotton saw that she had some good things. Antiques, but only fairly well kept up, he thought. And nothing that was truly distinguished.

Iris slid down in a soft chair, almost on her spine, legs extended in front of her. She asked about his job. She wanted details, specifics. Did he actually run any part of the business? Did he do the acquisitions? When she'd heard enough, she cut him off in the middle of a sentence. "Then it's very high-level, isn't it?" she said.

A disclaimer could only have been a kind of evasive modesty and not, that Cotton could see, useful to him. So he said that yes it was high-level. "Obviously."

"But it isn't really a *line* job, is it?"

It occurred to him, leaving, that it wasn't out of delicacy that Iris hadn't asked about his family. It would have been natural at least to have touched on the matter of his relationship with his former wife . . . or at least his children. Natural to most people.

But a week later, when he was still planning an approach, she called him at his office and said she didn't especially love those bars he seemed to want to go to. If he felt like it, he could take her to the ballet. *Giselle*. . . . She sat erect and wore her glasses when she looked at the program. "At my age," she said, "I need these." He tried once to put his hand on her arm but learned better. In the next few weeks there was a play she wanted to see and there were some exhibits. One night she said to him, "Don't you ever *do* anything?" In bed she said that at least now he did have a line job.

There began a relationship of service. Mutual and never close and interrupted by Iris' jagged moods. She had a terrorist's disregard for rules and there were no privileged occasions. Cotton learned only gradually that he'd always before played by civilized standards . . . in some accepted frame. It was a question of boundaries . . . from above him, still impaled on his skillful meat: "I want to know." This was before she'd even completely finished. Before the final shudder. With Iris these reflexive spasms weren't quickly over.

His forearm covered his eyes. "What did you want to know? Right now?" She hadn't released her grip from inside.

"Right now," she said, "I want to know about the life of the rich free man."

"His inner state?"

"Yes. It has to do with his inner state. With why he's so concerned to help out us more mature girls." What interested her was, didn't he know about the allure of really shining hair, firm flesh? "I mean, aren't you *attracted* by that kind of thing?" She was sure he was. So why this *odd,* if he didn't mind her saying it, affinity for the older lady? Not that she didn't have her thoughts. What had occurred to her was some mildly kinky attraction to the type. Rooted, no doubt, in feelings that most men outgrew. Thin breasts hung over him, brackets to what she'd said.

But there was progress too, and at unexpected times. He looked into a book she was reading. How some primitive tribe handled its refractory women. Gang rape. *We tame them with the banana.* He had a sense when he read that out loud that he'd gone too far but Iris was thoughtful, almost friendly, when she answered him. "Yes," she said. "I suppose they do. I can't see you, though, in any situation like that."

October passed and most of November.

When he made an appointment with Philip Kreg he told Iris about it. But he didn't give details and she didn't ask. He didn't tell her he'd made appointments a month back and then canceled them. *Stall him, Marcu had said. It can't hurt to play him a bit.*

On the next to last Sunday in October, Adam had driven his Alfa Romeo convertible, top down, through downtown Los Angeles. He circled the area. He crossed Figueroa and he crossed Los Angeles Street. There was almost nobody around and for a while he drove very slowly, swerving gently from one side of the street to the other. He was driving that way only for his own dreamlike amusement . . . and because he was in no hurry to arrive where he was going. "You were bad," he said out loud at one point. "You were a bad boy." He crossed Spring Street for the second time.

He was almost coasting when he came to the one-story cinder-block building off Hope. The building was painted sand pink. It had small signs for Kaplan Realty and for Johnson Imports but there was no Kaplan or Johnson associated with any business done at that location. Next to the building there was a small parking lot enclosed by a chain-link fence with razor wire over the top of the fence. Adam pulled up and unlocked the gate and parked.

The big 450 SEL, forest-green, was already there. Adam looked at his watch. Not yet eleven-thirty, so he wasn't late.

Inside, Ish and his friend Billy were at facing desks, both slouched back in their chairs with their feet up. Ish was reading the *Times,* the sports section, and Billy had a magazine with pictures of girls in swimsuits. Neither of them said anything but Billy held up the magazine to give Adam a look at one of the pictures. A dark-haired girl in a green suit was coming out of a pool. She was holding a ladder with both hands and for the moment letting her weight fall back. Deep breasts, big thighs and shoulders. Everything was very wet and sexy. You could see the shape of her nipples and the slight fold of the suit at her crack.

Billy just shook his head and grinned. A good-looking man in his forties with features that were lifeguard-perfect. He was wearing green slacks and a yellow polo shirt. You saw the flat stomach of a young athlete, not big but with wide sloping shoulders. Adam remembered the slight bounce when he walked. He noticed the one thickened ear. And he remembered too that if you looked closely you could see traces of damage at the eyebrows.

He grinned back at Billy. Then he said to Ish, "He isn't here yet? You didn't come together?"

"Well," Ish said. "The fact is, we don't do so much comin together. Usually I come on my own and I guess so does he. You know, we don't even double-date. . . . Now just give me a minute. Lemme finish this." He didn't look up while he was talking. While he was still reading the article, he said, "Actually, kiddo, there's been a change of plans. Our friend Karl Van Atta decided to take himself a day or two in the desert. A little sun, a little golf, he thought. You and I together, he told me, we could handle what he wanted us to go over. Just the two of us . . . with Billy here cause he happened to come along."

Then Ish got up. He yawned and stretched his arms. He got to his feet and stretched again. Monster man with his huge shoulders and barrel chest. Blue-shadowed outsized jaw, and the black hair that covered his arms and sprouted from the vee of his open shirt.

"Adam," he said jovially, "I don't think you understand the *import,* you know, of this Mexico thing. How serious it is. I mean, you skip off, this skunk Debbie with you to pour the wine, the two of you off to Mexico for the little holiday. . . . Right, Adam?"

Adam didn't answer. He heard Billy moving behind him.

"Right?"

"Right," Adam said. And then he screamed when Billy's fingers jabbed into his kidneys. He stumbled forward against Ish.

"Son-of-a-bitch," Ish said. "Whattya tryin to attack me?" He slapped Adam quickly, not especially hard, three times across the face. One cheek and then the other. Then dropped one hand gently over Adam's shoulder.

"You see," he said to Billy, "Adam, this young businessman, he cuts out down there to the sunshine, there's not enough of it here. Well, that's the first thing, that he doesn't tell anybody he's goin. You can imagine how everyone gets all upset about that. Where is the guy? So that, right there, that's the first infraction. How the hell you run a business, people go off on you, they don't tell you? . . . You follow?"

"Sure, I do," Billy said. "I certainly do."

"Van Atta," Ish said. "You can imagine how upset he was at this?"

"Hey," Billy said. "The guy is human."

"I mean, you know right there, most organizations, that's cause for a little discipline."

"Absolutely."

"So anyway, while Adam is down there he visits a guy. *Our guy* is who he sees. And he knows Adam and that Adam is from us. So any arrangement, it's like he's talkin to us. Wouldn't you say so, Billy?"

"No question, I think."

"Hear that, Adam? Voice of an impartial observer."

Adam tried to clear his throat.

"Adam?" Ish said. His hand began to dig into Adam's shoulder.

"Yes," Adam said.

"He hears it," Ish said. "So anyway, what does this businessman do? He starts to make these funny noises to the guy about maybe some personal connection. Some this, some that. This is where it gets so really bad. And he knows that and he's scared. So scared at what he's tryin to do, he's too busy wipin the shit out of his pants to say it straight. He makes it clear enough, though, the guy understands Adam would like to move some powder. You know, cocaine, blow, white dust. You got that, Billy?"

"Fuckin awful," Billy said.

"Kind of a disgusting little prick, isn't he?"

"A bag of shit."

"What it comes to, Adam is tryin to do drugs with our guy and Adam knows we don't ever get into that. Never. Not ever. . . . Adam," Ish said. "What you were doin, you were fuckin with our reputation. You understand that? Some hell of a no-no, you think of it that way. Could lose it all for you. . . . Adam. You want to lose it all?"

"No," Adam said.

"That's right," Ish said. "Of course you don't. . . . Billy," he said. "I think I know what Adam wants. Adam wants me to go back to Van Atta and tell him he's gonna be a regular guy from now on. A company man. In there every day. A nine-to-fiver like they say. Do everything by the book. All that shit. I think Adam plans just to be regular as hell after this. . . . No more free enterprise, Adam. Do I have it right? Is that what I tell him?"

"Yes."

"Kind of a baby *yes,* I thought. Wasn't it, Billy? He could hardly get it out. . . . Adam. Let's try that again. Executive voice this time."

Ish's fingers began to work deeper into Adam's shoulder and Adam tried to twist his body away from the pain. "Yes," he said in a louder voice. He tried to yell it out.

Ish shook his head. "You should stand up straighter when you talk to somebody," he said. And he asked Billy if this was the kind of young management material that Van Atta wanted around him.

"Maybe he doesn't anymore want him around? Who would want this piece of crap?"

"But he's a very forgiving guy, Van Atta. He said to forgive the kid. . . . Uh-uh." Ish was speaking to Adam now. He held his free hand in the air, palm out, as a moderator would to cut off an expected interruption. "Don't thank him yet," he said. "We really talked on this one, him and I. Forgive you, he said and I agreed on that. Maybe I wouldn't, he hadn't talked me into it. But I agreed." Ish laughed. "I agreed with the boss," he said.

He took his hand from Adam's shoulder. He smoothed that shoulder and then the other.

Adam swallowed. Dry. He was completely unable to start a flow of saliva.

Then Ish shot the heel of one palm into his chest and he went backwards. Billy caught him and from behind put one leg between Adam's legs, and he wrapped his arms around Adam so that Adam's arms were pinned against his body.

Adam was coughing and trying to breathe through the pain that was centered somewhere in his chest.

"We also agreed," Ish said. . . . He stopped and frowned. He said to Billy that Adam wasn't paying any attention to him. That wasn't nice.

Billy squeezed and Adam began to groan.

"We agreed," Ish said, "this can't just go by the boards. Attention has got to be paid. Your sake too, Adam. This is a valuable lesson. Most places, they make a guy fall down forever, a cheap stunt like you pulled. I mean they disappear him. . . . So you got to learn your lesson. I'm afraid what we got to do here is hurt you a little. A fair bit, I guess." Ish was smiling and he stepped forward.

Kreg in late November, the day before Thanksgiving, woke in his office. A short nap at the end of the day. The inside of his mouth was slightly foul. His free hand found the pipe that he kept on his desk and that he hadn't smoked for more than ten years. He cupped the bowl. His thumb touched a chipped place on the rim. And the clause he'd been working on when he dropped off came back into his mind.

His client was arranging a long-term lease on property owned by a Midwestern city. Kreg had arranged for local counsel and had a draft of what they'd done. The property was to be exempt from local real-estate taxes and it was this clause that had been troubling him. Because the exemption might not hold up. He decided to suggest an addition. If any taxes were imposed they would be borne by the city. He questioned whether his client had the resources to carry a project on the scale of this one . . . and whether that was necessarily a concern of his.

The bad taste in his mouth was bothering him and he wanted to wash.

On his way to the men's room, he noticed that Roth's secretary, the new girl, was still in the office. It was after seven. Late to be working. The girl looked up when Kreg passed her desk. Coming back, he stopped there. "I don't know your name," he said.

"Deane," the girl said.

He started to say something, calling her Miss Deane, but she interrupted him. No, she said, Deane. Deane was her given name. Kreg guessed at her age. Early or mid-thirties. "Do you like it here that much?" he said, holding his left arm so she could see his watch. Thanksgiving Eve, he was thinking. Why was she still here?

"It's only for a few days," she said. Roth acted as managing partner and took care of the books. Which meant that he had to have a secretary who could do them. He had approved Deane's system and she was trying to get things in order. Her idea of order. It wasn't a big job but it wasn't one she could get to during office hours. So a few days of this evening work.

Kreg explained that he was on his way out. He said, "It's not pleasant being alone here."

"I don't mind," Deane said.

"Not dangerous. The building is safe. Just gloomy."

"It won't bother me. I operate on trust and I don't get depressed."

She had a clear voice. Kreg listened. He watched her. She was wearing bracelets and a hand-dyed blouse in an Asian pattern. The effect was of an interest in authentic crafts. . . . By definition, style was supposed to be of its time. If she cared about that sort of thing, why didn't she go to a chic store? There was no point anymore to a folksy look. "I'll tell the elevator starter to watch out for you," he said.

"John?" she said. "The old man? We'll watch out for each other."

Kreg asked where she'd learned accounting.

"I pick things up," Deane said. "I can read a wiring diagram. If I had to, I could build a house."

"Have you done that?"

"I think I could."

"Do we pay you for overtime?" Kreg said. He had an appointment with Cotton and was already thinking about that. And about the responses he might make to certain propositions.

Each table had a candle in a heavy drop-shaped glass wrapped with plastic net. A teasing annoying half-light. Kreg moved the candle so that at least it wasn't between them. He could see enough. He could tell that the walls were covered in a paisley fabric. This was an Indian restaurant, more of a cocktail lounge. And there were paisley swags that hung from the ceiling. A darker pattern than the wall covering.

At first there had been a man in a tuxedo who played one song at the piano, but he had gone to the bar. Now music was being piped in. "Moon River."

The seats were too low and too soft. Kreg kept shifting his weight, trying for a position that would give him the sense of being *on* something. He eyed unhappily a cardboard turkey on the table.

Next to them, a man his own age was blowing very fat smoke rings and being admired for that by a woman with olive skin and a beauty mark. Cotton was watching them. He raised his eyebrows slightly. "Cheaters' heaven," he said to Kreg.

"It seems." This place was near his office and had always seemed acceptable from the street. He stared until Cotton looked away.

The waitresses in this Indian establishment were dressed like the girls in the key clubs. Black stockings and leotards that were cut to emphasize the mound and with a high curve at the hips. Very low on top and everything black except a thin white ribbon around the neck. . . . It was their second round of drinks. The ritual seemed to be that when she took your order or served you she was supposed to lean down for a significant period of time. Direct, meaningful eye contact.

She put Kreg's glass in front of him. Then Cotton's. Cotton, especially, was given a long full view. Which might have been expected. Women, Kreg guessed, were often taken with Cotton . . . with his classic regular features. And his good clothes and fluid moves.

The waitress moved away. Kreg noticed that she wasn't symmetrically built. There was a slight tilt to the left. What they probably also responded to was Cotton's air of attentiveness. A truly personal interest that he seemed to take.

But wasn't she a little past it, Cotton said, to be working in a place like this? He put his glass down. With no break in the beat or rhythm of his voice, he asked Kreg to tell him about Brandt Systems. "We think we have an interest, if that's all right."

There you are, Kreg thought. Fifteen minutes. Fifteen minutes since we met and you waited that long to get down to it. To business. Of course it was all right, he said. Brandt was a public company. Then he said, "You're interested or you think you're interested in us. That would mean . . . ?"

"Only that we have a portfolio. And that we're always looking for good investments. Some new position that we can add."

"Anyone would do that." Kreg could feel a thickness coming into his voice. He began to feel that way all over. Thick, heavy, flushed.

Cotton said, "We're like anybody else. Except for size."

Kreg thought of size and amounts. How more and less turned at some point into a difference in kind. If you were small enough, light enough, you could live on the surface of the water. If you had little enough, you took a different view of the world. He assumed that to be true. He couldn't be certain because he wasn't in that position. He had possessions. He earned and he spent. There were always surpluses which accumulated and compounded. A growth of financial fat that was distasteful to him. Not great sums but more than he wanted. He felt fat with money just as he did with his belly and the soft tits of the older male that he'd developed. Susan remarried and the alimony stopped and Adam was on his own now. So he kept more of what he made.

He was occasionally taken by the idea that he could rid himself of it. How much was owed to him? In principle, he knew, he should refuse to lend but on principle he rarely did. Some need to live as if he could throw it away? Iris had said she'd lend to Adam if asked.

In fact, though, he had less money now than in the past. Most of Kreg's capital had gone over the last few years. Down a real-estate rat hole, a developer's pipe dream.

This was a cousin with whom he'd played as a boy. They shared memories of common infractions, skinned knees, long days at the beach. They stayed somewhat in touch and had dinner once in a great while. Marvin was a frequenter of the kind of steak house where you could also get the four-pound lobster if that was your pleasure. He was finishing an office building in Stamford and had other projects going there and in Putnam County. He had a Jaguar and a Cad and went to England for his clothes. He kept pulling at his suit jacket so you could get a view of the three buttons on the shirt cuff.

"Anyway," he said, "you want in, I have this deal up north. Dream deal. Yokels up there, they don't see the values." This was in Columbia County. Marvin hadn't worked there before. The site had been a prep school and now wasn't anything. "Those people, they think it's an eyesore. Vacant that way, going to hell just outside their beautiful town. This is a place, the New Yorkers are pouring in. Buy themselves the second home, the condo. This is the great new area, and those school buildings, they're beautiful. Built too. They're so solid. Old trees."

There was room for eight hundred thousand and Kreg took it all. The biggest investment of his life but no true approval as he regarded the intimately familiar curves of his own handwriting on the check. He visited the site because Marvin insisted.

"A year," Marvin said. "Fourteen months and we mortgage out. You get your capital back and we see how fast we sell the units and we go to the next thing. I'm gonna make you rich."

Now a few early buyers were installed in the two sections that had been completed. Work on the main building had never started and the equipment had been pulled off the job. There were lawsuits of course. Marvin had other problems too. He said he was on the balls of his ass for now. Also that he'd come back. "The real-estate game," he said. "It goes that way. But every penny. Someday you get every penny back." In the meantime, though, didn't it look like Chapter 11?

He did refer one client, the company with the lease on the Midwestern property. Kreg didn't feel an ascetic's pleasure at being relieved of his money. He hadn't wanted to have it but didn't enjoy losing it like a fool.

Still, Marvin had meant no harm. There wasn't the need to be always on your guard as you would have to be with Cotton. As Kreg felt he had to be now, here in this Indian restaurant, where Cotton had just said his group were investors like any other.

"No," Kreg said. "Not like other investors. Not necessarily just investors, are you?"

"What else would we be?"

"You have a long reach. You might want it all." There was the Company's 10-K, Kreg said, and the annual report. Those were available to all the world. If Cotton had such a compelling interest in Brandt Systems he could look at them. He sensed his own fullness. His bulk. He could move on Cotton. He could crush him.

Cotton suggested that he'd hoped for a more intimate perspective. So often in other situations he'd been allowed to look at the books.

You were, Kreg thought. You were destined for this, this being a certain kind of big company vice president. Just as Cotton was destined never to lose his flat stomach and his nice direct way of looking at you. Or his clean jawline. In school, he guessed, Cotton had been sought after but not really liked. Class secretary and manager of the track team. Usually in pressed chinos.

He was imagining a private school. Probably not first-rate, old traditions but weakly held. A bad place for Cotton, for someone inclined to go the easy way in style. The same had been true of Adam a generation later. Education was something Kreg had thought about a good deal. Any parent would naturally do that. Because after a while there were the results of the choices you'd made.

A stocky man with a wrathful face went by their table. He limped, used a cane, and was leading, with one hand on her upper arm, a young blond woman. The man was wearing a corduroy suit. A fabric for casual wear that was out of place here. It was the kind of suit that Brandt had worn. An antelope color, according to the salesman at Brooks, and Brandt had made a joke about that. *The antelope at Brooks is very deer.*

Brandt and Kreg had gone into the store together. This had been a time when the valve company, the company which some years later would need an umbrella name to cover activities added by growth and acquisition and so become Brandt Systems, was starting to do well and Brandt was beginning to take some money for himself. Kreg remembered that he'd wanted to pick up a jacket he'd ordered. And he remembered the fabric of the jacket. A gray-and-white tweed. Still in the back of his closet. Patched. Something he kept to wear around the neighborhood on weekends. And never did.

They had come from Brandt's bank. Loan papers to sign, to buy machine tools. "A million dollars," Brandt said. "Nobody ever lent me a million dollars before. Nice guys, these bankers." The store was two blocks away and after the meeting he came in with Kreg. "Keep you company," he said. Fancy store, he said. But then he started to look around. Wherever he was, he always looked around.

Kreg remembered *deliberations.* Brandt standing back to look at the rack of corduroy suits, and moving closer to rub a fold of the material against his thumb. Brandt had been stocky too, like the man with the blond girl. But not wrathful. Awkward sometimes. And implacable. The creature and achievement of the slow workings of his own will. He had ordered three of the corduroy suits and afterward wore only those, in rotation, fall through spring. Always.

Kreg repeated what Cotton had said, *A more intimate perspective.* "Why would we do that?" he said. "Let you look at the books that way? Why would we do you that favor?" His face was puffed. He could feel it. And pressure working behind the eyes. A bull walrus when he was angry, Iris used to say. But she only said that when she was happy with him so he was sure it was a fair description. And fond. Fair and fond. He began to picture with specificity and in detail certain times with her, certain occasions, particular acts.

Cotton, showing no disturbance at Kreg's remarks, said that maybe as a courtesy to a potentially substantial investor . . .

In fairness, Kreg thought, you could understand that a woman would want to be with him. He pictured Iris with Cotton. He pictured, briefly, them doing what he remembered doing with her. *And, in fairness, I have to put that out of my mind. That's not my affair.* He cleared his throat. "You people," he said. "I've been trying to say that sometimes you buy stock and then there's a tender."

"Mostly we invest like anyone else."

"But not always."

"Not always," Cotton said. But he said also that there was no problem in this case. Not with the Brandt Foundation owning so much of the stock. "Twenty percent," he said, "the magic twenty." He smiled pleasantly. "And you're the Foundation and there's how much more, another twenty maybe, that management owns. And they all look to you. So this isn't a case where anybody could do anything that wasn't friendly."

"It wouldn't be friendly."

"Then how could it be at all? Probably not possible." Cotton thought they should forget about Brandt Systems. Food, he said, was coming to be a somewhat more immediate concern. He waved and the waitress came over. If he promised no business, would Kreg take dinner with him? He made a suggestion. *Nouvelle.* "But real cooking. Not just fruit with the tournedos." He seemed genuinely disappointed when Kreg declined. Then he noticed the waitress and sent her for the check.

When he was paying, he called her by name. Cindy. It wasn't clear if he actually knew her or if it was only a term he used, the way some other man might call her honey. Earlier, he hadn't particularly said anything to her but with him, Kreg thought, that might not be meaningful. Perhaps Cotton had been here before. . . . The man at the next table had stopped blowing smoke rings and he and the woman with the olive skin were pretty much all over each other.

At the door, Kreg said, "Of course, I'll mention this to the other directors."

Cotton couldn't imagine that the Board would go against Kreg's wishes. "Not that they wouldn't be delighted if you were for it. Institutional support for the stock."

"They probably would. They'd be very happy." Which, Kreg was sure, would be the case. Because the big banks and the pension funds hadn't used the stock. Brandt Systems was a thin issue. Difficult to buy and difficult to sell. Not that we aren't reasonable, Kreg thought. All we want is for the stock to move up. But we don't want it to be noticed. Not by certain kinds of people. It was a reasonable thought, in the way that any wish is reasonable. . . . *Although what are my wishes now?*

Cotton said, "We really understand your feelings. We respect your involvement here and that you want everybody to be looked after. We'd plan for that . . ."

Would you?

". . . if this were anything more than just an investment position." Cotton held up his hand and a Checker pulled out. "Let me ask you again," he said. "Dinner sometime soon. We'd enjoy it."

Just charming, Kreg thought. He makes his living with his charm. And maybe lucky. How many Checkers were still in service? "It's all right," he said. "I told you I'd speak to the Board." Another cab was coming toward them and he flagged it down. Sprung seats and no light for the meter. A driver who started to argue when he said to go up Madison Avenue.

But Kreg liked to look at the stores there.

They stopped for a light in the sixties. A mannequin in a natural pose (as if she might be talking to you at a party where you were all good friends) faced toward him from across the street. She had on a dress in soft brown with white dots and there was a scarf at her throat. Susan had had a dress like that. Kreg remembered her wearing it to a wedding in a garden. And she'd worn it twenty-five years ago in her lawyer's office. She signed and he signed.

She wanted a minute alone with him.

Why? she asked.

But there was no satisfactory answer. How could he answer her? He didn't see any way, not without recriminations. And he wouldn't recriminate.

Susan admitted her adultery. She mentioned it, her gentle affair, which had never been discussed between them but which Kreg was certain had been as much as anything else a protest against him. Against the unforgiving constancy of his trapped anger and his contempt for her. And against the liaisons she thought he always had.

I can't tell you, he said. You know why.

You've always had women, she said.

Not always. Rarely. But you wouldn't believe that.

How can I?

You can't. . . . As I said.

But it was this one time.

It wasn't that.

There was at one point the flash of her weak anger. She knew that she was being pushed away simply for being what she was. What she had always been.

The light changed and the cab began to move away from the mannequin. *Cheaters' heaven,* Cotton had said. Cotton was right. It was that kind of place. It occurred to Kreg that Susan had no doubt believed him to be fairly regularly in such places. A frequenter of them.

It also occurred to him that Cotton tonight had not actually expected to be allowed to see the books or in any other way to be welcomed aboard. This meeting had been only an opening declaration of intention on Cotton's part. On Marcu's part. It had cost nothing and there had been some chance of a pleasant surprise. There was always that chance.

More to come no doubt. Kreg began to wonder what it might come to . . . Marcu's final offer. . . . And what his own position should be. Cotton had spotted his unreasoned quick impulse to hostility. But why be hostile? Would a buyout, if it ever came to that, necessarily be such a bad thing for a company that was well enough managed but no longer truly led? Or for a foundation (the company's shield) that could only increase its yields by an exchange of its stock for cash (Kreg thought briefly of reinvestment opportunities)? And no weight to whatever might have been the thoughts and opinions of the dead man, Brandt, on this particular subject, assuming he'd had them and you could have known what they were. Leaving himself, the lawyer with half his practice in the balance here, as maybe the only interest at negative risk. And not willing to take account of that. . . . Able though to resent his having to be the high-minded and confused fiduciary here. *It wouldn't be friendly,* he'd said to Cotton. But what was uncontested wouldn't have to be friendly. And that was the question, whether there would be a contest. Which was a question that ultimately he would decide.

A cab to West End Avenue had gotten to be an expensive thing, although not something he was going to give up. Kreg didn't save on perishable comforts. He overtipped the way he usually did. Tipping that way was something else he did on principle.

The doorman had a green uniform jacket over gray suit pants. Kreg didn't mind. It went with the building, which wasn't badly run, only shabby. But they held packages for him and didn't lose his mail. He wanted an apartment that was too large for a man alone . . . and had it. He had been told that he ought to get four and a half nice rooms on the East Side. The second bedroom would be his study.

It was much colder now. Clear arctic air had been predicted. And had come in fast. There was a bellow of night wind down the street. Sheet metal clanged a block away. Maybe a garbage can. The doorman, with no overcoat, shivered slightly. Kreg realized he'd been standing there while the man, who was a quiet alcoholic and not young, held the big glass door open for him. Kreg had been thinking about his family. Himself and Adam. The two of them. As they were. . . . He stepped inside, bumped against the edge of the door and skinned the hand that was holding a lawyer's red envelope, full of work, that he'd been carrying all evening.

Over the elevator door, the indicator pointed to an upper floor. Kreg waited for the machine to creak down to him. He was thinking that seven big rooms with a fireplace were better than four and a half boxes in an East Side needle. *We never had a proper storage box for the wood. We kept it in the empty maid's room and some of it stacked right there in the living room next to the fireplace. But we had the fires.* Adam at five and six had been a reader there, stretched on the floor as close as he could get to the flames themselves . . . soon drowsy from the heat. Sometimes two or three books around him. Kreg in his chair watching the fire, watching the boy. Also reading. Susan there and later not there.

Although, about that time, Susan's drinking took over and Adam stopped coming into any room where his parents were. And Kreg didn't bother anymore to build those fires.

Now Kreg decided in favor of families. Ties. Even families of two with a continent between them. Fragmentation wasn't a reason to let go completely. Crawl into separate holes. His mind went back to his conversation with Cotton. Important not to let his dislike for the man take over. Why, really, should he dislike him? *Make plans. Don't be bull-headed and take care of your own, the Foundation and the Company. What Iris does with him isn't your affair. . . . It wouldn't be friendly.* That was something else. Totally. That had to be thought of as negotiating talk.

The doorman said it was going to be a cold Thanksgiving. Kreg said yes, he thought so. He went into his pocket. "Here," he said. "Take this. Something to go with the bird."

What counted for him was the space. Whole rooms he didn't need (Adam's still as it had always been) and mostly a little overfurnished with good things that he was used to. He had small statues, bowls, boxes, fragments. He had some Chinese and some Islamic porcelains, a small oxblood vase and a larger one in imperial yellow, a deep bowl with a startling motif of bright green leaves. No carpets but good oriental rugs and runners. The color in Kreg's apartment was on the floors and on shelves and tables. What hung on the walls was mostly black-and-white. These were his only contemporary things. Not that new. European expressionists. Work done in the nineteen twenties and thirties. Minor things, small, that he had been able to afford. One Ernst and a Grosz. Sometimes he added a piece but the apartment was, overall, the way it had been ten years ago and twenty years ago. Of the rooms he used, only his bedroom was relatively spare. He worked and read at his desk in the living room or at a table in the kitchen. The bedroom was only for sleeping.

He put on a flannel shirt and old slacks. He always changed when he came into the apartment. Washing, he looked into his own intolerant pale eyes. He cleaned his hurt hand. The abrasion was painful but not deep. Even alone, he wouldn't grimace. When he examined the cuts, he noticed the way the skin was aging there, visible fine cracks running between the pores.

Good light was something else Kreg had. His apartment was high enough and faced south and east. Morning. Over easy. He counted to twelve and turned an egg onto his plate. While he ate, he made notes on a yellow pad. He was thinking about his work, piecework in the service of a commercial class whose objectives he didn't especially share or respect. But it was a fair arrangement. He gave value and got the right to do what he liked best, his piecework. Not too bad as the world went. Nobody who wasn't soft would think he had a claim to more.

There was a spot of yellow on his shirt. At the sink he rubbed it with cold water. Yolk. . . . What was his cholesterol count? Shouldn't he know that? . . . He tucked in his shirt and felt the area he'd wet, cold against his skin.

In the middle of the morning, dressed for the street, awkward with his own size, he tripped over a rug end. Catching himself, he barked his skinned hand against a wall. With no expression, he shook the hand like a rattle, thinking that he could at least choose his own way of receiving unwanted messages. The pain eased and he went out.

On Broadway here in the eighties, at ten-thirty in the morning, with most of the stores closed, it was possible to imagine away the storefronts and conceive the buildings as they had originally been. A bouquet of derivative styles. French châteaux, aspects of

Baroque. Others. He didn't know the names. The men who had done this work, the architects, must have been, many of them, men like himself. Not originators. Conscientious, though, the beneficiaries of a good education in an established tradition. Workers. Later he came into Central Park, a variant product of the same cultural thrust that had produced the buildings and created out of the same rise and tide of urban purpose. In the near distance there were huge stuffed shapes. Bright-colored. Trying, idiotically, to free themselves for a mindless ride into the upper air. The balloons of the Macy's parade.

He saw through the window into a big cafeteria in the west fifties. Beach umbrellas there over the tables, to give the effect of a café. Old people already having their Thanksgiving dinner. Mostly alone. Some with a magazine or a book. A few couples. It was clouding over and there were things he could do at home. No food there but he'd pass a delicatessen on his way back. Get a sandwich for his lunch.

"It was like Tati. Right out of Jacques Tati." This was a stocky man. Broad-faced, with a yachtsman's creases around the eyes, heavy eyebrows and thick crack-nailed fingers. He was telling a revolving-door story. He went in and his friend went out. And then again. Kreg remembered that he'd met the man before. "A gravel voiced colleague of Iris' with the manner of a good-natured sportscaster. Always in a tweed suit and gray slacks. A man who winked at you when he talked.

And always at Iris' parties.

Veep, he was called. He was a senior vice president or executive president in the large firm where they both worked. "All I am," he'd said to Kreg when they'd first met, "is an old-fashioned account jockey. Packaged goods. Make some buddies here and there along the way. I take the guy from the magazine or the newspaper out for the big lunch, or a couple of pops at the Numbers after work. Send the birthday card to his kids if you get the picture." Iris said he had a cold eye for the odds and was one of the industry's truly successful business getters.

Veep was one of a group of regulars. These were people who

worked for the good banks and advertising agencies and real-estate firms of the city. The men were well set in vice-presidential slots but not at the highest level, and the women mostly scaled down from there. The married couples tended to be two-job families, children not in evidence and not much talked about. Alcohol and divorce the characteristic burdens. Some childhood friends who had gone to the same good schools as Iris. There were, of course, more women than men. "Girls from the office," Iris had once said. "Or from some other office. We do for each other. I have them over and they have me."

Sometimes, for Thanksgiving, Iris had a smaller group for dinner. Usually, though, she had these parties.

One year the dinner had been at Kreg's. He and Adam had done the cooking. Four of them there. Etkind Rossoff brought wine and Iris baked a pumpkin pie and cookies. Rossoff had been amazed that a dish so formidable as a turkey would come out properly if you followed the book. . . . The evening had been a success. It stayed in his memory as a *jolly time* of a certain definable old-fashioned kind.

Cotton was standing there with Kreg and Veep. "But finally," he said to Veep, "you did get together?"

"Sure we did," Veep said. "But only after I stepped out on the inside and he stepped out on the outside. Then I went around. *Then* we got together."

Cotton said you had to grab these little moments. "You see," he said to Kreg, "we keep meeting."

Iris, in the middle of the room, was leaning slightly so that a man there could light her cigarette from his. She was looking at Kreg. Then she looked at Cotton, who was facing away from her, and then back at Kreg.

Cotton said to Kreg he wanted him to know it hadn't been just talk last night. And also that in recent days Marcu had added to his position. "A little block someone showed us."

"A small investment?"

"Although we don't think about them that way. Small. We're serious about them all. Anything we buy. It's not a matter of size."

Iris wheeled on the arm of the man who'd lighted her cigarette. She turned her back.

"Watch the pennies?" Kreg said.

Cotton said that was what they tried to do.

"So do we," Kreg said. "That's why we're such a good company." *Play him,* he thought.

"Should we make it a big investment?"

"Up to a point. . . . We've been through that."

"We might. We start small. Sometimes we add but we always start small."

What was that, Veep said, what about a good investment? He was always looking for something.

"We were only joking," Kreg said.

"He's teasing me," Cotton said.

"Leading him on."

Iris said, "I'm not going to fill the refrigerator with little packages." She was looking at the food that was left.

"I'll help you out," Kreg said. "I'll have another piece of turkey." He took a scrap of dark meat from the side of the platter.

There was a kind of rigid posture Iris took on when she was nervous or irritated. Choppy, abrupt movements of her neck and hands.

Such movements now.

She was annoyed, Kreg decided, because he hadn't said anything about Cotton and she couldn't ask him what did he think of her new lover. He didn't see that there was anything he could do about her feelings. She had once wanted him and then she hadn't. He too. He had wanted her and then he hadn't.

Iris looked for certain kinds of change and he didn't. His life of action was a life of work and he believed in fidelity to that. This wasn't with any sense that he had found a true path. But it was his system and he lived with it. He didn't see that he was worse off than she. "Here," he said. He took another piece of turkey and held it out to her.

Iris ate the meat from his fingers. Not an act of submission or reconciliation. "You have some business together," she said, looking to where Cotton was standing. He was talking again to Veep.

"It's not really business," Kreg said. "You could call it light contact. Casual."

"That's good," Iris said.

"Why is it good?"

"You couldn't do business with him. He's better at it than you are."

"You think it would be difficult, working with him?"

"For you. If you were on different sides."

"We would be." Kreg tried a joke. A lighter tone. "But if I got in trouble," he said, "I'd come to you."

"Don't do that. Not with your problems."

"I'd be obligated to come to my friends."

"You'd be making a mistake. I wouldn't help you. . . . I'll tell you. Nobody would."

Her quick rage. Kreg suspected some intuition of hers that she should be concerned for him now. She certainly knew that Cotton had made a proposal . . . and been refused. She would also be aware that Kreg had no great respect for her new lover . . . and would be ready to go on the offensive about that.

She was out of cigarettes and asked him to get one for her. "All those smokers," she said.

Kreg came back with the cigarette and she said that maybe she'd had enough party. If Kreg wanted to go and if he could get a few of the guests to leave with him, then the rest of them would follow. Whoever was still there.

"Why wouldn't you help me?" Kreg said. "You or anyone else?" Cotton, of course, would not be leaving with the others. Not just yet.

"Because you think you can go on your own." Iris touched his cheek with a flat palm . . . as she had a month ago in the country. "It's the way you're *coordinated.*"

"So awkward?" He was thinking that Cotton in other circumstances might be acceptable enough. But he didn't like to think of Iris being with him. Responding to him in certain ways. He reminded himself that this wasn't his concern . . . or shouldn't be.

"Awkward," Iris said. "Different."

"Which isn't an offense. Nothing intolerable."

"Yes it is," she said. "It can be."

"As you once told me," he said. There was the weight on him of his whole history of refusals and willful deviations.

"When we separated, you mean?"

Kreg said, "We were never together so how could there have been a separation?"

"You see. So pure and honest."

"I don't try to be," he said truthfully.

Iris touched him again. "That's what I meant," she said, "about coordination."

Adam backed into his apartment with a bag of groceries in his arms.

Debbie, on the couch, was wearing red bikini panties with a lightning motif in royal blue. Also a peppermint-striped shirt of Adam's, not buttoned, sleeves rolled. She was shifting her head to get the best reflection of the changing light against her nail job, fingers extended and splayed. It really was a changing light. A Pacific sunset at Marina del Rey. Tammy Wynette was singing an oldie, "I Don't Wanna Play House."

Adam crossed through the living part of the room into the dining el. He reached over the pass-through and set the groceries down. Then he went to the stereo and took out the Tammy Wynette cassette.

"I don't listen to that," he said.

"That shit?"

"You're getting there. That's very good. Perceptive." He found another cassette and put that in the machine.

Debbie listened for a few seconds. "Bird?" she said.

"Yes."

"Bird. Bird Parker. Charlie Bird Parker." She stood up on the couch and flapped her arms like a bird. Her breasts jiggled.

Adam watched them as if they were curious. Interesting in that sense but not compelling. He pointed toward the kitchen and the bag of groceries. "I got it," he said. "Now you cook it."

"Drink?"

"White wine. There's a bottle, two bottles—they're chilled—in with the other stuff." He told her to be careful with the wine.

It wasn't Masson. This was a small vineyard that hadn't got popular yet and the stuff was hard to get.

"White wine," Debbie said. "*Bird.*"

Adam ate pasta salad and went through the mail. The last piece was a note on an insult card addressed to Debbie. "Tuke," he said. "Your friend Tuke."

"Just to thank us for when we lent her the place."

"To thank us a month later. You're supposed to be prompt." Adam poured more wine. "Tuke sucks," he said.

Debbie giggled. "Me or you," she said.

"The apartment. The way your nice friend took care of the apartment I lent her. You had me lend her."

"I cleaned all that."

"You had to clean all that. That mess your nice friend left us." Adam finished his pasta and squinted west at the corner of the ocean that was visible from the second-story patio. "Me or you?" he said.

"Tuke. Oh, yes. That's Tuke."

After a minute, Adam said, "Me *and* you?"

Debbie wet her lips. "Maybe," she said. "Sometime."

"But for now," Adam said, "she can go back to Santa Cruz. She can do her pottery and her folk arts."

"Tuke doesn't do those. She's a communications major."

"Does she like Tammy Wynette too?"

Debbie trembled slightly. "One other thing she doesn't do. She doesn't talk down to me, you know."

"I don't."

"Oh, yes."

"Not so much." But the truth was, Adam said, Debbie hadn't exactly taken advantage of the opportunities that were open to her. Not in the education department. He went inside and came back with a book. "Did you read this?" he said.

"A little."

Adam put the book behind his back. He said, "You read it a little? Maybe?"

"Yes."

"You maybe read this book a little. This book by *who was it again? Who,* baby?"

Debbie pushed at a tortellini with her fork. She looked straight at the middle of the redwood patio table.

"This is e. e. cummings and the point is it's *accessible.* It's *easy* to read." He had her read to him about Buffalo Bill and about a girl with hard long eyes.

Debbie read what Adam told her to read, three or four short poems, and then put the open book face down because she knew he didn't like that. She cleared the table, and in the kitchen, cleaning up, she made more noise than she had to. When she finished the dishes, she came back to the patio door and watched Adam who was looking at the night. "How did your day go," she said, "at the office?"

"Oh, that," Adam said. "The office. How did *that* go?"

"How did it go?"

"Fine," Adam said. "It was all fine. It's always fine. As a matter of fact, a little strange maybe, this particular time. That's some piece of work, that Karl Van Atta. Three weeks he's been back and you know he's hardly said anything. About Mexico I mean. It's been almost like it never happened or it was a minor thing. But you could be positive, believe me you could, that sometime he was going to talk about it. He was letting it build, I think. Let the dramatic effect build up."

"So today was the day?" Debbie said.

"*Vraiment.* Today was the day. Today we had our little chat. He had me in there and Ish was with us too. The ape. And Van Atta explained the rules. I said I hadn't really considered my actions. I hadn't thought about them at the time but now I had. With Ish in there, it was like mood music. An atmosphere, you know, of menace. But then he let me get away with it. I explained that all we did was to pay a visit. We were down there so we visited somebody."

Debbie went inside and came back with a pair of jeans. "Listen," she said. "Ortega. We visited somebody who happened to be Van Atta's big contact in Mexico. And all the time we were there, you were sniffing around for some opportunity to talk about this private deal with him. The big plan. Ortega knew that and he told Van Atta." She began to pull on the jeans against the night air. "Just thank God," she said, "you didn't ever come out with anything definite."

"Lucky," Adam said, "there was no opportunity."

"Didn't have the nerve, you mean. . . . Anyway, today, that was all that happened?"

"That was enough."

It was getting chilly, so they went inside and Adam read e. e. cummings and Debbie looked at a movie on the TV. After a while, Adam put the book down and watched with her. It was *The Guns of Navarone,* another oldie.

When the movie was over, Debbie said she was going to bed. While she was in the bathroom, Adam took a book of photographs from the shelf. Photographs of the American West. He took a map from between two of the photographs. The map showed both continents of the Americas and was marked with a X at a point on the coast of Colombia that was more or less equidistant between Barranquilla and the Guajira Peninsula. From there, a line arced north to Mexico City, and from there another arc terminated in California in the desert, near Twentynine Palms. There were inked notes next to the X and where the arcs terminated.

Adam looked at the map for a while. He lighted a cigarette and then the map at one corner. He held the map up to get a better flame but once it really caught, he seemed to change his mind. He fanned out the flame and scanned the map for legibility. Then folded it and put it in the book again and put the book away.

He was remembering the end of the afternoon, the part that followed his talk with Van Atta.

Ish standing in front of his desk. Not saying anything. Only crooking a finger at him. Adam followed him outside and they got into the forest-green Mercedes. Ish drove and he still didn't speak. When he parked, they were in the cobblestone alley between the new and old buildings of the Beverly Wilshire. "You were scared," Ish said.

"Why would I be scared?"

"You looked scared to me. You didn't know where I was takin you. Not the biggest stones in the world but, kid, that's all right.

Not everybody can be the hero type." Ish spoke like a friend. He reached quickly across his body and knuckled into Adam's not yet healed ribs.

Adam curled a hand in front of his mouth and screamed into the fist he made. "Ish," he screamed.

"Don't worry," Ish said. "Like I told you, it's all right. . . . Listen," he said. "What you can do, I got a try-on at Jerry Magnin, a jacket. . . . It's a silk, raw silk. Oyster color. So you watch the car for me. Fifteen minutes, I'm done." He came back in half an hour, wearing the new jacket. "Love it," he said. And he said he wasn't actually going in the direction of the office. So if Adam didn't mind a cab . . .

Debbie came out of the bathroom and said to go to bed. Not yet, Adam said. Look, she told him, all that about Ortega and Van Atta, there was no point thinking about that. That was done. Finished.

"Then what should we be thinking about?"

"I don't know," she said. "Maybe Tuke. That seemed to be interesting to you."

"Did you get that impression?"

"Well, I did," Debbie said. "I really did."

Frank Roth said that an eight-man firm was going to have trouble holding its larger clients and Kreg accepted Roth's judgment. He respected his partner's business sense and had always left it to Roth to run the office. And it was Roth who had developed the practice. Roth managed and hired and watched the billings. The arrangement worked for both of them.

Kreg thought of Roth as literate and well educated, carefully groomed. At home in many circles.

"But we can keep them," Roth was saying, "if we grow the firm."

Grow the firm. Brandt had also used that phrase. *We got to grow this business.* But Brandt hadn't condescended when he said it.

The larger clients were Brandt Systems and a client of Roth's that had some magazines and a cable TV business. Roth called it an entertainment complex. It generated almost twice the billings Brandt Systems did but there wasn't the hold on the business that Kreg had with Brandt.

Roth was a deal maker and a negotiator. He drew agreements that held up in court. I'm glad we have a little time," he said, "to talk about this."

Kreg said, "We always have time. We're close. You were saying, remember, what a small office it is." Roth, of course, had a plan. Why else this conversation? Fine. Kreg would go along with any suggestion. His body wanted to twist in its chair but he refused to allow that. He rubbed his thumb on the bowl of his pipe. Observed the deep red-brown and black-brown pattern of the burl. Gray scars of tooth marks in the black stem.

Roth waited.

Kreg caught Roth's eye and held it. "Arthur Harris," Roth said. "You know Arthur."

"Of him, really."

"Arthur's very competent. Good guy. You'd like him." Arthur Harris, he said, would bring three lawyers with him. This wouldn't change the character of the firm but it would be a start. And just the fact that you were growing would have an effect on the way you were perceived.

Perceived.

"We'll talk to him," Roth said. "I want you in on that. On any meetings we have."

"You talk to him. Have your talks."

"It would be very congenial."

"Which is another reason to talk to him. Talk to him."

"We should do it together."

"I'd rather," Kreg said, "you did it alone." It wasn't that he never wanted to give but it had always been understood that he wasn't expected to put in time on the business side. He practiced law. Only that. He worked with his clients and when they called on him he responded.

As he had with Brandt.

Even when Brandt had been unable to pay his bills, he had been careless and unremitting in his calls on Kreg's time. They met usually in the late evenings at the Long Island City loft that was Brandt's first factory. Sometimes Kreg brought sandwiches or containers of Chinese food. Brandt would show him blueprints, production charts, cross-section drawings. Or financial data on the back of an envelope. After they ate, Brandt always took him into the shop.

Kreg would sit on a workbench and Brandt would pick up a tool or would adjust the calibration on one of the machines. Brandt had been solid and slow-moving, pale in the particular way of a certain kind of muscular man who had formerly worked outdoors. He'd been younger then than Kreg was now.

They weren't legal questions that Brandt put to him. In fact there weren't usually any questions at all. It was more a kind of dream talk. Free-floating. Late in the evening he might begin to outline some new plan.

Sometimes there was a conference. Brandt and himself and Henry Juszczyk who ran the shop and Mouse Kelly. Mouse was five-four, the oldest of them, and had been a fly or a bantamweight. He had a flattened nose to show for that and a fortune to show for what he'd afterward done with Kelly Battery. He was the outside director here and Brandt sat on his board. The meetings had been mostly about new products and the cash flow that would be needed to get them started. There was never enough money, so you would have to plan for a cutback on some other line and how to stretch out your bills. Brandt never did discuss whether there would be a demand for whatever new item he'd conceived.

And didn't usually contribute a great deal to the discussion itself. *Maybe, he'd say, we could work it this way. I was thinking that could be possible.* But no more than that. So when Mouse Kelly (usually it was Mouse) had a question about a change in a production line or wanted to know if whatever new machinery that would have to be bought would actually do what it was supposed to, it was always Henry Juszczyk he asked. And Henry, six and a half feet tall, the production expert here, and having to know that he was with friends and expected to speak out with the rest of them, would nevertheless turn to Brandt, would blink his bad eyes while he waited for some sign that it was all right to say what he thought.

So fuck it, Mouse Kelly would eventually say. Just do the fuckin thing. You didn't need us. You always knew you were going to do it anyway.

Then there was only Kreg saying yes, go ahead and do it. And Henry saying it, everybody agreeing. . . . A litter of the empty white cartons that had held the beef with oyster sauce and the moo shu pork. It might be ten-thirty at night, with most of the shop in darkness. You'd see Brandt's cautious eyes and catch the hint of his brief smile. Thank you, he would say to each of them. He would thank Henry Juszczyk and Kreg. Then Mouse Kelly. *Thank you. Thank you, Mr. Kelly.*

And Mouse exploding: *Whothefuckisthat? Even in the plant I'm Mouse. Even some kid I hired two weeks ago.*

That was a game. It was Brandt's game. He'd catch Kreg's eye, then turn to Kelly. *Mr. Kelly,* he'd say, and each time would get this same reaction. And would promise each time to remember after this.

Henry never seemed to catch on. He always showed surprise when Mouse began to yell. Very likely, Kreg had thought, the shy production head was not able to conceive of the idea of play in terms of angry voices.

You could really say though that Brandt had never asked for anything. He'd said he needed you to come over, to perform some service. But those were statements of fact and put that way, flatly.

Kreg had responded and now had his legal fees and the Foundation.

"Maybe a lunch," Roth said, "with Arthur and me. Could you manage that? Could you go that far?"

Kreg wondered if Roth had really felt the need of a partner's approval. "You don't need me," he said. "When you have it arranged, then I'll see him."

"Do you know," Roth said, "that when it comes to your own interests, you have a tendency not to watch out for things?" He suggested a deal. There was a brief he was doing and there were questions of federal jurisdiction. Kreg was the expert there, so if Kreg would give him some time on that problem, he would go it alone with Arthur Harris.

"When would I have to give you that time?" Kreg was thinking about Frank Roth's office. It wasn't a place he particularly liked. Roth had a Stella and a Vasarely and good chairs and tables from Knoll. All those chosen by Roth's wife. Gerri Roth was a thin woman who held a graduate degree in fine arts and a simple nominalist trust in good design. But when Kreg had to discuss something with his partner, he always wanted to meet in Roth's office. Someone else's office was a place you could leave when you wanted.

Roth said, "Over the weekend? I have to work on it till then and I'll need it Monday."

Yes. Done. "At the apartment," Kreg said. "You get it to me there on Saturday."

"I can deliver it to you in the country."

"The apartment." How could he go to the country? Wouldn't he have to have access to a law library? Roth knew that.

At first when he opened the door Kreg didn't remember her name. He was immediately conscious of his bulk. A paunchy man in chinos and a flannel shirt, his eyes bulging because he was startled. Therefore a comic figure.

She held out the folder. He tried to think how to address her. Deane? Miss? "You work evenings and weekends," he said. He didn't take the folder and, not knowing what else to do, motioned her to come inside.

Today she was wearing a suit. But she had a blouse with a Peter Pan collar that wasn't right for the shape of her face.

Although how she dressed wasn't his concern. "You can have a cup of tea," he said. "Or coffee."

She was still holding the folder with Roth's brief. "I was only dropping this off," she said, putting it on a table and looking at the oxblood vase. She touched two fingers to the vase.

"If you came up here, this far, you can have something to drink," he said. The tea was from the supermarket. Teabags. But the coffee was a blend he sometimes got. He said so and then thought he didn't like the way that sounded. Affected.

Tea would be nice. She came into the kitchen after him.

He put a kettle on. Then he went into the dining room and started to set mats on the table.

She said, "Why not the kitchen? It's a better light." Later she heated more water for a second cup. She moved freely around Kreg's kitchen and talked about herself because he asked.

She had been Andrea Deane, Andrea Deane Malcolm, and had dropped Andrea when she was ten without having to fight too hard or too long for the right to change what she was called, which she later realized was an indication of the unimportance of the event. But she did develop ideas about her ability to modify certain conditions in her life.

She'd been born in Lincoln, Nebraska, where she was the second child, a middle child, of a Ford dealer and a librarian. A younger brother was brain-damaged and would always stay with his parents. Her sister lived in Santa Barbara, where she enjoyed the California climate and her husband being a full professor in the English department at U.C., and where she practiced a moderate commitment to environmental causes and raised four children.

In terms of geographic scatter, happiness and unhappiness, luck and achievement, this seemed a normal middle-class family. Kreg tried to conceive a graph on which these variables could be plotted.

By the time she became Deane, she was getting singing lessons, music lessons, dancing lessons. She was popular in high school. She went to the University of Texas at Austin, stayed two years, joined a drama group and took up alcohol and tobacco. She was then in with what she called a rowdy crowd. But after a while she took up more decorous ways.

She didn't say in detail what she'd done for over a dozen years since. A series of positions, though, with no seeming need to dig in or advance herself. She had lived at times in Aspen, San Francisco, Santa Fe. Kreg asked about now.

"I get jobs for a while. And see my friends."

"And tell people the story of your life."

"If they ask. No secrets."

"You don't smoke anymore."

"Or drink. And I'm not rowdy."

Her friends were mostly poor or anyway not wealthy. They were environmentalists, actors in progressive theater groups, socialists, blacks. Marginal figures in the polity of the Lion of Grenada. She distrusted large groups.

Kreg asked if she was religious.

No, she said. Although that was something she'd once thought could be interesting to her. But she had really no belief. "So I have to do without it."

"That's good," Kreg said.

"Why is it good?"

"I think it is. Because it's the way I am too."

"But it was never a question for you?"

"No." He decided that she was only moderately attractive. He had been looking through Roth's papers while they talked and had decided to go to the office now. If he put in time there today, in the library, he could probably finish at home tomorrow. He stacked the empty cups and told her she could wait while he went in to change.

"Yes," she said. "I can wait a few minutes." But could she see his books?

"You can look at the books. Whatever you want."

His books, she said. The books he'd written. . . . She had been talking to Roth, Mr. Roth as she put it. Roth had told her about them.

Kreg said yes, he'd used to be an amateur commentator on some aspects of the law.

"No. He didn't mean that you had a hobby."

"Here," he said, showing her where the books were.

In his room, knotting a blue wool tie, he considered the manner, the way of handling himself in the world, of the legal scholar who had written the books into which, he assumed, the young woman some few feet away from him, through a wall, was now looking. *It was never a question for you.* He admitted by way of a compliment to himself that, if his beliefs were constant, it wasn't because he didn't look around.

When they were downstairs and on the street, he saw thin rag ends of clouds scudding in front of a quick wind. An uncompromising iron sky.

Deane said, "If you just wanted to get out, we could walk for a while."

"For a few blocks," Kreg said. "A little while. But I have to get downtown." He reminded her that there was Roth's brief to be worked on. When he wasn't able to think of anything to say, he quickened his pace. They walked down Broadway. Deane, several times, stopped in front of a store window and then Kreg said that yes the dress or coat or picture was attractive or cheap or whatever she said it was.

When they were at Seventy-second Street he tipped his hat, disliking his own abruptness, seeing no reason why a middle-aged man shouldn't spend a few pleasant hours with a pleasant young woman. He said he should probably be on his way now. The point was, he thought, there were certain kinds of behavior that were inherently grubby. Middle-aged employers with their younger female help. *Getting Gertie's Garter.* Not that it had to be like that. It could be just those few pleasant hours. Innocent. Possibly it could be innocent. But he wasn't going to find out. He couldn't remember just what, leaving her, he'd said to the girl. He walked away from her for a few blocks and then, not planning it, into the park and to the museum, the Metropolitan.

Under the cloth, the two ends of the table appeared to be on different planes. Kreg stepped back. Possibly a better perspective. Cézanne. *Still Life: Apples and a Pot of Primroses.* The table, of course, had a middle and the join of the planes was as inevitable as it was improbable. "Break time." Eventually (during Cézanne's life) break space too. Disconnect it.

Perhaps, Kreg thought, the picture should be retitled. Something to suggest that when it was painted, quantum mechanics and the theory of relativity, these and other concepts of indeterminacy, limitation, fragmentation, had been massing immediately offstage, waiting to occupy the world's awareness of itself.

Outside the museum, at the top of the steps, Fifth Avenue below him. A crowd there watching a thug stalking a woman. The thug was a mime with black-and-white clown's paint on his face and a derby hat and baggy pants with suspenders.

Kreg went down the steps. The mime caught the woman. And let her escape. First, though, handed her a paper flower. Then stood in front of a man with a cigarette and begged a smoke. You could see his heart was breaking.

The hat came by and Kreg, thinking that miming tended too easily toward nostalgia, put in some coins.

He edged through the small crowd and began to walk south. Wind slapped at his face. Next to him, the long bulk of the stone façade of the museum. If he got to the office by one, he might be out in the early evening, about seven. Then he could work at home from notes. That would take longer. It was interesting that Roth resented him because he wouldn't help manage the firm . . . and would resent it if he interfered. Roth was going to resent him also for doing this favor. Roth wanted to be valued. Kreg valued him but not, he supposed, in the way Roth wanted. It didn't matter. Kreg would have a finished brief by Monday morning and Roth's secretary could retype what he gave her. She could do that couldn't she? Deane. . . . Where would she be now? Right now. Looking, possibly, through the inventory in a boutique or in a bookstore. Deciding what would be nice for an early lunch. . . . Assume the bookstore. Then what? A novel? Something about the ecosystem? No doubt she was interested in that. She was that kind of girl. Kreg corrected himself. *Woman,* not *girl.* Very possibly she might be working her way toward the museum that he'd just left. Part of a pleasant Saturday stroll, no particular goals. So into the park. Then see some art and take care of a few errands. Dinner later with friends. Or alone with one friend. Kreg doubted there was a man on the scene. Why did he doubt? He had no basis for an opinion.

Another gust. Light stuff, leaves, scraps of paper scatted east in front of it. Kreg blinked, clutched tighter at the red envelope with Roth's papers in it. He began to outline in his mind the direction of his work. Cardozo allegedly never forgot a citation. He, Kreg, had to look them up. Actually, Roth had got it wrong. It was more a matter of conflicts of law than of federal jurisdiction. Roth wouldn't care about that. Kreg did.

What if he had suggested that she come with him on this little detour to view some paintings? Not really any harm to that unless you thought of it as a prelude to something else. . . . Which he supposed was how he had thought of it and why he hadn't asked.

Jarvis Dalton seemed to lose his ability to concentrate. For more than a few moments his gaze wandered the quiet space of the Princeton Club dining room. Finally he broke a piece of toast and used it to adjust scrambled eggs neatly over the back of his fork, English style. "One thing we should be doing," he said, "is fixing some of us with some contracts. Those golden parachutes. Somebody buys the Company, I want to be able to show him a piece of paper that says he has to give me a lot of money."

Kreg said, "You'd have twenty percent of the stock against you on that. . . . And at least one director."

The president of Brandt Systems showed an emperor's jawline, but Kreg thought he looked indecisive. "Why?" Jarvis Dalton said. "Why would you be opposed?"

"That would be partly a moral issue, Jarvis."

"My future. I think I feel a moral need to take care of that. That moral issue. Family, you know. Kids, wife. Even me." Jarvis cut sausage with the edge of his fork. He chewed toast, then the sausage. "Moral," he said. "Let's hear about moral."

Kreg doubted he could explain to Jarvis his own revulsion at an entire fat system of buying and selling these companies and of the greasy rewards to some of those being bought. "Nothing," he said. He'd meant nothing. *Moral* had been a poorly chosen word.

Jarvis' quick smile. "And *partly,*" he said. What did *partly* mean?

Kreg explained about changes in the tax law and about the diminished benefits from arrangements entered into after June of 1984. About the write-offs the corporations could no longer take and the taxes the receiving executives would have to pay.

Jarvis said, "So if you'd recommended those contracts before last June. If you'd recommended them then . . ."

"But I was always opposed."

"The moral issue?"

"Whatever. You name it."

"I'd thought," Jarvis Dalton said, "that you had something in mind. Some way to deal with these guys. I mean you did call me and you kind of insisted that we get together. You know, pronto. At least that was the impression I had. Was I wrong on that?" He looked again around the room. He had a half smile, as if he'd triumphed in some small matter.

Now he thinks he knows where he is. He's decided that I'm his problem. Or the cause of it.

Jarvis said, "So my question, I guess, is what does counsel advise? About Mr. Marcu, I mean." He was wearing a victor's grin.

"I wasn't especially thinking we ought to be doing anything. I'd suggest that we wait." And yes he had, if you wanted, insisted that they get together. He'd thought it important to advise the president of this situation that might be developing. Didn't Jarvis agree that he should have done that?

Jarvis had a power breakfaster's way of getting a waiter's attention. With a clean table in front of him and hot coffee, he commented that one thing any acquirer would certainly want would be the Kyber division.

"The whole Company's attractive," Kreg said. "Everything's growing."

"But Kyber's hot."

"That's true."

"What I would see, I think, if *I* were going after us, is that balance sheet with no debt and how any child if he hadn't been arrested too often could borrow against it. And if I wanted I could sell off everything else and just keep that part of it. Just Kyber."

"You could do that. Probably. If you had control."

"The valve division and the people in that part of the business. This Marcu. . . . Whoever comes along. He might not have the same burning interest in those people. Or in senior management."

"Possibly not."

"Kyber Microsystems," Jarvis Dalton said. "Our crown jewel."

> Overall corporate revenues for the year increased seventeen percent. All segments contributed in a satisfactory manner. The greatest increases continue to be shown by our most technologically advanced lines, as represented by the Kyber Microsystems division.
>
> Brandt Systems Annual Report
> page 3

Yes, our crown jewel. Yours in particular. Because without it you might still be only a moderately successful marketing man at Perkin Elmer. Allow for an upward bias but nothing like the jump Brandt gave you. And then the further rise that came out of his dying. Your rise and the growth of Kyber. So that now ten years later you have all that to lose. So much that even if you lose you'll win. You'll have enough. You'll still be rich.

At first he'd noticed only some little loss of weight. Some further hollowness in the concavities of Brandt's cheeks and eye sockets. Or Brandt getting out of a chair and beginning to walk for a few seconds with one hand at the small of his back. The Company had moved to Stamford and Brandt bought a house off High Ridge Road, almost to the Pound Ridge line. In the city he'd had one bedroom. A country home seemed more than he could occupy. A few pans and plates in the kitchen, the arrangements of a man who did for himself and didn't care about food. Chairs and a dining table. Cartons that would never be unpacked.

Kreg saw the monk's cell of a bedroom only after Brandt was dead.

Downstairs a cellar had been converted into a family room and now by Brandt into an office. Why did he go down there? Upstairs there were rooms he never used.

Two bachelors, Brandt would say. Himself and Kreg. The two of them each with all that space and not needing it or even really wanting it. *You're worse, he said. Worse than me. Two places. The apartment and the house. All that space.*

Kreg claimed he was a better housekeeper.

I know, Brandt said. I don't do so good for myself. Then he went back to business, always business. The thing, though, he said to Kreg, it's that there's only so far you can go in this kind of operation. The valves and the special parts we make. That's what I know and it'll always . . . I know it's always gonna grow. . . . But that isn't tomorrow's news. The cutting edge like they say. He curled a fist behind himself. Pressed his body with that hand still behind him against the barrel back of the small stuffed chair he kept here in his new workroom. There was beginning sometimes to be a sweatshine on his forehead.

Why not enough?

You see. I found this operation. They have some new things, I think.

Which you don't need.

Semiconductors, microcircuits. That's not a field, is it, where you can ever tell for sure?

You can tell it's a capital eater. You can tell about the failure rate.

Brandt grinned with his pain. He shifted his weight in the barrel-backed chair. *He said, They have something new is the impression I get. Like a new language to learn. That's what it would be for me. Get into the computer age.*

So after a brief time of negotiations whose terms he seemed not to care about or think important because he left them pretty much to Kreg, Brandt bought that company and made it the Kyber Microsystems division. He overpaid. He knew that and only smiled when Kreg (the rational heavy) tried to hold him back. *Chance of my life, Brandt said. Last chance.*

And Brandt began to spend most of his time at Kyber or in his basement office at home. The balance after a while shifted more toward the office. Toward the chair in the office. The chair was covered in a tobacco velvet with burn holes and a shot nap and a rip along one armrest.

Kreg found a man who guaranteed a one-week job. Recover, restuff, replace the underwebbing. Brandt always said yes, that would certainly help the looks of the thing and also its function. Probably a good idea and he would certainly think about having that work done. It occurred to Kreg that Brandt usually agreed with you and then did what he wanted. This was what he'd done before they completed the arrangements for the Kyber acquisition. Some minor point, one item he hadn't left to Kreg, and Kreg pressed him for an explanation. *What do you need this for?* No, Brandt said. He really didn't, did he? As if *need* was irrelevant, something that didn't enter his thinking.

So Brandt never actually refused and the chair stayed where and as it was. He had his habit of smiling when he was in pain and now he smiled more.

He did hire a president and he established the Foundation with its twenty percent of Brandt Systems' stock. He'd known he was dying. Kreg hadn't until then been sure but those acts were preparations.

Before Jarvis Dalton signed his contract, Brandt had a question for him. *You never asked about the Kyber name.*

Kyber?

It's unusual.

Technology companies, Jarvis had said. These smart scientists who start them, they're all readers. They go for something nobody else would know. Gnostic Systems. Pansophic. Is it like those?

People ask about it, Brandt said. It's from the Greek. Kybernētēs. *The word that cybernetics is from. It means helmsman or pilot.*

It has to do with control.

I would think so.

Kreg, now in the Princeton Club, wrapped one hand around his cup. Idle feel of the warmth of hot coffee through the thick china. He reminded himself that he was dealing with a man who was probably frightened. How old was Jarvis Dalton? Fifty.

Younger than I am. Why does he let things make him afraid? "It might be," he said, "that an owner would decide to sell the crown jewel for more than it's worth. He could try that. Then he could keep the valve company. Stay with solid value."

"You think?"

"He'd know what he had. . . . It's an interesting moot question."

"What's moot if he's buying stock?"

"It's moot," Kreg said, "because there's been no tender. And if there were one he couldn't get what we didn't give him. We start, I start, with twenty percent. I wanted you to know what's going on but I don't see that we have a crisis." *But what,* he was thinking, *if there is a tender? What's my position then?*

"I'd rather it was some pension fund," Jarvis Dalton said, "if somebody has to be on a buying program for our stock."

"I suppose you would," Kreg said. Eight-thirty now. He wanted to be in his office by nine. There was a paragraph that ought to be changed. It was toward the end so Deane could be typing the beginning pages while he rewrote. Indulgent, with no purpose to it, going for that walk with her. Roth would be pleased about the research he hadn't had to do. Roth always claimed to be only a negotiator, which wasn't true. But even so, what was wrong with being a negotiator? Was it *less than*? Why *only*?

Jarvis, naturally conciliatory, talked figures, put Kreg in the picture. The picture of things as they then were and looked to be going. He had an optimist's nature and nothing in his experience to prepare him for serious adverse change. Why was it, Kreg thought, that he himself was so irritated by the softness of the man? A strong aggressive instinct, where was the virtue in that?

When they were getting their coats, Jarvis gripped at Kreg's arm. "I guess it really is," he said, "our crown jewel."

"Kyber, you mean?"

"Yes, Kyber."

Kyber Microsystems is a designer and developer of metal-oxide-semiconductor, large-scale-integrated and very-large-scale integrated circuits (MOS/LSI and MOS/VLSI). The division's products are manufactured and sold by it to original equipment manufacturers and to end users in the fields of data communications, computer terminals, computer peripherals, word processing, telecommunications and consumer electronics. In addition, the division has entered into many licensing and cross-licensing arrangements involving patented products and proprietary skills.

Brandt Systems Annual Report
page 6

"You have been busy," Deane said, not ironically. She fingered the sheaf of papers as if to derive from heft an approximation of work to be done.

Kreg said, "I tried to be careful about corrections. You ought to be able to follow them."

"You type?"

"You have to if you work at home."

Deane began to look through the papers. Kreg watched her narrow face. A loose strand of hair, an ordinary brown color, no special sheen to it, fell over her face. She brushed it away, and while she read chewed at the inside of her cheek. She looked up. "I should have it before eleven," she said.

He was moving away, going toward his own office. And stopped and considered the consequences of certain initial steps. He only half turned, so was facing away from her when he said that he hadn't gone straight to work when he'd left her. He'd stopped to look at some pictures.

"Good ones?"

"Cézannes . . . at the Metropolitan."

"Those are good ones," Deane said. Then she said, "I'd like to have seen them. I'm fond of Cézanne."

Kreg completed his turn. "You should go," he said. "They're very good. You'd want to see them."

"Will you be going again?"

Kreg didn't answer immediately. Then he said, "Probably not. Not for quite a while."

"Most people who go to museums go fairly regularly." She brushed the strand of hair from her face.

"I don't," Kreg said. "Not often." He turned away again. Met

Roth coming in with his coat collar up and a camel scarf and gloves.

Roth shook himself. Tucked his gloves in his coat pockets and rubbed his hands. "Cold," he said. "It's too cold. We could get an early snow."

"Maybe," Kreg said. "I don't think so but I'd like to see it. I hope you're right."

"My brief?"

"Before lunch, I think. Ask your secretary."

"Go over it with me?"

"Is that part of the deal?"

"Of course it is," Frank Roth said.

Before lunch didn't work out and turned into a conference with sandwiches in Roth's office. The office had a decent view. A brown marble coffee table with a Bertoia brush sculpture was set between two dark-chocolate leather couches. Even when he wasn't in conference Roth worked more at the coffee table than he did at his desk. He had a weak back and hunching over wasn't good for it but working in that position, that setting, confirmed, Kreg guessed, some private view of what his style should be.

The sandwiches and coffee were on nice plastic trays done by an Italian designer. The coffee was in white porcelain, Limoges.

Deane set down the two trays.

She went out of the room. Roth watched her.

"Maybe you've finished looking," Kreg said.

"Looking is all right, Philip. It's permitted. A man can look at his secretary's ass."

Kreg was feeling the rush of blood against his eyes and something along his shoulders. A need to clear his throat. He said, "You wanted to go over my brief."

Roth didn't immediately answer. But there was that shrewd quick ability to appraise, his negotiator's skill. He moved his tray to one side and arranged draft pages of the brief in front of him.

Scene: two attorneys reviewing document. There was no reason for this conference that Kreg could determine. Roth wasn't going to change in any substantial way what Kreg had written. Essentially, he would have to be pleased. Kreg had found two precedents for a ruling that jurisdiction would lie in the Southern District . . . and Roth wanted in this matter to be in the New York court. *Subtext: my mind on this girl.* But what was that about? She wasn't beautiful. He didn't sense an especially powerful sexuality. What it came to was that she was young, an amiable young woman. That was all. A banal story. *Back to the action: my workday as a series of skits.* Jarvis Dalton, now Roth. Why hadn't Jarvis picked him up on what he'd said? Yes, an acquirer might decide to sell Kyber and hold the valve company. Stay with the solid unexciting assets. But it was more likely to go the other way. The promise was in Kyber.

> Significant advantages in device operating speed have been derived from gate MOS/VLSI circuits employing a metal silicide rather than polycrystalline silicon as a gate and interconnection layer. Kyber Microsystems is the first semiconductor manufacturer to develop such circuits for commercial sale through a patented technology for depositing, defining and etching Titanium Disilicide.
>
> Brandt Systems Annual Report
> page 7

"Here," Frank Roth said. "Where I have the pencil mark. Next to 'or.' Shouldn't it be 'and/or'? So there's nothing ambiguous?"

"If you like it better," Kreg said. "But I don't do it that way."

"You don't think it buttons it up better?"

"That's why I don't do it," Kreg said. Jarvis, he was thinking, had even said it: *Our crown jewel.*

Marcu had flown to Washington, D.C. in the morning and didn't get back to his office until after eight o'clock, which was when he was expected. On time as always. Not obsessively punctual but never delayed. Not to Cotton's recollection. He didn't indicate any urgent need for news and Cotton didn't volunteer.

Cotton said he could send out for dinner if Marcu wanted.

Marcu was folding his jacket over a chair. He looked at his left wrist (a wafer Patek with a gold mesh strap). Not yet, he said. Would that be all right with Cotton? They could wait for a bit, couldn't they? There was almost a silk shine to the white broadcloth of his shirt, the white cuffs ending in surprising ruffs of black wrist hair.

It was only, Cotton said, that he hadn't known Marcu's schedule. When Marcu had eaten, he meant. He heard himself explaining. His master, he thought, never *has* to eat. He never *has* to do anything. He never gets that hungry or that thirsty . . . or a sudden gripe in his bowels. . . . He has to want to know what happened. How big a bite did we take out of Brandt Systems? How much stock did we pick up? Why doesn't he ask?

Marcu looked through messages in a folder on his desk. "Then it was a busy day for you," he said without looking up.

"It was a good one for us. We're over. We'll have to file."

"How much did we buy?"

"Seventy-nine thousand," Cotton said. "That's one and a half percent of the outstanding. We total now four hundred and thirty, four hundred and thirty-two thousand shares. We had to move it two points."

"Seven," Marcu said. "Seven percent. We hadn't planned to go in with only that."

Cotton brightened. "Eight," he said. "Another fifty-odd thousand in the morning. We'll print that on the open. From the trust department of a bank in New Haven."

"Up?"

"We'll pay three-quarters over the close for the block."

Marcu looked at the Patek as if it were time he was thinking about. "So we will file a 13-D," he said, "and then we will be in the open. Everything public."

"Yes. Naturally." But wasn't that where they wanted to be? At the next stage?

Marcu extended his fingers. Touched tips. Thumbs on the horizontal made the base of a triangle. He peered through the structure he'd created. Then closed his eyes. "We could lose this," he said.

"Why would we lose it?" Cotton felt a slight flush over his

cheeks. He reviewed in his mind what he'd done and what he hadn't. Grateful that Marcu for now was not looking at him. Marcu's brown eyes . . . it wasn't a matter of fear and there was never any seeming intent to intimidate.

Marcu said, "We file for ourselves and affiliated interests." He said, "I had spoken to Bronheim. There may be more stock. Another hundred thousand shares. A little more . . . we could be lucky." He opened his eyes. Asked Cotton if that would be enough to start with? Ten percent? Possibly that much. . . . He was wondering if he'd made a mistake, if he wanted Bronheim with him in this . . . or in any other matter.

Cotton wanted to be able to articulate some sensible reply.

Marcu said, "Although it is still my judgment that our bid will bring out stock for us to buy." He spoke tentatively, as if, if he looked deeply enough or thought intently enough, he might bring to his own attention some new fact.

"Then you're saying we *could* lose, not that you think we will?" Even with his image of himself as a kind of careless Elizabethan lieutenant, Cotton believed in business matters what Marcu believed. A shrewd mercenary picks the most reliable general. "Because I don't think so," he said. It was his pride not always to agree with Marcu.

Who didn't respond but then said, "How did you handle it today? Who did you use?"

"Bear, Stearns. I didn't want two houses."

"First Boston?"

"That would have been the other choice."

"Or Goldman, of course."

"Only if it was a friendly deal."

"But as between the other two, you preferred Bear, Stearns?"

"Our fellow there. It's not the house but I think we have a better man there. I think the one at the other place can get a little nosy."

"And you were satisfied?"

"Never satisfied." Cotton made eye contact. "But they were careful," he said. "They didn't just go into the market. Blow the damn stock out of the water. They shopped the institutions. Wherever they could find a little block."

"A light touch."

"That had to be. The only way."

Marcu asked about the government market. Where had the long bond closed?

"The long guy," Cotton said. "Up maybe a quarter point. Something like that. Maybe eight, nine thirty-seconds."

"The long guy," Marcu said. He made the triangle again with his fingers and thumbs. He asked if it might not be possible to work through another broker at First Boston in the future? Assuming Cotton agreed.

Cotton thought that could be arranged. *The long guy.* He heard Marcu repeating that. He flushed. He said he'd discuss arrangements for the future with their fellow there on the banking side. The bankers ran the store. "And we want to be able to go with them. It's a helluva house."

Marcu on this occasion didn't collapse his triangle. He turned his head. Slowly. Looked through the triangle at Cotton, then away, seemingly out of the window of his office with its view south over the city toward Wall Street, the Trade Center and the Statue of Liberty (shrouded now in its armature, torchless). "If we need them in the future," he said, "we'd prefer our arrangements to be already in place."

Yes, chief, I'll get right on it. Cotton wasn't going to say that but he made a note.

"Sometimes," Marcu said, "in these situations, there isn't that much time."

"Usually," Cotton said.

"The lawyers?"

"I talked to him this afternoon. Fire when ready, he tells me."

Marcu separated his hands. "Very nice," he said to Cotton. "Very nicely handled. There's nothing left for me to do."

Cotton said he disagreed with that.

"Except to worry a little. My only contribution."

"You don't worry."

"And the calls. After it's out, you'll have the analysts and the newspapers. Another little something for you to handle."

"All that on one plate?"

"But you're prepared?"

"Our intentions are simple. We bought some stock for investment purposes. We have no further plans." Cotton said it in a monotone. *Iris stripped for him. Slowly. Almost dark in the room.*

Marcu said it was an odd thing to have created a society in which such a remark would be taken immediately and correctly as transparently untrue. A mere ritual lie.

She did what he instructed her to do. First on her knees. Then he said to lie on the bed. Kreg had come around. Given in. Kreg came to his office. What else could he do? I laid it out for him. Then he wanted to talk with Marcu. Only through me, I told him.

No, Marcu said when Cotton asked again about dinner. Claire would be waiting for him or would be coming in soon. In any event, expecting him.

He'd sent his driver home but there were cabs. He gave the driver his address, the Carlyle. He imagined the isolated shaft of the building. He took a cab with torn upholstery, cigarette butts and the radio playing. He wasn't getting what he was paying for. Although why should he? The driver made conversation and called him *chief.* Marcu favored more formal relations. At Madison Avenue and Fifty-seventh Street he paid the man off.

He looked forward to walking. A quiet street at night and the displays in the windows of closed expensive shops. He'd come to think of Fifty-seventh Street as a kind of barrier and divider. Below it the dominating masses of the IBM and Telephone buildings had made midtown a canyoned place. No near skyline for the pedestrian. Claire would tell him about a movie that perhaps she'd really been to. She would sound as if she had. *Stop here.* A narrow store window with perfect Chinese porcelains. One large platter in blue and white. A small screen, oriental, with hunters on horses. All seemingly accessible.

To whose reach?

He wanted the screen. Come back tomorrow and buy it. After lunch. There was free time after lunch. *Ten percent.* He promised himself that when he passed the ten percent mark he would buy the screen. His own stock only. He wouldn't include what Bronheim had.

Marcu wore a grayblack topcoat and a gray hat with a narrow black band. He wore a silk scarf, royal blue with white dots, breathed cold winy air. It had been wet but now wasn't. He walked four, five, six blocks . . . and stopped at a bookstore. There were rows of books with red covers with white letters and rows with beige covers and brown letters. A repetition of patterns in the way of the best merchandising technique. The black-and-white covers, large, of a coffee-table book of photographs with a slender, somewhat kidney-shaped, red mark in the lower-right-hand corner. Rows of red marks.

Marcu distrusted any appearance of good order. Because actually, in the world, things were always collapsing or dissolving or sliding away. Which didn't necessarily imply despair as the condition of any given life. One morning, in a few days, Brandt Systems would not open for trading. *Announcement pending.* The little drama of that.

A couple walking toward him. She holding the man's arm, her fur coat open. *Mais je ne veux pas,* she was saying. A silver blonde, about forty, pearls at her throat. Her eyes met Marcu's. Hint of a smile from her.

There could be a deal next week. Two weeks. These things sometimes happened that quickly. Probably longer, but the stock would be coming out, as he had told Cotton it would. Marcu was certain he would have a chance to buy. Brandt Systems might look for a white knight, another purchaser. So it was conceivable that he himself would eventually tender his position to someone else. Why so often this search for white knights? They were only other acquirers, not true rescuers. And no more likely to keep their promises than any owner. What happened here, he thought, would depend on the lawyer. Philip Kreg. Kreg was the pivot. Anyway, a successful operation. No likely chance of loss. And Bronheim's interest wasn't significant. Marcu knew it had been only to satisfy his own ego that he'd allowed Bronheim into the deal. . . . Not characteristic of him to act like that but also not a mistake that would cost.

An accidental meeting at the dump. Why was that amusing? But that was where Kreg saw Nate Hobart.

Nate's hand was between the black shepherd's jaws. He was gripping the lower jaw and he rocked the animal's big head. When he wouldn't stop, the dog began to growl low in its chest.

Kreg poked the toe of his work shoe against the ground. The earth was hard enough but with a cellular give to it. They'd had a period of cold rainy weather. Each night the soil was freezing lightly and not all the water had yet leached out of the subsurface.

"I didn't expect you up here," Nate said.

"This weekend in particular."

"I read the financial section. I gather the hounds are after you." Nate freed his hand. He and the black dog contemplated each other. Not in any especially friendly way. The dog wasn't wagging its tail.

It was a scene of gravity, Kreg thought, with possibly some undertone of mutual respect. He said, "Marcu, you mean? You read he'd filed? But you see, there was nothing more to do about that. Not at the moment."

"People hang around and fuss."

"We went through that for a while."

"A flap."

"There was something of a flap," Kreg said. He recalled the

special meeting of the Board of Brandt Systems. Himself reporting to the Board what he had already substantially discussed with Jarvis Dalton (the soft worried look that drained the structure itself out of Jarvis' face). He recalled Mouse Kelly's quick combative anger and Henry Juszczyk following Mouse. Sam Marion's reserve. Sam, the founder and head of the Kyber division and still the key man there.

"You too?"

"Did I fuss too?"

"Like the rest of them?"

Key question. How to respond to it? A corncob at his feet, a relic of the summer. Kreg toed it. He eyed the black shepherd, received a measuring flat stare back. There were dogs that went, when you looked at them, into instant raptures of slavish love. *Pick it up, master. Throw it. I'll get it.* But this wasn't a fetch-and-carry beast.

Kreg kicked the cob to one side, reached into the open trunk of Nate's El Dorado and hauled out the black trash bag. What he hefted wasn't much for a week. He walked to the rim of the excavated area, twirled the bag and tossed it into the open pit of the sanitary landfill.

As it was now called.

A jay scatted through a spill of cans, paper cartons, loose small trash. A quick riff. Junked tires and odd appliances as major reference points in the landscape. Overhead a flock of geese headed home. That was a more businesslike procession. A sense of purpose there. The jay was less socialized, undisciplined, *cyanocitta cristata cristata,* an independent small-timer.

Kreg said, "I'd had a sense it might be coming. But all of us to a degree, we were all concerned."

He had been clearing his attic, odds and ends that he'd brought here for disposal. Nothing major, though, not a destruction of history. The air here had a mold smell. Not rich. More like a remembrance of its own self, a trace dissipated by any minor breeze.

The jay nosed into a yellow shopping bag, decided not to follow through on that and took off.

Something also about Brandt's funeral. A bird there.

Nate said, "It's that the stakes are so high. A lot to lose. People panic a little."

"Mere mortal men."

Nate curled his upper lip. Showed yellow teeth.

At the Board meeting, there had been the smell of discord. Which came from fear (Nate's point). *Calm them,* Kreg had thought, knowing he didn't have the accommodating manner he needed.

Brandt Systems had no boardroom. *What do we need that for? Brandt said when he went over the plans for the new building off the Post Road. Put the money into landscape. Make it a little park out there so at lunchtime people can have their sandwich. Sit in the sun maybe.* With only five directors they might have managed nicely in Jarvis Dalton's office. If they were going to manage nicely at all. Family photos on Jarvis' desk. Other photographs on the walls: framed enlargements of New England scenes and some that appeared to be of the more barren regions of northern Europe. Possibly certain of the islands off the coast of Scotland. Jarvis' wife was the photographer. He himself, right now, had the uncertain look of a former tackle whose game plan for life had gone irremediably awry.

"What the hell did you do?" he said to Kreg. "Did you sell us? You could have stopped this thing."

"Jarvis is trying to put it on the messenger," Sam Marion said.

Cool bluesteel eyes, blond, slender. Sam would only show you that he was detached and that he saw crises as occasions for ironic response. Something of the image of an upper-class slightly fascist aesthete. . . . Although it was true he could afford his attitudes. Everybody wanted what Sam Marion had. There were no foreseeable difficulties for Sam. Changes would be seen as adventures or entertainments.

He'd sold to Brandt for over four percent of the Company, with about as much more stock for his key people. Certainly he spoke for all the Kyber group and controlled their votes. He led and represented them, just as Brandt, alive, had been the unquestioned head (and not only by reason of title or ownership) of whoever worked for or served or even orbited his enterprise. Sam, as Brandt had been, was a maker, an original, and there was surely from that some emanation of force or will of a special kind that Brandt had sensed and that had drawn him to the younger man . . . more that personal quality than the specific nature and potential of Kyber itself.

Brandt had had no relatives and what didn't go to the Foundation, he'd left to his employees. Henry Juszczyk was a fairly rich man. All the old valve company people had stock. Men in the shop went home each night to neat ranch houses they hadn't ever expected to afford, drove big Oldsmobiles, had maybe a fur coat for the wife, something that came out of the closet three or four times each year. In Henry's case, the idea of that much money would be disturbing. He wouldn't want to know that he was wealthy. Put it out of his mind.

Add it up, Kreg thought. Between Brandt's people and the Kyber group you'd be close to twenty. And the Foundation would bring you to forty. Close to half. Not easy to beat.

If he could hold these people together.

Kreg himself spoke for slightly over a thousand shares. A joke number that could have been more. Brandt had wanted it to be more. He had come in with a list. Names on a yellow pad, over a hundred names. Written by him, although you'd have thought of those fingers as not any longer able to hold a pen. Kreg changed the number next to his own name. When he signed the documents Kreg gave him, the left hand cradled his right wrist. When was that? Two, three weeks before he died? More or less. *What was left of him? His will. Strength of will, which he exercised to come to my office to make his will. Three weeks then to the time of the funeral service in that church with the view over the Hudson. More or less three weeks. It was just after Roth had suggested that we make it a partnership. Formalize our union was how he put it. Gerri gave a dinner party to commemorate the event. Insisted on it. Almost twenty years in that building with him.*

And twenty years to the Board meeting in Jarvis Dalton's office . . . where Kreg had said, "No, I didn't sell you, Jarvis." If he and Sam Marion could agree, Jarvis would go along. Jarvis, possibly in a few days or weeks, would be able, partially correctly, to say again that he'd been sold. And that would be only partially correct, because Jarvis couldn't be sold unless he sold himself.

And Kreg wanted to get him to that point. *All of them. They have to be willing to deal with Marcu if that's best for them. Which it may be. Because if not Marcu, then somebody else . . . no better than he. . . . But I can't tell them. They have to see that on their own. . . . And I have to see that too. And I have to think what's best for me. I have to think about myself a little.*

He went over in his mind his conversation with Cotton. Cotton would be back. He was sure of it. Cotton or Marcu. *Next time, be easier on him. Don't drive him away. This isn't a matter of personalities, of how you feel about him.*

Mouse Kelly nodded as if he were listening from behind closed eyes. At eighty-three, no longer a bantam and weighing maybe a touch over a pound a year, he had, Kreg thought, a right to his rest. Even morning rest. Mouse trusted him.

He said, "There's no conspiracy, Jarvis. What you see is all there is. It's an offer."

"Bastards."

"Bastards can make an offer."

"The good guys don't have to accept it, Jarvis," Sam Marion said.

Jarvis Dalton flushed.

Kreg said, "We can sell the Company if we want to but they can't take it away from us."

"It's called control," Sam Marion said.

Observable direct relation, Kreg thought, between Dalton's regression and the little cuts Sam Marion was taking at him. Jarvis wasn't meeting eyes. You could imagine him twisting as a boy under the thrust of some teacher's patient, sweet-mannered ironies after, say, the entire perfect structure of solid geometry slipped in a quiz from a mind that had never truly embraced it in the first place.

And there was Jarvis' fear in the background, his fear of change. Why shouldn't he be disturbed? As Kreg was disturbed in his own situation with Roth.

"So fuckum," Mouse Kelly said. He shook his head. Moved his hand from his brow.

"Possibly," Sam Marion said. "We'll have to see."

"Believe me," Mouse Kelly said. "These bastards, you can't ever act soft." He was awake now. The thought of a scrap. His bright blue eyes locked with Sam Marion's cool blue eyes.

Sam smiled politely at him and then at Kreg.

Jarvis Dalton seemed to be observing generally understandable reactions and ways of acting, and to be taking encouragement from that. Positive changes in the set of his jaw and shoulders. He apologized straightforwardly to Kreg for saying what he had about selling out.

Kreg said that everybody was feeling a little stress.

"So all right," Jarvis said. "I guess the only question is how we word it when we tell them off." Suspicion, though, still in his eyes.

"Or if we answer them at all," Henry Juszczyk said. "Does there have to be an answer?" he said to Kreg. "Can't we just let em hang on their own petard?"

Henry shifted forward in a chair that was too small for him. Bald, soft-bellied, with thick glasses and a sweater under his suit jacket instead of a vest. Maybe never at ease with his own height. From a bench in the shop with Brandt to chief operating officer for the valve side of the business. Jarvis Dalton's loyal man because Brandt had put Jarvis in charge.

Again, Sam Marion's cool smile. Detached in a way that you learned in certain good families and schools.

Kreg said, "We have to answer them, Henry."

"Why would that be, Philip?" Jarvis put a growl in his voice. Man of action, now on course.

"Partly because we're public." Kreg didn't have to look at his papers. "We show thirty-one hundred eighty-six shareholders of record. Not many but enough. They might feel they had a right to hear from us." Jarvis, he was thinking, didn't particularly carry off an air of rugged hostility. You didn't get a sense that he'd be truly willing to go to the mat.

"It could be a good exercise too," Henry Juszczyk said. "Clarify our thinking." Henry rubbed at the side of his face, embarrassed at having an opinion.

Jarvis said he wasn't going to disagree with counsel. Just so we told them off was all he cared about. And so we weren't too polite about it.

"Then we should get at it," Henry had said.

Nate Hobart slammed the trunk closed. "You see," he said. "Nothing's that hard, even emergencies. You got your business finished so now you can come up here for the weekend. Hang around the dump and see who turns up."

"Except that I have to go back tonight. There's a conference in the morning."

"Worry the same bone over. And you kill a Sunday morning to do it."

"But partly a different cast of players."

Nate's shepherd prowled the perimeter of the dump. The jay or another one made a reconnoitering pass at a pile of scrap metal.

Kreg said he was bringing in new counsel. Someone who specialized in takeover work.

"On the defense side?"

"This time."

"That's smart," Nate said. "Why should you bear it all? The whole damn load."

"I won't. I won't bear any of it because I won't be working with them. I stepped aside as counsel. I'll brief the new people and then I'm out." There was the Foundation and the Company, he said. Possibly with different interests in a situation like this. It hadn't seemed to him that he ought to be representing both of them.

"I know," Nate said. "But to give up control."

"Did I have control?"

"Even so, I'd maybe have hung in there."

Which had also been Mouse Kelly's thought.

Then we should get at it, Henry Juszczyk had said and Jarvis Dalton said all right then. This was all legal maneuvering as he saw it. That was Kreg's area wasn't it? So would Kreg take over and set them some kind of an agenda? Sam Marion stretched elegantly and said yes he wanted Kreg's views. Watchful eyes though.

Lead them. From that, Kreg had a sense of false dealing. And what else could he do? Through the window of Jarvis Dalton's office, he watched a fine cold rain that lashed into the lawn there. Brandt's park. Skeletons of locust trees whipped by the wind. Green, though, underfoot.

He had a need to get out of doors. He decided then to go up to the country. The weather might break.

"What I've done," he said to Jarvis, "is to arrange a meeting for Sunday morning." He heard himself talking about the lawyer he was bringing in. How right the man was for this job.

Jarvis began, after he looked at each of the others, slowly to nod his head. "But you better stay on," he said.

"Yes," Kreg said. "Available when needed."

"When needed," Henry Juszczyk said. "You're always needed."

Kreg explained again that theoretically he might at some point have to go one way for the Company, "for us," and another for the Foundation.

"Theoretically," Sam Marion said.

Outside, the rain came at them obliquely. Mouse Kelly never wore a hat. His driver, in a gray suit and holding a golf umbrella in yellow and white sections, came to meet them. He and Kreg each took an elbow. They huddled over the old man. Hurried him to the edge of the lot where the black Continental already had its engine running. Heat on, warm inside. Kreg noted through the car window the sheen of the wet oily black asphalt surface of the Brandt Systems parking lot.

Mouse Kelly scrunched into himself for more warmth. "Theoretically," he said. "Theoretically you could piss up your leg."

The driver passed back a flask. "A small one," he said. "And give it back to me or she'll have my ass. . . . Not you," he said to Kreg. "You take what you want."

"Just close the glass," Mouse Kelly said.

"After I get the flask back."

Mouse drank and then Kreg. A small fire in his belly. He

realized that he was hungry. No breakfast and it was after one o'clock. He handed the flask forward.

The driver closed the glass partition.

Theoretically, Sam Marion had said. A few minutes later he'd been the first of them actually to get to his feet. "Then we can adjourn this thing," he'd said. "Short meeting. . . . What do you think?" he'd said to Kreg. "Should I get a lawyer of my own?" Partly he was putting it to Kreg but he was also serious.

Mouse in the back seat of his black Continental cupped his hands and blew into them, shivered as the warmth of the car began to get to him. He said, "You're not that big on conversation. Or answers."

"I might not have them."

"You're supposed to. That's why he set it up like that. The Foundation with all that stock. That was his plan."

The old man segued into sleep. Fine silver hair, perfectly in place. Easy smooth breathing. They were on the Merritt. Just past the Greenwich toll, without seeming to wake, he said, "The other part of it is that he left it to you. Up to you."

"Conditions change, you mean?"

"I mean he knew that. He had his ideas but no dead hand of the past. That wasn't part of them."

"What was part of them?"

"No ya don't."

"Then all right. You. How are you going to go?"

"I'm the outside director. Best interests of the shareholders. That's my only consideration. That's how I go. After I decide what it is. Best interests." Mouse had opened his eyes. He was wearing a moderately perceptible check to the house expression. "What it is," he said, "is that you're confused yourself. Your own views. You don't know what you think is best so it gets you down that they all look up to you."

"You too?"

"I got a more certain nature. I won't lean on you but I'm not gonna turn on you after, either."

"And they will?"

"It goes together. Depend on someone, it makes for resentment. You know that."

"They resent the dependency?"

"Don't they?"

Kreg started to remember some things that Jarvis Dalton had said. On two occasions. At the Princeton Club he'd wanted a golden parachute and today, about twenty minutes ago, had been asking for shark repellent. "If we had that new preferred stock they're using with the warrants attached," he'd said, "the shark repellent. Any raider who came along, we'd still be safe. We could dilute the stock to hell from under him." That had been as the meeting was breaking up. Sam Marion had already left. Possibly to find a lawyer. Then this remark from Jarvis. A thin clear note of petulance in Jarvis' voice. It had occurred to Kreg that Jarvis was friendly to him only when fearful or intimidated. He watched ahead of him the perfect clean arcs cut by the windshield wipers, obliterated as they came into being.

If that had been Brandt's plan, if Brandt had wanted, for some while ahead, the major problems of the corporation to be borne by a thick-bodied lawyer who cared about the business itself only as an equivalent for the burden that had been placed on him (the idea of the stubborn assumption of certain burdens being maybe the basis for the bond between the two men), then he'd lived long enough to effectuate his plan, long enough for Kreg to prepare the will that Brandt had always in the past said yes he should take care of and never had. *Yes, Brandt always said. Yes, I will. But I got to think about it a little. Figure how I want to do it.* Kreg drew the will and organized the Foundation that was created by it and reviewed the documents with the young lawyer in Stamford who was beginning to act as local counsel for the corporation.

They came into Brandt's study. Brandt was in the barrel-backed chair. He had a cot there. Sometimes it was too difficult or not worth the bother to get himself upstairs to sleep. There wasn't any longer a regular cycle of sleeping and waking. It was whatever the pain dictated. Male nurses around the clock. It was a wet spring and there was a damp smell here downstairs that mixed with the smells of the dying body. The damp and the acid urine and the sweet decay of the flesh. All these together. Sweet-sour.

One moment of querulous anger. Nothing to do with the

documents themselves, which he assumed were right, done as he'd wanted them done. But he wanted his own witnesses. He wanted Henry Juszczyk there and Kreg, their signatures on his testament. *The point is, the young lawyer said, they both take under the will. You left something to them. So they can't be witnesses. You have to be unbiased. And the other thing, it's only a formality really.*

No, it isn't, Kreg thought. Not to him, it isn't. . . . That's right, he said to Brandt. You can't have a beneficiary witness this. The associate from the lawyer's office and the secretary waited upstairs until the actual moment of the signing. Both in their twenties. Tense. Maybe they'd neither of them ever seen a dying man before. Skin over bone, loose here, too taut there. Eye sockets revealed.

The young lawyer gave Kreg a ride to the Stamford station. Kreg had assumed he'd stay on a bit, but Brandt waved him away. *I vant to be alone, he said, and winked when Kreg left. Not an easy business, the lawyer said.* Except for the brief flare-up about the witnesses, Kreg had never known Brandt to show any lapse of control. The little accented joke had been a kind of apology for that.

Now Kreg said to Mouse Kelly, "Jarvis mostly. I suppose he does resent it. Not being truly independent."

"Only thing," Mouse said, he put his head back, spoke up to the roof of the car, "it was me, I'd never of brought in those outside guys. I'd of kept it right here." He made a fist.

"What I said about the Company and the Foundation, the possibility of conflicts . . ."

"Words can never hurt me."

Nate twisted sheets of newspaper. He set them in the grate with kindling over them and logs, and he lighted his fire. He didn't ask about drinks. He made martinis in a glass pitcher and served them with cocktail onions.

"Jesus," he said. "I'd hate to work on a Sunday."

"I have to."

"Do you?"

"We don't have a choice."

"You, not we. You're the key, aren't you? That's what I read. So just sell out."

"That's one possibility," Kreg said.

"But you're not saying?"

"No."

"And you'd never want to make it easy on yourself."

"That would depend."

"Jesus," Nate said again. He raised his glass. "After this," he said, "there's some hamburger in there. And a bottle of California white in the refrigerator that's not too shabby."

Kreg had planned to whitewash the inside stone walls of his cellar. There would be another martini now because Nate didn't ever have one drink. After those and the wine, how much work would he do? . . . But in the circumstances . . .

Nate's glass was still raised. "*Morituri,*" he said.

Kreg said he was closing the house for the winter and would it be all right if he had the plumber call Nate about getting in to drain the pipes?

Nate sipped his martini. "Good drink," he said. "I'll see he gets in."

Other than that, Kreg said, he thought he had the place in shape.

"Keep an eye out for you."

"I always count on that."

And there was always a bed, Nate said, if Kreg felt he wanted to get away some weekend.

But Kreg's thoughts of the country, just then, had focused on going *from* there. Back to the city. Almost thirty years ago . . . as it had been then. The melancholy of Sunday evenings. He arranged the luggage in the trunk of a green Dodge convertible. Tape over a slash mark in the canvas. Adam took one end of a suitcase, as if he could heft it. Kreg took the other. *One, two, three,* he said. And the careful placing of the bag with the tomatoes. Adam wanted the promise of a stop for ice cream. *All right, Susan said.* And she promised he wouldn't have to sleep in the car. She was wearing a green wash dress and had a flower-print scarf tied over her head. She caught Kreg's eye and he promised too. An occasion of sadness. Himself, once, with his own parents. The certain anticipation that his drowsiness would build. His mother would hold him. Her flesh.

"I might take you up on that bed," he said to Nate.

"You never have," Nate said.

Frank Roth studied the green-and-purple Vasarely, which he decided was hanging slightly to the right. He adjusted the picture. He stood back and looked at it again and said it seemed perfect to him now.

"Straight, you mean," Kreg said.

"You're not in a good mood," Roth said.

"No." Kreg's hand went into his pocket. His pipe there. His office pipe. He wanted to hold something.

Roth, in his shirtsleeves, was wearing silk suspenders with hunters against a background of cream. He hunched over the coffee table, which was too low for his back. Kreg was across from him. "Takeovers," Roth said. Actually, he said, he'd been wanting to tell Kreg about their own little takeover. Or amalgamation. This firm's amalgamation with Arthur Harris' firm, which was proceeding so very nicely.

"That's good," Kreg said, guessing that Roth also had something else to discuss. Whenever he got to it.

"It's mostly mechanics."

"Details."

"I've never minded detail work." Roth leaned back, away from the table. Hooked his left thumb under his suspenders. Ran his fingers over silk, as if concentrating for the moment on that small act.

Kreg said weren't they going to need more space and could they get out of the leases they had? Roth said that they were and that yes they could. Kreg thought about moving. He saw himself having to pack his files. Losing papers. He decided to veto any layout that called for a row of secretaries' desks in the corridors outside the offices. He was certain that his new partners would be men who kept in shape and who would always know some good new restaurant they'd tell him he had to go to. They would be friendly with their own wives. He was across from Roth, with his hands on his knees. His big hands seemed strange objects.

"There are benefits you pick up," Roth said, "that I haven't even told you about. One of the kids there, I say kid, he's about five years into practice, is a top SEC man."

"That's good," Kreg said.

"It's a new area for us."

"Nice."

"What made it go so fast, we agreed in principle immediately. So there were *only* the routine items to work on."

"I can understand that." *Also, Kreg thought, it went fast because you had a head start. You were dealing before you told me. Although that doesn't matter.*

"About money."

Kreg didn't want to have to negotiate his value. But Roth said the arrangements were essentially the same at both firms and he didn't see substantial changes. So that was all right too. Fine, Kreg said. It seemed fine to him.

"Philip," Roth said, "it is fine. And it's important to us. So take a minute and read this memorandum that I have. A little outline of what we're doing."

Three minutes later, Kreg was handing back the memorandum and deciding that this joining of forces might not be intolerable for him.

Roth leaned forward a touch. "There is one thing," he said. There was the question of nomenclature. What to call the new firm. Whose name would follow immediately after Roth's. "You notice," Roth said, "I didn't set that out. It wasn't in the memo. It's not something I have strong feelings about. I should tell you that on a numbers basis, it would be you. Very narrowly, but you. Me, then you, then Arthur."

"And there's some question about that?"

"Their only thought was that, starting a new partnership this way, and it's so close, maybe the firm that's coming in should follow. I mean a name from that firm. Arthur's."

Kreg said, "It would be to everybody's benefit?"

"Arthur is very reasonable," Roth said.

Strong feelings surfaced. "No," Kreg said. "I won't do it that way."

Roth said it had been anticipated that Kreg might feel as he did. What Arthur Harris suggested, in that case, was that they flip a coin. That seemed appropriate to him.

Appropriate. "No," Kreg said, not sure why he cared.

Roth murmured that what they might have here was a go or no go situation. But he didn't ask Kreg to reconsider. After a few moments he said pleasantly that perhaps he could work things out. "It's not," he said, "as if we didn't have the same interests. Objectively." Then he said that possibly Kreg would inscribe a copy of one of his books. Arthur owned *The Climate of Constitutions* and had asked. Kreg's reputation meant something to the man. It ought to count for something, he'd said. To impress a client or somebody they might want to hire, some first-rate graduate who wouldn't otherwise be interested in a small firm.

"Whatever," Kreg said. "But tell Arthur Harris he's wrong about the clients. They don't impress."

"I would agree," Roth said. "I would say, wouldn't you, that in the long run we're talking about relationships that are ultimately material? For instance, one's value depends on his *value*, if you follow me."

Kreg followed. He hadn't thought otherwise.

Roth said, "I myself, for instance, I try never to let any major situation get away from me. . . . I'm talking about this other thing, this shot Marcu is taking at Brandt. It's very necessary to you to keep in charge there."

Roth's wary eyes.

A warning. And Kreg's own roil of anger. To be contained. He rubbed the pipe bowl. Mouse Kelly and Nate. Now Roth. He seemed to be faced with a consensus. Everyone was telling him to stay on top of his life. He thought of Brandt. How would Brandt have handled a consensus?

No need to ask.

With Brandt it was always a consensus of one. That had been true at the meetings under the factory lights in the Long Island City loft and later in Brandt's office in the new building off the

Post Road. And finally it had been true in a barrel-backed chair in Brandt's house in North Stamford (a fist pressed into his back to ease the pain). . . . Brandt was always the same. He would listen (to whatever complaint might be made about, say, the six-month failure rate of a new line of valves) and then at some point politely decide that *Maybe I think we can fix it like this? Maybe we engineered the thing too fine? Now we should put a little more strength into it, don't be so elegant it doesn't work.*

Always the question in his voice and him looking at you as if he really wanted you to go along with what he'd said. As if he weren't sure you would.

The strong will and the courtesy. Kreg had been remembering those qualities the morning of Brandt's funeral. Driving north with Mouse Kelly. An earlier Continental but no chauffeur then. Mouse had had the money but not in those days the need. They drove just out of the city on the Saw Mill. To a suburb on the Hudson, a town Kreg knew as a name. A place he'd passed over the years on the way to his own place in Connecticut.

"So now it's on you," Mouse said.

"And you. Both of us. The outside directors."

"That Foundation. He didn't care what you did with that. Promote some one-legged dance group. Make it nice for the Indians. That was his means. So you could control that big block. The stock. The lever to whip those hired hands in line, you hafta. Jarvis or Sam. Help you a little if I can but you're the one."

A moderate June day. First the clear silver light on the Hudson. The calm broad river, fresh, new. Then the rich green of the foliage as they began to get out of the city. Kreg said that was an interesting thought of Mouse's but Brandt had known he wasn't actively going to help run the business, that he couldn't and wouldn't.

"Shit on that," Mouse said. "Don't you understand? What I'm talking about, what he had in mind, was *direction.*"

"Which you'll help me with," Kreg said.

"I'll help you but the primary, the load, that's still on you. Your shoulders. That's what he wanted. You know he did."

Not only silver. The river had been green, graygreen, even green and blue.

"Some fuckin government by committee," Mouse said. "You think he wanted that? Run the place like a convention."

They came into the town and found the church. Brown shingle, on a rise. Kreg guessed at a view beyond to the river. They were early. The thought had been that they would receive the others. A formal gesture to make up for or mitigate the fact that there was no family or really anyone else here for Brandt in this place where he'd been born and where he'd chosen to be buried. His will, though, identified him as a former parishioner of this church and left "ten thousand dollars to said St. Thomas Episcopal Church, if I shall be buried from said church." And there was a letter to Kreg, instructing that, if there was a service, there was to be no eulogy. *No talk about me or what kind of person I was,* he'd written in the shaky spiderscrawl of his last months on one of the yellow sheets he used. And no efforts made to locate old acquaintances. *I would be absolutely satisfied to have present only the friends of my late years.*

"What I meant," Mouse said. "Not that he expected you to devote yourself forever to the thing. Or anything full-time. What he wanted, he hoped you could stay with them a while. Jarvis Dalton is new. Sam Marion. I mean he must have been thinking that who the hell else is there. So you see they get this Kyber thing all blended in. Harmonious, I mean. Get it all harmonious. That's the most important."

Kreg looked through the car window and up the hill toward the church. The priest had come out. He was standing in front of the open door of the building with arms crossed in an attitude of surveillance. Kreg could discern the cropped red hair and, even under the cassock, the athlete's shoulders.

They turned into the driveway of the church. And around the building to the parking area in back, a view from there over the crest of the hill to the Hudson. When they came around the front of the building, the priest had gone inside.

Minutes later, others began arriving. Kreg and Mouse Kelly faced almost directly into an eleven o'clock sun to greet the mourners. Mostly old-timers from the plant. Kreg knew them all and their wives, many of them remembered from Christmas parties and from other funerals. Women no easier in high heels and brooches than their husbands were in their dark suits and dress shirts and neckties. *Thank you for coming.*

Inside then. Lovely thin music playing. Scarlatti or Palestrina? The priest had said on the telephone to Kreg that he had a passion for the composers of the late Renaissance. Kreg and Mouse Kelly, last in, walked slowly as if escorting each other to the front of the church. Seats in the first row there for the officers and directors.

The music stopped and the priest moved toward the pulpit. Shafts of perfect light through the upper windows of the church. Kreg focused his attention on the downward slant of those rays. The priest began the service. Kreg listened to familiar phrases. Odd bits heard over the years at other funerals, other services. This time there was something new that took his attention. There was what the priest had just said about joining *the saints in light.*

Then what was he going to do with this Foundation that Brandt had imposed on him? Brandt had wanted to perpetuate some considerable degree of control, and Kreg had arranged that for him. Not though with any idea that he himself would wind up having the details of its operations handed into his hands. His big hands . . . long fingers with spatulate tips. *But then, the priest read, face to face: now I know in part: but then shall I know even as I am known.* Kreg repeated in his mind the scattered phrases of the Kaddish, the little he knew. *V'yskadal, v'yskadash.* Heard at other times, at other events like this. Brandt had had a strain of melancholy . . . so any sound of deep sadness.

Then after the service people were forming in small uncertain groups on the lawn in front of the church. No common purpose now. There would be only himself and Mouse and Henry and Mag Juszczyk going to the cemetery. Contrary to Brandt's instructions. No one, he had stipulated. No one to accompany the casket. But Henry had decided no. *This time we can't, he'd said. We can't do it his way.* Not asking Kreg or Mouse but not looking at them either. A flush over his neck and face, and he'd started to blink rapidly and to clear his throat.

Kreg edged into a patch of shade. He ran his dry tongue around the inside of his mouth. Would it have been better to have had a reception? That way possibly some stronger sense of closure. But a reception was something else that Brandt had stipulated against.

A light touch. A hand on his shoulder. Sam Marion had come up on his blind side. Sam would be a master of the quiet approach.

"A day like this," Sam said, "if you have to go."

"When you have to."

"But almost worth it, don't you think?"

"I really don't." Kreg noticed, across the lawn, standing alone, Joan Marion watching them. Exchange of looks at a distance. She ran a hand through her hair. A river breeze whipped lightly at her dress. With Joan, Kreg thought, there would always be some likelihood of exciting sexual warfare. He thought about Sam's beautiful wife and her long legs and go-to-hell manner.

Sam Marion said, "His personal things. Is that going to be a big job?"

"You know what he had," Kreg said. "It was what was in the house. There wasn't much."

Sam looked away and then back at Kreg. "The papers there," he said. "Some of his papers."

"Could be important?"

"I think so."

"In connection with Kyber?"

"That's what's important to me."

Kreg understood now why Joan Marion wasn't here with her husband. He said, "Do you mean am I going to do something with them that I shouldn't?"

"I mean what's going to happen to them?"

"I'll deal with them."

"Which doesn't really tell me what I want to know."

Kreg breathed in. *Keep it harmonious, Mouse Kelly had told him.* He said, "There was a letter from him. It said that any technical or business papers, notes, sketches, diagrams belong to the Company and they're to be turned over to it promptly by his executor. By me. So no need to worry." The thought occurred that Brandt at a funeral would have been less assiduous than Sam in staking a claim for what might or might not be due him.

"Not worry. Just information."

"But now you're satisfied?"

"I understand there's a foundation that's going to hold his stock?"

"That's a different subject. It's not necessarily something you have any special right to know."

"But perhaps you'd accommodate me?"

Sam's pleasant frosty smile. A breeze washed over them from one direction and then another. It was important of course to ease Sam's mind. *Keep it harmonious.* The Foundation itself was partly a device to that end, a device to achieve harmony through control.

So now he was explaining to Sam Marion that the Foundation was no threat to him. "The true purpose of it is to leave you people free."

"Free of?"

"Constraints from outside."

"Last question, then?"

"However many you want."

"About him. He had a little bit of an accent. Some kind of Scandinavian. So how did he get to be an Episcopalian? Lutheran or Catholic, isn't that what you'd expect?"

"They were Norwegians," Kreg said. "Cook and houseman. Brandt was grown when they came here. A grown boy, twelve or thirteen. The people they worked for were parishioners here and this church was probably the easiest place to go."

"Say hello to Joan," Sam said. "She wants to talk to you." He took Kreg's arm.

"I want to talk to her," Kreg said.

When they came up to Joan, she smoothed Sam's blond hair. Nothing said but information was being exchanged. She made Kreg promise he'd come to dinner when asked. The priest was near them with Henry and Mag Juszczyk and another couple. Joan called for the priest to come over. "Talk to us," she said. "They've had you long enough. . . . The music," she said. "You have to write down exactly what it was."

The priest reddened slightly.

Nice, Kreg was thinking, that Sam was satisfied about the Foundation. But what about himself and having to administer it? He imagined a mountain of grant applications. How would he handle those?

Brandt, though, hadn't cared about Kreg's time. He'd had his own objectives. *I think I got you now.* Brandt grinning at him after Kreg had promised that yes he'd direct the thing and he'd drafted the purpose clause and read it to the man whose color by then had been a match for the yellow tobacco velvet of the chair in his study. *Make you have some fun, you want to or not. You pick something. The theater, research. Whatever subjects you like. Maybe a cancer study. You think you find a cure for me?* A spasm hit and he grunted. It was only in those last weeks that he made any noise at all. And then not much.

In the back of Sam's pocket diary, the priest was writing down the titles Joan wanted. Joan, Kreg thought, was no doubt amused by the man's willingness to please.

A man in a chauffeur's gray alpaca suit came up and whispered to the priest.

"The hearse?" Joan said. "We know there's a body and that there's a hearse. He doesn't have to make a secret of it."

The priest went red again.

"Always in practice," Sam said.

Kreg went to Mouse's car. From the far edge of the parking lot, he looked toward the Hudson. A line of barges moved north so slowly as to seem not to move at all and there was a sailboat, almost out of his field of vision. He started to open the rear door. Leaned against it for a moment. The red flash of a male cardinal across the lot and through a clump of honeysuckle into the thick green of a maple. Lost there.

And then ten years, and now he was here with Roth.

"I wouldn't try to tell you how to handle yourself," Roth said.

It was Kreg's idea that he was a fiduciary. And that if a fiduciary wanted to free himself of the burdens he'd taken on, there were things that had to be done. They had to be done first, before the burden was dropped. And no need for comment, even from his amiable, too dapper little package of a partner. He said, "I know you wouldn't. I never thought you would."

"Just so you consider. Brandt Systems is your practice. Almost everything. You can't lose it."

"I stepped aside. Not out. Temporarily aside."

"If they're taken over?"

"They won't be. How could anybody do that?" Kreg said. Not admitting for the moment, even to himself, any thoughts about the outcome or consequences of a decision to sell to Marcu . . . if there should be that decision.

"Probably not," Roth said. "I suppose they couldn't." He asked Kreg to look carefully at the Vasarely. He was thinking it had had its day and maybe a replacement was in order. "Not a long-term winner, is he?" Roth supposed that was one quality of truly fine art, its ability to hang on in the imagination, to keep its hold there. This was something he'd discussed with Gerri, who agreed with him.

That was also, Kreg thought, the way you'd measure the duration of a fashion. "What would you replace it with?" he said.

"Maybe de Kooning." Roth and Gerri had been considering de Kooning. Also Motherwell.

"They would be good," Kreg said. "Either one of them."

Through the cluster of women around her, Deane caught his eye. Her thin white face. She was red-eyed from crying. Red at the tip of her nose. The women were trying to comfort her. . . . A look of great hostility. . . . Because she was defenseless? Observed by him in her grief?

One of the younger women was on the phone. "United or American," she was saying, "why would I care? Look, this is an emergency."

Then Deane was gone for three days.

Kreg's secretary said it had happened so fast. Twenty minutes after she got the call, she was on her way to the airport. "Of course, she had to detour to her apartment for some things." It was the sister's boy, the woman said. The oldest, in his twenties. Always a problem, Deane had said. Never straightened himself out. "But to do it that way in the hills," she said. "In a garage there. He turned the engine on."

When Deane came back, Kreg stopped at her desk.

"It's an odd thing," she said, "whatever it means, being close to someone. I mean, in one way we weren't anymore."

He had an impression of calm.

No reason to think she'd waited for him but, leaving at seven, they were again the ones who closed the office. It was some time before the elevator came.

An exchange of half smiles.

"At last," Deane said when he stood aside to let her in first.

On Forty-fifth Street, Tech Hi-Fi was closed; Harvey's (Advanced Consumer Electronics) was closed; Charrette was closed. The camera store and the hardware store were closed. In the empty luncheonette across the street a counterman was serving a waitress.

Deane, in low-heeled shoes, looked up. "Well," she said. "How did this happen?"

Kreg said, "We work late so we come downstairs together."

"Not that."

"That's all," he said.

The waitress looked away from the counterman. Delicately, with the tip of one finger, she revolved the raspberry vinyl top of the stool next to her.

Deane looked across the street at the scene. "Buy a girl a drink?" she said.

"No," he said.

"You're busy."

"I'm not busy but it's not a good idea."

"Even so."

"Then that would be nice. A drink." *Easy,* he told himself. *Go slow.*

"Just a drink," Deane said.

Kreg thought of the Algonquin but they wouldn't be able to get a table there. Where did she go? Which direction?

"Near you."

He started to look for a cab. No, she said. Why didn't they walk? For a while anyway. After a few blocks, he asked her if he should try for one now and she said not unless he preferred. She kept up easily. When she had a point to make or saw something that interested her, she would touch his arm for emphasis. Each time she did that, he tensed. He felt light inside and some kind of effervescence over the surface of his skin. When they were uptown, she suggested a place on Amsterdam Avenue. He wouldn't like it in the late evening, she said, it got too crowded and noisy, but now it was fine. It was still early.

She ordered a Perrier. She was a regular here. She and the

waiter called each other by name. Kreg watched the waiter's expression to make sure there was nothing in the way of a smirk. Deane and the man she was with were as old as they happened to be . . . and that was their business only.

He remembered that she'd said she didn't drink anymore. Not to excess, he'd thought she meant.

"No," she said. "I don't drink at all."

"But you come to places like this?"

"I'm sociable, I guess, and my friends come here. It's not just that I don't want to drink. I'm an alcoholic."

"We don't have to stay," Kreg said. He wondered if she could have said that only for effect.

"But it's nice here, isn't it?" Deane said.

"Nice," he said. "If you have a good time, it's nice."

"I know," she said. "I'm not always totally precise." She asked about his family. A little later she said it was fascinating that Adam was in Los Angeles. That was so near to Santa Barbara where she'd just been. "Are you close?" she said.

"Three thousand miles," he said.

"He would have to be younger than I am. He is, isn't he?" She was thirty-three, she said.

"He wouldn't have to be."

"But isn't he?"

"He's thirty-two."

"You were young when you had him."

"I was in law school."

"So you were young. . . . Is this a mistake?" she said.

"Not necessarily," Kreg said. "But probably. It doesn't matter though. Except that we shouldn't do it again."

"I might ask you to buy me dinner."

"And I would have to decline."

"Not because you have other plans?"

"No other plans. But we really can't be seeing each other." There was a flatness in his voice that was distasteful to him. Why couldn't he explain himself now in a way that wouldn't be hurtful to this nice young woman (whose only culpability, so far as he knew, was in the very fact of her youth and the accident of her employment)?

"I've always liked a direct manner," Deane said amiably, although there was a pinkness now in her face. "Not that I understand your reasoning."

Of course you got into situations like this when you began to go around surreptitiously with your partner's secretary. He had been having a ridiculous vision of himself, a man in his late middle age with a thick phlegm of excitement in his throat, being led toward the bedroom of his apartment, his hand in the hand of the modest young woman who was taking him there. He was childlike, he thought. Easy dreams of what he would always be obligated to reject. Quickly frustrated, and then he closed in on himself. "In some ways," he said, "I would consider myself old-fashioned. I mean it isn't completely a matter of what we might prefer."

"Or confused," Deane said. "In various ways."

Not inhibited, though, not in any sense of being sexually shy. He had always believed that if a man and a woman wanted to get into bed together they ought to do it. But circumstance as a constraint on action was another matter. Which would bring you back, if he reasoned correctly, to this business of relations with young women in your office.

Deane squeezed lime into her Perrier. "You see," she said, "this necessity to look the facts in the eye. . . . Can't there sometimes be mitigating circumstances?"

Bend a little. Let her walk you to the bedroom. Lead you there. She stepped out of her shoes. Her hair was down. He said, "There can be. I'm not very good at those."

"I usually try to allow for them," Deane said.

Kreg didn't answer her. Actually, he was thinking, he also allowed for them. Facts or events or circumstances in mitigation. How could he not? a man with an equity practice. Fairness. Arguing for fairness, pleading, was so often at the heart of what he did.

Deane looked vaguely around her. "Do you notice," she said, "at this time of evening, how fast it fills up?"

As she'd told him, the place got crowded. Too crowded, and already a solid line along the bar. He guessed that the age of the customers here would fall, ninety percent, between twenty-six and forty. He noticed a great predominance in costume of black and of gray. Wide-shouldered raglan coats and jackets and argyles that crossed an easy divide from sex to sex. Kreg felt agewise and girthwise out of place.

Although not alone in that. A man at the bar in a business suit, maybe forty-five, with the look of a rugged building contractor. A man who stayed close to the senior union people and gave to the B'nai B'rith and the K. of C. and the United Way, went to the charity dinners and the political dinners, drove between job sites in the gray Cadillac. Never out of touch because there was the phone in the car.

Deane in her business suit and blouse and bow tie. What irritated him was her awkward straightforwardness here among the supple and the playful.

He was suddenly aware of the background music, that it was constant and too loud. The businessman caught his eye and then looked away. Careless, no interest. *Adam,* Kreg quickly thought.

It was a nice blending here, Deane said, wasn't it, of outer yuppie with a little of the art and entertainment worlds?

Very nice, Kreg said. Although he couldn't tell about the blending. He was realizing why that thought of Adam. And why a connection with the man at the bar. The man conformed to his image of the one who'd a month ago been asking about Adam at the apartment house. Van Atta's man, as he'd assumed. During the time of Adam's trip to Mexico, he'd got into the habit of watching for men like that. A habit of watchfulness that was no longer needed . . . but had been brought again into operation through some neurological tic. Probably related to whatever he felt about this meeting with Deane.

. . . who was saying, "But you wouldn't classify it as one of my world-class ideas? I mean, bringing you here."

"It was probably as well that we did it," Kreg said. *What did he feel about this meeting? Or rendezvous? There was a fermenting roil . . . a turmoil.*

"Lay certain notions to rest," Deane said.

"There weren't any notions," he said. Despising (as he said that) his own utterance, his blimpish evasiveness.

"Yes, there were notions. There are."

Just then he was able to catch a waiter's eye.

"You know," Deane said when they were on the street, "I'm always getting new jobs. I could get another job."

"Why would you do that?" Kreg said. "You're fine with us. You ought to stay where you are." He walked across with her to Central Park West and stayed while she waited for a bus. *Near you,* she'd said when he asked where she was going. Then why did she have to take a bus?

Midmorning when Roth came to his office, Kreg was interleaving pages into copies of a draft brief. He was working from guide notes on a yellow pad and he had books there, most with page marks in them. There wasn't quite enough desk space for a smooth operation. Kreg anyway was heavy-thumbed, not good at the job he was doing. Sheets of paper slipped away from him. But he was almost finished. Two more items, he said.

This was for a motion to be argued in the Southern District. The client was a small trucking company with an interstate business and a disputatious president who claimed certain load regulations in many states to be a burden on interstate commerce. Kreg had warned him he would lose. . . . But he would attempt on behalf of this irascible trucker to sustain a proposition that he knew to be unsustainable. Reasonable regulation, the courts had held. *A fight that's already lost,* he'd told his client. *Then fight it again,* the client said. Three days until the motion was heard. Kreg was reasonably comfortable with that deadline.

He inserted the last sheet and straightened himself. His back, he said.

Roth's fleeting smile, to indicate the superior understanding of the more experienced sufferer. He was shaking his head. Some friendly remonstrance to come. Today his suspenders were french blue. And he was wearing gray-and-white tweeds and a blue shirt with a yellow tie.

Lively. Very neat.

Roth put his hands on the high back of a chair. "You see," he said, "we're already starting to feel the consequences of this thing of yours."

Kreg had been meaning to get to a men's store. His own

clothes seemed all to be going at once. Last week a suit he liked had ripped at the knee. "My thing?" he said to Roth.

"Brandt Systems. You know."

"Consequences. They would be adverse consequences? You're saying that someone disapproves of my relations with my client."

"No one disapproves but there's concern."

The judge in the Southern District was going to ask for briefs. Kreg would be more or less ready in advance. Free time then for a lightning raid on Brooks. Two gray suits, shirts, socks. Whatever he needed. Iris, a year ago, had told him to throw out his winter coat. He said, "That would be Arthur Harris? He doesn't like it that there's a pass being made at Brandt Systems?" It *was* Arthur Harris, wasn't it, he said to Roth, who had that concern?

"You have a very special relationship with Brandt. You can understand . . . he doesn't know how all this might develop."

"Well there's no way he could know that, is there? I don't know it myself."

"What he sees are risks he hadn't contemplated."

"Of course he does."

"I absolutely know it's going through eventually. But it's the form of it that's uncertain, if you follow me. The thing is, Philip, he's figuring Marcu could possibly win this thing. We know he won't but . . ."

"We don't know that," Kreg said.

"We do know it, Philip. You and I know it but Arthur doesn't. What he sees is the possibility that a chunk of business he'd counted on just might not be there. A *big* chunk. And that he might have a senior partner with him who isn't really contributing all that much. . . . So we get back to what I said about the form of this thing."

Kreg had a thought for his brief and scribbled a word on a yellow pad.

Roth said, "If you could hold up on that for a minute. This is important. I don't know. Maybe if you hadn't stepped out as counsel, given up the little influence you had over this thing. What's he supposed to think when he sees you don't even fight? Philip, it bothers me too. And I want you to understand what I'm talking about. I'm talking about the configuration of the membership of this new firm. Ours and Arthur's. The organizational morphology. The partners. Who are going to be the partners? You. I'm talking about you. About what happens if you lose your practice."

"So I shouldn't let Brandt Systems be sold?"

Maybe five seconds apart, Frank Roth clapped his hands together. Three times. "You got it," he said. "That's right. You shouldn't let that happen. After they cut off your arms and legs, that's when you let them do it. Marcu. Marcu wouldn't keep you on, an operator like that. What would he want with you around? And what the hell would you do without that retainer? What is it, seventy percent of your income?"

"Maybe more." Kreg remembered a joke with that punch line. *The kid is worth a million bucks.* Pause. And, *Maybe more.*

Roth toed the carpet. He said, "No talking to you, is there? All right, you're bringing Willie Unger in to replace you. Three cheers, you're bringing in the best. Maybe he is. What did Willie say?"

"He doesn't think it's going to go away. Marcu won't drop it. He thinks we have a fair chance."

"So it's a dogfight?"

"It seems."

"But if you needed someone to do the job for you . . ."

"Yes. Willie would be your choice."

Which had also been Jarvis Dalton's opinion as voiced last Sunday at just after noon, with already the drive to the city and a conference behind him. "He is," Jarvis said. "He is something. I mean he is really going to carry the mail for us." This was in the cheerful fluorescent ambience of the hallway outside Willie Unger's office. They passed high-domed young lawyers with intelligent eyes. "Jesus," Jarvis said. "Sunday morning and the place is half full."

"At the national budget per hour," Sam Marion said. "Four twenty-five," he said.

As if that big number itself held some promise of magic to come.

It was the number Willie Unger had used when they came into his office. Willie in his vest, five-five, a mini-bulldog with (in his forties) an Einsteinian confusion of white hair and Coke-bottle glasses, was planted in the middle of the room. "On the money," he'd said, looking at his watch. "At four twenty-five an hour, that's what I'd be too. Right on time."

He stabbed at Kreg's chest with his forefinger. "Goddamn lucky for you," he said to Jarvis, "you got this guy with you. This is your defensive line. Two minutes on the phone if he wanted. One call to Marcu and you'd lose the farm. Where would you be if the Foundation sold its stock?"

He was shaking hands with Jarvis and Sam before he stopped talking.

"We all understand about Philip," Sam Marion said. "Jarvis does too."

You couldn't see through the thick glass into Willie's eyes. "No time for personal crap," he said. He moved toward a round game table covered in green felt. Yellow pads and sharp pencils for each of them. A half pack of Luckies at Willie's place.

"Somebody give me a date," he said, "for a special shareholders' meeting. This isn't complicated. We just have to move. I have an ad ready. You know what it says. Standard stuff. Same like you always read in the *Times.* You know, Marcu is a raider, which means he's a shit. Look at what he's done to other companies he's taken over. Strips the assets. . . . Now, think of our great record. So, shareholders, stick with us. . . . Got it? . . . Now read this and tell me if anything's wrong. This is the name at the agency but you won't talk to them. I'll handle that."

Then he said there should be new contracts for Jarvis and Sam and anyone else who was essential. Henry Juszczyk, was that right? Who else had to be protected? He had ideas about terms. He began to talk numbers.

Jarvis' golden parachutes. Something slavish came into Jarvis' eyes.

Before the meeting ended, Willie mentioned the outside chance as he saw it here of a leveraged buyout, the possibility that management might borrow enough money to buy in the public stock and have the Company for their very own. Big numbers if things went right.

At the elevator Jarvis said, "Do you think it might work out that way? That we could do an l.b.o.?"

"Willie is very astute," Kreg said. "He's very resourceful." *And he knows how to handle his clients. The suggestion about the big-number contracts and then the thought that maybe, at some near happy point in time, an l.b.o. could be just the ticket, the appropriate means to put this takeover problem once and for all to bed. And also, Jarvis, to make you rich. Not a matter of misdirection either. If Willie mentioned an l.b.o., he sees a possibility of doing one. Some possible way. Of course he never guaranteed that. He was only giving them good news first. To whet their appetites a little.*

It was a technique that worked.

A reasonable hope of delightful solutions had turned Jarvis into an aggressive bear for action. He'd made notes. He took, like a treasure, the letter to shareholders that Willie gave him and said that Sunday or not he'd get a couple of the senior girls into the place and, however late, those letters would be Xeroxed and ready for Next Day Mail by nine A.M. tomorrow. To every registered holder.

"Personal contact," Willie had said. "Half your stockholders are employees. Talk to them."

Jarvis' voice went thick. He said he'd go through their facilities like Sherman through Georgia. Get on the phone to distributors. Everybody was going to be a player here.

Willie Unger approved. "I know you will," he said. "You'll go through the place like shit through a Christmas goose. Only I want you to be judicious. Counsel with them. Don't try to sell them anything. 'Come, let us reason together,' it says in the Bible, or Lyndon Johnson used to say it does. You follow?" Then he said, "One thing you can sell them. A little fear. What about jobs? What is this takeover artist going to do with their jobs? *Kapish?*"

Jarvis' features were softened by his expression of childlike adoration.

Willie had that effect, Kreg thought, on certain clients. He led them and was there to take responsibility and to give orders. With Willie there was always hope, some forward thrust.

But not everyone was totally a believer.

Not Sam Marion.

"You too," Willie had said to Sam. "Pitch in. It's not your style but work a little for the cause."

"A little," Sam said.

Always close to the vest. Cool, Kreg thought, because that was necessary to some self-image of superiority through detachment.

Even so, Sam was willing enough for now to trust, as ready as Jarvis Dalton to approve the proposals Willie Unger suggested for presentation to the shareholders. Like Jarvis, he looked only at Willie, but unlike Jarvis he was always evaluating what he heard.

Logically, any success of Willie's would be a vindication of Kreg's own stewardship but he had a quick sense of bad luck to come.

"I want you to understand me," Willie said. "I'm not trying to go all the way here. Tie us up so there's no mobility for the future. There's no need for that. If anybody sees it differently, we can argue about it. This is a middle-of-the-channel course. First we positively disabuse *anybody at all* who has any notions of greenmail. We disabuse him of that notion because the Company is going to be *absolutely prohibited* from buying in its own stock for any more than the average price of the stock over the last two years, except if we offer that price to everybody. All the shareholders. Then the second thing we do is put in a fair-price requirement. That knocks out the two-tier wiseguys. The ones who think they can offer one price to us. They think they can cut a deal and then go out and screw the little holder. It isn't only because it's ethical, which it fucking is, that I'm putting this in. It's also to tell the world they want to piss on our side, they're in a major contest. Sharpies, keep away."

Kreg, he knew, followed him. Kreg knew this stuff as well as he did. "Only he's too smart to do it all the time. These lousy hours. And you wind up the Maalox kid." He patted his stomach. But he wanted to be sure that Jarvis Dalton and Sam Marion understood perfectly what he had in mind and why he wanted to handle the matter in just this way. "So let's go over it again." After a few minutes, he said he was satisfied and it was then he'd begun leisurely to discuss the remote and distant possibility of a leveraged buyout.

Which Jarvis Dalton referred to at the elevator just before the red down light came on.

"Visions of sugarplums," Sam Marion said. "Would that be nice, Jarvis? Our own company. Wouldn't it be nice?"

"He said it was doable."

"That it seemed to be doable," Kreg said. . . . Not adding that this wasn't an idea that appealed. A leveraged buyout would leave Jarvis Dalton as the long-term caretaker of the Company. And Kreg saw, too, squabbling between Jarvis and Sam Marion, the Balkanization of management relations.

"Would you go along?" Jarvis said.

"It would be a matter of price."

"The Foundation stock, I mean."

"I would sell it. We couldn't hold stock in a private company."

"Sell it," Sam Marion said. "But not to Marcu?"

In the lobby a suspicious guardian without his jacket watched them sign the in/out register. His magazine was open to a photograph of a girl in white stockings on a couch. A setting of florid Victoriana and two fingers partly lost in her chestnut pubic fuzz.

The starter followed Kreg's glance. "Table pussy," he said. "She could kill you, couldn't she?"

Sam Marion let his eyes travel the distance from face to beer drinker's belly. "Do you think you'll ever know?" he said in his nicest manner.

Now Roth worried further with a black calfskin toe into the thin carpet of his partner's office. He watched detachedly the play of his own neat foot and said after a bit that Willie Unger, when you thought about it, didn't too much care about taking on any losing causes. So you would have to regard it as favorable, wouldn't you, that he was going to handle this Brandt Systems thing?

"Yes," Kreg said. "It's Willie's baby now."

"In God's hands."

"Fortune's. Of course. Always." A nice sententious rounding

off, that was. And with the same imaginative verve that, possibly, two Staten Island housewives might bring to their consideration of a cancer-struck neighbor. *It's all through her, I heard. So now she's in God's hands.* But if what Willie had taken on (or anything else) was in God's hands, then everything was. *Even with those new techniques. . . .* Think of Willie's techniques. Willie was a master of the techniques he needed. *But sometimes there's a remission, the second housewife said.*

Tuke, with a Tab, kicked off pink running shoes and settled herself on the couch. She put her drink on the coffee table and stretched. A major contender, Adam thought, in any contest of sexual languor. She was wearing a scenic tee shirt, a trout stream with a string of caught fish, actual little stuffed cotton trout hanging from the front of the shirt.

From inside there was the drum sound of water against the tub enclosure. Debbie in the shower. Adam said he'd tell her they had a guest.

"Don't tell her," Tuke said. "Give her a surprise when she comes out." She pointed a red-wine toenail at her bags and at Adam's bags next to them. "The second I get here," she said, "and right away you have to leave."

"Not want, though. Have to."

"Same thing."

"Really, it isn't. But I'll be back. So be here then."

"Can't. Can't stay."

"For me it's a business imperative. Florida. Florida beckons imperatively. I have about zero minutes. They were due ten minutes ago."

"Who's due?"

"The people who are coming for me."

"You could put it off."

"Believe me. Not so."

"Then we seem to be pretty much just ships that pass."

This was in its way a kind of formal dialogue of light flirtation. Easy living and all, but Southern Californians did this kind of thing as well as anybody. Relations here were as carefully ordered as any, anywhere, ever. Before Southern California was invented, who had better understood the nature of formal relations? Not Amenhotep. Not Molière or Metternich. And what couldn't you expect of a culture in which dark glasses were the prevalent totemic object?

Of course Adam himself had adopted the tribal rituals. He always wore his shades.

The shower had stopped and Debbie, in a bathrobe with a towel turban-style over her hair, came into the room. She squealed, hugged Tuke, sat next to her on the couch. Close. They held hands and began to talk as quickly, as easily, as if preambles didn't exist.

Maybe it was the luggage, Adam thought, his and Tuke's center stage in the middle of the room, that gave the place something of the air of a set. The bags could be seen as props that had to do with business, entrances and exits, getting the actors onstage and off. What you had here could be a play about the girl from out of town and maybe fast-developing three-way erotic relationships. Why not? There'd been in fact intimations to that effect from Debbie.

When the downstairs buzzer sounded, he was still musing along those lines. And Debbie and Tuke were still talking only to each other. But then they fussed over him, seeing him to the door.

"You see," Tuke said, "it must be me. Right away he wants to leave."

"No," Debbie said. "That's not exactly true. He'd really like to stay."

Adam said he honestly would.

"Believe me," Debbie said. "He'd want to be here if he could."

Nobody was behind the wheel of the forest-green Mercedes. Ish was in front on the passenger side and Van Atta was alone in back.

"We thought you might have been downstairs," Van Atta said.

"So we wouldn't have to wait," Ish said. His jacket was oyster silk. No doubt from Jerry Magnin. "Put your stuff in the trunk," he said. "You drive."

On the way to the airport Van Atta didn't speak, so neither did Ish. He closed his eyes and slouched in his seat. When they were there, he said for Adam to drop them at American Airlines departures. Then Adam could take the Mercedes to the long-term lot. Ish also gave him the envelope with his ticket. "Fifty," he said. "Nice easy number. Flight 50. You can find that, can't you?" He squeezed Adam's shoulder until it hurt and grinned for approval at Van Atta. Van Atta smiled briefly and looked at his watch. Ish said that Adam could leave his luggage. He'd check everything through.

Adam was thinking that he could. He could find Flight 50, Los Angeles to Miami. Palm to palm, you might say. The palms of Miami becoming now the palms at the end of his mind.

He had a window seat, first class, with Van Atta and Ish just behind him. That was one thing about Van Atta, he looked after you, was in some ways a caring employer. Adam read *The New Yorker* and looked out of the window at the gorgeous colors of the American West. A few times Van Atta leaned over the seat to ask if he was comfortable but there was no real conversation. Van Atta's gray eyes. Hardly any California tan. Courteous, remote. Sometimes Adam could hear him talking to Ish but mostly he was quiet.

When they were over certain portions of Arizona, Adam closed his magazine. He considered that the mesas, buttes and declivities below might be precisely some of the ones photographed in the book from which, moments before Tuke's totally contemporary forefinger had touched the buzzer to his apartment, he'd removed a map. The X in Colombia and the arcs leading north from there to the airstrips near Twentynine Palms had become mere marks. Notations having to do with an operation that was dead and had no power anymore to stir the mind. This time, when he'd touched a match to the edge of the map, he'd let it burn. He crumpled the ashes to almost nothing. Debbie and Tuke later didn't even notice the gray dust in the big ashtray on the coffee table.

Of course the map when it existed had not been a useful object. The information on it had never been translated into a plan. There hadn't been the opportunity or, truthfully, the hunger for action. Adam knew that if there'd been a moment he wouldn't have seized it. And that he would not make another trip to Mexico or directly to Colombia. *I have a weak will . . . certainly when fear comes into the picture.*

The quiet woman of sixty in the aisle seat next to him saw more than Adam knew. She saw a smile come over his face. As if he were pleased with himself. He was. He'd thought of a noun that described the quality of his passions. *All my strongest desires, he was thinking, are velleities.* The woman looked back to her book.

A friendly girl at the Hertz counter gave Adam a map and showed him how to take 836 east and then I95 south to Rickenbacker Causeway. She even told him to be prepared for the twenty-five-cent toll on 836 and the other toll on the Causeway.

"Maybe you better come with us," Ish said. "He's not good with directions."

"He'll do just fine," the girl said.

Outside there was soft air, pleasantly heavy. Seventy-two degrees, an airport thermometer had read. They had a beige Oldsmobile, an 88. Ish told Adam he didn't know shit about how to pack luggage in a trunk. He rearranged the bags and yawned into the night air.

Adam, of course, drove. As if at home. The expressways could have been California expressways. He marveled at the vertical extravagances of the Miami skyline and then, across the Causeway, the sudden lushness of Crandon Park.

Key Biscayne.

Key Biscayne in the morning. Breakfast outdoors next to the hotel pool. A view of the ocean.

Van Atta behind dark glasses (all three of them wore dark

glasses) ate the last segment of a grapefruit half. He squeezed juice carefully onto his spoon. The operation was always under control. No chance ever of a rebel squirt onto his white shirt. Ish was wearing a tennis shirt in light blue with the alligator at the left breast. Adam thought of that shade as one favored by retired municipal workers. He contemplated Ish. There was the aging gladiator's inhuman breadth of chest and shoulder. And the thickness of the neck and the arms and wrists. An Oyster Rolex, cut-steel band.

Van Atta pushed his grapefruit away and began to eat toast. He chewed thoughtfully at what was in front of him. He asked Adam about some properties in Brentwood that he'd said to look over. How did they net out for what kind of a spendable on your investment? Would Adam buy them? "With your own money," he said.

"Residential," Ish said. "Rent control. The L.A. market's in the shithouse for residential."

Adam shivered pleasantly in the warm morning sun. "What's to lose," he said. "They're cheap and they're easy to carry."

Van Atta pushed a piece of toast to the other side of his plate. "Cheap?" he said.

"To the market, they are," Adam said. "The only thing, does it pay to do anything that small?" *This is crazy, he was beginning to think. Three thousand miles across the continent and nobody says why or what we're going to do here.* Some way out in the water a gull flopped drunkenly to the top of a piling and perched there in a stupid trance. *Maybe they want to try for an East Coast tan.* Adam itched for information all through to the fine thin bones he'd inherited from his mother. What was going on? He really wanted to know about this trip to sunshine East. What the hell were they doing here?

"Too small," Van Atta said. "You don't bother with those?"

"You got to understand," Ish said. "This is a big operator. Adam. Adam don't fuck around with just any piss-ass little deal. Adam throws the small ones back."

Van Atta folded the *Miami Herald* and signaled a waiter.

Ish smeared a last piece of sausage into egg yolk, popped the load into his mouth. He wiped a bit of yolk from his chin. "Give Adam the check," he said. "Adam's the big guy here."

Upstairs, Van Atta found a number in his address book and put in a call. Adam, across the room, heard three rings and then a female voice. Van Atta put the telephone to his ear. He asked for Señor Quijada. Then he was talking. He spoke a flat, uninflected Spanish, as if the language were not closely approachable on its own terms. Adam was able, pretty much, to follow him, but nothing interesting was being said.... Yes, an easy flight.... Yes, very comfortable here. Hibiscus Island at eleven. . . . He would find it. They would be there.

After he rang off, he looked at the phone for a moment before putting it down. "That's a start," he said to Ish. "Step one." He asked Adam to get directions for Hibiscus Island and some idea of how long it would take.

"The last step," Ish said. "That's the step you want to think about."

Adam drove on MacArthur Causeway past the monstrous Port of Miami. A mile of sheds, cartons, winches, cranes. And anchored in front of them (in waters he'd always imagined reserved to cruise ships, sports fishermen, sailing craft) were the workhorse cargo ships themselves. White, blue, black, red. Shipshape, rusty. Whatever. There was the place itself and there was the idea of the place. He said he hadn't thought of Miami as a port city.

"You mean they got longshoremen here?" Ish said. "I'm a longshoreman from Miami," he said in a high fag voice.

"You didn't know?" Van Atta said to Adam. "This is a major port. I ship a lot through here."

At the gatehouse to the islands the guard was waiting for them and at Quijada's house there was another gate. A guard in a navy blazer and slacks took them inside. There was another guard in the front hall. Ish and the two men measured each other with the disinterested unwavering regard that Adam supposed to be characteristic of their profession. The second man took them through the house to a back terrace on the ocean.

Señor Quijada was a Dickensian Latin, petit and plump, with a manner that Adam could only think of as *jolly.* Bald. He had a wiry beard that hid nothing. He said they could stay out here on the terrace. He made a gesture to indicate sky, air, sun. Beverages? He insisted. Anything. Coffee? beer? soft drinks?

A Coke or a Tab, Adam said, he didn't care which. He was looking at the sunlit bay. Light sparking off any little ripple in its placid surface. The inaudible (from the height of the terrace) lap of baby waves against the balustrade that rimmed this island. So how could he care what they gave him to drink? He was interested right now only in the goofiness of his sudden delight at being here, at being a part of whatever monkey business Van Atta and the plump señor were planning here in this pastel place. Hibiscus Island.

The thing was to have the map in your head, to realize in some specially numinous way that this island and Palm Island and Star Island and the islands to the north were trimmed and outlined as neatly as the lawns of the houses on them. A long ellipse, rounded at both ends, was the dominant shape. Even the imperial port itself had only one area of irregularity, that at its southwestern end. Most mysteriously, there were the cartographer's black dots that indicated the three-quarter-mile-long outline of Pelican Island, *submerged.*

Then what were the origins of these places? Were they totally man-made? Probably not. Adam envisioned small natural reefs or outcroppings (coral? stone?). Then structures of pilings and shiploads of fill and the blasting away of any inconvenient protuberances. And finally the landscaping and merchandising of the stuff by skilled Southern developers.

What you ultimately had in this neat and affluent emptiness was a proof of the cross-cultural pervasiveness of toy. It went through classes like the kudzu vine through landscape. Here was the essential matter, the very *geist* of the domestic existence of the well-to-do. Across the bay were the fantastic post-modern shapes of the newer office buildings.

The second bodyguard brought a tray with their drinks. Adam poured and heard the instant fizz of the icy brown liquid.

Maybe, Van Atta said, Adam would like to wait inside. Because there was no need to bother himself about anything here.

The bodyguard took him into a kind of a family room with

rattan furniture and green-and-white pillows in an overscale pattern of tropical leaves. There were some magazines. Adam looked through *House and Garden,* then *The New Yorker,* the same issue he'd read on the plane.

When Señor Quijada walked them to their car the other bodyguard was in the courtyard. He was lifting packages out of the trunk of a gray Mustang convertible with its top down. The girl next to the car waved to Quijada.

"My daughter," he said happily to Van Atta.

A pretty girl, diminutive. No doubt, in a father's view, to be protected. So there would often in this house, Adam thought, be the question of which visitors to introduce her to and which not.

"The guy is a shopper," Ish said. "The list he's got, you got to consider he's world-class."

"We thought he needed," Van Atta said. "We flew across the country to meet his needs."

"Even so it's a lot. What he wants to buy, you know it's a lot."

"We're in business," Van Atta said, "to sell a lot."

"But it bothers me what he come to us for. Military stuff, we're not exactly a low price on that. A million places he could go, he could get it cheaper."

"Why do you think?"

"I'm asking. I knew, I wouldn't ask."

"It's maybe because I plan for the long term. Do a quality job and I get a reputation for that."

"You mean like the special night sights, they're not going to be half of them just little pieces of plain glass?"

"And the machine guns shoot and the ammunition is live. And, you know, if there are spare parts or antibiotics, those are going to be in their original cartons. If there's something secondhand, tanks or something like that, he's going to have, not a guarantee, but he'll know some qualified maintenance guy has looked them over. At least if they're from some origin I can get a maintenance man into. So anyway he knows he's going to get a square deal and he wants me to think that's why he put out this bait with me."

Adam, a silent mouse at the wheel, turned onto Route 1 south. *Bait.* He wanted to know about bait.

Ish asked that question for both of them.

Van Atta said, "I think it was maybe a little too easy. Here and there I stiffed him a little. Which he has to know. But he said yes like a soldier, didn't he, Ish?"

"Couldn't wait."

"You see in these things there's usually a little bargaining. But our friend there didn't bargain. Why would that be, Adam?"

Your young executive on the move is always ready. Now there was a sense of expanding horizons. Admission to the war council. "You would guess," Adam said, "there's something more he wants."

"Wouldn't you guess that?" Van Atta said to Ish.

"Yeah, we know that. The other stuff. Adam's a smart kid." Then he said that maybe Adam could tell him something to take for his stomach. Because it had been kind of funny all morning and now it was worse. Could Adam tell him that?

They were crossing the Miami River. Adam gunned past a red Cutlass, old man at the wheel. A kid's enthusiasm, he told himself, that little burst of speed. *Just watch it.* He didn't answer Ish.

"Adam," Van Atta said, "what he slipped in at the end was a little matter of sugar refineries along with these new pellet machines."

"I didn't ask," Ish said. "The pellets, that's for sugar cubes?"

"The pellets are for briquettes. So you burn your waste cane and you cut down on the oil you don't have and that the Russians don't have to send you anymore. Adam, would that sound right?"

This Socratic game.

Adam could play. "Not for Colombia or Central America, it doesn't. Not Mexico. Do I get another call?"

"Play again," Van Atta said.

"I think it could be right for Cuba." Adam looked into the rearview mirror.

Van Atta was showing nothing.

"Cuba," Ish was saying. "This is no Cuba. This is big-time right wing. This is a kill-the-lefties, connected to the ad-min-is-tra-shun guy."

"Eight whole refineries," Van Atta said. "No pilot order and ten years' spare parts. Somebody wants to slip it past them while he can."

"Yeah," Ish said. "Just get it out of the U.S.A." Then he said, "You sell him those? Do business with the Cubes? Those *Coobans.*"

"I think we can fill him," Van Atta said. "Also, I believe he's from some other country . . . doing business with the Cubans. That doesn't matter. Not if we work it all out with his boss." He explained to Adam that there was someone above Quijada. They would have to clear a few details with him and then they'd be home free.

Ish cackled. "Some top guy," he said, "from wherever it is. Colombia, Brazil, who cares." Later he said, "This isn't some kid's toy, you go into K mart and ask can you have eight of them, and thanks, will they wrap them good for this foreign destination you've got down on this piece of paper here." He was having a good time with his own wit. But moments later, in a different voice, he said to Adam, "Would you move this thing? My fuckin stomach. I got to get to a can."

Van Atta put down the papers he was working on and went to the deep end of the pool and dove, entered smoothly, almost without ripples. Seven or eight laps then in an easy crawl.

Adam saw that in swim shorts Van Atta was deeper chested and generally better muscled than he'd expected. Nothing massive like Ish but a solid halfback's build.

When he came back, Van Atta put his papers in the alligator envelope he worked from and closed up. Finished for now.

Ish saw Adam looking at the envelope. "Bijan," he said.

Van Atta ran his hand over the glossy reptile skin. "Nice piece of leather," he said, "isn't it?"

"Terrific," Adam said, noting privately that he remained a passionate conservationist.

Van Atta possibly sensed less than an absolute sincerity of tone. Adam, after four or five seconds, buckled under the peaceful weight of his employer's regard. Looked away. Looked toward the pool. A teenaged girl in a black bikini was testing the bounce of the diving board. Black hair, a flat stomach and small exciting breasts.

Ish was saying to Van Atta, "This business with Quijada, we got to decide what name for the permits and all, what company we call it."

"Iona Transport," Van Atta said, not concentrating.

"The other stuff. The sugar plants. Customs, those Operation Exodus guys. They could be all over us on that. Them and the Export Enforcement from Commerce."

Van Atta said there would be more than sugar refineries. He expected those were only a first item. "It was a test when he asked about them. He wanted to see how I'd hop."

"Then fuck him," Ish said. "Up his."

"I didn't mean that he didn't want them. He'll love it, I can deliver whole refineries. Actually I think we could hear from him on other things you can't usually come into the country and tell them your name is Castro and you'd like to buy them because you've got the dollars to pay. Say possibly those Motorola 68010 microprocessors. Different kinds of communications equipment."

"They need those things in Cuba?"

"How do I know?" Van Atta said. "They need the sugar refineries. Other things they can use for export. For their balance of trade. . . . All that stuff, we'll use a Dutch company for it. They can be the exporter."

The idea that you could call it up that way if you wanted or needed it. . . . A Dutch company. Adam focused on that. The girl came down on the edge of the board. Formal, ready, poised.

Ish said, "I like it. Our Dutchman can ship the fancy stuff."

Our Dutchman.

The girl in the black bikini rose in the air, jackknifed through air, then water.

Ish groaned and hauled himself up, started for the bathhouses. He didn't have to say why. It was a trip he'd made four times in the hour they'd been at the pool.

"The runs," Van Atta said. "Such a big guy but he's got a delicate stomach. Any new thing. Travel, some different food, and Ish is living in the crapper."

"It's too bad for him," Adam said.

"It's nice you sympathize." Van Atta adjusted his chair to a reclining position and leaned back. Adam took up *A Passage to India.* Five minutes later Van Atta reached, lifted it from his hands, looked at the pages he'd been reading, handed back the book.

"Very nice," he said. "Look. A young guy like you, you probably want to get out. So take the car. Make yourself an evening. Ish isn't going to want to leave the hotel. The two of us, we have an early dinner. Look at the tube a little."

Leaving, Adam passed the girl in the black bikini. She was just coming out of the water. She was gripping the metal stanchions of the pool ladder, rocking herself back and forth before climbing the last few steps.

Adam found Cocoanut Grove and the old movie house that was now a theater and the moderately bohemian streets around it. Mostly young students there (lawyers, advertisers and accountants to be). He found a bar with tables outside and placed himself near a woman of sixty who was with a handsome man twenty years younger. From the theater poster Adam recognized the woman as the lead in the play, and the man, he guessed from their conversation, was with her in the cast. The man had an Errol Flynn mustache and a bandanna at his neck. Adam knew the woman by reputation but had never seen her work. He admired her wide-brimmed hat and her careless tiger eyes and raunchy mouth. She was still able to carry off, without it being laughable, an air of desirable womanhood. She'd used herself. He could tell that. He imagined gallant rearguard actions in the universal game. No word or gesture to show it, but he saluted this aging doll.

She and the man were saying about another actress that they'd heard she had a bit in some new thing with Bobby De Niro.

Adam considered what it might be like to sleep with the actress. That woman at that age.

"Can I take a light from those?" It was a girl in a short pink wrap skirt and a navy tee shirt that said TIMES SQUARE. She was pointing at a pack of matches on the table, white with the name of this bar in blue letters.

Adam lighted a match, cupped it a moment to burn off the sulphur and held it to her cigarette. He pointed to the legend on her chest. "New York."

"A suburb. You?"

"Once. L.A. now."

"No. Here now," the girl said turning.

She had a tennis player's firm slender legs. Little cotton puffs, sock tabs, at the heels of her sneakers.

Something important seemed to be beginning. Students were coming out of the fern bars or from around the corner and filling the sidewalks. Cops helped a crew of young men to keep them out of the street itself. Equipment trucks were parked at one end of the block and heavy electrical cables snaked from portable generators to light stands that focused on a burgundy Continental Mark IV. No illumination as yet, no actors in view. The students moved in shoals up and down the block, waiting for action.

It wasn't any longer peaceful and Adam decided to leave. The man at the next table was flicking his eyes to take in the street scene. The actress showed nothing. Adam assumed she had an extraordinary capability for disdain.

He went inside to the bar to pay his tab. When he came out, the actress was saying, "Everybody tells you Broadway. They all want that. But if she's going to be poor, she ought to be poor where it's warm."

The man said, "Charlie. I think Charlie would always help her. They were so close so long. Charlie has a good heart."

"Like you?"

"I try."

"No," the actress said. "No you don't. You try to butter me up and you try to get some little girl in bed. That's all you really try. . . . Doesn't he?" she said to Adam who was putting down his tip.

In one sense she wasn't really talking to him. But he raised his eyebrows, flashed his best smile and lifted one hand in a happy salute.

And moved up the street.

Where there was only the event itself, the press of that crowd of students exciting themselves by their mere anticipation of the shoot that was about to happen. *Not a commercial,* Adam heard. *A whole segment they're gonna do here.* Somebody said it was a new perfume by Chanel. Deneuve was going to do it. She was around the corner now in a trailer.

Adam noted that he was listening mostly to Northern accents. Bodies all around him. He started to work his way to the other end of the street where there might be some room to move.

He found himself next to the girl in the pink skirt. She was on one foot, holding the other, and trying to hop away from three linebackers in cutoffs. One of them was apologizing for something and didn't seem anxious to see her go. She tested the hurt foot against the ground and said to Adam that this nice boy had just backed his heel over her instep. "Heavy tread, you know. I only thought I'd go through the sidewalk."

"Hey," the giant culprit said, "I'm sorry."

Adam took the girl's elbow. "You better come with me," he said. He walked around the block as if he knew where he was going. And found something. They ordered beers and only then exchanged names, Adam and Lisa as it turned out.

"Nice standard nomenclature," Lisa said. "I mean for your upper-middle Eastern *juif* of our generation."

"Like Sarah and Michael," Adam said. *Our generation.* He had a dozen years on this slender child.

"Kimberly and Noah."

"You're a tennis player?"

"In high school. But here it's too much practice. So just for fun a little." She swigged at her Löwenbräu, from the bottle, and then giggled. "I'll show you something." She rummaged inside her bag and then put her clenched fist with whatever was in it on the table between them.

"Open."

"In a minute. You guess."

"You open it."

Adam reached and against no resistance unfolded the strong brown fingers. In her open hand was a Cricket lighter in white. He held the lighter between thumb and forefinger. Examined it from various perspectives. "You had it all the time."

"I didn't know it was there."

"You wanted to meet me. You're a pickup queen. Probably some kind of dangerous nympho."

Lisa giggled again. "It was only to check you out."

She was a junior, a psych major who had pretty well decided to take more English lit and find something in publishing when she was sprung from this place. In the meantime though, maybe a couple more brewsters and a hamburger?

"Better. Some scotches and seafood. Where can we get a seafood dinner around here?"

"Big spender," Lisa said. What did he do, she said, to earn that bread?

Adam talked California condos to her. With now, he said, a look at the upscale Florida market.

She shared a small white house, off campus, with two other girls. One of the girls was away and the other one not home when Adam and Lisa came in after dinner. Lisa got Miller Lites from the refrigerator and they went to her room. She had a hi-fi and a sixteen-inch Sony color set, a poster that said MONET AT GIVERNY and one that advertised the Santa Fe Opera of 1980. She also had a Smith Corona Coronamatic 2500 electric typewriter and a reasonable number of texts and Cliffs Notes for *Catch-22* and *The Bell Jar.* There was a little stuffed teddy bear next to her pillow. The bear didn't look new. Adam asked and she confirmed that it wasn't today's bear. No part of the bruin madness of the moment. The bear was Sammy and she had always had him.

Lisa set down the Millers and pulled at the window shade. She left the bathroom door barely ajar with a night-light on. "I like that," she said. "Just a little bit of light."

"Not that," she said when Adam was ready to enter. "First Sammy or you make him jealous." She handed the bear to Adam and had him rub it between her breasts and between her legs. She wanted its nose inside her. Then its little feet. "Yes," she said. "That's what Sammy likes." She spoke baby talk to the bear. Suddenly flipped like a seal onto her stomach. "Around on my back," she said. "All over my back. Sammy wants that." She had one hand under herself. With the other she reached back for Adam's wrist. She guided him until the bear was between her buttocks. Then disengaged and groped for him, Adam.

He woke after three with Lisa's arm across his face. No easy way to turn in her narrow bed. This time no foreplay with the bear. Lisa seemed not to come fully awake. "Yes," she said dreamily. "Yes. Like that."

He dressed in the dark hoping it wasn't going to be too difficult finding his way back to Key Biscayne. If he could get to U.S. 1, the South Dixie Highway, he'd be all right. He kissed Lisa before he left and he copied her phone number on a sheet of scratch paper from her desk. In case.

No trouble at all.

In minutes he found his way. And wasn't alone. There was traffic on the road. Plenty of it. *So watch yourself.* A fair number of these drivers would be late makers out like himself. Headed home and many of them still no doubt half drunk or drugged or both. Upped or downed but not reliable. *Danger on the highway.* The thing to do was simple. Just stay in lane and take it easy. Twisted Sister on the radio. Watch the white line. As he so often had at home. In California, if that was home. Same thing. No difference at all. Even the girls. Lisa and Debbie. Where were the differences? The *significant* differences. Debbie was fairer. Lisa was a tennis player and had a bear named Sam. Debbie had maybe Tuke or other kinks.

Everybody likes something.

But were sexual bents really an appropriate start toward a definition of the whole, the entire personality? He liked that, sexual bents. He began to think he might drive back to Cocoanut Grove. Get rid of that middle-aged Romeo she was with and have things out with the old actress there. Right now, wouldn't she be there still? Straight talk, words as direct as the bullets that once whizzed across the O.K. Corral. Slow down. He was doing eighty and wasn't perfectly in lane. He eased right, decelerated. Now Mötley Crüe. Nothing but heavy metal. Who could listen to it? Why not country in this part of the country? If not the actress (whose name he hadn't been able to remember), he'd call Iris from the hotel. How many years now that Iris had not been going with his father? Who did she go with? *Go with.* There had to be somebody, didn't there? That was an interesting question. Not that it mattered if there was or there wasn't, not between himself and Iris. They'd talk about that too. Iris would take his call, she always would . . . as so many years back she'd taken his other call from the New Haven railroad station. . . . And they would talk and he'd discuss with her this business of what people liked to do unto others and have done unto them. . . . And they would discuss other things. Because why not get it straight? All of it. Light gleaming an instant. Only an instant. The human condition. *The human condition,* he said out loud.

Airhead. That's what Lisa at one point had called him.

He was doing fifty now. That might be considered a stodgy overemphasis on road safety. Or highway citizenship. He increased somewhat the pressure of his right foot on the accelerator.

In the morning, the note under his door read. *Eleven. Car clean, gassed, etc. To Bal Harbour. Directions? Hope you had a good evening.*

At breakfast, Adam unfolded his map to show it to Van Atta. He said, "This way. The way we went the other day and then up Collins. It'll be longer I assume. Traffic lights and all but we have time. We'll see Miami Beach."

Van Atta didn't seem particularly to have his mind on routes. On the other hand, he didn't say no.

Adam said he'd chosen a way to go that would keep them at all times close to a public can.

"That's nice," Ish said. "Thoughtful. Two things about you. You're thoughtful and you always got some little thing to be funny about." He helped Adam to his feet. Adam knew there'd be a bruise on his arm where Ish had gripped him.

Adam drove past the port and the little islands, Palm and Hibiscus. He wondered if Quijada was at home. Or Quijada's daughter? The bodyguards? Storm the place and take the girl.

On Collins Avenue there were first the small hotels of the twenties and thirties. Many of them now refurbished. Painted cream, turquoise, tan, aqua. Art Deco retirement homes for elderly Cubans and Jews and pensioners of the mighty industrial corporations of the Midwest. The lives of these people were also restorations of a kind. After a while he began to note some of the great names he'd always known. The Fontainebleau and the Eden Roc. Places that advertised in the travel section of the Sunday *Times.* Dean Martin playing, or Don Rickles. Finally Bal Harbour. Today's place. The shopping plaza as Madison Avenue, rue St.-Honoré. Classy guards to let you in.

Certainly civilization on the Beach had developed positively from south to north in an admirable synchronization of that upward thrust by how many realtors, land speculators, bankers and insurers. Positive thinkers, mysteriously coordinated to create. What do consumers know of the forces that work for them?

And better to do your waiting here than in the dust outside Twentynine Palms. *It had better be better.* Because his situation here in this affluent and, as it was beginning to seem, probably dangerous place could not be changed in any easy way. At least there was no way that occurred to him . . . nothing quick and simple like the quiet burning of that map at home in Marina del Rey.

Quijada was where he was supposed to be, at the jewelry counter in Neiman-Marcus. He saw them first and waved. They were early, he said. Please. One minute. The girl was wrapping something.

"You too," Ish said. "We're both early."

"A present for my daughter," Quijada said to Van Atta.

"He isn't here?" Van Atta said.

"He is. He was looking through the store. He is coming now."

The man in the white linen suit had an athlete's easy walk but was going to fat at fifty. A tomato face and platinum hair in a brush cut. Fine-cut features that were too small for his face. A girl's mouth. Hans Kalb. Certainly a German.

Kalb did a formal handshake all around (Adam last). His accent was Latin. Adam understood how this might be. There had always been Germans in Latin America. One small group had arrived in the late forties. Perhaps Hans Kalb had been one of them, a boy then. Adam made that guess. The man had the face of someone who ate beefsteak in a poor country where chicken scraps flavored the beans. Tiny, bright blue eyes.

"Only two, I had understood," he said to Quijada. "Mr. Van Atta and Mr. Frankel. There was nothing about a third person." He was still holding Adam's hand.

Adam, Van Atta said, was an important member of his team. "I wanted you to meet him so if sometime you're in touch with him you know each other. And I like to bring him in a little bit to any new situation."

"Part of his training," Ish said.

"This is not a school," Kalb said. "We are here for business."

Van Atta said, "That was why you came to me, I thought. Because you like the way I run my business. You heard good things about it."

Quijada received his package from the salesgirl. Signed the slip and fumbled with his platinum card, putting it into his wallet. "Now," he said. "Miss Grimble's. The cheesecake." He put his thumb and two fingers to his lips. Blew a kiss. "I tell everybody about the cheesecake at Miss Grimble's." He didn't seem to know how to go from there. He had the anxious look of a man who is afraid things could be coming apart for him.

Hans Kalb said, "Our men are not with us. They are waiting in the car." But he was conceding this point. He nodded shortly toward Van Atta, let go of Adam's hand.

"Like I mentioned," Van Atta said, "Adam is more a young executive with me. He doesn't especially hang around in parking lots."

Adam caught Kalb's eye, wiped his right hand slowly against his trouser leg. Smiled pleasantly at the man.

When they were outside Miss Grimble's, Van Atta said, "Adam. So whatever you want to do. Figure an hour. You check back then. . . . That's good isn't it?" he said to Quijada. "An hour? . . . And now you know Adam," he said to Kalb. "You would know any messages that they'd be coming from me? That he's, he speaks for me? What he says, I told him to say."

Quijada seemed happy again. Ish too. Ish, Adam guessed, was enjoying the sight of red spots rising in the pink skin of Kalb's full soft cheeks.

On the other hand, no illusions about placement, about any sudden move up, past the salt. Not at this table. Being so nice to him was only a way of sticking it to Kalb because the German (which was how Adam thought of this Latin blond) had gotten out of line. Adam knew his rank. He was someone who drove the car to meet a man he'd met yesterday but hadn't been told was going to be here and another man about whose standing in this affair he was still uncertain. He was allowed to hear what was being said but then was dismissed, told nothing.

So by design he was five minutes late coming back to Miss Grimble's. And found his party gone. Van Atta and Ish were waiting for him in the parking area next to the car. Van Atta only looked at his watch.

On the way back, he didn't talk but Ish at one point said, "This thing is gonna be a big enchilada." He stretched the adjective for emphasis.

At the hotel Ish said, as if to remind him, that he should be ready at four. To be a little early at the airport.

Adam hadn't known they were leaving.

"We're not," Ish said. "Him. Not us."

Not easy going at first. He drove alone with Van Atta, who was no talker. A silent presence behind him in the back seat. Then there was a slight delay on the Causeway and with nothing being said and the car not moving, he could feel his neck begin to redden. He imagined disapproval from behind, himself being held responsible for the congested traffic of Key Biscayne.

After five minutes the bridge lowered and cars revved their engines.

Adam cleared his throat. "I can see what Ish meant," he said, "about allowing extra time."

"You have to," Van Atta said.

Adam counted slowly, silently to thirty and there began to be traffic to his left, heading onto the Key. Then sluggish starts ahead of him and the transmogrification of that belching line into discrete segments flowing easily over a stretch of American road.

After they turned into the airport itself, Van Atta said that one problem in this business was the question of loyalty. "That's absolutely key. Without it you'd be animals. Kill each other off. . . . Remember what I'm telling you because someone could make himself a stake here. You know what I'm saying?"

"I appreciate it," Adam said.

"Obviously I trust you."

Adam pulled up in front of the terminal. He got Van Atta's bags from the trunk. "Well," he said. "It's a long trip back."

"Not that bad. It's only to Chicago. I'm there overnight. I try to use my time. No wasted motions." Van Atta smiled briefly.

"I'll try to watch the store."

"Like I told you."

Adam read from a scrap of paper and dialed. Waited for a voice. "Lisa?"

"Cheryl."

"Roommate?"

"Next room."

"So she can knock on the wall."

"Sometimes she does when she's here."

Lisa, whereabouts unknown just now, was expected but not at any particular time. "Whenever," Cheryl said.

"You'd leave a message, wouldn't you?"

"For you."

"To keep the evening open. Expensive dinner and all. Big-time stuff."

"You have a number."

"I'm in and out. So I'll call back." Cheryl, Lisa. But all these girls sounded the same. If Lisa was from Scarsdale, Cheryl would be from Westport, or some good suburb of Philadelphia. Although there were certain important differences. He began to call up in his mind with great particularity images of Lisa's body and of what he and she and Sammy had done with it. It was hardly after five o'clock. About six-thirty, he said, he'd call again. Nap now and then a shower.

More pictures when he woke, pictures in his head of himself and Lisa. And himself and Lisa and Sammy. They were a trio, weren't they? They could take Sammy with them to dinner.

After his shower he went lightly over his face with a razor. Second scrape of the day. He should have inherited his beard from his father. No problem there. That light hair. He slapped at his face with Polo cologne.

Now make your call.

The phone began to ring before he got to it. Ish's gravel bass. "Down there at the bar," Ish said. "A half an hour."

"The pool bar?"

"The other one is the one I mean. Nice dark inside bar. Peanuts on the little round tables. Later the guy plays 'My Funny Valentine.' The piano player. So we can be comfortable there. I can tell you our plans."

"We have plans?"

"You think it's only a vacation here?"

Part of Ish, his head and shoulders, was visible at the bar when Adam came in. He was bending forward talking to a heavy blonde in a long green dress.

Adam moved toward them.

No flab on Ish. Muscles that stressed against the shoulders and the upper arms of his jacket. The blonde, in her late forties, wore pearls. Three strands. Quite a few wrist bracelets. She'd been laughing. Her eyes were still shining from it. Adam remembered Ish in the pool with a laughing woman in a yellow swim cap. Adam had speculated on the likelihood of shark bites under water. Ish now had a gold signet ring and the metal (Ish's ring, the blond woman's brooches and wristbands) caught light and reflected it. Flashed in the dark bar.

"Sylvie Aaronwald," Ish said.

"Mrs. Sylvan Aaronwald," the blonde said.

Adam assumed or hoped that Ish would want the company of this delightful bimbo for himself alone. He went with that sentiment. "So our conference," he said to Ish, "we'll do that in the morning, I guess. I'll let you be for now." He waited for a little nod from Ish, only that, so he could start to edge away, so he could say to Mrs. Sylvan A. what a peach of a time it had been with her. So he could get his ass to a phone and then to Cocoanut Grove.

"Conference," Sylvie said. "I didn't know I'm interrupting any conference."

"Conference," Ish said. "Hold your water, honey." He jabbed at Sylvie with his forefinger. "Would I have a conference when I could be with you? I mean would I? Do I have that bad taste, I rather talk to him than you?" He jabbed again. "I look like such a bad-taste guy?"

Sylvie slapped at his arm.

"No," Ish said to him. "It's no conference. I never said conference. I just have to clue you in. It's for tomorrow morning when we see the guy. We pick up our package and put a seal to our contract."

"Quijada?"

"Names. You got a big urge for names. It's the other one. The guy we first met today."

"And that's all? Just the meeting tomorrow?"

"That's the deal."

"So nothing tonight?"

"Fun time is all." Ish leered at Sylvie. She slapped again playfully at his hamthick upper arm.

Adam thought for a moment. Then said, "So if there's nothing this evening, I might go out for a while."

"No you don't," Ish said. "The idea," he said to Sylvie, "he takes the car, he's gone you know. Gets back here at four in the morning. So tomorrow, what's he good for then? He's good for shit."

Sylvie said to go easy on that, the shit. She wasn't really especially crazy about his dirty language.

Ish apologized. What he suggested was that Adam hang out with them. Have a drink here, and then dinner and maybe come back and listen to the guy at the piano.

"Spend the evening with you?"

"Well, not all of it," Ish said. "Later you could be, you know, discreet. Leave us alone together."

Sylvie did another of her flirtatious slaps.

Kitten on the keys, Adam thought.

Ish said, "Only you don't go out. You leave us, you go to your little room. *Comprendez?*"

"Who are you," Sylvie said, "to tell a grown young man like that he can't go out?"

"Ise de boss," Ish said happily. "Ain't I?" he said to Adam.

So Adam joined in what developed in its way into a kind of ragged evening. A few more there at the bar and he began to feel outclassed. But no chance Ish would let him pass a round. Sylvie was beginning really to enjoy herself. "Couple of hollow legs is what we are," she said to Adam.

Then in to dinner in a bright room. Shards of light taking crazy bounces off the modern chandeliers. Adam, between the steak and the pecan pie, thought again of calling Lisa, but what to tell her? *Something came up?* What would she think of that?

After dinner they went back to the bar. "Saved a good table for you," the captain said to Ish. "Love yuh," Ish said. He hugged the man. Punched at him in a buddy's way. Reached in his pocket. The man left them and Ish said, "The table, he saved that for my twenty."

The piano player was a roundish black in his sixties who was trying to sing like Louis Armstrong. Ish talked to him and *shmeered* him another twenty and then said maybe they wouldn't have to listen to any stuff with the goddamn autumn leaves in it. Anything Ish didn't like, the piano player said, just wasn't going to be played. He had an enthusiastic slightly beaten manner. He started with a sophisticated line of oldies. He did "Miss Otis Regrets" and "How Long Has This Been Going On?" He even did "My Funny Valentine." Then some contemporary things. A song called "Da Ya Think I'm Sexy." A modified softer beat for the older crowd you got here. He rolled his eyes at the right places and got his laughs.

While the pianist was playing that one, Ish whispered in Sylvie's ear. "You look the other way," she said to Adam.

Ish kept ordering more drinks. So there was a great increase through the evening in spin and whirl and the lights coming at you from all angles. From everywhere. At times the conversation of Ish with Sylvie was thick, private, muttered. Heads down and close. Adam thought of the coming together of hippopotami. Through the mud and toward each other. Swimming through silty waters. He began to laugh and made flailing motions with his arms.

Ish and Sylvie stared at him. What the hell was he doing?

He choked. "Swimming," he said. He could have let himself go out of control, but didn't. Knew enough, even in this moment of exuberant release, not to mention hippos or any persons who reminded him of hippos. For a moment though he put both hands in front of him on the table. Now he could push up, push off and attack. He would be potent, victorious. Seen by the world as *puissant.* Piss ant, he thought.

Some time later, Ish excused himself. He had to go, he said. Adam, not seeing clearly, watched, as it receded, the fuzzed outline of the head and below it the triangle of the leg breaker's torso, with, to one side, a ghost outline of that structure. The lower body was lost in swirl.

Doubles. Twice as good a way to see.

Adam noted at the bar the rows of bottles, the glasses, the long mirror. More fuzz and ghost images. Which gave a soft impressionist texture to the light reflected from those shining surfaces. A nice means of softening this hard-edged evening. "Re-flect-ion," he said. "Re-fract-ion."

Adam, in the morning, followed Ish out of the ziggurat-shaped hotel and into the ziggurat-shaped cluster of condominiums next to it. Pools and tennis courts between the huge buildings. Clearly the work of a single developer. Adam knew the formula: build it all. Then sell the condos but keep the management of them. And keep the hotel. You could walk from the hotel to the other buildings and from one of them to another.

You could if you had a key with a green head.

Which Ish did. He had a ring with three keys. Green, red, yellow. With the green one he unlocked a gate that led onto the grounds of the condominiums.

"We want that far building," he said.

He seemed to know his way and moved with no hesitation past areas of lawn, clipped bushes, pools and courts. In a few places there were interior gates. He opened these with the yellow key.

He did stop at the tennis courts, which just before noon were all in use. On the second court there were two good-looking women, in their late thirties maybe. They played a volley game. Hard flat drives deep into the opposite court. Good backhands, better forehands. Ish watched for possibly three minutes. He grunted at a spectacular return. Then looked at his watch and started to walk away.

Adam following.

Adam, hammered by a less than mild hangover, began to feel a rise of sweat that started on his shoulders and his scalp and forehead, and spread. He had a headache and a dry mouth. And he was pleased in his mild agony that they were moving, because wherever Ish was taking him, there would no doubt be water. Trailing his guide he conceived a kind of twisted admiration for this thuggish muscleman who had, through an evening of song and quarrel, outdrunk him two to one and was now merely red-eyed (that is, showed nothing else, no visible distress). And who only an hour ago had telephoned and got him up and come to his room. Fresh, steady-handed, a happy man. To watch as the young wreck prepared himself for the day. Watch over the shower and the shave. Approve even the costuming, the kelly-green polo shirt and yellow linen jacket, gray slacks. And when Adam was ready, had slapped him two, three, four times, forehanded and backhanded, left cheek then right. As certain parents might do once gently, inspecting a difficult child, finally dressed and ready to send to the important birthday party. Here it was not once and not so very gentle. A dose of the daily cheerful torture that served to mark the nature of their relationship. "That's good," Ish had said. "A million-dollar kid. A million-dollar assistant."

Maybe more.

Adam had said he'd get the car.

But they weren't going to use the car. A little walk, Ish said. To pick up a package. Like going to the corner for a carton of milk. "You do that, don't you?" he said. "You go out? You buy the milk and all that?" But after that little collection, he said, assuming there were no problems, which there weren't going to be, then they were going to get the car. They would get themselves and their package into the car and to the airport and on the first flight out of here. "Home," he'd said.

Now they came around to the front of the building. Shade on this side. Ish stopped again. "So why is it," he said, "he left us yesterday? He went on ahead?"

Business in Chicago. Adam repeated what he'd been told.

"Yeah. Well, Chicago. How would you know? Chicago wasn't exactly a necessary detour. More make-work, if you follow me. For a different purpose. It was to avoid this little pickup we're makin here. One thing, you see. One thing you have to learn. Anything in an operation's not completely kosher, he steps out of it. On the other side of the world if he could. He's Mr. Clean, you know. Whatever he touches himself, they could audit him right to the nickel on it. He has a fetish that way."

Adam thought it was all right to ask about kosher. What wasn't kosher?

"Actually it's easy," Ish said. "This part of the deal. Everything gets shipped with papers and there's documents and checks and money in the bank. Of course maybe not all the stuff is exactly what it says in the documents but that's all right. No problem." He scratched at his chin. "Only thing," he said. "We arranged a little sweetener. Outside the price there's a little that doesn't show. There's a million dollars we're goin to get right now."

A carton of milk. A million-dollar carton at the corner.

"That's against those refineries and the pellet machines." Ish squeezed where he'd been scratching. "Ingrown hair," he said. "Although you want to consider that where there's substantial amounts like this it's always possible there could be some kind of trouble."

The big time, Adam thought, might have its drawbacks.

"And that's another thing," Ish said, "he likes to avoid."

No more than me, Adam was thinking. And he began to consider how profoundly he had passed beyond the bounds of a certain kind of conventional life. *On the edge, as I always wanted. Then why don't I feel a natural outsider's elation? Is this a time to jump? Is disengagement called for?*

When they came up to them, the glass doors of the lobby opened automatically. Ish didn't seem surprised to see one of

Quijada's guards at the front desk talking to the concierge. The guard said something more and the concierge spoke into his telephone. Then the guard turned to Ish and pumped twice with his thumb in an up direction. Ish put his hand under Adam's left elbow and led him through a corridor off the lobby to the elevators. In the elevator, he read from the red key and pushed the button for seven.

Seven. Ish looked at the sign in front of him and guided Adam to the right. As you might a favored prisoner. A prisoner you also sometimes, as Adam was remembering, slapped. How often did you do that? Or work your knuckles into his ribs or squeeze his shoulder where it joined the neck until there was at least the start of a scream and a buckling at the knees.

Wasn't it a principle of equity that to be enforceable a contract had to be fair? *So Dad always said.* Adam had bargained only for a little time along the margin . . . so as to define himself imaginatively as a kind of loner. That way true freedom. And he had wanted to distance himself credibly from certain perceived values of the republic. But thugs in the lobby and a possibility of actual violence, these were outside, as he saw it, the terms of any deal he'd made. Was this a problem for Dad? *Dad, I need a lawyer. I have this problem.* Adam had a quick recollection of his father at his desk in the apartment, of looking at him over a mound of books, blue-covered briefs, yellow pads. *The heap that he made, the wall.*

Ish was holding the red key but didn't have to use it. A door was partly open. Hans Kalb there waiting for them. Angry at something or else always like that. Lips of his small mouth compressed under his small mustache. Kalb's hand was out and Ish dropped into it the ring with the colored keys. Kalb then, still half blocking the entrance and Ish pushing past him and into the living room.

"Noon," Kalb said. "Twelve o'clock. A quarter of, we had agreed."

"A little *tarde,* right?" Ish checked his watch. "Five after, I make it. That's twenty minutes. But what's that between friends?" He sniffed the air.

The apartment had the dry rich smell that a closed place eventually takes on. It was too warm and all of the window drapes were drawn. The drapes met imperfectly and let in a thin ray of outside light. Ish went to the window. He pulled the drapes. Worked a catch and pushed apart glass doors that led to the terrace. "Clean out the stink in here," he said. Breathed heavily and grinned amiably at Kalb.

"That's good," Kalb said. "*Bueno.* You proved your point. You're late and you don't care and you let in the light. *Bueno.* What did you prove?"

Terrace furniture in blue duck was piled at the window end of the room. Overstuffed chairs and a couch, with a dining table at the pass-through to the kitchen. A stack of paintings against one wall, nothing hung. The first painting, the one you could see was in a primitive style and showed a street in a Latin village with women in shawls and men in wide hats, much foliage and some white buildings. In front of the couch, there was a large coffee table with a very large glass ashtray, thick, in a greenish hue with bubbles in the glass and also an attaché case in brown calfskin.

Ish waved his hand. "Forget it," he said. "Forget it. Everybody's friends. Okay?" But if his friend here, Adam, who wasn't really at his best today, if Adam could have a glass of water? Then they could go about it and finish their business.

"No water. The water is turned off." But maybe there was soda water in the kitchen. Adam could look in the cabinets there. Kalb faced Adam. Authoritarian belly thrusting forward out of his linen suit. Did he always wear those suits? "Or should I do that for you?" he said. "For the executive. Mr. Van Atta said you were an executive."

Adam found canned crab, pâté, jars of olives, booze, glasses, plates, cutlery. The refrigerator wasn't connected. There were typed sheets in English and in Spanish taped to a cabinet with instructions about locking up and water valves and building and outside services. The paper had begun to curl a little where it wasn't taped. Someone had penciled *Not bad* next to the number for a takeout Chinese restaurant. Adam leaned his head against the cool metal of the cabinet and counted the frequency of the throbs in his temple. Under the sink, in with the pail and the rags and the Clorox, he found six-packs of soft drinks and beer, everything warm of course.

Beer, Ish said. Whatever beer it was. And Adam took a Tab for himself. Kalb declined absolutely. He was on the couch, drumming his fingers against the coffee table. The attaché case was perfectly centered in the rectangle of the table, with the ashtray in the upper left quadrant. Kalb's drumming fingers were exactly in front of the combination lock of the case. He had the petulant look you might expect from an irritable maestro faced with a late and noisy audience.

Ish drank beer and put the can down on the coffee table, spoiling the perfect symmetry of the arrangement there. He wiped sweat from his forehead and stripped out of his jacket. A small pistol, a .32 with a two-inch barrel, was holstered under his left arm.

Adam only wondered where he'd got that. He couldn't have brought it through the airport check.

Kalb's pale skin went paler. "Guns," he said after a moment, "at a private meeting."

Ish grinned. "Hey," he said. "Not for you. I trust you. So pardon my bad manners." He very quickly drew the weapon and stretched across the coffee table to put it down quite close to Kalb's right hand. Now, on the coffee table, there was no longer any arrangement at all. Only clutter, mere objects.

Hans Kalb looked at the gun and at Ish. His mouth twitched. He took the attaché case onto his lap and began to work the combination. His face was pink now. The case, he said, would be a present. Ish could take that with him along with what was in it. And the gun, he said. Take that too. He spoke to Adam. "Please make a note of the combination. Write down 9-8-1. Do you have a pen? Something to write on?"

Ish said, "Adam's a good secretary. Always prepared, you know."

Kalb pressed the release catch and the case opened. He put the case back on the table where it had been. Precisely where it had been. He faced Ish and made an open-palmed gesture of handing over. Ish smirked and gestured politely back and Kalb opened the lid so it was fully upright.

All of the bills that Adam could see were hundreds. Not a small case but it was almost filled by the bulk of its contents. The sweetener, Adam thought, the million. If the bills were all hundreds, there would be ten thousand of them. *Think ten thousand pages. Think a dozen long Victorian novels.* Adam looked. The truly benign face of Ben Franklin returned his stare in multiple. Even repeated so, the Sage was without ability to infuse this scene with his own attitudes of moderation and cautious goodwill.

"You will want to count these," Kalb said.

Ish said, "Why would I want to do that? I trust you. You're an honest man is what I hear. I hear that all around."

"You should count them."

"What do I need to count. It's all there. The proof is in the pudding. Why would you, why would you make a mistake here? What we got, you want. The stuff you're buyin, that's my guarantee."

"For everybody's protection."

Ish put his hands up. He surrendered. All right, he'd count. Him and his associate here. It would be all right, wouldn't it, if Adam helped? "But no receipts. This service don't give receipts."

Kalb rotated the open case to face toward Ish . . . who lifted one wrapped stack and hefted it and tossed it gently two, three times as if to gauge its weight . . . and then started very suddenly to sweat. Oh, shit, he was saying. Shit. He wanted this goddamn shit to stop. "The crapper," he said to Kalb. "Where's the crapper here?"

Kalb didn't answer. He blinked.

"The runs," Ish said. "I got the runs again. Now where's the fuckin crapper?"

Kalb said, "Impossible. The toilet has no water."

"Those little valves. They turn the water on. Anyway that doesn't matter. I got to get in there."

Then Kalb pointed. "Left," he said. "Go through the bedroom."

And Ish was gone.

Adam said he thought it would be a while. "At least he hasn't been so very quick about it the other times."

The German didn't answer and turned the bulk of his belly away from the mere errand boy or fetch-and-carry assistant or whatever he took Adam to be, in the direction of the terrace and the sunny day outside. He presented now the ruin of a formerly powerful torso (not Ish's class but a legitimate brute) as seen from its flat-assed rear. The body tapered into thick legs, slightly knocked at the knees.

No speech in the room. The reverberations still (after ten seconds) of the slam of the bathroom door.

Adam also turned.

What he did then he later realized was not because of the money or for it. It was for no reason at all . . . except only some overflowing accumulation of resentments of insults to his spirit and his body. *Go for this. Drive there. Wait for me.* Scorn and minor violences had taken his reason. He wasn't reasoning. . . . What he did was to stoop and, in the literal thoughtlessness of the rage he hadn't been aware he had, pick up the thick-walled conference-sized greenish-glass ashtray (with the bubbles in the glass). Which he raised biblically and brought down on and a little into Hans Kalb's right temple.

The German collapsed in a sluggish fall. Descending, he gave a low moan, although he wasn't any longer conscious.

Adam with, for seconds, no ability to organize his mind, stared at objects. Separate, unconnected things. He couldn't make a pattern. He saw Kalb, the attaché case, the gun. The awful felt presence of Ish who would be a while, a short or a long while, but would eventually come into this room.

He moved. He closed the case and went into Kalb's wallet. Stuffed bills into his pocket. Then Ish's jacket for the car keys there and more money. He didn't conceive of what was in the case as immediately useful. He took the case. *The gun there on the table.* He didn't touch that. And he headed for the door.

Then remembered the colored keys. He might still need those. But how could he go back into the room? How could he make himself do that? He counted as if doing that would overcome his fear . . . *three, four.* The keys would be in the side pocket of Kalb's jacket. He'd seen Kalb drop them there. He went back.

And only at the elevator remembered the thug in the lobby. If the thug was there, he'd leave the case in the elevator. Abandon it, walk out with nothing in his hands and say he was going for the car. But with his finger at the main-floor button, he saw another button below it. G. . . . And came smoothly down into the garage. Daylight at the far end.

He began to run.

If he could get to a beige 88. *And get off this island.* Just don't let any black sedan screech to a stop in front of him when he was coming out of the parking lot. He could see that. Ish in the car and the thug. And Kalb with some bloody bandage at his head. *Just please keep that Causeway open.* He was already beginning to think ahead. The airport. How many men would they need to cover the airport? He used the yellow key and eventually the green key. He got to the beige 88 and used the car key.

The middle of a calm day. Minutes only and then the rich cool enveloping greens of Crandon Park. Then you come out into a cleared flat area and that narrows as you get to the Causeway itself. Adam stopped trembling. His sweat began to dry and he started to shiver. When he was first in the car he had turned the key and it had been possible that the engine would not respond. There had been his momentary certain foreknowledge that the battery was dead. The battery or some one of a thousand other potential electrical or mechanical betrayals. *He was due for a major failure.*

But then the cough and the loving purr.

So he was now free, free for now, with the sour cool of drying sweat spreading over his back.

Somewhere in the wild confusion of tall shapes, the office buildings of South Miami (at street level no sense of their loony tops or the dizzy angles that could delight an enthusiast at a distance), he pulled alongside a young executive in a blue suit. "Uh, buddy."

Not a friendly smile but the man stopped. Suspicious. Not a buyer of the stolen platinum watch or the bag of special powder that someone had brought in for his own use and now by circumstance was forced almost to give away. Not from a cruising car, and most likely not at all. This one had the look of a fine-boned hard-driving puritan. An odds player who would prefer to go carefully and move up in the firm.

But willing to direct you to a decent men's store.

Adam found the store and on the next block a parking garage. Before he left the car, he sorted the bills he'd taken from Ish and Kalb. With those and his own little bit of money he had over sixteen hundred dollars. He copied the number 9-8-1 from the paper he'd written it on to the back of a small appointment calendar and checked the attaché case to make sure it was locked. He tucked his aviator sunglasses under the front seat. Then he walked back to the men's store.

"Son of a bitching Eastern," he said when he walked in. "Bastards lost my luggage." He bought a navy blazer and a blue button-down shirt and a maroon tie with white pin dots.

"That blazer," the salesman said. "That's almost a perfect fit. One little wrinkle at the shoulder. You have it tomorrow."

"Can't. Got to get down to Key West. Sales conference. Bring it back next week?"

"If we're still here."

"You will be. You carry any luggage? And maybe a pair of sunglasses? I like that horn-rimmed look. Or maybe a plain black frame." From here, he decided, it would still be safe to use his plastic. But cash only when he got under way. Leave no trace.

What kind of business meeting? the salesman said.

Adam talked advertising. Kind of high-level.

A little conference then. The salesman pushed his view that, for that kind of meeting, you wanted to turn up looking your best. So Adam ought to wear what he'd bought and carry his old stuff. Yes, Adam said. And five minutes later he was looking good and carrying an under-the-seat bag in high-quality heavy canvas. The attaché case and the things he'd been wearing were in the bag.

The horn rims, the salesman said, gave him a kind of very distinguished look.

Adam said, "Where would I phone for a cab around here?"

He got almost to the airport with no panic at all. He put his mind to other things. Lisa and Sammy, as if that were a topic. At some point he would have to get in touch with Debbie. But later. This was an anonymous society and he was about to sink into it. *A new me with new i.d.* But when he got out of the cab it was only, *Why didn't I buy a hat?*

He had to wait an hour and a half for the flight he decided on, the flight to New Orleans. His great fear was of being trapped, but in a modern airport where can you hide? So he stayed in open areas and kept a newspaper in front of him. Three times he moved. He forced himself to get up and move so as not to be noticed as a fixture in any one place. He did manage to drop into a wastebasket the ring of colored keys and his hotel room key. When the plane left the ground he told himself that now he was absolutely safe on a short-term basis. He began to think of others. He saw Ish zipping up and coming into the living room where Hans Kalb was possibly dead or beginning to come to. He thought of Ish afterwards in communication with Van Atta . . . and of Van Atta taking steps.

"This is Raymond."

Kreg didn't immediately move on and so, just outside Tech Hi-Fi, in a snowfall, just steps from the sheltered entrance to his office building, found himself in conversation with Deane and this tall thin young man. Raymond. Snow whipped down the street in undisciplined whirls. Mostly, Kreg thought, straight at him, into his face.

Deane and Raymond seemed not to care. Gravely Raymond shook hands. He was, Deane said, an old friend passing through. A mathematician of fractals at MIT. "Planar and solid."

To which Kreg had no reply.

"Irregular shapes," Deane said. "The volume of an intestine, the area of the surface of the brain. The true length of a coastline." She looked quickly to Raymond, who nodded. Then she smiled as if somewhat embarrassed at having such knowledge.

Kreg understood that these mathematics would appeal to her as more natural than the math of straight lines and circles. They would seem more organic, with almost a tie to whole grains and nature's sweet honey. Raymond, next to her, had no hat, even in the snow. He had brush-cut black hair that grew low on his narrow forehead. Small sharp amiable face. Wire-rim glasses.

Deane seemed truly pleased at this meeting. Eyes flashing between Kreg and Raymond. Did they really like each other? The lace-trimmed bottom of a prairie skirt showed under her parka. "All this learning," she said.

Yes, Kreg said. Wasn't it impressive? It was to him because when you got past simple math he was lost.

"Both of you, I meant," Deane said. She said that she and Raymond were going to duck across the street for some soup or something. Raymond's bag was in the office. He was lucky. It was going to be a museum afternoon for him; later he'd pick her up at the office.

Kreg had the impression that Raymond would be staying at Deane's place. Which was fine except that she was too birdy about it, anxious for him to know. How long now . . . ten days since he'd bought her that drink? Possibly she was embarrassed because she'd been foolish to insist on that.

It was more or less ten days. He thought of that in connection with Marcu. It was long enough for a stalemate to have developed in Marcu's campaign for Brandt Systems. He'd stabilized at about seventeen percent of the stock and the Company had bought in almost four percent. There was so little around that any further push seemed likely to send the price into another dimension. Nobody was doing anything, and Willie Unger was coming increasingly to the view that an l.b.o. might be a real possibility. With some sweetener of course for Marcu. Willie hadn't suggested how the Foundation would be protected and Kreg hadn't asked. He was in a position to wait.

Yesterday Marcu had called.

"I'm surprised you took my call," he'd said to Kreg.

"I take all my calls. Why not yours?"

"Would you meet with me? We should meet."

"Yes."

"My suite? We do a good lunch."

No, we won't. We won't arrange it so nicely. In your suite. "No," Kreg said. "Not lunch."

"Then later. A drink."

"Just business."

"Ah," Marcu said. And then he was saying yes. Of course. When would Kreg want to come by? No refreshments, he promised that.

Kreg said, "I'd rather it were here."

Marcu's voice went a little different, flatter. "My associate," he said. "I'm not able to leave but you know him. Mr. Cotton. He speaks for me."

"Tell him to call."

"It isn't unreasonable," Marcu had said before they rang off, "that you'd want to put me in my place." He said that in his normal pleasant courteous voice.

Yes it is, Kreg thought. I won't say so to you but it is unreasonable.

This now was a wet snow. A dark day with some cars using their headlights. But nothing coming and Raymond took Deane's arm and they stepped down into the slushy street. Kreg kicked snow from his wet shoes, moved toward his office building. He was wondering about Iris and Cotton, whether they were still seeing each other. And if they were, how long would it last? He didn't see a long-term relationship there . . . although that wasn't his business, was it? Not his concern. His shoes had soaked through and he was due upstairs for his meeting with Cotton, who of course had called, as Marcu had said he would.

"Our point," Cotton said, "would be, why not?"

Kreg contemplated the drape of Cotton's suit. How many hours a week to keep the body fit? So as to permit that elegant fall of gray worsted over it? He said wouldn't it be better for Cotton not to concern himself with motives? The Foundation preferred not to sell its stock. That could be taken as fact. "What some people call a given." Cotton's good features, easy manner. You could understand the attraction for a woman, for Iris.

Cotton said that if they knew Kreg's thoughts they could design inducements that would satisfy him. "Custom tailoring," he said.

Kreg said, "We would like you to go away. You could design toward that."

"But that can't happen."

Cold from Kreg's wet feet was moving up his legs. Especially into the left knee he'd once injured. "Then what would it be?" he said. "What kind of inducements?"

"Not so much a change in price."

"I hadn't expected. Not yet."

"We thought, especially for the Foundation, it would be income. We would modify our package toward the fixed-income side. We would offer you a high-yield bond, something very high-paying."

"And you have a proposition?"

"A sketch, you might call it. Only an outline." Cotton handed across a memorandum. Two sheets.

No letterhead, Kreg noticed. And no salutation or signature.

"You'll see," Cotton said, "when you look at it, what we could do apart from the coupon itself. The bond could be convertible if you want, and we'd arrange a put feature. You could put it back to us at par any time you wanted, say after a year or two.

"And if I accepted for the Foundation, everything would fall in line?"

"You're the engine here. You could make it a done deal."

"You'd offer everybody . . ."

"Choices for everybody. Everybody can go income, go for the bond. Or else take stock. All very fair. . . . And at the corporate level, they keep their independence. Total, functional independence. And salaries and bennies. The whole opportunities package."

"Do they call it that?"

"I'm afraid." Cotton said his people would consider any reasonable sweeteners.

Your people. Marcu, you mean. Marcu will consider. Kreg said he couldn't speak for the Company. He said for Cotton to talk to Willie Unger. He remembered that Willie had talked about sweeteners for Marcu.

"But you seem to be the one to talk to. And of course you're not out of touch with any of them."

"It would be naïve to think so."

"We're not naïve."

Kreg said that what they'd discussed so far he'd already assumed. He'd heard nothing new.

"Well, no secret about it, we're anxious. If there's any chance, we don't want not to take it. We'll just keep trying." Would Kreg tell him, Cotton said (repeating his earlier question), *why not?* Why didn't he want to sell? That was what he didn't understand. Cotton didn't and Marcu didn't. Sooner or later, this Company was going to fall. So why not sell it now? Why not to them?

Kreg stood. Fire now in his left knee, which happened sometimes when the leg got cold, as it had earlier when he'd stayed outside in the snow talking to Deane and Raymond. He walked with Cotton to the elevator. Cotton was explaining that he hadn't been talking in confidence, everything was intended to be passed on . . . if Kreg chose to do that.

When he was alone Kreg allowed himself to massage his knee. And thought of Adam, because the knee itself was always a reminder. Adam had been just old enough to walk and he himself was trying to establish a practice and barely able to afford even the collapsed shell of a country house he'd bought when he inherited some money. And maybe the house and fixing it up and making a garden would in some way salvage the marriage that he already knew to be the disaster of his life.

Coming then on a blazing August morning, the heat like a weight on you, into the cool cellar. Smell of must. There, just as you entered, a lolly column bore an actual weight, the sagged thrust of the southeast corner of the house above. Every week Kreg gave the column another quarter turn. At the rate of an eighth of an inch per week he was raising the floor above. Leveling out his house. There was an inside tap and he ran water into a jelly glass. Drank first and then sloshed his head and face.

He started to be aware of what he was hearing . . . and began to run.

Past the barn and past where the land sloped downward. Adam, rigid in his fear and anger, was bawling toward the sun and wearing a cap of red. Blood over his head and face and streaming down his body. Susan was already there but not useful because she wasn't holding the boy. She was next to her child, not moving, clenched hands pressed to her mouth, immobilized by her terror of the blood or of the child's agony.

Kreg, twenty yards from them, fifteen, felt his foot catch in the uneven ground. He felt the twist of himself falling. Saw ahead of him, next to Adam, the iron splitting wedge. *Against that, of course. That's how he did it. Falling on that.*

"You all right? Can you wait a minute?" It was his neighbor, Hobart.

Hobart took charge. He scooped up the crying boy. Held his hand out to Susan until she took it. Then marched with her and his sobbing burden to the house.

Kreg rolled on the ground for a while. In a few minutes was able to hobble. He found Adam in a Mickey Mouse shirt. Clean except for the drying blood in his hair and with a bandage on his head. "We just got downstairs," Nate Hobart said. Adam was pulling at one of Hobart's extended fingers. "The trick of it is, with these scalp wounds there's a lot of blood. You just have to pull it tight and tape it closed." Susan ran soothing maternal hands over the body of her happy child. Kreg's knee was beginning to stiffen. A drink? he said to Hobart. It was lunchtime and Susan would make a little something. "There's food, isn't there?" he said to her.

With a guest there would be a different kind of conversation. The conversation could be about country life. The how to, for instance, of restoring a neglected lawn, or how much wood you'd need for weekend fires through the winter. It could be about the very propping up of this house on an iron column that was doing its brute job on a line almost directly below the ache in the owner's left knee. There were all these and other potential topics. The sag and propping up of this marriage, on the other hand, would not be discussed at all. Failures to measure up would not be mentioned.

Susan's shy glance. "Wonderful," she said. Her mood had changed and now she wanted to make this a little party. And really that was fine. Because what was the point of personal talk, in the face of that sweet blankness?

"Five minutes," Nate Hobart said. "Change this shirt for something with a little less red in it. . . . Whisky would be good," he said to Kreg. "Anything. Just no gin-and-tonic."

A quarter century later, Kreg flexed his left knee and decided not to take an aspirin. The thought of Adam was only that they hadn't been in touch and that he didn't want long time gaps opening between them. He started to wonder about Cotton, who normally was smooth, easy, controlled. As he had been today. Almost until he was at the elevator, when he'd turned suddenly toward Kreg and started to speak and then hadn't and faced away.

Possibly there'd been an impulse to suggest that Kreg had been less polite than he should have been (which was true and to a degree regretted). In this situation with Brandt Systems, something was going to happen and Kreg wanted to keep his lines of communication open to the enemy. *Don't paint yourself in any corners.*

Most likely though, Cotton had simply thought of something he wanted to say and then decided against it.

Kreg put weight on his left leg. It seemed possible to manage. Take a hot bath tonight as he had done when he first hurt the knee. Susan had helped him. She fussed over the scrape and eased his leg out of the torn khakis. When he came out of his bath, she made him lean on her shoulder to step into a fresh pair (he had felt the slightness of her bones).

Adam watched from the bathroom doorway. Nate Hobart came back and Kreg gave him twenty-five-year-old Scotch whisky. Ambassador. There'd been a special reason for him to have had that. It had been a present from Susan when he was admitted to the bar. Now he and Nate Hobart were drinking it. Susan had her gin-and-tonic. She was teasing Nate. Was it all right for her to have this drink that he couldn't stand? She had wonderful cold chicken and tomatoes and sandwiches for them. And some cake from last night. But if Mr. Hobart was going to disapprove of her taste in drinks she simply wouldn't feed him. She hugged her son and was really charming in a more flashing way than usual.

Nate Hobart had been telling Kreg it wasn't only the house. Kreg's barn too had a sag in places. Very picturesque but also dangerous. Not so big a job as it might seem but you'd have to take care of it if you wanted to keep the barn . . . and if you didn't mind the unsolicited advice. Maybe, he said to Susan, she'd eventually convert him to those things she was drinking but he'd hold out just a little longer as he was, if that was all right. He turned his attention back to Kreg, turned back, it seemed, not to the husband of the woman so much as to the adult in charge. And Kreg, *exactly then*, permitted into his mind a conscious awareness of his desperation. He had thought he could stand anything.

"Come in here if you like."

Raymond said he didn't want to interrupt.

"Finished really," Kreg said. "Anyway, taking a break."

"I didn't mean to be lurking in the wings."

"Don't lurk. Come in."

"She has another little bit to clean up."

"Then we'll talk for a while." By now, he was thinking, Marcu and Cotton would also have talked. *I didn't make a great deal of progress, Cotton would have said. In fact, no place. I got no place with him. He listened to me. He wasn't even too badly mannered about it. For him. Just gave you the sense that he was examining you like something on a slide or out from under a rock.*

On the other hand, Marcu said.

I know what you're thinking, Cotton said.

Yes, Marcu said. The fact is, he talked to me and then he saw you and he listened to what you had to say. He talks like war but actually he doesn't act that way.

Cotton said, Not like total, one hundred percent, no-traffic-with-the-enemy, take-no-prisoners war. Not that kind of war.

But that's good, Kreg thought, if that's how they're thinking. They think I'm flexible and that I don't have to make any immediate decisions. Not heroic but sensible. *Then take your time. . . . Just let me have some time.*

Raymond sat across from him. Stretched so he was in a slouch. Crossed long bony legs at the ankles. He said that in some ways he envied Kreg.

"Why would that be?"

"You have to understand the appeal to someone who plays games for a living. The idea of the law. Real differences between real people. Out in the world that way."

Kreg said, "This being out in the world . . . it's only a kind of stumbling forward. Very makeshift."

"But that's what appeals."

Kreg said he'd be willing to operate for a while with the perfect certainties of a cleaner discipline. Could he say that? Clean?

"Clean, yes," Raymond said. "Consistent, you mean. But not always so certain. We make whole systems that could be very shaky structures indeed."

"Because?"

"Well, after a certain level, after a certain point, you operate from these inductive leaps."

Kreg asked if Raymond's work might be superseded? Did mathematics work that way?

"I think it would be more a matter of boundaries, the extent of application. For instance, Euclidian geometry still applies, if you follow me. Just not everywhere. It doesn't define the universe."

Kreg asked about Deane, how they knew each other?

At Austin, Raymond said. They'd been undergraduates together.

"But she was never a mathematician?"

"She wasn't a student," Raymond said. "I mean not seriously. Although it was a good place for her. She liked it there."

Deane had said she'd been with a fast crowd in college. *Rowdy*, she'd said. Kreg didn't see Raymond as having been part of such a group. Raymond would have been separate from her other friends. Or possibly those other friends had never existed. Possibly the rowdy past was a made-up story. But with Raymond there would have been coffee together, movies.

Raymond said, "I think she likes it here too."

"I hope so," Kreg said.

Deane from the doorway, in her heavy coat and hat and boots, said, "Two minutes with all this on and you'd begin to melt in here." A woolen glove like a child's in one hand. Where was the other one? Her eyes going from Kreg to Raymond. Was everything all right between them?

Raymond uncoiled, stood. "We don't want you to melt," he said to her.

"If you're in the neighborhood again," Kreg said to him.

Deane smiled at both of them. "Come on," she said to Raymond. "I'm planning a *wonderful* evening."

Raymond shook hands. "Well," he said.

Kreg observed the young mathematician. Alert intelligent eyes in his small head which perched, birdlike, on a long neck. The head always moving, turning to observe the novelties of the curious world.

When he was alone he surveyed his desk and worktable. The stacks of papers. There was a matter of a limited partnership that he'd been planning to attend to. This was his client with the Midwestern real-estate deal. The referral from his cousin Marvin. The man was investing or anyway putting money into a play and a check would be written once Kreg approved the structure of the deal. And then the money would be substantially lost as it had been so often in the past. To which the client didn't object since the true investment here was not in theater but in a kind of social range. An exchange of dollars for the right to give certain dinner parties and to use certain names with authentic familiarity. Each party to the transaction satisfied with his end of the bargain. What he lost, the client always said, his uncle shared, his Uncle Sam. *That's why God made write-offs. And what can I do? She loves the theater. So how much has that cost me over the years? I had to marry a girl who went to Bennington. They go artistic, it's going to cost you.* So couldn't Kreg understand why he'd rather it was fifty thousand here and there against an unhappy home and three times a week at the shrinker? This way she wasn't a patient.

Which was not a term that had been used about Deane this evening. But the sense of it had been there. It had been implicit in the atmosphere of the conversation. He and Raymond had understood what wasn't being said.

How is she (Raymond had wanted to know)?

In a way this is a good place for her. She functions. Actually she's very efficient.

Because she's always very close to the edge.

But never over?

I can't point to episodes.

She told me she's alcoholic.

She's delicate, you see.

Delicate. I wouldn't disagree.

Kreg started to make notes. This was simple work, a deal like its predecessors. Really he was only proofreading. Certainly he wasn't writing. He didn't do that anymore. He was a lawyer only now. His client somehow had made a new connection. This was to another producer, a major name. Future deals would be with him. An increase then both in prestige and the likelihood of a return on his dollars. It was a talent like any other, his client's ability always to be ready to capitalize on chance.

He imagined that Raymond and the sturdy delicate girl might not actually have been lovers in the past. But surely now . . . with the two of them there alone in her small apartment. He envisioned it as small. He imagined her as straightforward, possibly enthusiastic, but not a truly exciting partner.

Adam thought again about his decision not to stay in New Orleans and concluded he'd been right to leave. He'd spent two days there, seen the Quarter and the wrought iron and the vault graves that flooded over when the river rose. He didn't need either the romanticism that was like a protective intellectual wrapping for the *idea* of the place or the humidity or that sense of nostalgic ticky-tack metastasizing and taking over.

Cincinnati was a better choice. It was central in the country, clean and middle-class. And there was no one he knew here. Which made it the perfect stopping place in which to plan and determine what he would become. You could strike from Cincinnati in any direction. Eventually he'd step out new-made. Ready to carve his destiny as he conceived it.

But first his time here, his planning period.

He saw himself in some spacious upscale pub, converted from a warehouse. Brick, stone and brass. Real gaslights on the posts outside. He would be drinking a moderately good local beer (this was beer country, wasn't it?) and trying to decide between the *paillard* of veal and three baby lamb chops with piquant mint sauce. Oysters first, flown in daily from icy New England waters. Not too bad for the boonies. Everybody was learning.

This was a late dinner, after a concert which also hadn't been bad. Local guys doing intricate modern stuff. As a tribute to Monk, their own version of "Ruby My Dear."

In a mirror on a near wall he exchanged looks with a light-haired girl. Blue eyes to go with hair that was the color of corn. The guy she was with, beefy going on fat, kept his head in the trough. Never looked up. Shy glances so as not to alarm her. This was no Debbie or Lisa. A more refined commodity than the one, less outgoing than the other. Although eventually a fuckee as they all were. Later, when she seemed used to him, he'd nod his head decisively and get up as if headed for the men's room. Bring some authority to that move. She would follow. Exchange of telephone numbers and something started. Don't scare her. Not even the softest kiss. Brush her cheek with the back of your hand and send her back to the table.

So I'll meet girls. Screw like a bandit. I'll follow my crazy dick. . . . Be led through life by my penis . . . my lingam. No question, the life of action made you horny. Your secret heart, that was what you followed. From a song of his father's time. Maybe before that. That was a life for you, the old man's. *Dad's.* The triangle that ran between the apartment, his office and the place in the country. Maybe there was more to it than you first thought. The books he wrote, of course. *But I mean, a life?* The ox at work. Always. He lets nothing interfere, which means nobody, so now there is nobody. He forced Susan out. Couldn't keep it going with Iris and he has squat for friends. Some professors at Columbia Law and Etkind Rossoff. Rossoff always trying to be friendly to me. The two of them worrying over those tidbit grants they give out from the Foundation. *Is the work original? Does he really have anything new to say?* Corned-beef sandwiches and pickles on the kitchen table. Just hope they don't drop some law professor's application in the mustard. . . . And he talks over the back fence with Nate Hobart when he's in the country. *Wunderbar. Tell me about his relations with his son. By the imposition of my standards I let you know that you are shit.* He'd lent money and Adam would send that back to him. Cash in an envelope. Dad would go through the floor. Now give this girl a name. Maybe German. Wasn't this a German city? They settled here, didn't they, after 1848? Considering the number he'd so recently dropped on Hans Kalb, that German from Bolivia or wherever it might be, wouldn't it be a nice ironic hoot also to get himself in the rack with some prize young Rhine maiden from here in the heartland of the U.S. of A.?

He'd arrived in fifteen-degree weather without an overcoat. At the airport there were two people ahead of him waiting for cabs and a malignant dry wind that whipped down from northern flats. He tried to curl into himself like an illustration of a Dickensian derelict. Nipple-sized goosebumps all over his body. . . . One cab and then another one. . . . The dignified old man in the sheepskin coat who was ahead of him already had his hand on the door handle, then crooked a finger at Adam. "Just take this guy here. Can't have you freeze to death."

He shivered for ten minutes in the cab. In the hotel he felt conspicuous and a fool, being out of costume in that particular way. A kind of nakedness. Of course nobody noticed him. Who'd wear an overcoat in that overheated lobby?

At the last minute, after he registered, he took the attaché case from the top of the counter. He'd been going to check it in the hotel safe but decided against that. He wanted it with him. 9-8-1. The number was always in his mind.

Upstairs, when he emptied his bag, the stuff didn't fill one bureau drawer. He put the attaché case in another drawer. Would he carry it with him when he went out? Would that attract attention? He started to nap. He dropped off, then woke and got up to check the case. Slept again. It was all confusion and surreal transition. Doom in the funhouse. Trick doors, weights. Ish, his father, the old actress. A half hour later he was soaking under a very hot shower. He blessed the fine plumbing of the country. But why had he dreamed of the actress? That struck him as odd. What was she to him?

He dressed. Downstairs, he prowled the soft carpeting of the lobby, the public area of a good chain hotel. The air had the stuffy closed-system smell indigenous to such places. An atmosphere that implied some necessary unhealthy consequence and of course had found it in Legionnaires' disease. There were friendly people with white identification badges. He saw them wherever he went. A sales meeting of an electrical device manufacturer, he learned from an amiable product manager.

For the discriminating, there was a choice of bars and restaurants. Not only different places but different styles. You could eat American or international or simply in a cafeteria. Barwise, you had a raised section of the lobby with little tables and chairs. Elsewhere the romantic gloom of Lady Harriet's (Victorian) and the more elegant Osborne Room with the sign outside that told you who was singing these nights.

He had an urge to give a spot of business to Lady Harriet. Chivas-on-the-rocks. Adam could taste the smooth warmth of the first sip. But you had to prioritize. An overcoat was necessity *numero uno.*

He was directed to a department store across the street. Across the street meant above the street. An enclosed passageway that bridged the frozen avenue below. You could beat the flight to the suburban malls by transforming downtown itself into a mall. A strategy of innovative cooption.

In the men's shop he found a salt-and-pepper tweed coat with raglan shoulders. An informal cut. Exactly what he wanted. He counted out six one-hundred-dollar bills. He still had some of the money he'd taken from Ish and Hans Kalb but this was a test of the large-denomination stuff from the attaché case.

"That's cash," the salesman said. "Hundreds."

Audacity, Adam decided, would be needed if he was ever going to be able to spend what he had. "Legal tender," he said. "You check the bills and then you call the U.S. Attorney if you don't want to take them."

In another shop he found a plaid cap and a long handknit scarf in bright red that he had to have. And he bought fur-lined chestnut leather gloves. Soft. You wanted to rub them over your face. A three-pack of jockey shorts, shirts, handkerchiefs. He used three more of his hundreds plus change. He knew exactly the sleeveless cardigan he wanted as a vest, a zigzag pattern with about four different earth tones and heather and blood red in it. He didn't find what he wanted. But no compromises, he told himself. Some other day in some other store.

In his room he tried on the coat with the red scarf and the cap and gloves. He didn't want any kind of tweedy-dowdy look, Brooks Brothers and the job at the good law firm. The scarf and the horn-rimmed dark glasses took care of that. They provided the slightly sportier effect he was aiming for.

"Now," he said to the mirror.

It was clear to him what he'd be giving up, cutting past ties. Nothing. Nothing that was important to him. So he was well prepared for the life of cool detachment that he saw ahead. *Work it out,* he was always hearing. Work out your feelings toward your father, your ambivalent relationship with your mother. But in his case there was no need. There was nothing to work out. Susan was somebody who'd gone away. Susan married handsome Ted and they lived in the mild and gently rolling green hills of Marin County and waited each day for the advent of the cocktail hour. Nobody really home, so nobody to work anything out with. More complicated with his father. Somewhat more. Even a kind of bond there. You'd be a liar to say there wasn't. But a bond could be broken; it was a condition of his freedom to do that. So chop as necessary.

He changed his shirt for one of the new ones, a blue-and-white stripe. And then downstairs. Lady Harriet's was beginning to be crowded but there were a few places at the bar. He squeezed in next to a square-jawed oriental with a white badge that read John Tamamura.

"Day like this," Tamamura said, "you need a couple."

"After whipping up the troops?"

Tamamura's badge also identified him as V.P. Sales, Western Region. He smiled the open smile of the rising exec. "Hit do take it out of you," he said.

Adam ordered his Chivas with soda on the side. "And whatever he's having. Another for my friend here."

"Great. But let me do it. Let the *company* do it."

"Wish I could but I'm in a spending mood. Jack Adam, by the way."

Tamamura finished his drink. "Meet you, Jack," he said. He tilted the glass to get an ice cube. Crushed it with his back teeth. A slender man with wide muscular jaws. The pattern and articulation of bone and muscle perfectly discernible when he chewed.

Adam started to say he was a freelance writer. But caught himself. *Stick to what you know.* From now on it would be caution and control. Don't get caught in some dopey lie. Be the man from nowhere . . . never truly at home but never uneasy. Real estate, he said to John Tamamura.

"You the construction side?"

"Development. Whatever it takes. Do it all."

"Company?"

"Just us. Two partners and me."

"Local?"

"Only passing through. See some people and back to the Coast."

"West?"

Adam pointed to Tamamura's badge. "Only place to be," he said.

"Tell it, brother."

"Sales v.p. I meant to ask for, uh, who?"

"That's Grissom-Talbot. Electrical, you know. Wiring devices. Connectors. Big line but that's the heart of it."

"I've heard the name."

"Have to if you build."

"I build a little."

"Commercial?"

"That and warehouses. Some residential. Anything."

"Then you probably use our stuff. Not in the residential though. Also a lot of marine, we get into that."

"Not really."

"Hell of a field." Probably, Tamamura said, there was going to be a change of corporate name. Get something not only more up to date but so they wouldn't be identified only with the old Grissom-Talbot end of their business. "I mean," he said, "we've got divisions in communications equipment, military electronics. We are growing the thing." He shook his head in simple amazement at the wonder of it.

"Then it's a good idea probably. The new name."

"Maybe G.T. Industries. And get some good designer to do a current image for us. New logo, new packaging. Change the whole damn look." Tamamura looked past Adam's shoulder.

"There she is," he said. He slid from the bar stool and kissed a dark-haired girl in a red dress. He introduced her, Julie who worked with him, to Jack Adam. He said Jack was a big real-estate deal from our part of the country.

Julie barely acknowledged the introduction. She didn't turn her eyes from John Tamamura. Not out of rudeness but because she couldn't. Then (Adam guessed), since she had to do something, even here in this public place, she reached to the badge on Tamamura's left lapel and unpinned it and dropped it in his left pocket. "Everybody knows you," she said. "You don't need this."

"You. You know who I am?"

"Tell me if I forget."

Perfect small features. She would be Italian or Greek or Spanish. A petite child of the Mediterranean. Adam saw disappointment ahead. What defenses would she have at home against the pulls and ties of the nisei family?

"I could buy you a drink," Tamamura said to her. He could do whatever he wanted, he knew that. "Or we could go to the hospitality suite?" he said.

But she wanted what he wanted.

Tamamura seemed to watch disinterestedly for some sign in the girl of a will to please herself. He rubbed his fist along her cheek. She leaned quickly against it. Any scrap. "Maybe we'll go to the suite," he said. "I have to circulate a little. Make nice to the guys. . . . You come with us," he said to Adam.

They went by escalator to the mezzanine floor. They rode up in a line of corporate personnel and spouses. Much calling back and forth. Everybody wanted to talk to John Tamamura, who seemed to be a kind of young prince in the organization.

"Listen," he said to Adam before they went into the suite. "I have to move around. Do my stuff, you know. So you make yourself at home. Maybe you can meet somebody . . . Julie, one of the girls want a date with a real nice guy? Take a minute and get him started. . . . Anybody asks," he said to Adam, "you're my guest."

Julie watched him leaving. Three steps and he had his arms around two men, mid-fifties with a middle-management look.

She turned. "About that date for you," she said.

Adam caught the uncertain note. "Listen," he said. "No big thing about it." He considered Julie. *Very important, he decided, that I get this girl laughing.*

Julie looked at him and then away, as if without control, toward Tamamura's back. Adam knew what Tamamura was telling her when they were alone. *Baby, I wish I could but you don't understand. You don't know how it is with a Japanese family* (famous American line). *How can I make that clear to you?* "You don't know how it is."

Of course, that part was true.

A sense of more bodies around them now. The suite was filling up. *Mucho* active now at the bars. Adam put a hand under Julie's elbow. "Come on," he said. "We better get a little something."

A fat man ahead of them saw Julie and seemed to decide that it would be impossible for anyone but him to order for her. He took requests and handed back a white wine for her and a tall scotch for Adam. He introduced himself. "Bronheim," he said.

Julie said she was with Western sales headquarters. Mr. Adam, she said, was a guest of the company.

"Me too," the fat man said. "I'm also a kind of a guest. Where you work there in Western sales?"

"Mr. Tamamura's office."

"John. I know John. Lucky John. One of my associates knows him pretty good. That's partly how we went into this situation."

"Went into?" Julie said.

"We bought some stock. I went on the Board. Announce it here. The big meeting. The two of us. Me and my associate. So you could say I have an interest here. . . . Why a kind of a guest?" he said to Adam. "You do business with us?"

"Social. Through your friend John."

Minutes later, Bronheim was talking to Adam about Southern California real estate. "Kid," he said, "I did them all. I did the shopping centers and the condos and the office buildings. All that stuff. But every deal I went in cheap. So show me cheap today. You find it, good luck to you." Julie started to slip away but he put a casual heavy hand on her shoulder.

John Tamamura came over to them. Tamamura, Adam thought, didn't make bad moves. You'd assume, then, that Bronheim was what he'd said he was. Adam had never really doubted that. He'd sensed the solid self-assurance of a successful operator who'd move from real estate to manufacturing to maybe retailing or a theater chain . . . whatever floated up. Always ready to grab at whatever was put in his reach by chance. And he sensed something else: *the guy's in action.* Adam thought he could tell. How many like Bronheim had he met in recent years? He imagined Bronheim bribing a state senator, owning a piece of a middleweight, making the right donations.

"You have two minutes," Tamamura said to Bronheim. "That's a threat." He placed his hand for a moment on Julie's shoulder, where Bronheim's hand had been. "Very nice," he said to Bronheim, "that you horse around with the prettiest girl in the room and my friend here but this is a working night for you."

"I don't work. I'm an owner and I'm a director. Owners and directors, they don't work."

"You see," John Tamamura said to Adam, "he doesn't understand. He doesn't know how it is. . . . Now you're in," he said to Bronheim, "you're just another body for the sales department to exploit. We use it all. Everybody, whoever there is. People out there creaming to meet you, the big investor who bought into the company. . . . Poor bastard," he said to Adam. "He's got to follow me around. Make nice with guys whose great treat is twenty, twenty-five minutes of detail on this miniature connector we developed for NASA or the new zillion-pronged pin plug that's knocking the spots off the competition." He crooked a finger at Bronheim. "Work time," he said.

"I hafta?"

"You get to love it."

"But you too," Bronheim said to Julie. "You keep me company a bit."

"Uh-uh," Tamamura said. "This is just the fellas together." He reached to a passing hors d'oeuvres tray. Took some small tidbit and popped it into her mouth. "Stick around," he said to Adam. "Connect with you later." With Bronheim next to him, he moved into the crowd.

"Well," Julie said. After a moment she said there was someone across the room she had to see and she drifted off. Mostly, Adam decided when he looked around, he wasn't seeing people he really wanted to be with. A few guys like John T. or not, but Grissom-Talbot was pretty obviously an old-fashioned manufacturing company. That was the culture. He was watching grown-up men in shopping-mall suits slap each other on the back and tell the funny story. Great.

He began to edge his way again to the bar. A solid press of bodies around him. Those newly served working their way back through the crowd. Two or three full glasses held at shoulder level or higher. Tentative slow movements. One drink, not two, was what he'd stay for. Unless, of course, he connected up.

If you could scrunch yourself just a c.h. to the side?

Adam made as much room as he could. Took a *Good boy* thank you from a tall man with two drinks and one of those outdoorsman's leather faces. Then he was at the bar.

And just in front of him were the head and shoulders of Ish. The neat wiry hair. Familiar slope of shoulders. Then the extension of Ish's arm. The hand accepting a drink from a bartender. The huge body beginning to turn. A confident slow rotation.

To face me.

Adam made no move to save himself. *Try something. Put your head down. Cover. Cover yourself.* He didn't. He went absolutely still. There had to be some way not to be where he was. . . . Ish elevated his glass, not so high as others had done. Because room would be made for him. The face was coming into view. Ish's eyes would meet his eyes.

Then they did . . . and weren't. It wasn't Ish. There wasn't the battler's jawline. Only a second chin, drape of flesh that hung from ear to ear, and not the thick ridge of brow. A blob nose on this man like carelessly shaped dough.

The man pushed past him.

Then he was conscious of the rush of sweat over his face and body. Himself turning . . . and he began to push his way through the crowd behind him.

He was on his back and looking at the ceiling. He'd get up in a minute. It was still early and there was an evening to plan. One thing—he wasn't going back to the Grissom-Talbot hospitality suite. Not because of what had happened . . . not because he'd been scared for a moment. But what was the point? Really. Who would he meet there who wasn't already taken?

He was bothered by the smell of his own dried sweat. Stink of fear. How many times in his life had he read that phrase? Which now he knew to be accurate. He could see one loafer on its side where he'd kicked it and his blazer in a heap over a chair. He wanted to shower and change. Do that soon.

He decided that Cincinnati was not his place. This was a provincial city. Midwestern, landlocked.

Adam thought it was. He had no sense of the riverine center as it actually existed. The run of the Ohio along the south porch, as it were, of the city and the connection going west to the Wabash and eventually the Mississippi itself. And so to the Illinois, the Skunk, the Iowa, the Cedar. Immediately south, the confluence with the Licking River for a cut into the north hump of Kentucky. Or go south on the Mississippi, past Memphis and Jackson, eventually to New Orleans and the Gulf. He had no understanding of the reach of these waters and the energizing notion of spread from a central place that could come from an awareness of it (so he failed entirely to understand anything of the benign cultural and commercial network of river life, although he'd picked up earlier, so immediately and accurately, on that other network of fairly corrupt relations through which a man like Bronheim advanced his interests, moving easily and without premeditation from one semilegal activity to another, an athlete of such transitions).

Why settle? he thought. Why, when there was, say, Cambridge/Boston. That would be a feast . . . with the architecture and the free life of the universities and the museums. A real place where you could walk. In the fall of the year, you could be in the Common. Crunch under your feet the dead leaves of New England. Look at the Charles, which feeds into the sea. All around you the sense of the sea. He breathed in and swung his legs off the bed. When he was on his feet, he found the other loafer behind a chair.

Willie Unger, red-faced under the ambiguous storm cloud or halo of his own white hair, mashed a Lucky Strike into a full ashtray and said that Marcu was ready to bump his offer to forty-three . . . a forty-three-dollar stock equivalent. That could be in any form. Marcu's man, Cotton, had already explained about that to Kreg, hadn't he? So Kreg understood how everybody could choose the stock itself or convertibles or bonds with puts? "Like ordering from an old-fashioned Chinese restaurant. There's column A and there's column B. Dah-de-dah-dah. Whatever makes you happy." And forty-three was a new level. But there would be nothing, no actual offer at all without some understanding about a positive response. And on that point Marcu hadn't seemed too hopeful. He'd said that Kreg had been more than a little negative in his meeting with Cotton. "Fucking hostile, I think he meant."

Yes, hostile. "Then he hasn't given up," Kreg said, reflecting on the way in which he had dragged himself so very reluctantly, and truly unwillingly, toward a possibly successful resolution of this matter.

"He's still in the game," Willie said. "We don't go along, he stays where he is and grinds it out."

"And succeeds?"

"That's a toss-up, isn't it?"

Kreg smoothed a wrinkle in the green felt cover of Willie's conference table. "Forty-three gets to be a substantial number," he said.

"I would think it might be top."

"And that we should take it?"

"You should if you want to do business."

"I think I do. I want to do business."

"So I'll talk to Jarvis. Jarvis and Sam, I guess."

"Tell them I'm for it."

"And then I'll call Marcu."

There was a sense of fatigue. Heaviness. Almost a need for sleep. It came on suddenly. A feeling you'd associate with the end of some long task. Kreg said to Willie that he'd always been willing to sell. That had been his intention, in his mind from the moment of Cotton's first arch conversation about the little investment that had been made in Brandt Systems stock. But earlier it hadn't been possible to say so.

"Why couldn't you say so?"

"Because people can't negotiate when they're divided, and Jarvis Dalton was complaining he'd been sold and Sam Marion was ready, I think, to take his key people and walk." So how could he have negotiated, Kreg asked, in the face of that strong likelihood of major internal combustion?

"Although you'd have had a deal," Willie said, "before it collapsed. A deal for you, I mean. The Foundation would have had its money and you and Marcu could have gone in there and made nice. Smoothed some feathers."

"That wasn't possible," Kreg said, considering the enormous burden of constraint that was going to be lifted from him. *Harmonious, Mouse Kelly had said on their way to Brandt's funeral. Get it all harmonious. That's the most important. . . . So I had to have their consent. I had to have their willing and freely given consent.* Kreg considered also the price he would pay for whatever freedom he gained. And why it was that he had chosen to play out this drama of his life under the terms of an understanding that had never actually existed between himself and a dying man who at one point had said, *I think I got you now.* Fine. Brandt had gotten his foundation and Kreg had run it. *But that was all I promised. Just to run it.*

"Philip," Willie Unger said. "It was. It was possible. Cutting a deal with Marcu was the easy way. And for you too. You could have done right by the Company and made a deal for yourself. You know that. You have to know it."

Yes, I know that. I always knew it and I was always willing to sell. And I have, although neither you nor Roth seem willing to credit that, a real and rational concern for my own well-being. . . . So there was a pull to arrange something with Marcu. . . . But can't you, either of you, understand too why I wasn't able to do business with him until after they were together on this at the Company? . . . And also you'd say that I just wasn't willing, that I went into a child's sulk because I despise people like Marcu (whom I've never met) and because he was forcing my hand. Maybe so. That feeling was there. Maybe that's all that was there . . . of any significance. "I know that," he said to Willie.

"But?"

"It wouldn't have worked out that way." They were discussing entirely different subjects and there seemed no way to explain that to Willie whom he liked and didn't want to offend.

"You know you nearly lost him?" Willie said. "He told me that he almost walked away . . . a couple of times. I mean, you nearly convinced him that you really didn't want to deal."

Kreg looked down at his hands.

Willie tapped a finger to his right temple. "With you, Philip," he said, "it's all up here, isn't it? You really keep it to yourself."

Kreg felt a kind of helplessness. An inability to explain why he operated in certain matters on his terms only. "Then we'll go ahead," he said. "You can tell Jarvis there's a deal and of course the Foundation is with them on it." Only one indulgence, actually, that he'd permitted himself . . . the attitude of hostility that he'd maintained always toward Marcu . . . even knowing (as Willie had now confirmed) that Marcu might be offended to a point where he'd throw in his hand. Walk away, as Willie had said. Or simply conclude that it wasn't possible to do a deal. . . . *But not really an indulgence because there was no possibility for me of acting in any other way. But why? In what way was Marcu so very bad? Really (as Willie had said and I concede) he represents a perfectly acceptable future for the Company. A better one, I truly believe, than Jarvis could eventually provide for it . . . if allowed to provide, which he wouldn't be. Because sooner or later there would be some other Marcu and the Company would fall.*

And you always wanted a deal because you wanted the money for the Foundation. You had your obligations there.

So why this intransigent hostility toward Cotton and Marcu? Petulant, you know, and that's never acceptable. Or put it like this: In what way did you so very much want to keep things as they were? As Brandt had left them, so to speak.

Willie looked at his watch. "Lunchtime," he said. "The meter's off. You join me? Just a sandwich right here." He didn't wait for Kreg to answer. He buzzed for his secretary and ordered roast beef for himself with milk and whatever kind of pie they had.

Kreg said chicken salad for him. Coffee, no pie.

Willie took a bottle of scotch from a desk drawer. His secretary came in with four glasses on a tray. Two empty and two with water. Willie hadn't had to say anything to her about the glasses.

She left and Willie poured at least a double for himself and passed the bottle to Kreg who took a smaller tot. "Sissy," Willie said. He drank half his scotch, shivered briefly when the whisky hit his belly, then poured water into what was left. His port-wine face went darker. "How about you?" he said to Kreg.

"In what sense?" Kreg said.

But he knew that Willie wasn't asking if he liked the whisky.

Willie looked through or into his drink. "Philip," he said. "Don't try to shit the shitter. Anything practical, I'm always five steps ahead of you. Your business is the sense I mean it in. I mean it in that sense, in the sense that Marcu doesn't love you. So you'll last as counsel to any company he controls for how long? Fifteen seconds if you're lucky. Tell me you haven't thought about it."

Kreg had thought about it, had imagined himself accountable to Marcu or Cotton. He disagreed with Willie about the fifteen seconds. No need to make it a quick-and-easy termination. Some playtime first, a period of minor humiliations, everything with a smile. And then, eventually, of course the meeting to explain that really their own attorneys could probably manage this additional load. Kreg would honestly have to agree with that, wouldn't he? *But we want to continue your retainer through the end of the quarter. Doesn't that seem fair enough? Tell us if you don't agree.* This would be Marcu and Cotton together. Looks between them just short of smiles. If he asked for more time they'd give him more time. They'd allow it, another month, two months. He imagined Frank Roth hearing this news. *No,* he'd said to Roth about the order of names in the new firm. Now he would have to make some new arrangement. Because the numbers now would not permit a partnership division that would satisfy his pride. . . . He would find someone with whom he could share space (as he had with Roth before they formed their partnership). There would be the crushing weight of how many books and files to be moved. "You had mentioned a leveraged buyout?" he said to Willie Unger.

"If this didn't work out. It's still a possibility. Right now, though, there's forty-three on the table. A bird in hand. You want to pass on this deal with Marcu, we can go to work on the other. Jarvis and Sam would jump at it."

"Probably." *Yes. Very likely they would. And I would keep my fees and my practice.* Why was it, he said, that forty-three seemed right? Why had Willie stopped there? He could have said to Marcu that forty-four was a number he might consider. Or forty-seven or -eight.

Willie glared at him. "It isn't exactly a science."

"Even so."

"Baseball. You ever play?"

Kreg remembered camp. Himself awkward, condemned to the outfield, waiting under the sun for the rare fly ball that most likely would not come and if it did would be misjudged and dropped. Everybody, he said to Willie Unger. Everybody played a little.

"I was a player. . . . So tell me. Deep in the hole. Shortstop takes it. How does he decide? Throw to first or he tries to double the guy up? *Exactly at what point does he know?* Forty-three. Same thing."

Kreg could understand that (although there remained the sense of some larger neurotactical mystery).

"So you say yes to go with him?" Willie said. "With Marcu."

"If I saw a choice."

"There was a choice. You just didn't want to take it. Kind of a sleaze choice of course to pass up a sure deal with Marcu for a possible l.b.o., just so you can keep your job. And you're too picky for that. . . . *L'chayim,*" Willie said. "*Salud.*" He bumped glasses with Kreg. They drank and Willie said that Kreg had never answered him. How was it going to be for him? For Philip Kreg?

"When was the last time," Iris said, "that anybody had an old-fashioned? You could order one of those for me." She had the grayblue eyes of a gunfighter. Two weeks earlier they'd been together and witnessed an accident. Afterwards they'd gone to Kreg's apartment and made love and then they argued and she'd left him in a rage.

But today she had called him and now they were in one of the second-floor bars of the Palace, the Hunt Room.

He ordered old-fashioneds for both of them.

Iris addressed the very point he'd been thinking about. She said he never could bring himself, could he, to make that first healing move? "It's not as if you're surrendering, you know."

He should have called, he said. . . . He'd wanted to call.

"I'd assumed that," Iris said. "Poor cripple." She touched his hand. Then called his attention to the details of this room, the fine woodwork and the ceiling with its alternating strips of wood panel and dark pattern.

The Hunt Room: as a name it called up a tradition of English country homes and of county families come together to gorge on rare meats and underdone fowl . . . a tradition of blood sports.

In his apartment after the accident they'd seen, Kreg had stripped off his own bloody clothes and bathed and come out to his own dark bedroom with Iris in the bed. They made love and she said, I don't cheat. So why is it I would cheat on him? He calls Marcu from the apartment. Do you understand me?

Don't tell me, Kreg said. Whatever you hear, it isn't something I'd want passed on.

I said I'd never help you.

Don't help like this.

You won't let me help you?

Not like this.

They'd had drinks with them in bed and quickly she flipped hers over him and said for him to get out while she dressed. You have such a talent, she said when she was in the front hall, for bridge burning. If you don't want it, torch it. Leave nothing behind.

The waiter came with their old-fashioneds.

To one side of them, an American and his wife were rising to greet two Japanese businessmen. On the other, a couple of men in sport jackets were eyeballing each other and talking about residuals.

Iris sipped at her drink. Then in a low voice she said they didn't want, did they, to be two people who sometimes met for a fuck and a fight? She met his eyes and then looked away and then back at him.

No, Kreg said. Whatever they wanted from each other, it wasn't that. He looked at his hand (flat on the table) as if he could will it to take hers.

She had called him then as she had today. Just to see him. Waiting for a streetlight to turn, she was saying about Cotton and Marcu and Brandt Systems that, To me it's only some little thing in the D section. A statement that Cotton's mistress or whatever, she was always in her way importantly in Kreg's camp.

She jogged his arm to cross and they moved into the street. You might remember, she'd been saying, that we're able to rely. We have from time to time.

On each other, she was telling him.

Yes, he was thinking when he began to be disturbed by noise.

First there was the high imperative cry of a bicyclist's whistle. And the violent screech and underwhine of an automobile braking, tires screaming. Then the sound of the collision itself. . . . No visual image. . . . Not until he saw the body actually still turning in the air. Amazing slowness of motion. The amazing isolation of the victim. A moving cynosure. Then to rest. On his feet, which wasn't possible.

He saw in the middle of the street the gorgeous broken silver object that was the bicycle. A still life perfectly and imaginatively set off on the black asphalt mat of the street itself. The auto had veered left into the line of cars parked on that side. The driver was sitting up. He looked at the standing man and put his head in his hands. He was alone in the vehicle.

The cyclist did not move. He was standing there, not even shaking or trembling. A tall thin young black man with his glasses still in place. A long Giacometti figure. Ribbons of blood over his face.

Kreg began to run. Heavy-footed. He felt the rush of his own blood, his heart going. The man didn't answer questions. All right, he kept saying. All right.

What was all right? Kreg was afraid to move the man and couldn't let him stand alone. So he hugged him. Gentle enfolding support. Kreg's overcoat was open. Blood was coming onto his suit. And his own blood still racing and the pumping of his heart. Iris put her hands on his back.

Then, quickly, there were other people. No, Kreg kept saying. He's all right here. I'll stay with him like this. And a cop was saying that the ambulance would be here soon and could Kreg maybe just stay there and hold the guy like he was doing. The cop started to ask the man did he know where he was? Did he know what day it was?

Kreg began to hear some blocks away the siren of the ambulance. It got louder until it was there.

After that there were questions and name-taking and descriptions of what had happened, what had been seen. Then very quickly it was over. Iris touched a finger to a bloodstain on Kreg's coat. Aren't you a mess, she said.

In the cab he began to shiver and she told him, no shower. A hot bath was what he needed. Scald you, she said.

"I've left him," she said now in the Hunt Room. "Not left. We were never together. Broken off. Whatever."

There was a stop in the conversation at the table to Kreg's left, the one with the two men in sport jackets. Possibly they were trying to hear what Iris had been saying. Kreg turned his head to face them. Actually one of the men was motioning a waiter for the check. The other one was simply waiting. Kreg thought of the damage he'd done himself in the past by being too quick to go on the offensive. He thought too, and very suddenly, of the awkward, sometimes humorous girl in his office. Although that thought was unimportant. It was a thought with no possible consequent effect. He said to Iris, "It was never something you really intended would go on?" Deane he was sure would not go on with Raymond. He didn't see her as having a romantic future with anyone at all. Something not fully developed there. Cuddling and touching very likely preferred over the sticky ramitin sexual act itself. But she and Raymond would probably stay in touch. They would be friends through the years. Which Iris wouldn't be with Cotton.

Iris said, "While it lasted, I intended it to last."

"For a while," Kreg said.

Iris removed the maraschino cherry from her drink. She said, "It didn't affect anything else when it started. But then it got too complicated." She put the sweet cherry on a saucer. "I hate these damn things," she said.

Kreg imagined the wary establishment between himself and Iris of whatever the name was for a certain relationship between a man and a woman. Not a couple. And in theory not accountable to each other. Occasionally a vacation together. That also theoretical because he didn't take vacations. . . . A sudden image of the long slope of Sicilian mountains (in the spring, wildflowers all over them). He had been there with Susan. Smell of thyme and the flowers and the sun on the dry earth. Susan at night, next to him, pretending to be asleep in the soft bed. On the far edge of the mattress to avoid any roll toward the middle. Rigid, sticklike. Not possibly thinking he didn't know she was awake. Only sending a necessary message . . . that she wasn't there for him. But by then she'd had nothing to fear. How could you even try to approach someone who wasn't truly present? Certain kinds of absences, if you thought about it, had created gaps that couldn't be bridged.

How did these absences show themselves?

They were expressed by means of detachment and remoteness. Occasionally a cute evasiveness.

But she never left you? She wasn't physically remote?

She isolated herself from my presence.

How did she do that?

She watched a great deal of television.

That's all?

She always watched it. And she kept herself a little out of things.

A little out of things. That's not specific.

Specificity is what she avoided. It was the extra drink at night. Sleep late in the morning. She made a life that was somewhat, can I say, fuzzy?

Fuzzy. I like that. And by-the-by, personal absence . . . then wasn't there sexual deprivation? Didn't that lead to feelings of anger or resentment? Could you quantify those?

You know what you know. Isn't it obvious what I felt?

. . . as it had now begun to seem obvious that he and Iris would in some way be together. Make an alliance. He reached for the candied cherry she'd put down. Chewed it from its stem. What they'd develop, all unspoken, would be a system of treaties, a constitutional package that would cover the terms on which they saw each other. . . . How often, where. . . . He might be entering into a period of calm. There would be this new and expanded relationship with Iris and he would survive the relocation and rebuilding of his practice. . . . Even take a few days for himself and visit Adam. He envisioned himself with his son. The two of them talking, eating, sightseeing without stress or argument. . . . Problems would fall away. . . . There was the sweet aftertaste of the cherry. At one time both he and Iris had had a taste for these drinks. Neither of them this evening had mentioned that. He said, "We'll have another drink and then I'll buy you dinner." Something occurred to him. He said, "Did you have trouble with him?" Cotton, he meant.

Iris' hard smile. "Getting him out? Why would I have trouble with him?"

"I thought you might."

"He doesn't, when you really get down to it, have any great desire for confrontation."

Which at one time would have been comforting to hear. And now didn't matter because there wasn't going to be that confrontation. Because now there was forty-three on the table and a deal in progress. . . . One thing there wasn't, though. No strong run of excitement through his flesh. He had in mind that first evening in the office talking with Deane. And then when she came to his apartment with the papers from Frank Roth. *Think about it. About the way you felt. Tell me civilization depends on repression. Tell me. Civilization depends on lies, you know.*

Iris was saying to him that the ceilings in his apartment were peeling and the whole place had got to a point where he was going to have to paint it.

"Yes," he said. "I'd noticed. I was thinking about that."

"People could begin to think you were *eccentric.*"

Maybe a room or two at a time Kreg thought. He was thinking of what he'd have to move and replace. This coming on top of what he would be doing in the office. Leaving and finding another space.

But Iris said to do it all at once. "If it gets too bad," she said, "you always have a place to stay."

Iris had said she'd never help him. *Nobody would,* she'd said. He mentioned this and she flared into a quick temper.

"Whatever you're counting on, don't count on too much," she said. "Just don't. . . . Offer a middle-aged man a bed for a night, that doesn't mean you'll sell your soul for him."

"The bed," Kreg said. "The bed would be enough."

It was some time before her mood softened. She would talk with him for a moment and then glance at someplace across the room with the intense blank stare of a raptor. Later in the bistro on Fourteenth Street that he took her to, they had more drinks and a bottle of wine and a quiet but rather good time.

Then too much was happening. Frank Roth was arranging the reorganization of the partnership. There was Iris now. And Willie Unger was always on the phone checking some detail of this negotiation that was rapidly approaching its resolution. Jarvis Dalton wanted to know that they were still on the same team. Mouse Kelly called. There didn't seem to be any modulations, just quick takes and the cuts between them.

When Mouse called, Kreg was in his office. He was with Frank Roth. Mouse started to go on about Marcu.

"You know all that," Kreg said. "We've been over that and you've heard it from Willie."

"Everybody explained it," Mouse said. "And I wanted to hear it from you again. But you don't have the time, don't take the time."

Some hurt in the old man's voice.

Then easy. "What do I really think?" Kreg said.

"Between us."

"Mouse, the bird is grown. It's out of the nest."

"And into that operator's jaws. That's where it's gotta go?"

"Where life is taking it."

Roth never loved to be kept waiting. He was drumming on Kreg's desk with his fingertips. Kreg wanted to calm the old man and he looked at Roth's fingers until the action stopped.

"I thought I lost you," Mouse was saying.

"Just something happening at this end."

"So that greaser, Marcu, it has to go to him?"

"It doesn't *have* to go to him."

"Just that's the best way."

"It seems."

"Best for everybody?"

"In the circumstances."

Frank Roth went to the window. He leaned slightly forward and slowly did a kind of pelvic grind. Repeated the motion possibly every ten seconds. At first there was the odd impression of a middle-aged man doing a lascivious dance. Then Kreg realized that this was an exercise. His partner's contortion was an exercise for his weak back.

"What I'm thinkin," Mouse said, "I know really it's best for those guys. Sell out to the shark. We been through that and I heard all the arguments. But what about you? What happens to you? . . . Truth."

This after all wasn't merely some funny-talking old man who held to his street accents the way you would to your father's watch. Mouse still ran the company he'd built. He'd been *consigliere* to Brandt and Kreg saw no significant diminution of ability. The judgment was still there. Kreg said that for himself he expected things to go on as before. "Pretty much," he said.

"Liar," Mouse said. "The fuckers are gonna chew you up. Thing of it is. What I wanted to tell you, I'm always here . . . so long as I *am* here, you know. The other, that bird-is-out-of-the-nest stuff. I knew all that shit before I called you. That wasn't why I called."

"I can tell," Kreg said.

Frank Roth came back from the window. He eased into a chair while Kreg was setting the handpiece of the phone in its cradle. "I take it," he said, "you haven't made any arrangements to protect yourself."

"From?"

"Philip, they're buying this company from under you."

"Which I can't really help."

"Do you know, Philip, that people have negotiated long-term retainers? Of course you know it but you didn't try anything like that."

Kreg said he doubted that would have been possible.

"Yes, it was possible. It would have taken maybe ten seconds to work it out. You know, Philip, Paris is worth a Mass? You know that thought? All you had to do was ask. The retainer was there for anyone who wasn't too fucking proud to ask."

Undertone of contempt there. Until a few days ago Frank Roth wouldn't have used just that tone with him. But Roth must have decided the game was over. So what would follow would be discussions Kreg had been expecting of a change in the structure of the partnership. Not immediately, though. Roth would feel his way. He lacked the brutal force you wanted for certain kinds of quick action. Which didn't mean he was indecisive. Besides, he, Kreg, wasn't yet quite out of the game. Maybe Marcu would unexpectedly keep him on.

He began to think that this was probably the period of the final dispositions of his professional life. Not a glorious resolution but no sense of despair or even major disappointment. Something maybe lacking in him. Some will toward triumph. More than that, he wanted to take himself out of the system.

The system of practice? The practice of law?

More than that.

Explain, please.

I'm tired.

He said to Roth that, about the arrangements with Arthur Harris, Roth should of course pick up on those talks. Wind them up. "But without me in the picture." He'd decided, he heard himself saying, not to continue with a firm. "Mostly a matter of how I want to practice. On my own, I think. Share space with somebody the way you and I used to. I think that suited me." The words came out as if he'd considered earlier what he was saying now.

"Philip," Roth said. "I never meant . . ."

Yes you did. You meant. And now you have this unexpected gift from me that I can't think of as a gift because I had no preintention of making it and which anyway was made with no wish at all to benefit you. And it's your relief and guilt that induce that coy untruth . . . you never meant. You never meant. You're free to say that now.

"But no quick decisions," Roth was saying. "And however you decide to do it, share space, I mean, you'll do it here. What's wrong with us?" His voice went a little thinner. Higher. You could tell he was speaking out of a rising sense of sudden freedom. A burden lifted, and now his anxious willingness to compensate.

Kreg said, "You'd want to talk to Arthur Harris about it." He would accept Roth's offer. There would be the great benefit of not having to search out some new association. And when the office moved someone would pack for him.

Roth said, "I can speak for Arthur."

"On this."

"On this. On what we're talking about."

"Sleep on it."

"I don't have to do that." Roth put out his hand. He said, "We want you here."

"You should think about it," Kreg said.

Roth dropped his hand. "I never understand what it is," he said, "that goes on inside the mind. I mean why it is you have to be so afraid somebody might be doing you a favor. You know something? There's no favor here. But even that would be okay. It's all right to accept one once in a while. You could just say yes."

You're right. Of course, you're right.

There was a sense Kreg got of events closing in on him. But he could burrow deeper.

"*You* sleep on it," Roth said. "I'm here when you want to talk to me." Then he was leaving. A small trim man, the artificially stiff carriage that he had when his back was hurting. Gorgeous white cotton of his shirt. Suspenders of watered silk in the cheerful french blue that he seemed to favor.

Kreg said, "Frank."

Roth turned.

"Of course I'll take you up on it," Kreg said. "Generous," he said. "And now you're stuck with me."

"No," Frank Roth said. "Not generous. I didn't mean to be generous."

"In spirit. That's all I meant." There was a feeling of release at the thought that from now on he would be truly on his own.

Roth then asked about an unannounced visitor of yesterday, a man who'd been informed that Kreg was in court on a motion and had said he'd wait. Composed, self-assured, pleasant. A *Wall Street Journal* folded in front of him as if he were reading the pages he never turned. But it had become a matter of hours, which was why Kreg's secretary had asked Deane to speak to Mr. Roth.

So Roth had gone out to see if he could help. The man thanked him but no, he said. He thought he'd just wait for Mr. Kreg to come in. Sooner or later Kreg would, wouldn't he? Wasn't that likely? This was kind of a personal matter. Brief smile when he said that. A stocky, somber man with the kind of skin that took a slightly yellowish tan. Karl Van Atta, he'd said. He was wearing a light brown suit with an almost matching shirt. Dark brown patterned tie and tan shoes.

"Four o'clock," Roth had said. "He could possibly not come back to the office. He doesn't always."

"I'll catch up with him," Van Atta said. "No hurry."

Then Kreg had come in and Van Atta introduced himself. He mentioned Kreg's son. Roth heard that. He heard Van Atta saying that he assumed Kreg remembered him from conversations they'd had some time in the past. And Kreg, with overstuffed red envelopes under his arms and his scarf half falling from his shoulders, blinked for a moment at Van Atta. Yes, he said. Earlier in the fall. He remembered their talks.

"I sort of thought you would."

"You'd better come with me. I have to put these envelopes down."

"Appreciate it," Van Atta said to Roth, "that you tried to help me."

And we went into my office. The two of us. I closed the door and I told her to hold my calls. He hadn't said anything and I knew he was waiting for me to speak first. I took my coat off and looked through my messages. Interesting, I thought, how he could wear those clothes and still have an appearance of business-class respectability. A solid patient man. That was the impression he gave. Winter light was fading so I went to the doorway and switched on the overhead. Adam. What bad news was this going to be about Adam?

Van Atta looked for a while at his square-tipped manicured fingers as if they were something to reflect on. When Kreg was in his chair, settled, he said, "You've always had trouble with him, haven't you?"

No sparring, Kreg decided, or pretending not to understand. "You mean Adam," he said. "Tell me."

"It would be better if the three of us could talk together. Why don't we set it up like that?"

"Why don't we?" Kreg said.

"When can we do that?"

There began a few moments of seeming misunderstanding. They talked at cross-purposes until Kreg said that he wasn't immediately in touch with Adam and Van Atta told him (explaining that there were details he was leaving out because it really wouldn't help Kreg to know them) about what Adam had done and how subsequently he'd gone to ground. Van Atta said those things about Adam but he kept himself composed, good-natured. He had the manner of an exemplar of the idea of power-in-grace. He repeated it about the advantages of a meeting. "But you don't want to set that up?" he said.

Kreg's hand groped in a side drawer. He came up with his pipe, chewed on the bit against the worn places that matched the outer contours of his teeth. "I thought I'd put it differently," he finally said.

"You thought he was in California?"

"Until now."

"He could. He could be there. You talk to him there?"

Not in touch, he'd said. He explained to Van Atta his feelings about being too closely questioned. Especially here, here in his own office.

"Same with me," Van Atta said. "I wouldn't like it either. You have to remember, though, this thing is kind of important to me. Also, it's that I trusted him."

The conversation began to take on aspects of a quiet contest. Neither of them would lower his peaceable regard from that of the other. Kreg was realizing that he was in the presence of a gangster . . . and that his son had been employed by gangsters.

Van Atta's major concern, he said, was that he wasn't totally in control of this situation. "Certain kinds of people," he said. "They can get these ideas about what they're going to do to you. They get very violent, if you follow me." Also, one way or another, he himself had an obligation here. "That was my employee who did that to my customer. I was the one who set it up."

Nothing now, if you looked that far, that was truly benign in Van Atta's gray eyes. Although still calm.

Kreg asked if the police had been brought into the situation. Not a good-faith question. *Careful, though. You didn't control yourself with Marcu but you are going to control yourself here.*

Van Atta only said, "My customer isn't someone I'd want after me. And he's out there on his own. Looking, you know."

Then the man was all right? He'd recovered? Was on his feet?

"But poorer. And there were those couple of days in the hospital. The point is how unhappy he feels."

This someone Van Atta wouldn't want after him . . . it was Van Atta's thought that Kreg should locate Adam and turn him over to that person? That was the thought, wasn't it?

"Not to him," Van Atta said. "To me."

"So that you could . . . ?"

"If he returned the money you see. Then I could control him. My customer."

"And that would end it?"

"Truthfully?" Van Atta went carefully. "Truthfully," he said. "He would, I think, insist on some small penalty. But nothing major. That I could probably guarantee." And what was there to lose? he said. Look at it the other way. The guy would find Adam. Sooner or later he would, you knew that. Wouldn't it be better to have him, Van Atta, working all-out to resolve the thing?

"The penalty," Kreg said. "That would be something physical?"

Van Atta spread his half-cupped hands in a gesture of irresolute affirmation.

At just this moment, of course, notions of retribution and

punishment would have to be in both their minds. Van Atta would surely assume that Kreg wouldn't, in this context, take *physical* to be a term without significance. There wasn't the implication of some mere light working over.

Kreg told himself, *Don't show it. No anger. Nothing for him to work on.* More generally, you had to consider, didn't you, the way your short-term failures turned into long-term losses?

Because wasn't there a certain progression from various early lapses and omissions in Adam's training to these happenings now? The space between Van Atta's hands framed a scene. Scenes really. Kreg was remembering those evenings with himself and Susan and Adam in the kitchen of the apartment. One or another of those evenings when he took Susan's glass from her and put her to bed and finished the dinner as best he could. *This time, if this is the evening I remember and not another one like it, Adam didn't follow me when I took her inside but later he didn't want to be read to and said he'd play in his room. I went to my study, acquiescing I suppose in a kind of compact of mutual withdrawal.*

Van Atta dropped his hands. "So you'll call me," he said, "when you hear from him."

"If I hear from him, I'll tell him what you said."

"If he comes to me. If he made it good, returned what he took. I know that's the best thing all around. So you talk to him. Explain how things stand."

"He might not agree about what's best."

"He could be scared. Maybe he isn't thinking that clear. You could straighten him out."

"I would discuss things with him."

Iris had said that if he let himself go, he would be a sponge for guilt. That it was his nature to soak guilt up, draw it to him in an unhealthy way. *But you don't, she said. You don't exactly run with what you feel, do you? You keep the bridge up. Cut yourself off, isn't that how you do it?* They had been talking about Adam.

You mean distasteful, Kreg said about the guilt. It would be distasteful to you. . . . If I soaked it up that way. Distasteful, not unhealthy.

Yes, Iris said. Distasteful. You think you can carry the world. You want whatever burden you can find. That's what's distasteful, that attitude. It's the wanting to be tested. Put upon.

No illusions about Adam, she'd said. She had her fondness for him but she took him for what he was. Kreg wanted it both ways: never admit there was anything wrong with Adam but take responsibility for whatever was wrong. *Some inconsistency there. Wouldn't you say so, Counselor? Wouldn't you think the jury might just not buy it?*

That conversation with Iris, only a few days earlier, related directly, Kreg thought, to this one now with Van Atta.

"He would listen to you," Van Atta said.

Kreg said, "Usually he hasn't."

"It's not a very good record that way?"

"Not especially."

"Break your stones," Van Atta said, "to educate them. Bring them up." He seemed to be regretting a pandemic lack of gratitude in the young.

It would have been so perfectly natural to ask this sympathetic visitor if he had a family of his own. *Do they listen to you? Do what you tell them?* Kreg took the pipe from his mouth. Rubbed his thumb over the bowl. With Adam, he was trying to think, had there been some specific point of failure? Some single act that turned him wrong? "If I hear from him," he said to Van Atta, "possibly I'll be in touch with you."

"At some point?"

"Yes."

"I don't use a card," Van Atta said. "Why don't I tell you my number. Any call, they always reach me. You write it down."

Kreg wrote, and when Van Atta left, he looked at his shaking hand.

Roth now wanted to know about Van Atta. "Unexpected visit, I take it?" A natural curiosity about someone who looked different and didn't state his mission.

"Did he say that?"

"No but there was no appointment. There wasn't, was there?"

"That's right," Kreg said, "it was unexpected. It was nothing really," he said. "The man thought I could help him with a problem." *Unexpected.* Kreg had known since the night before last that there was going to be something. He had known that although he hadn't known he would see Van Atta.

They had been at his apartment.

Iris had answered the phone. "No," she'd said. "Not a wrong number." She held the instrument out to him. "Young thing at the other end," she said. "Is Mr. Philip Kreg there?" Not troubling to lower her voice or hold the mouthpiece away from her.

Then he was listening to what Deane began to tell him. "That's your son's name, isn't it?" she said. "Adam?"

"Tell me," he said. He started to listen to her and his face went into a foolish pudding shape. He tried to concentrate on familiar objects in the room, his oxblood vase, the fat man with the monocle in the Grosz drawing. Could she get him something to write on? he said to Iris. And a pen? Not showing emotion or mouthing any silent message that this call was important or alarming or that he'd explain later to her what it was about. There was only that stupid expectant blobby mask of his face. When he had the pen she gave him and a magazine wrapper to use for his note, it was an address that he wrote down. Then he rang off and told Iris what he knew.

She didn't, when she'd heard him out, say that it was probably some kind of mistake or some other Adam.

Now, Kreg thought when they were in the cab, he knew where Deane lived. East Thirty-fifth Street.

It was a mini-apartment with thrift-shop furniture. Too much of it; no free space. A dark red throw partly over an apple-green couch. On one wall, there was, tacked among the framed posters and other pictures, a child's crayon drawing. *Happy Birthday Aunt Deanie. . . .* The place was very much as he had imagined it. He had imagined it. He had thought in the cab about her apartment, what it would be like.

But the immediately central thing was not the apartment or Deane or what she was saying. It was Raymond who took your attention. Raymond had pushed himself up from a small plum velvet chair. He moved stiffly with his torso twisted to the left. His shirt was open and you could see the wide band of tape around the body. A bruise along his right cheek and a cut in the eyebrow above that. Careful deliberate breathing because of his pain.

Deane began to explain again what she'd already told him over the phone. Adam. That was his son's name. He'd told her that. So mustn't they have taken Raymond for Adam? Didn't that make sense? She had to be right didn't she?

All this before Kreg introduced her to Iris.

"Tell me again," Kreg said.

"I was the one," Raymond said. "I'll tell you." Chinese, he said. They'd decided on classic Cantonese and Deane was going to take him to a place on Doyer Street. So he'd come to the office to meet her.

He talked slowly, held one hand flat against the bandaged ribs on the left side. Deane had her hands together in front of her, concentration wrinkles in her forehead. She watched him, nodding at what he said. Something cramped in the way she held herself. But every few seconds a deerflick glance toward Kreg or Iris.

At Kreg's office, Raymond was saying, two men had got into the elevator with him (Kreg saw that, the old-style elevator cab with its cream paint. Metal fluting at the corners and a motif of vine leaves above). Nobody had spoken. The men got out when he did. Both nicely dressed. Each of them in a dark coat. One had a silk paisley scarf. They were big men, not huge but big. About six feet, each of them. Youngish, his own age. Raymond didn't notice immediately that the elevator had been propped open behind them.

There was no sense of hurry.

"Adam," one of the men said.

Raymond was shaking his head, starting to say that he wasn't Adam, when the slap came. Heavy. Flat-handed against the side of his cheek. Hard enough to rock his head and body.

"Adam, you cocksucker," the other man said.

When he put his hands to his face, they hit him in the body. Then one of the men held him and the other one worked at his ribs.

"That's an appetizer," the man who was holding him said

when the other one stopped hitting him. "It's to help you think a little."

"So you tell us how you gonna make it right," the second man said.

"Shut up, Sally," the first man said. The one with the paisley scarf. He let go of Raymond from behind. Pushed him against a wall and held one hand flat against Raymond's chest. "The point is," he said, "my friend here, he gets a little over himself tryin to get into the negotiations. But that's cause he's such a good guy. He wants to help you. He wants to see you help yourself. . . . What we're gonna do, Adam. We walk out of here. The three of us. You come with us and we make a call. You tell the man how you want to return the thing and where it is. And we make our arrangements."

Down the hallway there was the frosted-glass rectangle that was the doorway to Roth & Kreg. Light behind the panel.

The man with the paisley scarf saw Raymond look there. He grinned happily and pressed his palm harder into Raymond's chest. Wagged the forefinger of his free hand. "Adam," he said. "Be smart. Not even a peep."

Raymond was taking air in sudden gulps. Little rapid breaths. Then he was able to speak. "Not Adam," he said. "My wallet. I have i.d."

The man with the scarf stepped back.

At first, when Raymond tried to reach into his hip pocket, he had to stop because of the pain in his side. Then he made it. Held out the wallet.

The man in the paisley scarf went through it. "Show you somethin," he said to Sally. "Some of this plastic. This ain't new fakes. You can see on the raised parts where the color's worn. And the paper, how it's got all soft and those fine wrinkles in it. . . . So you're right," he said to Raymond. "You ain't Adam." He let the plastic cards he was holding slide through his fingers to the floor. "Lucky for you," he said, "that you're not." The paper items he tore across and he let those fall too. He watched concernedly for Raymond's reaction. Then took the money out of the wallet. Fanned the bills in his hand. "Sixty-five," he said to Sally. "Sixty-five big ones here."

"Big ones for the big spender," Sally said.

The man with the scarf smiled and tore the bills. Folded them and tore again and dropped the pieces into the mess on the floor. Watched the downward flutter of the bits of paper. He bent and scaled the wallet down the hall where it stopped perfectly, only a fraction of an inch from the glass door with the light behind it. He straightened. "Raymond," he said. "Like I said. Lucky for you you're Raymond and not the other one." His face twisted a little and he took Raymond's left cheek between his thumb and crooked forefinger and turned his hand. Twisted the flesh. Then he stopped and went to the elevator.

"Bastard," Sally said. "Waste our time." He went first to the stomach and then three or four times to the face.

"I think," Raymond now said to Kreg, "they learn to act like that from the movies. Movies or television."

Deane went over to him, could not hug him or touch his bruised face. She put her hands on his shoulders. Her cupped hands (echo of that gesture to come two days later, in Kreg's office, when the man from California cupped his own hands in just that way . . . but facing up and in the empty air. . . . No connection between those gestures except as they were linked in Kreg's memory. No common meaning).

Yes (during his talk with Van Atta), Kreg might have said. Yes, my son Adam. Adam has been difficult. And there's an effect from that on others. For which I'm sorry. Because it was this event with Raymond, and Kreg's knowledge of it, that two days later would be so central in his mind (although not mentioned to Van Atta). Because he never doubted which Adam it was that Sally and the man in the paisley scarf had hoped to meet and discipline. *Lucky for you,* Raymond said, and Iris met his eye for barely a moment. Concentrated with a gambler's tact on some space in the middle distance.

Kreg said, "It could have been my son they wanted. I don't know. I haven't talked to him. It's been some time." He could understand, he was thinking, how there'd been this confusion. Adam was as tall as Raymond. They were both dark. Fine-featured.

So there'd been the confusion and the mistakes. All right, but what was his position here? The position of the dough-faced representative man? He had a weight of responsibility for his son. For Adam as he was, who inevitably (as he was) had created for himself this hopeless foolish predicament that could destroy him. He could be maimed or killed.

Deane offered coffee. She had this decaf espresso. The caffeine was washed out by a water process. No chemicals.

She was waiting for a response from him. Some reply . . . which he was unable to make. Because he was thinking how Raymond's body had been battered because of things Adam had done *(my son, therefore, in some way, me, my responsibility).*

"Is that how they do it?" Iris said awkwardly to Deane. "They wash the caffeine out?"

It seemed of enormous importance to be honest with Raymond and Kreg said to him, "Probably it was Adam they wanted. I'm sure it was." He said, "I don't know what it is. What they wanted with him. If I did, I wouldn't discuss it with you. You understand that. . . . I really don't know. I don't know what he's done." The idea, he was thinking, of his responsibility for Adam or to him would be one with no effect in the world. Therefore these were private and insignificant thoughts that ripped at him. Now he had also a responsibility to Raymond.

Who said, yes, whatever this was, you couldn't talk about it. He understood that.

Yes, Deane said. Of course she understood that.

Kreg hadn't answered about the coffee. "No," he said, no coffee. He said he had work to do and that Raymond would be tired. Pain was always exhausting. "Did they give you anything for that?"

"Oh, yes," Raymond said. "I have my Percodan. My perks for pain."

"The police?" Kreg said. Because he had to know.

Deane moved next to Raymond's chair. "We talked about that," she said. "We thought it might be better not to call them. That you might prefer it that way?" Impossible to keep the question out of her voice.

Kreg said again that he did not know where his son was or what he'd done. . . . And they were being too good about this.

Both of them. Raymond and Deane. . . . He really did not know what he was going to do. . . . If there was anything. Were there medical bills?

Raymond smiled. Insurance, he said. One benefit of the academic life, a great insurance plan.

Kreg made some poor pleasantry about sending a bottle of wine. "Too good," he said again helplessly. He touched his hand to Raymond's shoulder. Iris led him out of the apartment.

In the cab, she said, "It was Adam, our Adam, they were after?"

"Adam. Yes."

"I would think so."

Iris looked out the window for a moment. Then she said, "Odd scene when we were leaving, didn't you think?"

"Was it odd?"

"Well. The three of us standing there looking at the ceiling and waiting for the elevator to come. All that awkward indecision. You couldn't say what a pleasant evening. And there wasn't exactly anything to *thank* her for."

"Yes there was," Kreg said.

"Yes, of course. . . . Don't mind. I'm just going on." She looked away again. Then she said, "He's really done something, hasn't he?"

"Something."

"Do you know about it? I'm not asking what you know." They were through the transverse and had to stop for a light at Central Park West. "Our dear boy," she said. "He's not really a good one. You know that, don't you? I always have."

She had taken his hand. It was very nice, Kreg thought. Iris was somebody who could do that and talk to you this way but without any sense at all of a sentimental squeeze.

"What I'm trying to tell you," she said, "is, don't let him drag you down."

"How would he do that?"

"Just, if something comes up, don't let him."

"Better for him to work it through on his own?"

"Not necessarily. I didn't say not to help him. But think of yourself. That's all I meant." Then she said, "Tell me. Did you and she ever?"

"She?"

"That girl. Deane."

Kreg said he'd once bought her a drink. The cab turned sharp left at Sixty-sixth Street (they were going back to his apartment) and Iris was thrown against him.

"That's all?" she said.

"Yes. Only that. A drink."

"Well," Iris said. "I'm glad of that." She was still holding his hand.

"The ridiculous thing," Kreg said, "is that I could never cut myself off from him."

"I suppose not. Your son. Of course you couldn't."

"Although there's no reason when they're grown to continue to have these feelings for them. Not necessarily, at least."

"If they turn out badly?"

"In certain ways."

"But you wouldn't choose not to have them? Your feelings, I mean."

"No," Kreg said. "I'll stay as I am. I would always do that . . . which is in some ways what I find so strange." *Not accurate*, he thought as he said that. Because he didn't find it strange that he continued to love his son . . . and thought it absurd that he didn't.

Something was wrong with the streetlights in Kreg's neighborhood. They were out along the avenue for three or four blocks in each direction from his building. So there was no light except from the side streets and the building lobbies. Possibly Adam hiding there. Waiting.

Iris faced him when they got out of the cab. "I couldn't either," she said. "I would be with you about not writing him off."

Upstairs, he stood under the arched entry to his living room. No pictures on the walls now. These and any ashtrays or vases or leather boxes had been moved elsewhere and the rugs rolled. Most of the books were in piles on the floor. Kreg had a feeling of melancholy in the face of disorderly arrangements.

But he'd admitted a need to paint the place. Every removal showed some further shabbiness. Even so, he had a sure sense of loss in change. The bright apartment that was going to come out of all this would be in some way less his own place than it had been. And there was possibly more to come. Iris had pointed out couch coverings that were worn through over major areas.

Kreg regarded her as responsible for this project. He had admitted a certain shabbiness and she'd kicked into executive gear. The entire apartment was being done. He'd made the point that she wasn't usually so intensely domestic and that she'd let things go a bit in her own place.

"Not like this," she said. "They'll start to write about you. It's no place to bring a lady." She'd been naked in his bed when she said that.

She found a painter and worked out a list of what would be needed. She took Kreg to a paint store on West Seventy-second Street. It was a Saturday morning. "If this was a hardware store in the country," she said, "you'd be having a good time. You'd find some tool you didn't have and that would do it for you."

"Some useless thing," he said.

She was ready to walk out with a batch of color chips to take back to the apartment but Kreg said no. They could choose right then. They were here, weren't they? He arranged for delivery and they walked out. Well, that was behind them, he said.

"Man of action," Iris had said. "Once you get him moving."

During the night, Kreg woke. He went back to the living room and looked at the ghost shapes of the bare furniture. He touched his fingers to a nick in the surface of a piecrust table. Adam had done that, banging a toy fire engine against it. Kreg had a perfect recollection of the quick show of terror on the child's face . . . a realization that he'd gone too far.

"What is it?" Iris (not really awake) said, when he came back to bed.

"Go to sleep," he said. "It wasn't anything."

And then there had been the new week and yesterday and today and Frank Roth was speaking to him. "Could you?" Roth said. "Were you able to help him?"

He was asking about Van Atta.

"As a matter of fact," Kreg said, "I didn't see any immediate solution to the problem."

"Best thing you ever did," the fat man across the table from Van Atta said, "was go in with me on this." The man was finishing his veal chop while he talked. "Figures," he said. "The figures'll knock you on your ass."

"Mostly business isn't so good these days."

"Lousy. That's right. A lot of business is in the shithouse but we got a backlog that's up eighteen percent. Good margins. They run, I tell you, it's a very tight ship." He ate baby pasta shells in cream sauce. "Tighter than a nun's cunt," he said. He drank the last of his wine.

The captain was almost immediately at their table. He started to pour more wine. First for the guest but Van Atta placed his hand, palm down, over his glass. What remained in the bottle didn't fill even a quarter of the fat man's glass.

"So not too bad," the fat man said to Van Atta. "Have this place five minutes from the apartment. Caesar here to take care of me."

"Very nice," Van Atta said politely.

The captain asked if he could bring the *signori* another bottle.

"He won't drink it with me," the fat man said. "I have to put it away myself, I better not. Build a load, she'll kill me I get home. You could tell me though, what is this stuff? The name of it?"

Caesar held the bottle so the fat man could see the label. "A wine from the Piedmont," he said. "A Gavi. Principessa Gavi. Crisp but with bouquet. A very good wine."

"Write it down. Maybe I get some for the house."

Van Atta watched the captain leaving. He said, "It sounds very nice, although I've never been in anything before that I didn't control."

"Listen, it's a better business than . . . California real estate, that's dead for this cycle. Your other things, your exports, where's that gonna go? This is a business. This thing has assets and smart people working for us. That Jap kid I told you, the sales guy. Five years he could run the store." The fat man looked down at the bone of his veal chop. Pushed at it with his fork. He said, "This afternoon, I nearly fell off the chair when you called me. I didn't know you were East."

"Well, I had some business with a lawyer here."

"I know a lot of lawyers. I could have always recommended a lawyer for you."

"Not legal business." Van Atta watched the compulsive play of the fat man's fork through the remains of his meal. He believed in self-control. "More of a personal matter," he said. "A man named Kreg? Philip Kreg?"

The fat man, Bronheim, began to laugh. "Heard of him," he said. "Only eight people in the whole goddamned world. Everybody knows everybody. Of course, I heard of him." Sound of giggles, low shrieks, and he stopped what he was saying to look toward the next table. Two girls there in their early teens, one fair, one dark. Having dinner with the dark girl's parents. Rouge dabbed at their cheeks and lipstick. Both of them just at the edge of losing control, feeding each other lines, wild stories. The shapeless dark girl looked like her mother. No show of real spirit. But the blond guest had possibly a sudden perception of her own developing sexual power. She was always turning her head, looking around. All evening, Bronheim had been watching her.

Van Atta, after he understood what was going on, hadn't looked again. He had ideas about how you handled yourself in circumstances like these. A middle-class child, you would protect her even from herself.

Bronheim said, "So Kreg. Tell me about Philip Kreg."

Van Atta leaned forward. He began to talk quietly. He explained, but without background detail, some of what Adam had done. No mention of Hans Kalb or of Miami. He said, really, only that Adam had taken off with some money that a customer was about to deliver to him. And that the money was for him, Van Atta.

A busboy cleared the table and Caesar came back with suggestions for dessert. Espresso, Bronheim said, and the Italian cheesecake. And he agreed to a Sambuca when Caesar suggested it. There was more shrieking from the next table. Caesar looked over there and then at Bronheim and shrugged slightly. Espresso, Van Atta said. But no dessert. Nothing to drink.

When Caesar left, he said, "I thought maybe he could put me in touch with the boy and we could work something out."

"Crazy," Bronheim said, "you think he's gonna do that. Work something out. He's not dumb."

"Sooner or later," Van Atta said. "He's got to know that, sooner or later, that this kid has got to surface."

"And better it's voluntary. Maybe so. But it would be hard to turn him over. What kind of a deal could you work? I mean, that he would believe you'd keep to it. Cash," he said. "I never handle cash. I am so clean."

A waiter set down their coffee and the cheesecake. Caesar poured Bronheim's Sambuca. He pointed out the coffee bean in the glass. That was the traditional way, he said.

Bronheim began immediately to tuck into his dessert. He finished in seconds. Van Atta was politely stirring Sweet 'n Low into his coffee, not looking at Bronheim. When he finished stirring, he twisted lemon peel, rubbed it along the rim of his cup and dropped it in.

Bronheim sipped his liqueur. He said, "You might sometime. I would think you could, at some point, use a lever against him. I could possibly help you there."

"Well, maybe I'll take you up on that. Maybe I'll need you. I don't have any impression he's soft."

"I don't think so. Not that I hear. You understand, I've never actually met him. But what my guys tell me, I think I'm pretty well clued in, and I gather he's kind of a real hard case. The father, we're talking about." Bronheim finished his Sambuca. Held the glass to his lips to get the last drops.

"So we agree," Van Atta said. "He's tough. I don't see that that necessarily changes anything for me."

"He's also, I'm told, smart. Very quick."

"That could be a benefit to me. No funny ideas that something isn't really serious."

The check came and Bronheim grabbed it. "Hey," he said, "we're in Los Angeles, you get. But here, like the Englishman said, this is my canteen." He paid with a platinum card. Before they left, he handed Van Atta a manila envelope with red letters that read GRISSOM-TALBOT. "Here," he said. "Some stuff I got out at the sales meeting they had. And some reports for the Board. Make your heart sing, you see that stuff. The opportunity."

Caesar was at the door. He snapped his fingers and a busboy handed him a paper bag, which he passed to Bronheim. "You do me the favor to take this," he said. "Inside is a label with the name of the wine the *signor* enjoyed." The bag was of a size to hold two bottles.

Frostclear night. A still cold that you wouldn't immediately notice. But they were on Second Avenue. Only three blocks to Bronheim's apartment on Park. Van Atta said they could walk together and he'd go on from there.

"Tell you the truth," Bronheim said, "I'm not so much of a walker." He shifted the bottles to his other arm, looked evasively into the night air. "Maybe we get a cab," he said. He stepped from the curb and was flagging one before he finished talking.

Just sliding across the seat, he began to puff. He gave the driver the address.

"Don't drop your meter when you get there, buddy," Van Atta said. "You take me down to the Regency."

"Tomorrow night," Bronheim said. "Thursday she makes, I think, a brisket. A boiled beef. Very simple. So come to dinner. There's just us. Family. Six-thirty I like to eat."

"It's whether I'm still here tomorrow evening. I have to call you in the morning."

"Call me." Bronheim patted his free hand against the bag with the two bottles. "Every once in a while," he said, "he does some little thing. Smart operator. I drop a lot of money there."

"Nothin," Ish said into the phone. "I tell you, I watched them early morning, the day, later at night. All hours. It's a week now. No sign. Debbie, I see, that little slot he lives with. Her and there's also some other girl that's stayin there. But no Adam. Adam, I tell you, Adam isn't here."

Van Atta, in his hotel room with the sound muted, watched *St. Elsewhere.* He was in his shirt sleeves and stocking feet. Next to him there was an open bottle of ginger ale. He said, "Or he could be inside, not showing himself."

"Never come to the window? Come on. Not unless, unless he's hibernating. And how could he do that, those other two running around the place all day?"

A senior nurse, with a show of substantial anguish, was explaining something or pleading a cause to the head of the hospital, who patted her shoulder when she finished. Van Atta said, "He could be in there. It's possible."

"I'm tellin you no."

"It's possible."

"Technically maybe."

"Then I think you better go in."

"I can get. Let me think who I can get."

"No, you."

"I don't like. I've told you, I'm past that kind of thing."

"This time."

Then there was only the sound of Ish's breathing into the phone. After that his voice. "This has to be?" he said.

"It really does," Van Atta said.

"That little fuck," Ish said. "That Adam. Put me through this. Somethin like this."

The senior nurse was walking down a corridor. Then she was in the hospital cafeteria, at a table with two smiling doctors. Van Atta had rung off and was able to turn up the sound in time to catch the beginning of their pleasant conversation.

. . .

The furniture was drawn to the middle of Kreg's living room and covered with drop cloths. This room had been done today and you smelled the fresh paint before you came into it. The place, as it was, empty except for moon-mounds under white canvas, didn't seem to him as if it could ever again be comfortable.

Really this would all be fine, Iris said to him. It seemed so bad because he was seeing it with no furniture and under the glare of a standing lamp turned against bare wall. When things were arranged, they would look softer. It would be very pleasant.

"Where can we have a drink?" Kreg said. "I can make them but where do we sit?"

Iris said he could come into the kitchen and watch her make their dinner. They could drink in there. It was comfortable and he wouldn't have to help.

Yes, he said to her. The kitchen would be good. Susan's, he was thinking, Adam might have gone there. Doubtful but he might have. Kreg wouldn't call to find out. What could he possibly learn that would help except to calm his own worried self? And possibly the phones were covered. Did people like Van Atta do that sort of thing? You couldn't know how they operated. Under the white canvas in the middle of the room, he was able to recognize the high consoling silhouette of a wing chair that he liked.

Iris put her hand on his shoulder. "Make the drinks," she said.

In the kitchen she worked with a cigarette in her mouth, squinting against the rising smoke. She was wearing boots, a brown skirt, a pale cocoa blouse. Sheer. Kreg saw, through it, her thin back, the narrow straps of her slip. Certain clothing of women, it seemed to him, evidenced an inordinate trust against violence.

She was a careless, efficient cook. She set chicken breasts in a casserole with wine and cut vegetables. She sipped bourbon and added herbs to the casserole. Turned the flame up under a pot of water.

Not a labored process at all.

Kreg was remembering the interminable preparations of Susan. Which had served her purpose of prolonging the cocktail hour, the drinking time. He exchanged glances with the smiling farm girl on the box in front of him. *Penne Rigati* it said on the front of the box. It was a tubular green pasta, with the ends cut at a slant.

Iris sautéed cherry tomatoes in oil to make a sauce for the pasta, the penne. She was using an iron pan Kreg hadn't remembered he had. It had been out of sight in a cabinet for years. She stirred pesto into the mix.

When she finished what she was doing, he topped off their drinks and they went into the study he so rarely used. He changed his mind. Another few days. If he hadn't heard by then he might call Susan. He'd find some excuse, something that wouldn't alarm her.

Later he followed Iris when she went back to the kitchen and set the pasta going. He thought of her as working together with the smiling girl on the package. Iris arranged the table settings in the dining room. There were candlesticks with stubs in them and she lit those.

"Waiting," she said when they were eating.

He repeated the word, making a question of it.

"You're fairly good at it," Iris said.

"Am I?"

"With some people it's a kind of negative power. Like not flinching or showing expression."

"What you can't be made to do?"

"Yes, exactly."

"Those people," Kreg said. "They sound like unattractive types."

"With some of them, their better qualities are buried. Repressed. You have to loosen them up, bring them out of themselves."

"Into the light?"

"So to speak." Iris cut a neat segment of white meat. "Did you think of anything?" she said. "Any plan?"

Running round in my brain. Like the line from the old song, his thoughts had been doing that. And with no focus to them. He was simply unable to concentrate. This of course was a classic symptom of panic or of some overwhelming and shapeless dread. They were drinking a California white wine with their dinner. It wasn't a wine he knew but he'd bought a case. *Trust me,* the man at the liquor store had said. What he remembered was his absolute certain knowledge that Van Atta had been right. That sooner or later Adam would be found. *You know that, Van Atta had said. It's like the sun comes up in the east.* Acceptance: he would have to accept and Adam would have to accept. Which admittedly would be difficult because you would be going in blind. You wouldn't know in advance the nature of the punishment. Only that it would be severe, fairly awful. He'd probably on some level of consciousness been fighting this thought. *Accept.* He began to feel calmer but you could make a mantra of anything. That was another trap. Accept wouldn't mean you'd have to give in completely. Usually in any situation there was room to operate.

"Nothing yet," he said to Iris. "Although I haven't talked to my client, to Adam." He spoke the name cautiously, as if the actual utterance of it (even to Iris) would constitute a giving away of something to be kept secret, a release of power into the hands of the enemy. He thought of himself, a man of law, going to the police. Which was what you were supposed to do . . . and what they were for. And which in the actual event (this time of fear and dread) he knew would be a ludicrously impossible act (or rather a thought because it would never become an act). *So what price the man of law when you really put it to him?*

"But you will," Iris said. "You'll talk to him soon."

"That's what the other fellow said. That fellow, Van Atta. He was very confident I'd be hearing soon from Adam."

"Then we all agree."

"I hope not," Kreg said. "I don't want to agree with him on anything. Only to make agreements with him."

Iris sliced across another segment of breast. Raised the white meat to her mouth. "Well," she said. "Whatever we can." She put down her knife and made, most elegantly, the sign of the finger against the enemy. "Whatever we can do," she said.

This wasn't something, Kreg said, to get involved in.

"Girls can play."

What began to be comforting was the idea of a small team. A community of like-minded believers could accomplish anything. But he rejected that notion. He said, "It isn't a group sport."

"Singles? You'll only go it on your own?"

"There's no other way."

Iris stared at him for a while. She placed her knife and fork on her plate next to the dinner she'd only half eaten and set her napkin next to that. "I hadn't planned to ride out after the bad guys," she said. "What I meant was an expression of sympathy. Emotional solidarity." She was standing now. She said he was going to have to learn about certain kinds of basic exchanges that commonly took place between people in close relation to each other. Reasonably close, if he understood.

Kreg stood. Only weeks ago there had been that terrible argument with her about Cotton. That was his first thought. He hadn't meant, he said. No intention, he was going to say, of pushing her off, of refusing her help. Not in any way. But he didn't say that. He had, he was thinking, meant what he'd said. So now he didn't say anything more. Not now. This was a ridiculous scene, he knew that. A somewhat oversized man clutching a napkin and not able to speak. Probably red-faced. Eyes popping a little. Facing the furious lady. *Discombobulated.* The word came into his mind. He hadn't heard it since he was a boy. He didn't know if it was a real word at all. And it was so much in his mind that he didn't want things to be this way between them. *Not these burrs and abrasions that seem to accompany our every disagreement.*

"Nothing from you," Iris was saying. There was nothing she wanted. She hadn't been trying to take from him. "In fact, I want you to have it all. That lovely sense of yours of being alone. The only fighter in the game. You keep that. Talk to it." She began to go out of the room. "Cuddle it at night," she said.

Kreg followed her down the hall. Raise your voice, he told himself. Touch her. If you make a sign you might stop her. When they came to the front of the apartment, he waited, helpless in his own inability to go the little further distance that might conceivably bridge this gap.

Iris put on a raincoat and gloves and a man's felt hat. All her motions were stripped, economical. She arranged a yellow scarf inside her collar. Looked into a wall mirror and adjusted the angle of her hat. She pulled the bright scarf to blouse it at her throat.

Not turning her head, she reminded him to be ready for the painters at eight. She tugged at her coat collar and faced him.

There would be some action that could stop her. He knew that but only as a fact. As an outsider would know it.

"I'm sorry," Iris said. "I keep walking out of here," she said. She went out very quickly. She said for him not to wait for the elevator.

Kreg locked the door. *Why was she sorry? What about?* He had some idea about finishing his dinner. He was certain that in a few minutes he'd want to do that. He took one of his red envelopes into the dining room. Pushed his plate to one side and took out a grant application he'd been meaning to get to. The application was for a book to be called *Skeptical Styles in American Legal Thought: Holmes and Some Followers.* With the application, there was a c.v., a bibliography and photocopies of several articles. Also Etkind Rossoff's report proposing a ten-thousand-dollar grant. A handwritten note with the report: "Yes, he acknowledges Hofstadter. Give him the money. Very smart, I think." Kreg began to read. He absolutely refused to think about Adam. After a while he pushed the papers to the side and finished what was on his plate. One thing was certain. It would be impossible for Adam to come into the open until they developed a plan. Which in the circumstances seemed impossible to do.

Before bed, he went through the apartment. He turned off the lamp in the living room but there was still enough light to make out the shrouded white shapes of the chairs and tables and couch. Iris was responsible for this scene of disarray. He'd agreed to paint the place but only in the thought that she'd, so much of the time in the future, be there with him.

"I don't understand you, Billy," Ish said. He slowed to twenty, then five miles an hour, and turned left into a parking lot. The sign at the edge of the lot read SEA HARBOR II. He parked in a spot that wasn't too well illuminated and cut the engine. He looked at his watch. "Two-twenty," he said.

"That's good," the man next to him said. "That's about how we figured it."

"Figured it, Billy," Ish said. "We didn't figure. Whatever I figured, you figured something else. And you got it all fucked up."

"Come on," Billy said. He shifted in his seat. In a bad light like this, you could have taken him for a fairly young man.

"I don't wanna hear come on," Ish said. "A job of work, you turn up. You've obviously had a few. I tell you, no circumstances, under no circumstances anybody's to know you went out with me tonight. You turn up with Rose. *Rose, I'll see you tomorrow. Ish and I we're gonna ride around a little.* What's that, the tightest mouth in town? She's got a mouth as big as her snatch."

"I didn't tell Rose. Not anything."

"Except maybe you and I are goin to the late movies? *Lassie* they're playin. A rerun. . . . A job? She doesn't know that means a job you're bein so cute about?" Ish got out of the car. "Quiet on that door," he said. "It's that second building."

He walked on Billy's right. On the side with the cauliflower ear.

Both men wore blazers and slacks.

Billy stepped behind a black Cherokee with stickers plastered over the back. There was one with crossed rifles and one that said to *Have A Good Day* and a Raiders sticker in the shape of a fist with *No. 1* across it. "Look at this one," he said to Ish. The sticker read, *If little girls are made of sugar and spice, how come they taste like tuna?* "That kills me," he said.

"Fuckin filth," Ish said. "Ride around the country with that filth showin. Kids see it." He walked to the second building with Billy after him. When they were inside, Billy pulled on thin disposable rubber gloves. He took a small tool from his pocket and worked on the security door. Then they took an elevator to the second floor and turned left. "Here," Ish said. "It's this apartment here."

Billy started to look under the door. "No light," he said. He was still wearing the rubber gloves. "Ten seconds," he said. "Take care of this piece of cheese."

When the door was open, there was a chain lock that he had to reach in and free. He took two pencil flashlights from his pocket and gave one to Ish. He motioned Ish in and closed the door with no sound. Then he used his light. Checked the living room and looked into the front closet and the kitchen. Only seconds to do that. Then he went to the bedroom door. He motioned again and Ish followed him in.

In the bed there were two shapes in a boneless sisterly sprawl. Debbie had her hands together against her body. The other girl had one hand stretched in front of her, one against her cheek. A stream of black hair behind.

There was the twitching of closed eyes under the beams of the flashlights.

"Debbie," Ish started to say. "Debbie. Come on, Debbie. Time to talk to me."

It was the other girl who woke first. Cat-fast, tried to turn. Maybe to say something or to scream, but Billy's hand was over her mouth. Ish was shaking Debbie's head. "Debbie," he was saying. "It's Ish."

"Jesus," Debbie said before she opened her eyes.

Ish switched on a lamp. "Who's this?" he said.

Debbie didn't answer him. Now she was sitting up. Ish sat next to her on the side of the bed. She tried to pull the cover over her but couldn't because of his weight on it.

"Debbie," Ish said.

"Tuke," Debbie said.

"That's good," Ish said. "Just talk to me. Debbie gave a slight pull at the cover. "Don't worry about that," he said. He was looking through her nightgown at her breasts. "What we have to talk over," he said, "we have to talk about Adam." Like a father he took her chin in his hand. "Adam," he said. "So where is Adam?" He looked at the darker outline of her nipples.

Debbie didn't answer him and he began to squeeze her chin. "Debbie," he said. "Come on, Debbie. You're gonna talk to me about Adam." With his free hand he began to slap very lightly at her face. First one side and then the other. "Talk to me," he kept saying. "I want to hear about Adam."

Billy was stroking Tuke's hair. "Kid," he said. "Now nothin dumb. No noise, I mean. That would be dumb."

After a while Ish said to him, "Maybe Tuke here. Maybe she's in touch with Adam. Debbie and she probably talk about him. Where he is and how the little cuss is doin."

"I think so. I would guess."

Billy bent and whispered in Tuke's ear and ran his fingers through her black hair.

Later Ish said, "I will tell you what we did here. We established a negative, you know. We established, I think it's safe, that Adam isn't here. He hasn't been. And these kids, they're not in touch with him."

Tuke was still crying a little. The top of her shortie nightgown was ripped and she was holding a pillow to her front. Debbie wasn't making any sound. She was watching Ish and Billy, whichever one of them was speaking.

"They understand," Ish said, "it's somethin we had to find out."

"You know what?" Billy said. "What I was thinkin?" He

started to smile. He had the affable regard of a talk-show host. He put a hand to his crotch.

Ish's eyes followed the hand. "The thing is," he said when he answered, "it would be to show there's no hard feelings."

"Friends again."

"Debbie, I know," Ish said, "whatever happens here tonight, she's not gonna say anythin. I know that. And her friend there, she looks like a smart girl too. So, like the guy says, we can stay the manner of our goin a few minutes more. Maybe it's a little pact to show everybody's, the way Billy said, friends again." Probably, he said to Billy, Tuke would like to go in the other room with him. And if Billy would close that door behind him.

Really, where was the big difference? He came out here alone or he came out with Billy. What difference did it make? Of course, Van Atta, if he learned about it, wouldn't be happy. It wasn't that it mattered. Only that Karl Van Atta had said to go alone. Very big on having things done his way. Always. And Van Atta would probably learn. Find out. Rose's mouth. Rose never stopped. But how he would have done this if he was alone and there were the two girls to deal with, Van Atta wouldn't care about that. Only that somebody hadn't handled it the way he said to.

Although it didn't honestly too much matter. None of it. Because really there was nothing that had been fucked up. Just he didn't want one of those sessions with Van Atta. He didn't want Van Atta *explaining* anything to him.

Clammy now. The way it could get out here after dark. You were so close here to the ocean.

They were passing the Cherokee with the stickers. Flame design on the side of the vehicle. Billy was being careful not to show any expression. Ish could tell that. And that was fine, *because he knows I don't, I don't want any sick jokes about some little girl.* Only a creep would own this car. Ish had a brief vision of the man, a slavering flasher who was abusing a blond child with curls. Then Ish caught him. The pervert tried to back off but there was no place to go. Ish started to do things to him.

Six and a half feet tall and Henry Juszczyk would trust you like a girl in love. No special reason why that height and the easy willingness to believe shouldn't go together but Kreg found the conjunction odd. So did Mouse Kelly, he thought. Mouse was nodding his head with no expression on his face.

Henry said it again. "If he could have been here."

Kreg didn't think so. He didn't believe Brandt would have been delighted or proud to be with them now at this little party Willie Unger was giving in a private room at the University Club. To set a capstone to the deal, Willie had said, make it a happy beginning now they were all one team. Just eight of them in a small room with its own bar and all the shrimp and oysters you wanted.

"No changes to our show," Henry said. "And a four-billion-dollar company behind us."

Kreg imagined Brandt's voice. *Bunch of rascals, they want to take us over. So I think we got to figure something.* The start of a lousy script because it assumed Brandt's presence. But what would some hypothetical Brandt have expected to be done absent his own strong and tenacious self? What would he have expected from a not-so-hypothetical Kreg in this actual situation?

But Henry assumed Kreg was agreeing with him and that seemed to please.

Mouse rolled his eyes a little. Then went back to his job. He was eating whatever there was. He put his martini down to spoon capers over salmon on black bread. Flash of gold crown when he popped the morsel in. A caper rolled onto the dark wood floor. "Love this stuff," he said.

"I stick more to what's got a shell on it," Henry said.

"The fish itself, that doesn't appeal?"

"Not really so very much."

"Too bad," Mouse said and he went for another piece of salmon. "I love it all." Willie Unger, a few feet away, was with Cotton and Jarvis Dalton. Mouse caught Willie's eye and raised the tidbit in a happy salute.

Kreg wasn't totally a subscriber to Willie's views about being all one team. Not if they implied a full reconciliation with the former enemy. He reasoned that only certain contests were essentially sporting and that sometimes there was a reason to hold a grudge.

Don't you think so?

Winnie Mandela defied the authorities and addressed a meeting of thirty thousand. She said power would be theirs. Sakharov refused to eat and for over two hundred days they clamped his nose and poured food into his gasping mouth. Not games for them, not sporting contests . . . and not for Adam now in his own poor cause. It was no mere game that Adam was playing these days. It was hide-and-seek for real.

You know that, don't you? Don't you?

Kreg noticed the way Jarvis, a jovial warrior with wrinkle lines across his forehead and talking too fast, was looking to where Marcu and Sam Marion were talking together. Neither of those two was holding a drink or eating. Jarvis excused himself and started toward them. Too late because Marcu right then was already coming over to Kreg.

Henry saw him coming and skedaddled, leery of the imperial presence?

Marcu had a moderately contented expression.

"Hello and goodbye," Mouse said. He made a kind of spitting sound and held up his martini glass. "Another one of these," he said. "White devil for what ails you." He moved off toward the bar.

"His resentment," Marcu said. "You see it was something he was close to."

Kreg blinked. He had been remembering his conversation with Iris earlier in the day. *Don't you? she'd said. Don't you think so?* It had been as if there were some constraint on her. Chopped sentences, a kind of holding back. She'd have had in mind the reconciliation she'd initiated after one dispute only a few weeks ago . . . and the emotional carnage that later followed. She wouldn't be trying to pick up those pieces so this would be something else, something important to her or she wouldn't have called. *All right, she said. Then before your dinner.* It didn't matter that Kreg wouldn't have a lot of time. She suggested an Italian restaurant on First Avenue. *We can have a drink. You can spare a few minutes, can't you? We should talk. Don't you think so?*

Not really. Kreg didn't really believe there was any great need for them to do that. Or that Iris felt there was. So there had to be some specific thing she wanted. Of course, he'd said, he'd meet her. The place she'd mentioned would be fine.

"Good of you."

"That wasn't what I meant."

"Yes it was," Iris said. "Only you didn't know it."

She'd been there before him, which was unusual for her. A Campari-and-soda on the table . . . and her cigarettes. Woman in a café, a bar. She looked as if she belonged in that setting. Lean, somewhat faded, often angry and accepting that. Kreg imagined the flat herby taste of the aperitif.

Iris began to speak about nothing in particular. Kreg wasn't going to ask her to tell him anything. Not about why they were there for example or anything else. After a while she said, "It doesn't seem there was anybody behind you. No one's come in."

Kreg said, "It isn't a party. There's only me."

"I had to promise I'd look for that."

Nobody behind you. I had to promise. Kreg wasn't going to play. It was possibly five minutes that he'd been in this almost empty place and now a waiter was coming over. Kreg ordered scotch. His tongue began to probe at a raw spot in the cracked lips he'd got from walking in the cold.

Iris looked at her neat unpolished nails. "Adam," she said, "is in a kind of panic. So I promised him I'd be careful. He's with your friend Rossoff."

Statements delivered for effect. Made to draw a certain kind of response. He wouldn't . . . respond that way. Adam. He'd wait until she told him about Adam. Which she would do. That was why she'd got him here. And she would tell him about Rossoff. What was her connection to Etkind Rossoff? Years ago they'd met, possibly three or four times. Ten years? More than that. She used to go after Rossoff about European intellectuals who kept their berets when they came to this country. Rossoff hadn't minded. *Lady,* he always called her. Adam, though. *About Adam . . .*

Iris said, "He came to my place first. He's in New York."

Let her tell you.

She said, "He was afraid to go to you."

Pure ache of your fear. . . . There must have been that ache for Adam. The panic. And your need to get home, where you had to be, even knowing about the thugs who could be waiting for you (safety though in rooms with couches, chairs, rugs that you knew . . . your fireplace, the view from your bedroom). . . . Kreg was sure it had been like that. He said that Adam had been right to be afraid.

"I told him about Raymond."

Kreg thought about the effect on Adam of that knowledge. He asked about Rossoff. How had Rossoff come into this?

"I remembered his place. The extra rooms. Because he couldn't stay with me. Only that one bedroom." As Kreg knew, she said. She looked at him with some measure of distaste.

The waiter came with Kreg's drink and Iris waited until the man left. Whoever was going to take him in, she went on, would have to be told. So it would have to be someone you'd trust . . . first with your story and then to open his doors and take in the frightened bungler you'd brought him. Rossoff had seemed to her someone who would fill the bill.

About hiding. Rossoff had once commented on that. Years ago but his remark had stayed in Kreg's mind. *Would they hide you?* That was a test that went beyond amiability and good times together. A final standard. You were supposed to open your doors and take them in. As he, Rossoff, now had with Adam. . . . Kreg had speculated about possible family of Rossoff's, cousins or parents who had not been taken in . . . and about what had happened to them.

Adam, Iris said, had stayed one night on her couch. "Then I took him to Jane Street. . . . All those warehouses. I don't really love it that far west, but it is out of the way, isn't it?" She said, "You hadn't told me exactly what he'd done. He filled us in. I think he had to because of the attaché case. He has the money in an attaché case. He can't let go of it."

Van Atta had mentioned a caseful of money. "I know about that," Kreg said.

Iris raised her eyebrows and examined the unlovely sight in front of her. A stolid mouth-breather, never really tidy and too big to be comfortable in these little café chairs.

The money, that big man said. Had Adam talked about that? Was it all there? All the money that had been in the suitcase when he'd taken it?

Iris said they hadn't really been talking numbers.

"You should have been. Possibly I can buy him out of this situation. . . . For a price."

"As I said, the attaché case is full. It's almost full."

"I need a count." Kreg felt in his pocket for change. He said he'd call Adam at Etkind Rossoff's and tell him that . . . to count the money. He began to realize that his hand was shaking.

"Don't call him," Iris said. "He thinks they could be watching you and he's in a panic. No direct contact. I promised him."

And there was sweat on Kreg's forehead. "If you could tell him then," he said. "Get me the count. Something I can start with." The sweat was only a light film which she might not notice.

Iris' crooked smile. She said, "Tell me about that dowdy girl."

Kreg said, "Unfashionable, I think you mean. She isn't with us anymore. She's left the office." He was thinking that actually there had often been an excess of color in Deane's clothing. *And no knife work now.* He wanted Iris not to start with that at all.

"I can understand that," Iris said.

"She's moved. She's left the city."

"For?"

"Boston. Around Cambridge, I think. In that area."

"Yes," Iris said. "To be with Raymond. Was that what happened?"

What *had* happened? There had been a note. Two notes, one to him and the other, the actual resignation, to Frank Roth. *Urgent personal business.* That had been in the letter to Roth. A phrase from a nineteenth-century novel. And she'd apologized for not giving notice. *The usual notice,* she'd written.

Kreg explained to Iris that Deane hadn't spoken directly to him. There'd been only those notes.

"Easier on her that way," Iris said.

Kreg imagined it had been. But the idea was that you were supposed to face up in person. "Yes," he said. He guessed it had been. *Fucking irresponsible,* Frank Roth had said but there was a terror factor of course that Roth didn't know about.

In fact she would doubt, Iris was saying, that Raymond would be so very happy to have Deane near him, actually living there. Old friends and an occasional night together, all that was fine, but she really didn't believe Raymond would want quite so much *fey* in his life. Not as a steady diet.

Very possibly, Kreg said, that might be true.

"I'm sure of it."

Although being right didn't enact an open season. It didn't legalize for instance Iris' slightly vicious, slightly triumphant way of speaking. So why didn't she stop? . . . Kreg didn't say anything about the note that Deane had left for him. *Violence (he remembered perfectly) has always frightened me. This was not, she wrote, to be laid at Kreg's door. . . . Not your fault. Your son is an adult, leading his own life.* A kind of teachers' college diction, he had thought, reproaching himself for his snobbish view.

She had written also about some special feeling you were never willing to acknowledge but I knew it was there. . . . I gave you every sign that I could.

His own feelings he'd kept to himself. *No large relations unless you open yourself to them.* And with Deane he never had. Which of course had been a good thing. "Maybe you're right," he said to Iris. "He might not want her there."

The check was already on the table and he put money down. He swallowed part of his drink, noticed that Iris hadn't finished her Campari. No rush, he said. Not to hurry.

But she stood.

When Kreg was helping her with her coat, she asked him was there any message for Adam? "I'll tell him to count the money. Other than that, I mean."

"What else would there be?"

"Nothing. There wouldn't be anything else. Of course there wouldn't."

Kreg said, "I want to help him. Tell him I'll try to help him."

"And that your emotions overcame you?"

"No. Don't tell him that." *And I won't say it to you or to Rossoff either. But I am overcome. I do have you in mind. So very much in my mind. My two friends. . . . Not only that you took him in but your exposure to harm. The actual danger.* He cleared his throat. He noted that Iris had told Adam about Raymond. Rossoff also?

"He knows."

"Thank him for me. Both of you, I mean."

"I'm sorry," Iris said, facing him.

"For?"

"A little bit of a bitch about that girl. I was, wasn't I?"

"Well," Kreg said, not sure of his ground here. He adjusted his scarf. He examined it as if looking for a stain or for some sign in the plaid material.

Iris said, "It isn't her. She was very good, she and Raymond, about that business."

"Yes," Kreg said.

"But that mask you wear. People want to. . . . Do you know how it makes them treat you?"

"Yes," Kreg said. "I understand that."

They went out into a cold that tried to cut you. Iris had a mink coat, old, no luster, that she pulled tight around her. She shivered when she first came into the wind. Kreg said he'd walk with her to her apartment. Only a few blocks out of his way. No real distance. No, she said, there wasn't any need to do that. Kreg said, "I need the number to work from. You understand, whatever shortage there is, I'll make up. You can tell him that."

"Yes," Iris said.

"And that I am concerned. For him, I mean . . . in every way."

"Oh," she said. "Yes, I could tell him that. And that's better, isn't it?"

She turned away from him and began to walk. It was a northwest wind and came against her at a slant. She walked into it, clutching the worn fur around her thin body.

Now in the University Club, Marcu was waiting for some response. Mouse's history with Brandt Systems, Kreg said. Was that what Marcu meant? Because, yes, there was a history there.

"Which makes for resentment when outsiders come in?"

"I'd expect," Kreg said. Mouse's narrow back was to him. Mouse was talking to the barman, a short plump cherub. White hair, red face.

It would have been nice, Marcu said, if there'd been a place for Mouse on the Board, but that hadn't been possible.

Kreg said, no, he didn't think Mr. Kelly would have wanted that.

"Would you have wanted it?"

His own directorship, Kreg said, had always been in the nature of a caretaking role. . . . Kelly's too, really.

"Pending a permanent solution?"

Marcu was immaculate. Trim in a navy chalk stripe. Silk sheen of the fabric of his blue shirt. Enjoying this pleasant exchange in the way, maybe, of an eighteenth-century general, a civilized winner, facing his defeated foe at the end of a limited war. Patently a more capable custodian of Brandt's enterprise than the soft-bellied creature facing him (whose mind was racing then with unprofitable thoughts about the future of his fugitive son. No plan emerging). Cracked fingernails there and a button gone from his suit jacket. And who finally made a kind of reply. "Permanent," Kreg said. "We never thought about that."

Which seemed to satisfy. Or at least to close out that line of questioning. Marcu went on. Now that it no longer mattered, there was a question. This was only to satisfy his curiosity, which was giving him no peace (a smile when he said that). When was it? he said. At exactly what point had Kreg decided to sell the Foundation's stock?

"From the beginning," Kreg said, lying about a certainty he hadn't felt. "I knew from the beginning that I was going to sell to you." *We're always looking for good investments.* He heard Cotton saying that over drinks in the Indian restaurant. Now heard himself telling Marcu how he, Kreg, had always assumed there might be offers to follow. No need to answer questions but he answered Marcu's.

Marcu looked into a glass of soda water or Perrier. Then at Kreg. Liquid quizzical eyes. He said, "But it was different. You didn't act like a man who wanted to do business. I can usually tell."

"I tried."

"Not to show your hand. Naturally. Of course. But there's always some little sign along the way, you know."

"And there was none from me?"

"Only of hostility. . . . You're too good an actor, I think."

"No," Kreg said. "I'm not an actor. I don't know how to do it."

Marcu's eyes went very clear and then remote. "But everybody benefited," he said pleasantly. "You served your ends and I served mine." Now, he said, he should talk to Willie Unger. His host after all, and certainly a man he'd want to work with in the future.

Why? Kreg thought. Why do I have to pretend to him that it was easy for me? That there were no hard choices (no worries about holding Brandt Systems together . . . and none about my own future)? Put it, at the same time, to him by tone and inflection that I despise him. And that I'd outmaneuvered him. Got him to raise his price to a level that even Willie hadn't believed attainable . . . and did it in a way to make an enemy of him.

When Marcu came up to him, Willie locked a hand over his arm and pulled him closer and went into his act. Willie no doubt had his own ideas about useful relationships. In Kreg's circumstances, Willie would have extracted a deal for himself . . . and somehow made of Marcu an ally and, as such relations go, a friend.

Mouse Kelly saw the enemy had left and he rejoined Kreg. He

had a fresh drink which sloshed a little over the wavering edge of his glass. Jarvis Dalton came over too. Jarvis stood where he could keep an eye on Marcu.

"Jarvis," Mouse said. "He's not gonna go way. You get your chance."

Jarvis talked the way Henry Juszczyk had . . . about what a good thing this marriage was, about the resources that would be behind them now. After a couple of minutes, he said that maybe he had better get over there and talk to his new chairman.

"Jarvis," Mouse said. "Don't leave us." He winked at Kreg. A few drops of martini went over his shoes. His eyes glistened. When Jarvis was gone, he said, "That's kind of a weak sister, isn't it? I mean there's not really a whole hell of a lot to him, is there?"

"Courage, you mean."

"Yeah. Fortitudewise."

Kreg said, "I think it's on his mind they might not really want him."

"Scared for his job?"

"Apprehensive."

Mouse made his spitting noise again. "Like I said, no guts."

"He doesn't know it," Kreg said, "but he may not need them now. Not to any special degree."

"What you mean, it's a protected environment? He runs his division, they leave him alone?"

"More or less."

"So now he's safe. That's never true but like you say, more or less. They use him to fill a slot is all. I hope it works for him, the poor rabbit." Mouse looked into the air in front of him. "I even hope it works for you," he said.

At dinner he disgraced himself. He took over the seating arrangements. He wanted Kreg next to him with Henry Juszczyk on his other side. All this did start the meal off on a hectic note. The waiter who had been the barman caught the mood and was a little careless serving the black-bean soup. Cotton jumped when a hot spill of it went over his hand. Mouse had his martini with him. "None of that goddamned wine," he said. He fixed a mean triumphant eye on his drink. At home, Kreg knew, he wasn't allowed. Not more than one a night.

"What you want to do," Mouse said to Henry, "is to watch your ass."

"Sure, Mouse. Mouse, I'm always careful."

"You wind up with a bunch of cannibals, they want to chew on your ass . . . if you follow me." Mouse jabbed an elbow into Henry's side. Sly look around the table. His body shook and a little of his drink went on the cloth. "You understand," he said. "It's the nature of the beast. . . . Beasts."

Another waiter came and whispered to Willie Unger. "Some of my kids," Willie said to Kreg. "Back at the ranch. They need a telephone consult. Ten minutes maybe." He looked fondly at Mouse Kelly (the frail old drunk who wasn't noticing him). "Why not?" he said to Kreg. "Why shouldn't he?"

Marcu for a moment caught Willie's eye. Between them they exchanged possibly some brief intimate communication about the world they shared. High-stakes battles, so a need to be available around the clock. "But don't you think he thrives on it?" Marcu said to Kreg. He nodded in the direction of Willie's retreating compact back.

Kreg, with something else on his mind, said to Marcu, "Everybody who overworks is supposed to thrive on it." That sounded abrupt. The aftertone of his voice stayed with him like a taste. This was intended to be a meliorative occasion. *Lay down your arms.* So he said also, "Although he does stay cheerful." He was thinking of something else. He was thinking about Adam. He was absolutely unable to clear his mind and stop thinking about his son. *How much for how much?* If you were trying to conceive some plan of action for Adam, that would be the only question to address. How much revenge could you buy off for how much money? But it was a world Kreg didn't know. He didn't know the customs of the country.

"Headhunters," Mouse said to Henry. "Get in touch with some headhunters. So you have yourself an out. You make some contacts in case these cocksuckers stick a knife in your ribs."

Henry's face was going red. He looked to Jarvis and to Kreg. Jarvis compressed his lips. The implication was of a Rushmorish disapproval constrained from comment only by respect for the aged. But you knew where he stood. And that he wanted especially for Marcu to know where he stood.

Marcu smiled at Kreg.

Mouse's head began to droop. Then he shook himself. His fingers, blind worms, crawled toward his martini glass, which he found and raised in the air. Fog-eyed but he swept the table with his glance . . . not actually seeing what he was looking at. "Toast," he said. The barman-turned-waiter was serving from a platter of sliced steak. Thick slices, rare. A spoon or two of blood juice over each portion. Behind him was another waiter with the vegetables. "Shaddup," Mouse was saying against the ambient hum of conversation. He hit his knife against a water glass to get attention. "Listen," he said. "Toast. Triumph of the fuckers."

Signs of amusement on Marcu's face. And on Cotton's and Sam Marion's. None of which Kreg enjoyed seeing. Not those or the snort of suckup disapproval that came from Jarvis Dalton.

"Fuckers," Mouse said again. Weakly this time with everything about him suddenly indeterminate. The glass went from his fingers. It rolled without quite tipping, somehow retaining most of its contents, across the table. A slow progress, as if controlled by a schizoid and determined mind working against a weight of barbiturate haze. Infinitesimal fractions of a second then but enough for the making of the most precise exquisite observations (although there was no opportunity to act).

Kreg noted the freezeframestoptime effect around the table of this erratic forward wobble of a mere glassy object.

And over all this, the sluggish buzz of a winter fly. Probably the lone survivor of his kind. Programmed to do and, with the advantage of his stupidity, not distracted by the sparkling event below him . . . and with certainly no appreciation of it as the miracle of delicate balance that it was. A miracle that died with a final roll or swoon of the stemmed container off the table into Jarvis Dalton's lap.

And at that moment of fall, occasion of the spill of liquid, Kreg's refractory mind, triggered by its own appetite for incongruence, recalled to itself something about delicacy (this notion resulting from the sight of the final balletic dip of Mouse's glass

. . . slender-stemmed, bosom curve above). *Delicacy, Deane had written, the delicacy of my position. So how (she wrote) could she have spoken? Made any further sign?* . . . He felt himself in a hallucinatory surround of false expectations and craziness.

Jarvis then . . . coming immediately to his feet with a napkin at his crotch and a banshee scream. A risen man of action. "Fucking wet," he screamed. His shoulder caught the edge of the steak platter and there was a fall of meat over the table. A disaster *au jus.* "Too much," he started to scream. "Too goddamned much."

Mouse shifted slightly forward and his head went on the table, cradled trustingly there in the crook of his own right arm.

The old waiter was wiping red from the front of his uniform. Kreg noticed that he didn't seem put out. In fact an amiable glance toward the sleeper in front of him. Nice, Kreg thought, to see that. Find some opportunity and slip the man a ten.

The waiter turned an experienced and pleasant eye toward the damage. He sent his colleague for a lot of extra napkins. He rescued the meat platter with a fair bit of its contents and began to stack, clear and mop up as best he could. A spread of good feeling from him. From the instant cynosure. Which caught. Sam Marion passed plates, silver and whatever debris he could handle. Cotton, too, and then Jarvis. Smiles all around. Including Marcu, although he didn't help. He wasn't a man for domestic chores.

Jarvis began to apologize. Because he was the one who'd actually done the deed (no matter how provoked).

"Jarvis," Sam Marion said, "it's all right. You had cold stuff on your balls. You were protecting the jewels. That's always allowed."

When the worst was under control, the waiter stopped. "About him," he said. He was looking at the sleeping miscreant across the table. "No more party for him, I think. Is there someone can get him home? Tuck him away in his bed?"

A faint repeated snort from Mouse when Henry lifted him. Then again the contented regular peaceful breathing. Baby sleep.

Henry followed Kreg to the elevator, with no sign from him that he was actually carrying weight, no apparent stress or pull at the shoulders. Downstairs there was some fumbling in Mouse's pockets for his coat check. Kreg didn't like the beginning of a grin he got from the attendant and sent out looks calculated to destroy any notion that this was a funny business.

Willie Unger came across the lobby. "The hell," he said, "is going on here?"

Kreg told him and he touched a chubby hand to Mouse's hair. "Old thing," he said. And gave a little squeeze to Henry's arm. Willie was very physical. When he was talking to you he wanted actual contact. Little caresses, digs, punches. He always wanted to be intimate.

Kreg went outside to call Mouse's car to the door. There was an audible wail before he pushed through the outside doors, the wind from the northwest now gone manic.

"Oh, Jesus," the big driver said when Kreg told him. "Trouble now. She'll skin his ass." That wasn't to criticize, he said. What else could she do? How else could she keep that frail *bon vivant* in line?

It was only seconds that Mouse, with his coat tucked as best they could around him, had to be exposed to the knifecold air. He gave two short puppy yelps when he was brought into it but his eyes didn't open. . . . Put him there in front, the chauffeur said, so he could keep an arm around him while he drove.

Upstairs everything was tidy again and, after a while, cozier. No reason why seven should be a more intimate number than eight but it was. There was a new closeness to the conversation and you had a sense that weapons had been laid aside. Even the fine curl in Sam Marion's lip was gone for now. This new warmth, Kreg decided, was generated by the slapstick memory they shared. Boffo might be only a crude and distant cousin to high drama but wherever it existed there was a community.

So they were a little group with something to talk about. A collegial buzz across the remaining meat. And an excess with it of St. Julien, a Château Talbot of 1977.

But they weren't friends and there was anyway too much tension for that mood to last. More or less over the brandy everything went slack and then there was only a gathering of men waiting for the end of a formal occasion.

Willie Unger didn't let the gloom drag on. He had a negotiator's sense of timing. He tapped his spoon against the thin glass of his snifter (as Mouse had earlier with his water glass). "This is a wrap," he said. "Some of us, you I mean, have got to get back to Connecticut tonight. And some of us, that's me, have got to get back to their awful offices. And everybody wants to rise with the gorgeous lark in the morning. So I mean let's drink up and flee this nifty place." He made the sign of the cross. "*Pace,*" he said. "Bless you, my children. I brung you together. Now go forth and prosper. Be nice to each other."

There had certainly been some prearrangement. Cotton wouldn't simply have left that way, not unless it had been set up. Only that one-fingered salute from a distance . . . and the nice polite smile of the well-bred man.

Then there was the chauffeur holding open the door to Marcu's limousine with Marcu next to him, shivering. And there was the bite of the wind.

It would have been surly, ungracious, to refuse Marcu's offer of a lift so Kreg bent his head and clambered in. *Not for free,* he told himself. *Something he wants.* But there was room here to stretch his legs which he did, liking the luxury and the idea that he permitted himself to enjoy it.

In the car Marcu pulled the brown fur collar of his navy overcoat close around him. A successful evening, he said. Didn't Kreg think so too?

Kreg asked if that thought allowed for Mouse Kelly's martini and the business with the meat platter? Did those things in any way qualify the success?

"No qualification," Marcu said. "Dramatically, they added. I would say they made the evening."

At Fifth Avenue they caught a green light and crossed. It was almost soundless inside this luxury machine. Soft gray fabric over the upholstered areas of the interior. Kreg ran a rough hand over the armrest. "Comic relief?" he said.

"He was perfect in the part." Marcu opened his coat now. He explained the importance of physique, of size, in such a role. You needed somebody very small who could be carried off like a doll or a huge fat man who couldn't be moved. But either way it was the idea of extremes that was essential. He himself preferred the version that had actually taken place. "The portability, you know. The fact that you could actually carry him off."

All right then. Mouse as a comic figure. *Just no display, please, of your puritanical disapproval. That gets you nowhere.* It was too warm in the car and Kreg had a need to yawn. He refused to give in to that and also didn't directly respond to Marcu.

Then they came into the park. Still white from a snowfall of a week ago. They passed the zoo, now being renovated. Marcu noted that many of the buildings were already bricked in and that a fair bit of the roof work had been done. He wondered if it was real slate they were using for the roof tiles.

Actually Kreg was always informed about the progress of the work. He was a walker and often came this way. Usually in the mornings on his way to work . . . along with the joggers and the yuppie men and women, dressed for business except for the Reeboks or Nikes on their feet, their good shoes in attaché cases or canvas bags. And this was where he sometimes saw the cats, two of them gone wild and living next to the roadway there, just inside the iron fence that bordered the drive. Someone had made a home for them. There was a plastic delivery carton with its open end facing out. A piece of blanket over the bottom and some other fabric covering the top and sides. The cats had been there for more than a year now. Often they crouched next to their shelter. They watched the walkers . . . sometimes blinking. Usually there was a can of food in front of the shelter. Evidence of some continuing benefactor. But how much of that food was eaten? Kreg imagined a diet of choicer morsels. He imagined carnage and devastation among the area's birds and rodents. Rip of claw into a squirrel's back. Small creatures at peace in death . . . as in certain genre paintings, with the day's bag set out. "Slate," he said. "It looks like slate."

"Public job," Marcu said. "Any cost." Then he said they would be working together. He and Kreg.

The remark hung in the air.

"It seems," Kreg finally said.

"Now it does. Not something you'd have bet on a month ago."

"Yes, I would," Kreg said. "I'd have bet on it."

"That's right," Marcu said. "You would have. You explained

about that before." They passed another construction site, the steps at Seventy-second Street leading down to the fountain there, and Marcu noted that the park was a major source of employment to the construction trades.

"That's true," Kreg said. He reminded himself that he was riding in this man's car and there was an obligation to be civil, to extend himself a little. He pointed out, just ahead of them, the fenced area of Strawberry Fields, the memorial gift of Yoko Ono.

This was new to him, Marcu said. He'd read about this place. Rare trees and bushes from all over the world, wasn't that right? But he hadn't seen it until now. A circumscribed life he led. He knew nothing of the actual structure and geography of the city. Only a few blocks of the East Side and the business area. Strawberry Fields, wasn't it possibly a little *Disney* as a name? He remembered the song and that one line, "Strawberry fields forever," but still. . . . Would Kreg agree with him about the name?

"Possibly," Kreg said. He tried to think of something that wouldn't be just another clipped response from him. But what he thought of he wouldn't say to Marcu. There was his thought about Strawberry Fields, the sweet hope of the song and the place, and his thought that neither served as a model for any world his son inhabited. Adam's world was better represented by the other scene, the scene with the cats. It was a cat world that Adam lived in, or a wolf world. He asked about Lincoln Center. Didn't Marcu ever come across town to Lincoln Center?

A concert once in a while, Marcu admitted. "She does like to get out to a concert."

She? Kreg didn't ask. "Lincoln Center," he said. "You do go west for those occasions? You extend your beat?"

"Exactly," Marcu said. "You have it exactly right."

Everything was sounding very intimate and cozy.

They went north on West End Avenue and stopped across from Kreg's building. He hadn't given Marcu the address and neither of them had said anything about it to the chauffeur. The chauffeur waited for a car to pass and then wheeled the big car in a U-turn and stopped in front of Kreg's door.

Marcu, on the street side, leaned forward with his hand on the door handle. Kreg began to move out of his seat but Marcu didn't open the door. Marcu said, "You know it's mostly coincidence. Somebody mentions something and that ties to something else."

What was *it*? Maybe everything. Marcu perhaps saw chance as an ordering principle. That wasn't original. . . . Steady liquid eyes. The man seemed to be ready to add to what he'd said. Or to explain the reason for this companionable lift. "Yes," Kreg said. "That's often true." Why didn't Marcu open the door?

Then abruptly he did and Kreg was able to leave. "Well," Kreg said. "That made it easier for me."

"Whenever I'm able to help."

"You did. You just did."

The night man in his mismatched uniform and with a sweater under his jacket was in the lobby. "Bitch," he said. "Isn't it out there?"

He walked with Kreg to the elevator and pushed the button for him.

"Cold one," Kreg said. *Welcome aboard* had presumably been Marcu's message. Not that difficult to say. Then why hadn't he said it? Spit it out.

"Steppin up in class," the night man said. "Set a wheels you rolled up in." Shrewd fox eyes and a twist to his thin mouth.

"Comfortable," Kreg said.

"And warm." The man's eyes shifted toward Kreg's right hand. Kreg's fingers began responsively to curl. *But I shouldn't. I can't be tipping him every time I walk in the door.* It was warm there in the lobby. He pulled at his scarf to get it away from his throat. What he had to work on now was some plan for Adam, something that would close the account with Van Atta or Van Atta's customer . . . whichever of them was the ultimate creditor here. Restitution of course as a starter. But then there would be the penalty, the something extra that Van Atta had indicated would have to be physical. *Physical? Could somebody be more precise about physical?* How bad would that have to be? He considered the recalled images of Raymond's bruised face and his damaged body. That picture would have its effect on your judgment.

The elevator would be at seven now. Always a slight shudder and jar of the cab exactly there, and then a screeching sound, the agony of the cables, surely due to some mysterious twist or obstruction. All this audible along the entire passage of the shaft.

Wouldn't it be reasonable to assume that *physical* would have a price on it? that it could be bought off? A reparation for a retribution, that was an old story. Precedent there. Kreg made a guess that Van Atta would keep to any bargain he made.

He said he's bound for Canaan,
Happy land.

The lines ran in his mind. He heard Fats Waller's voice. . . . And he considered the idea of a happy land. . . . Because you started, if you thought about settlements, necessarily to think in terms of *after.* That was the nature of any settlement. It was a step toward the future, and any future is possibly happy.

But would Adam learn anything from this mess? If you could save his body, what about his mind? his soul? Also Adam might possibly realize that he didn't have the equipment to be a bad boy, not successfully. He might give up that life the way Deane had said she'd abandoned her earlier rowdy ways. Adam could take that lesson from Deane. Not that he would have to go all the way with her to yoghurt and save the baby seals. Just get away from the violence and the corruption.

Why would you think (Deane might say to him) you have to test yourself in that world? You don't belong there.

Tell me, Adam said. Tell me about belonging.

Don't feel sorry for yourself (she was emphatic about it). You have nothing in common with those people. You're not a criminal.

A Florida prosecutor might disagree with that. But what I have nothing in common with is some whacked-out ex-flower child fifteen years past her time.

Just stop with those people. Move away. Leave. Deane also favored a period of counseling. Maybe in a group of some sort.

Yes, Adam said, gripped by a major perception, an evolutionary leap in his moral life. You're right of course. I'll try it. Or, more likely, he said, Fuck you. Go sing a folk song. Find yourself a rifle so you can stick a daisy in the barrel.

But Kreg's mind cut away from that scene. The elevator indicator went horizontally to the left and the door opened for a tiny fat lady who lived somewhere above him in the building. In her seventies with orange hair and small eyes and two yorkies on spaghetti leashes. A suspicious look at Kreg for being there and she was immediately talking to the night man, about the heat. They always promised and then they didn't do anything and somebody was going to have to arrange so you didn't freeze to death in the winter. She was moving while she talked and the man trailed uncertainly after her.

Kreg stepped into the car and pressed the button for his floor. He disagreed about the heat and except in the worst weather kept his radiators off. About the night man, he suspected he'd have weakened. He'd have pressed a bill into that willing hand. Only saved from a sentimental gesture by the coming of the little pig woman. Heavy, too sweet smell in that small space, of her powder and her perfume. The elevator almost stopped at the seventh floor. One thing about Marcu, possibly his greatest asset. There was a draw toward him, a pull to tell him your secrets. *Help me with my son,* Kreg had wanted to say . . . and of course had not. How many years ago that he and Susan had cruised the Caribbean? There had been a hypnotist on the ship. Kreg had not permitted himself to be hypnotized. It was no different now with Marcu or with any easy temptation. It had been Susan's idea to take that cruise. He'd found nobody to talk to but he'd enjoyed the clean clear light of the region.

In a black-and-silver robe over black pajamas, Marcu drank cocoa from a porcelain cup. From his window he could look across the park; he could see west and south and north or below to Madison Avenue.

Claire touched his arm. She had a cup like his. She made the cocoa because she thought it was good for him, that it would make him sleep. It always seemed to him odd, *incongruous,* that she was truly fond of him.

She wore a negligee in pale gray. Marcu liked her in negligees. He liked the look and idea of the fall of shimmering fabric over her body. You sensed but didn't hear a rustle when she moved. . . . There had been a moment. He'd bought this one, the one she was wearing, from a dark-haired saleswoman. Late middle age, older than Claire. She was heavy-breasted, chic, with a slight Spanish accent. The woman draped the gray silk over her forearm to show him . . . to show. She was as aware as he (Marcu knew that) of this garment as something meant eventually to be removed.

"My old man," Claire said. "But you don't get tired."

She had never been afraid of him. *Old man.* She'd started to call him that almost from the beginning. She took care of him, though. Watched his diet and kept after him to exercise. "To keep you *vigorous,* she'd say. He was inclined anyway to take care of himself and it was amusing to be bullied by her. Yes, still vigorous. Shrewd appraising eyes of the saleswoman. *This old man. Is it all style or is there still performance there?* He sipped from his white cup. The cocoa was too sweet but he relished it for its warmth. He set the cup down and looked out at the pleasant lights of the park and the city. Almost seventy. He was always aware of that.

Claire put her arms around him from behind. He felt the warmth of her body against him. One clever hand worked past his pajama top into the coarse fur of his chest, all gray there. "Long evening," she said.

"Long enough."

"And everything is settled now? Everything is calm and peaceful?"

"Peaceful," Marcu said.

"That lawyer?"

"The lawyer is out of it now."

"Gone?"

"Soon."

"Does he know that?"

"I think so. We didn't talk about it but I think he does."

"Good," Claire said. "I'm glad he knows. I hope he asks to keep his job."

"He won't," Marcu said. It was not imaginable to him that Philip Kreg would ever ask for anything, for any favor. Some intimidating quality the lawyer had, and he was isolated in a way such that you wouldn't break in on him. You would suspect it could be a dangerous entry. . . . In the car he hadn't been able to tell Kreg about his son. Kreg's careless possessive slump, heavy face shadowed in the semidarkness, revealed whitely when they passed a streetlight. It was a face that Marcu had seen often enough in a show of irritation or displeasure. But he had intended to do the man a service, to tell him what he had learned.

Bronheim had loved the happy coincidence of his friend mentioning Philip Kreg to him and then the story about Kreg's son. *Do you know a lawyer named Philip Kreg? the guy asked me. The fat man's eyes teared when he laughed. Use it, he said to Marcu. The information. Any good you can do yourself. Only my name. Just keep that out.*

Claire disengaged. She went out of the room for a moment and came back holding a maroon box. Knelt with it next to a coffee table. "Purchase of the day," she said. She opened the box, set something on the table. Her body blocked Marcu's view of what it was. Heavy, though. He heard the sound of whatever it was being set down on the glass tabletop.

Then she said to come and see.

An eagle's head in glass. Crystal, Claire said, from the thirties. Lalique, to be used as a paperweight in his office. Although his desk was always clean. Just an object then, something to look at.

Marcu took up the heavy sculpture. Ran his fingers over the textured cuts that shaped the feathers. He touched the beak, the eyes, then set the figure down. The head and neck were erect but there was the sense of a potential for forward thrust and he was intrigued by that.

In bed he worked through a novel of espionage by a new master of the form . . . who wasn't. Claire looked at an Italian architectural magazine. Bronheim, he thought, might someday be a buyer for the Kyber division. Bronheim had a weakness for hi tech. Marcu imagined a price that would leave him the valve business at no cost. He considered the assets there. For now, then, stay close to Bronheim. No deal though for Kyber unless Sam Marion wanted it. That could be worked out.

Claire nudged his arm. She showed him an article on a Tuscan farmhouse, all stones and stucco done over and furnished in a skillful mix of rustic and clean high modern. But not this new

Memphis, cutouts in foolish shapes, which she really disliked. Should they have a place like that? Every once in a while, a quiet week there or ten days. Near Florence, she said. Siena. Of course she'd heard there was so much vandalism of unoccupied houses. And would they use the place? Would Marcu take the time off?

"Yes," Marcu said.

"Yes," Claire said. "What does that mean, yes?" She put down the magazine and reached for the lamp on her side.

Marcu turned out his light. He welcomed the darkness, sleep coming over him. Brief moment to think. The truth was he'd been intimidated by an air of sullen and uncaring power, by his sense that Kreg played for private goals and didn't necessarily even try to calculate how it was that he would win or lose. *Coincidence, he might have said. Your son. I know about your son. I know they went to see you. He might have made some offer then of sympathy, or asked if there was a way to help. . . . Then what kind of response? Probably only that flat unforgiving stare that always made you want to be in some other place.* Really as well that he'd said nothing to Kreg. This was a situation with gangsters the son was involved in. Why mix with that?

Next to him, Claire yawned. She said, "That man. He has a way of making people not like him?"

"I think he does." And always, Marcu thought, something about him that was unbuttoned or frayed or out of place. Some outlaw difference.

"That's good," Claire said.

"Why is it good?"

"Sooner or later."

"It's going to come down on him. Is that what you mean?"

"Yes," Claire said.

Marcu had liked it earlier when they had been talking in the living room and he liked it now that she would be so casually vicious in his interest. "Yes," he said. "I think so. I think it will."

But then he didn't sleep well, which wasn't unusual with him. He would be up two or three times in a night. He'd have some thought to write down so as not to lose it. He would look out into the dark and come back to bed and go off, almost always, into a light easy sleep . . . until he woke again.

This time there was nothing to write. He came conscious thinking about Kreg. And about the stone set of his face. A need leaped in him to energize the lawyer's features with the plasticity of the true supplicant. He wanted to see a mouth that twisted to tell him, *Please.* . . . Please. . . . He wanted quivers in the flesh of those heavy cheeks. Eye to eye, he wanted to tell Kreg about costs. About the price that Kreg would have to pay for help. Kreg would have to take money from him . . . and Kreg would be made to understand that the money was nothing to Marcu. It was purely a price, in the sense of something exacted . . . as something would most certainly be exacted. . . . Imagining that scene should have been comforting to him, soporific. But he began to have a difficult night. When he got up after three, it was to go to the kitchen for water. . . . What price? he was thinking.

He put ice in a glass. Bronheim too. Bronheim would have to be dealt with. He could be dangerous to know. A man with associates who were outside the law. . . . The Kyber division. Maybe, after all, he would hold that, build on it.

When he came back to bed, Claire in her sleep turned slightly toward his side. Sometimes in the morning she woke reaching for him. She'd have her hand on him before she opened her eyes. Soft milk-sour breath, like a baby's. Just holding him for a while before she moved closer.

This evening in the car when he'd been unable to speak to Philip Kreg about Kreg's son. . . . He had created that opportunity for them to talk and then had wasted it. Because of some reluctance in him to be despised . . . by that man. But he liked the idea that he was honest with himself, even about his own inadequacies. And his vindictiveness.

Adam was sending signals for help.

There was his talk of a new life elsewhere with the money. But Iris believed he wanted to stay here (at home) and be helped. She carried a flow of questions, messages to his father. How could you get a social security card in a new name? Would you have to be fingerprinted to get a real-estate license? He'd read that you could write for birth certificates in the name of someone who'd died and they never checked. Was that true? If it was, you could get a passport and you'd be home free. Europe could be a place to go. Maybe London. . . . But there was the cash. How to get that into an account somewhere? You couldn't in the modern world go through life with only bills to your name. Legal tender didn't always do for money.

He insisted on detail. Hard fact. *So much of what he wants from me, Kreg thought, is illegal. And it doesn't even occur to him that I might find it repugnant to do what he asks.*

But actually, Iris told him, Adam was just sending those signals, aimless static. He was a fly in a bottle. The real message, she said to Kreg, was that he wanted his father to help him.

And his messages had to be transmitted in person. *No telephones.* That was the hysterical imperative. Which meant that Iris had to be in touch with both of them. She would go to Rossoff's apartment and visit with Adam and listen to whatever he had to say. The next day she would meet with Kreg, and would have some response or message from him when she went back to Jane Street at the end of the day.

This was a cycle of questions and answers that tended to be repeated, a ritual of demand. Because Kreg of course couldn't make the kind of hard and certain replies that Adam insisted he had to have. And it was certainty that Adam was screaming for. Absolute reassurance. One night there'd been a crisis at Iris' office. "The usual last-minute craziness," she said, "that you get when you release a new campaign. Nothing special." But she'd stayed at work until eleven and had missed an evening at Rossoff's and couldn't phone to explain. Because that had been forbidden. And Adam had not been very understanding about it. "You see," she said to Kreg, "there can't be any break in the routine. Not the least little change in whatever he's got going for himself down there."

Kreg said, "No sympathy because you work so hard?"

"That isn't Adam's way."

"Also, he keeps forgetting to count the money."

"He doesn't forget. He's putting it off."

"Why would he do that? He's not advancing anything."

"I think he's afraid to advance. When you get your count, you'll call Van Atta. I think he's afraid of that. Things actually beginning to move. . . . Also, of course, he's controlling us while he waits . . . wouldn't you say?"

"Adam's rules," Kreg said.

"And his regulations."

Oh yes, his rules and his regulations. Because aren't they his only means, in this situation of fear and loss of power, of managing his life to any degree at all? In hiding, his willfulness is his strength.

Now he was asking, was there some way to return what he had taken? to return the money and be safe? That was the thought that after a while began to emerge as central. Everything else was mere desperate talk. How to give back those dollars was his real question. Kreg's too . . . and Kreg had no answer.

"Tell me," he said to Iris. "What about Rossoff? How is he with Adam?"

Usually enigmatic, she said.

But Rossoff was providing the refuge. And he would always take care of you if he could.

Kreg saw no end to this cycle of meetings and plans. Just meet again with Van Atta, he finally thought, and give him back the money and extract whatever promises you can that he'll call off his dogs. He told Iris to discuss that with Adam and Etkind Rossoff.

When Iris called him, he said they could meet at the Modern. Would that be all right?

She said there seemed to be progress. She had a number he'd been asking for.

Thick strokes in black on yellowtan paper. Mies' rendering of an office building. Like so many other designs in this commemorative exhibit, an unexecuted concept. Never truly brought into the world, a mere idea of a kind of perfection. MOMA. Kreg always said it out, the Museum of Modern Art. They had really not come here to view an exhibit. "Here," he said to Iris. "We'll just walk through it. And we have to eat. I'll take you to the members' dining room."

"Feed the messenger," Iris said.

"I thought I would."

"Why not?" she said.

With no reservations, there was a ten-minute wait for a table. People around them and what they really had to say was private so they just chattered on, and neither of them was very good at that. Next to them, there was a tall old man with a shapeless woman of forty. The man had an eagle face and magnificent eyebrows. He wasn't particularly bothering to make conversation with the woman.

"They didn't seem likely together," Kreg said when he and Iris were at their table.

"Little dumpo," Iris said. "He didn't love being with her. Being seen together. Maybe she was a messenger too. Only a messenger."

"Why *only*?"

"Well," Iris said.

The tables had white cloths and were spaced generously

enough apart so that the improbable business of this luncheon could take place in private. They ordered and Kreg said they might each want a glass of wine, those little mini-carafes they had here.

"That would be nice," she said. "White." She found a sheet of notepaper in her purse. "You wanted a number," she said.

The paper Kreg took from her had a ragged edge where it had been ripped from a spiral binder. He read,

$1,000,000
−4,100
$995,900

"The forty-one hundred?" he said.

"It was mostly wardrobe. He got some nice things."

Kreg crumpled the paper. "That's very nice," he said. "I'm glad of that." He smoothed the sheet, ironed it with the heel of his hand and folded it and put it in a pocket. He said, "Now he wants me to talk to Van Atta?"

"He thought you might make up the difference. He said he'd pay you back." Iris reported that in a perfectly uninflected voice. She wasn't arguing for a client.

"Yes," Kreg said. "I'll make it up. . . . Do you think he will . . . pay it back?"

"Not likely," Iris said. "Not bloody likely," she said putting on a sudden cockney accent.

Kreg said, "The money. You keep it there, in Rossoff's apartment?"

"He keeps thinking about burglars or a fire but he keeps it there." Iris added that, even in the apartment, Adam couldn't be separated from the case. He was always going to where it was kept and checking it, touching it.

Kreg said he'd go ahead then. Was that what Adam wanted? For Kreg to talk to Van Atta?

"If you can negotiate out the other. That was the only condition."

The other would be the penalty Van Atta had specified. Pain certainly. Possibly a more lasting treatment . . . some measured crippling. Who would opt for that? "I'll try," Kreg said. "I'll talk to him." He started to think about a bonus. Because there was a history to that, to the idea of the buying off of vengeance. Hadn't there been a term for it at common law? *Wergild,* he remembered or *bote,* or *manbote.* So not hopeless. Likely a way out. If Van Atta asked for any substantial sum, Kreg would sell securities. He thought briefly about his cousin and the failed real-estate conversion upstate. He said to Iris that he'd been considering some proposal that included a guarantee against future violence.

Iris scratched a pattern across the tablecloth. She watched the tip of that finger. "Does it bother you," she said, "that you know he's never going to pay you back?"

"Yes," Kreg said. "It does. It bothers me." *No explanations but how would it not? With sixty coming up a few years out and my career seemingly at a point of irrevocable collapse. And I have a son who, knowing he could simply ask, would rather play me like a fiddle with his lies about repayments he knows he'll never make.*

Iris said, "He wants to see you."

Kreg said, "He was concerned they might be watching me."

"Now he's calmer."

"He's willing to run that risk?"

"He's decided it isn't a substantial risk."

"It isn't. Then when would we meet?"

"This evening, he thought."

Kreg imagined himself with Adam in some west Village restaurant where it was too loud and the tables were jammed against each other. He didn't know the restaurants down there. He asked Iris.

Rossoff, she said, would know a place.

"Only for health food or a delicatessen."

Then she'd find something, Iris said. That would be easy. There were people in her office who gave major time to the restaurant scene.

Someplace that wouldn't be too crowded, Kreg said.

Iris said she was sure she'd come up with exactly what he had in mind. Not a difficult assignment at all. Her voice went slightly higher and thinner than normal. And was there anything else? she said. Any other messages or little arrangements she could help with?

The waiter brought their wine; he promised food in just a minute more.

Kreg said, "We do seem always to be brought together by something."

"It seems that way, doesn't it?"

Kreg was aware of the heavy questioning sag of his features. He was breathing through his nose. Mouth open a little. A walrus. He decided he had no ability at all to do anything truly effective to help himself or Iris or Adam. If needed, he could provide some money for Adam. That was the extent of his ability. He said to Iris that it was a long trip for her, going to Rossoff's apartment every day.

"After work. We have our talk and I cook a little something. Then I go home."

"You do the cooking?"

"Rossoff is European. He's old-fashioned that way. The woman does the cooking."

"And then she does whatever work she's brought home from the office?"

"Yes, she does that too."

"At least I assume you bring work home. You used to fairly often."

"Fairly. . . . I still do. Fairly often."

"Adam. Does Adam help?"

"Well," Iris said. "Adam. On the other hand, he asks about my work. He wondered if it might appeal to him."

"What did Adam decide?"

"I explained that in public relations we don't usually get very much into originating new products. Not even the name or basic marketing strategy. Whatever they hand us, that's what we push. I think Adam felt that was a little *secondary* for him."

Kreg said, "About your being a messenger . . ."

"About that?"

"I mean, it isn't always just from here to there." *I mean I thank you for it. . . . I have to let you help me. You and Rossoff. Do you understand that I have to? And that all I can do is hope there's no harm to either of you from what you're doing?* He kept thinking that there was nothing he could do to protect these people he cared for. He had no ability to do that.

Iris said, "But it's something you can learn. And it's steady." Crooked smile at that but she was clearly in a better humor now.

Adam came out to the stoop of the brownstone. He was wearing his tweed coat and his cap and his long red scarf. The clothes of Cincinnati as he thought of them. A mild and humid night. He lit a cigarette, blew smoke freely into the sluggish air. Then stepped down into the street. Walked east on Jane Street. Walked with his coat unbuttoned and his left hand hooked into his pants pocket. Optimist time. Signs of motion and, no question, some resolution ahead. A settlement. The air held the fresh tobacco smell of his cigarette. He'd have a few more this evening. As many as he wanted. He was always able to regulate the amount he smoked. Where was it he'd read that it was overwhelmingly women who could smoke the way he did? Real guys, they did or they didn't. If they puffed, it was a pack or more. *All right, so I'm a closet fag.* Or maybe the data were wrong. Was that possible? When in the history of human events had the data ever been wrong?

Why not a settlement? he was thinking. Wouldn't you want to let bygones be the neverhappenedgones as it were and get your million dollars back? Triumph of simple reason. Money talks. *It turns out that I'm the boy who holds the cards.*

So this nice feeling that you might not have to be looking over your shoulder for the rest of your life. Which made you easier about right now. What were the chances, say, of Van Atta or Ish or even Kalb, the pig-eyed kraut, of any of them being here in New York on just this west Village street with its old brick houses and the white trim at the windows? Soft lights of evening all around. Signs of family life where you could see into the parlor floors. Amiable calm of the cocktail hour. Maybe an eight-year-old curled in a far corner, reading while you talked. Or a dog at your feet. Kazaks and Bokharas, not new ones, on the wide pine floorboards. You had been born in that house, and your father too. It was Adam's point that he had no strong connection to this part of town and the odds were enormously against their even looking for him here. Right now the risk was minuscule. It was a teeny-weeny risk. *I'm daring. I kind of rush to take a risk like that.*

For now he enjoyed the idea of them looking. He liked the idea that they were out there and not finding him.

We seek him here, we seek him there,
Those Frenchies seek him everywhere.
Is he in heaven?—Is he in hell?
That demmed, elusive Pimpernel?

He had read that in school. That and books like *Tom Swift and His Flying Machine* and *The Hardy Boys* at wherever they were.

Sit in a circle. They were fifteen or sixteen years old and they would pass the book around. Read in turn out loud and blow weed or do pills if somebody had gotten lucky and generally laugh themselves silly. Especially at the dopey dialogue. Some of those sessions got kind of ragged after a while. They would just fade out into some kind of dreamy dreamy time. *Then wander away on your own, man.*

Adam turned south.

He took a deep puff, held it, flipped his cigarette (half smoked) in a high arc over a gray Honda toward the middle of the street. He watched the revolve of that tiny white baton until it disappeared behind the hood of the car.

He was early enough to stop somewhere for a drink and he'd have another cigarette with that. These were Rossoff's cigarettes. Rossoff kept Winstons in cartons and Adam once in a while just helped himself. Rossoff didn't mind.

Adam looked through a restaurant window. Nice place. Nice white tablecloths. And touches of warmth, pictures and some plants, not too many plants. Pleasant to see, these signs of order, after the mess of Rossoff's place. Journals that didn't get thrown out and half the books off their shelves. A kind of perpetual disorganization that could put you up the wall. Burn marks on the furniture. How could you live like that? Rossoff seemed to relish it. He was always showing you something. Rossoff, the cheerful monkey. Here, Adam thought, the waiters had a look of competence. The tables were beginning to fill up. People from those houses on Jane Street might come to a place like this.

He went in and took a seat at the bar, one stool away from a blonde of forty-five. He ordered his Chivas-on-the-rocks with just that little head of soda and a slice of peel. He liked the ritual of ordering and specifying. Life on the outside, a free life. Everything just so. Well, he was, wasn't he? On the outside now? Coming out after a period of hiding, of *not being able to come out.* A kind of incarceration. When he sipped his drink, he tried to decide if you could actually taste the lemon. Probably not, but there was the sense of it being there. *Comment dit-on,* he'd said to the square-faced Frenchwoman who had the café in Carmel, *la peau du citron?* Campari umbrellas there and the classic blue-and-white checked tablecloths. *Zest,* the woman said. *C'est le zest.* So now he always ordered peel with his scotch. How could you pass up *le zest*?

The blonde, looking straight ahead, sang "Kiss today goodbye." Softly, as if to herself.

Adam was remembering again about school. Two years past circle jerks when they read those books and laughed at the simple thoughts of an early time and doped if they could. Somewhere else in the dorm, younger kids sat in another circle and did their competitive handjobs. Or that was the story you heard. Adam didn't know if it was true. He'd been older when he started at that school. So it remained an open question like did they put saltpeter in the food.

"And point me toward tomorrow."

Weak perfect features. Forty-five years there of trying to please. You wouldn't guess her age unless you really looked. But there was the set of the body and the fine wrinkles that were beginning to etch themselves into the fair skin around her eyes and mouth.

"Chivas," she said. "You drink the Chivas."

"Mostly."

"I can't drink that. It's too heavy for me. I'm a scotch drinker too but I like a lighter blend. J&B. J&B for me." She said that as if it were a line in a jingle.

No, Adam said. He really didn't care for a very light whisky, a J&B or a Cutty.

"But those are the ones I like," the blonde said. "That's what I keep at home. Someone wants to come over, I always tell him that. Of course whatever he likes in some other booze. But if it's scotch what I have is the J&B. So if he wants a different one, he can bring his own."

"That's fair enough, isn't it?" Adam said. "Fair warning." This must have been something twenty years ago, he thought. Something to see. Little flower of the city. Special. He watched the extended stretch of the woman's throat. Thin cords showing because she had tilted her head to get the end of her drink. He caught the bartender's eye. Pointed to the woman's glass.

"Well thank you," she said when the fresh glass was in front of her.

"J&B," Adam said. "Right?"

"Right," the woman said. She toyed with the glass, revolving it between her palms. "What I get for home," she said, "are the quarts. It's a little cheaper for the half gallons but can you see me hauling those monster bottles around? I mean with my wrists?" She leaned a little toward him and placed her wrist next to his. She was looking at him fairly directly now.

"Well," Adam said. "You wouldn't want to strain anything." He tapped a cigarette out of the pack and offered it to the woman who shook her head. No, she'd just finished one and she didn't smoke that much anymore. So he lighted it for himself. Watched in the mirror across the bar the young guy exhaling after the first deep puff. Smoke and the reflection of smoke.

The blonde hummed a few bars of "September Song."

"Very nice," Adam said.

"You know Willie Nelson on that? Just kills me when he does it." The woman's eyes glistened. Not truly bloodshot but traces of red around the rims and at the corners.

The bartender, dark with thick brows that grew together, caught Adam's eye.

Yes, Adam thought. That's fine but it's not what I'm here for. I'm only passing through. Couple of minutes and I'm off to meet old Dads.

Who right now was probably in something of a sweat. On his

way down here or just getting ready to start. Going over in his mind the things he'd say to the bad boy. Let him know what he'd done was wrong *but don't alienate him.* There was that constant fear of causing some permanent break and you could always play on that. Guilt. That had to come out of his sense that he hadn't been a Perfect Pop. Which he hadn't. Except in a few areas like pointing out the kid's deficiencies. He'd been good at that, the deficiency game. Not so much, if you wanted to be fair about it, a matter of directly articulated criticism. But there was always some evidence of his disappointment and there was his ponderous and labored example. And he'd been pretty good too at shipping the kid off to school. Why not? He was always working. Very little pals-together time.

But Dad's guilt was a handle wasn't it? Useful in the past and no doubt would be again. As in starting over. There wasn't going to be all that lovely money so a stake would have to come from somewhere. *Gee, Father, I'm still thinking about Boston or Cambridge. They say the economy is very strong and all that culture would be a good influence on me.*

Susan of course didn't have it at all. No guilt. She'd be incapable of having it. A constituent advantage, you might say, enjoyed by the truly detached. Tell Susan there were Indians waiting to shoot you in the ass and you'd get this warm smile. *You grew up so well. You're so resourceful. I know you'll think of something.*

"Danced," the woman said.

"I don't get that."

"That's what I did. Some acting but mostly I danced. You know, sing a little, dance a little. I was on Broadway. Lots of things. You probably saw me."

The fact was, Boston was interesting. Truly interesting. See Louisburg Square in the snow, sail on the Charles. He would get his license and sell real estate. *And then branch out.* He might begin to write. Short articles, knifework on the local scene. Cut and slash and walk alone. Drink only champagne. And no need to be afraid. That was essential. There was going to have to be a commitment on that from Van Atta. *Pas de violence.* You'd want to be specific and unambiguous about that. Very. Tell the old man to treat this like any other contract negotiation. Leave no loophole. He could see the two of them together, doing business. Van Atta's calm eyes.

Adam finished his drink. He put money on the bar. "Maybe," he said to the blond woman, "but probably not. Probably that was before my time."

When he walked out, there were streetlights and old plane trees. But no palms. The palms were thousands of miles to the south and the west. And wasn't that nice?

Kreg, at a corner table, massaged his left knee. The ache wasn't supposed to be there in this mild weather. Maybe it was going to come on more frequently as he got older. He looked at his watch. *Don't, he told himself. You don't have to do that. He'll be here. Punctuality was never his strong suit.* But what were Adam's strong suits?

He ate a pencil-thin breadstick, breaking it into small segments. Clean sharp sound when the pieces snapped. A young man in the front of the restaurant was checking a tweed coat. Kreg attempted to study the menu.

The young man was being shown into the restaurant. He hadn't removed his sunglasses. Kreg started on another breadstick. He read carefully through the listings for the antipasto. The young man stopped at his table.

Dad, Adam was saying. *Dad.* But wouldn't it be galling to have to use a filial that way. *Father?* That wasn't better. The problem was in the situation itself, the relationship.

He came to his feet. Huge next to his slender son, clumsy. He had no sense at all of what to say. They didn't embrace.

Adam seemed easy about being here. "Well," he said. "It's me. Bad penny."

"No," Kreg said. "No, no. Not at all. . . . Here," he said. "We'd better sit down." His napkin had slipped to the floor. He was going to have to bend under the table for it.

He came up red-faced with Adam watching him and smiling pleasantly behind his dark glasses.

"You could take those off," Kreg said.

"Yes," Adam said. "Why not?"

"I'd like to see you when I talk to you."

Then there was the special expression that always passed across Adam's face when he'd succeeded at some mild annoyance. *Score one.* "Why not?" he said again. "Yes, sir."

Moments later a waiter was asking about drinks and Adam said did Kreg still take his on the rocks with soda? Only a splash, wasn't that right? The same for each of them, he said to the waiter. The soda on the side. When the drinks were brought, he added soda and rubbed peel along the inside of his glass. Kreg watched his son's eyes. Adam seemed to have an ability to concentrate absolutely on what he was doing and at the same time to be taking in the room. This might be characteristic of people who lived by their wits. No doubt necessary on occasion.

Kreg asked about Rossoff's place. How was it for Adam, staying there? He was thinking that he couldn't immediately begin about the money and Van Atta and Van Atta's client.

"Your friend, Rossoff," Adam said. "He isn't very much into the domestic side, is he? I mean about repair and fixing the place up."

Kreg took too large a gulp of scotch and his eyes bulged from the jolt. He wouldn't let himself cough. He had a picture in his mind of an overload of magazines, books, chipped ashtrays and unhung pictures. Rossoff's nest. It didn't matter that by any rational concept of good housekeeping Adam was right about Rossoff. That didn't seem to touch on the relevant issue here. On the other hand, the relevant issue, which might be gratitude, was another one of those matters Kreg wasn't going to talk about. . . . Let Adam bad-mouth his host or go on being provocative in some other way. Whatever it took to test his father. Kreg would rise to no bait.

He rubbed surreptitiously at his knee. The steady ache had flared into something sharper. And he considered the difficulty of understanding his own feelings. Whom he cared about for instance. And why. This was a subject he often considered. But that was all he did. He considered.

When they were having their second drinks and just after Adam had ordered the special seafood appetizer and permitted Kreg to take the fish soup, Adam with a little smile opened the discussion. He smoothed his right hand across one cheek and then the other. "You see," he said. "No major marks or defects." He worked the fingers of that hand and then of the left hand. Articulated them in the air. "Parts in good functioning order," he said. "I mean we want to keep them all like that, don't we? Isn't that the top priority in this high-stakes game?"

"Van Atta, you're talking about?"

"Right. That's very good. That's exactly who I'm thinking about."

Easy, Kreg thought. We're not going to act in those old ways. Try in your mind for a scene of harmony, the genuine pleasure of two men, father and son, in each other's company. Even under difficult conditions. So no arguing and face up to our problems. He noted that he might not be able to come to terms with Van Atta. Although he doubted that. And Van Atta might not keep his word, which he also took to be unlikely. But how could you know? So where was the objective basis for trust? "How good are the guarantees?" he said. "Could be foamy waters ahead." *Foamy waters.* Fatuous.

But Adam permitted that lapse.

"Although where's the choice?" Kreg said.

"I thought I had one," Adam said.

"I think they would find you."

"You know about these things?"

Shouldn't there be a point after which certain feelings stopped? The male lion has no regard for his cubs. Kills them if they get in his way. This was a man past thirty. Kreg said, "I think they know about them."

"You mean I should tell you to go ahead? Go forth and negotiate?"

"I think you should."

"You think. You keep on thinking." Adam's hand began to toy with his folded sunglasses. Then he put them away in a leather case. Honey-colored soft leather.

Kreg's left hand squeezed into his leg. You could choose to act as if nothing were intolerable. Adam was watching him. The leather case, he thought, wasn't something Adam had gotten when he bought his sunglasses. It would have been a separate purchase. Adam had accessorized his sunglasses. Kreg had seen that verb in advertisements for costume jewelry. He said, "Is there a better way to operate? Better than thinking?"

"You know," Adam said, "there could be some risk. I mean just for being the go-between." He met Kreg's eye. Smiled.

Kreg shrugged. How to respond to that? Not an expression of concern. Only another way of testing him.

Adam seemed even more pleased. "The four k that I had to spend," he said. "If you'd advance me that . . ."

"Yes."

"I mean advance it to Van Atta."

"Yes. I understand that. I'd said to Iris . . ."

"And that's really all right with you?"

"Yes. It's necessary."

"Isn't it?" Adam said. "It really is, isn't it? . . . Or else," he said. "They don't especially love those little shortfalls," he said, and his attention seemed to wander for a moment. Then he began to explain about talking to Van Atta. This was important. Van Atta had to speak for himself and for a man called Ish. Ish Frankel. And for all persons, as the phrase went, under their control. "No minions," he said. If he was going to do this thing, he didn't want any strangers coming around later. None of those guys with the big shoulders like the ones who'd played a little with that young professor.

"Raymond."

"Raymond. But what if it had been Adam they'd had in their hands? What do you think they'd have done then? So just make it clear. Van Atta and Ish don't do anything and they don't hire anybody to do anything and they don't let anybody do anything."

"The minions," Kreg said. "We should talk about them. You said there could be some risk." He pointed out that the risk could extend to Iris and to Rossoff.

"And to you?"

"And to me too. Yes."

"I hadn't thought anyone was immune. . . . You're telling me something?"

"Only that there doesn't seem to be a great deal of concern."

"On my part?"

"Yes."

"Well, I didn't sit down here and say right off that I was sorry. That's true."

"Or gratitude either."

"I'm sorry, I'm sorry. I was bad and the good people are helping me."

"Our friends are helping you. Yes. . . . If you wanted to, you might tell me what was behind it. I know what your employer told me you did. But he didn't go into the background. I don't really know what you people were doing."

"You people?" Adam said.

Kreg noted that he and his friends did not normally operate outside the law. And that perhaps they ought to know what they were involved in here.

"Get the subtext and clear your consciences?"

"Subtext. Not necessarily. . . . I don't particularly see that it would clear anything but we probably ought to know."

"If you don't want to participate," Adam said, and he let that thought trail off. "You know, I didn't mean to soil that fine white moral sense of yours."

He wants to see you, Iris had said. . . . But then there had been that charming exchange with Adam. . . . Adam saying, You think. You keep on thinking. . . . And now this. There was no wish that Kreg could discern to be together in the way of family members united by love. Adam wanted to see his father . . . but to use him as a bulwark . . . and as a target. Father across a table from him and having to put up with the bad boy. *Contemplate his failure and take whatever he throws at you. You made him so you be sorry for him.*

But wasn't that the fairly usual way of it?

Not a view to be conceded. Kreg was able to imagine a life in which the field was less abrasively contested. No Tolstoyan conceit of happy families. Just not this unremitting quality to the skirmishing. It didn't seem naïve to think there could be some mutual goodwill out of a common remembrance of rooms, furniture, the foods he'd liked as a child. Actually Adam had been a picky eater. But some foods he liked. Foolishly, Kreg began to remember how he'd always enjoyed the loin lamb chops Susan cooked for him. She broiled them pink and cut away the fat. This was some ritual of good nutrition out of her own childhood. Her mother had done lamb chops for her. And just that way. So there was, you might say, a habit or continuum of cutlets across the generations. Later sometimes Adam would ask and then Kreg made the lamb chops for him. He remembered once himself watching the boy who sliced precisely across the nugget heart of his meat, then looking over to where Iris was standing and watching them both.

It seemed proper to this occasion that he and Adam would dine tonight in a North Italian restaurant from a cuisine that was not the cuisine of home.

Adam raised his eyebrows when Kreg's dinner was set down. Kreg had ordered sole, a fillet broiled in a lemon sauce. No doubt that simple dish was thought to be wrong in some way. For himself Adam had chosen rolled beef on a bed of spinach. Also a forty-five-dollar bottle of wine. "That's all right, isn't it?" he'd said. "You don't mind red with your fish?"

When the wine was brought, Kreg covered his glass and pointed toward Adam's. "Why not?" Adam said. He accepted a tasting measure of the ruby liquid, rolled it in his glass, sniffed, drank. He waited and then nodded to the waiter and told him to pour away. Kreg tasted his wine. "Worth it, isn't it?" Adam said.

"The best revenge?"

"Something like that. But worth it on its own. Just worth it, wouldn't you say?"

All this good living, Kreg thought. The well-to-do young and the well-to-do old. There seemed to be a consensus that really taking care of yourself was a good thing, the best thing.

Adam was tapping lightly against the side of his glass. "Well, I'm here," he was saying. "Join the party. . . . Wandering thoughts?" he said. "You want to watch out for those when you're getting on."

His most affable manner.

Kreg's mind responded . . . and began to work: *If the law presumably hits the evil where it is most felt, it is not to be overthrown, because there are other instances to which it might have been applied. In* Weaver *v.* Parker Bros., *Holmes quoted that.* Weaver *was 270 U.S. 402. I used it in a brief two weeks ago. Rembrandt lived and died, 1606–1669. So where was the significant loss?* "You think," Kreg said, "it's beginning to pass me by a little?" He hadn't willed himself to remember anything. Those items, dates, had jumped like popcorn into his mind following the stimulus of Adam's pleasant comment. His mind went on. Satan came into hell: *Here at last we shall be free.* Why that? that in particular?

"Sorry," Adam said. "Not to offend." He leaned back in his chair and ran his forefinger gently over the rim of his wineglass. "So about Van Atta," he said. "We agree how you should go about it?"

The little ritual with the wineglass. Kreg considered for a moment the notion that his son lived by such gestures. The little attitudes and the rituals. Yes, he said to Adam. He'd get on it. In the morning he'd call Van Atta. "As we discussed. Just that way."

"Unless you can think of some better approach."

"No," he said. "Not really. There's nothing better I can think of."

"Then no fancy wrinkles. Plain vanilla. Exchange of dollars for peace in our time. That's what we go with."

The issue of physical retribution, Kreg said. There was only that one issue. And that was a precondition. Not negotiable. His point was that there was nothing to negotiate here. No room for counsel to maneuver. He wanted Adam to understand that.

"There's only that," Adam said. "That one issue." Then he said okay, so why didn't they drop it? Change the subject. Van Atta would play or he wouldn't. Lap of the gods now, wasn't it?

Adam was bored. He'd lost interest in the subject of his own freedom, his ability to move freely where he was known. He began to concentrate on his food, ate rapidly for a few moments. Then he half lifted the cased sunglasses from his breast pocket. Caught his father's eye. "Habit," he said. He grinned and tapped the case back into its pocket. He pushed neat cuts of rolled beef onto his fork, drank wine in short gulps. Stopped to look around. He leaned slightly toward Kreg. "Those two," he said. "Dykes."

They were two women in middle age. Trim, decorous. One with the fine and slender high-seaboard look of possibly a cousin of Nate Hobart's. A squash-blossom necklace on the other and close-cropped gray hair and barely heavier features. Our Crowd, you might guess. She caught Kreg's gaze and passed her own polite, pleasant and uninterested regard over and away from him. These women could be lawyers or psychiatrists or advertising executives. There was some aura from them of competent presence.

Kreg guessed that Adam was right about them. But what could you judge at fifteen feet? And why judge at all? "Probably not," he said to Adam.

"Hey, it's nothing to me but I think they are."

"And you can tell?" *Don't. Don't get into this with him.*

"Usually," Adam said alertly, "I can."

"Although really it doesn't matter whether they are or not."

"Yes it does," Adam said. "Everything matters. Everything about people. You know. Nothing that is human is alien to me."

He sees himself, Kreg thought, as a conversational opportunist. Happy opportunist.

After dinner, Adam wanted to walk. When they were outside, his hand went immediately to his breast pocket. Kreg doubted that he was even aware of the gesture. No anger, he told himself. Not his business if Adam wanted to make a fool of himself. Wear dark glasses to bed if he wanted. Adam's coat was open. The long red scarf was draped over his shoulders.

Adam stopped and looked into a silver Jaguar. He put his hand on the door. "It could be," he said. "The key could be in the ignition. We could go for a little spin. Come back and they'd never know it was gone."

Kreg had no way of responding.

"Or not come back," Adam said. "Great car . . . and I forgot to tell you, great meal."

"Yes," Kreg said. "It was very nice."

"No, I mean it. Wonderful food. The wine too. What was that wine?"

"It was a Chambertin. You ordered it."

"Didn't I? Didn't I order well? Just all of it. The raspberries, and you could die from the espresso. And then that cognac."

Adam was being a grateful child. It was a manner of ironic exaggeration that was a weak man's way of attacking you at an angle. Keep that tone and he could always be superior.

Just so long as he can do his act.

A black boy, a white boy and an oriental girl came by. Probably eighteen or twenty and all in retro clothes. The white boy was carrying a guitar case and had a gray fedora with the wide brim that had been the preferred style from the twenties through the McCarthy era. The black boy was wearing a derby. A scarf in a band around the girl's head, some silklike material, a pattern of diamonds in black and white. "That's disgusting," she was saying to the boys. The three of them were laughing.

"Not disgusting," Adam murmured. "Only natural."

Then there was a stew of locals. Couples and singles, the gay and the straight. One black-leather menace (solitary) with metal studs.

"Tacky," Adam said. "Shouldn't we get a cab and flee this tacky scene?"

Pleasant, Kreg had been thinking. Human mess. Cultural soup from which . . . But all right. *Where?* he said. That would be fine. Whatever Adam wanted. "But where?" he said again.

Adam pointed north. "Uptown," he said. "I want to see Fifth Avenue. The big Doubleday's that's open late." See that, he thought, and walk around a little and then cabs home. "Our separate ways, you know."

"You'd wanted to avoid that part of town."

"I was upset. I wasn't being the courageous person I have it in me to be." Adam stepped into Hudson Street and raised an arm.

A cab skitted across two lines of traffic like a psychotic herring breaking from the shoal. Near-perfect yellow paint and bright chrome and an unscarred never-smoked-in interior. Kreg sniffed the new-car smell of leather and oil (although those seats were not of any material that had ever served as the skin of a living beast).

Adam looked over the front seat to check the driver's card. "Hey, Avram," he said. "Yours?"

"I wish," the driver said. He patted the wheel. He said, "The medallion I got. And the title too, that's in my name. But I have an uncle in it for forty percent. I pay my uncle off, *then* it's my cab."

"That's good though. With family it's more flexible. You get a slow period, you defer things a little."

Avram gunned the cab around a bus. Held up his right hand. Thumb against forefinger, the money sign. "My uncle," he said. "You don't know my uncle." One-handed, he threaded a way between another cab and a stretch limo. "Drivers," he said.

"Even so," Adam said. "You have to understand. It's a new car and you *are* going to pay it off. New car, new life. Trust me." He winked at his father. "You're going to have a fleet," he said. "A monster fleet is what you're going to wind up with."

A brown plush ape swung by one arm from the rearview mirror. Plastic eyes fixed on Kreg. The radio was telling her, if the singer was singing to a woman, to hold "your warm and tender body next to mine." Too loud. Could it be turned down? Kreg asked. A little.

"No," Adam said. "That's a good song. I like it. It's like that other one, 'Help Me Make It Through the Night.' Not really like it but I always think of them together. Similar spirit there. Similar view of the world, wouldn't you think?" He winked again.

Avram turned the volume so it was barely audible. He looked up, past the dangling ape, into the mirror. Kreg looked into the mirror. He was wondering if there had been some tip-off in Adam's voice or if Avram had actually seen him winking.

"I never hear it," Avram said. "I never even notice it's on." Then he said, "My fleet. The big fleet I'm going to have."

When they got out of the cab, Adam made a fuss about paying. "These small treats," he said. "I have to watch, I have to *start* watching what I spend now. So I'll take this little thing. The Adam Kreg Memorial Treat we'll call it." He was looking at Kreg. He counted his change. "Tip," he said and handed two singles to Avram.

Kreg, in the poetry section, raised his eyes, didn't close the book. "He is born the blank mechanic of the mountains." He rubbed his thumb and forefinger over the page they held, in a gesture like the one the cabdriver had made. But flesh this time was separated from flesh by a thickness of paper. In Current Fiction, Adam was talking to a woman in a loden coat.

Kreg closed the book. Stevens, on the cover, stared into some distance. Like himself, a big heavy man. But there was that oxymoronic deep lightness of mind.

"Not sure if you remember," someone was saying. "We never actually met, not for years." Then, the man said, it had been only an introduction, at some Bar Association function. "Arthur Harris," the man said. He was neat, smallish, friendly.

"Of course," Kreg said. True, he actually did remember. And also that he'd liked the man. Hadn't he said he liked Arthur Harris when Frank Roth first mentioned him?

Harris inclined his head to see the book. Kreg turned it to show the cover. Then put it back on the shelf. He was still thinking about the poem, about getting from blankness, the condition of the *tabula rasa,* to the beneficent receptivity that was always the requisite for hope. The woman, forty feet away, was smiling at something Adam had said. Brown hair. Pretty, with amiable regular features. She pushed her hair back from her forehead. Implication of pleasant trust just in the arch of her wrist.

"Did Frank tell you," Arthur Harris said, "that we'd found a place? Signed today."

"He hadn't. He didn't say anything about that."

"Because you didn't want. . . . You wanted to stay out of all that. Just leave your office one day. Go into the new one the next. That was the instruction. He respects that. The other thing was a big office for you, someplace you could *sprawl.* He really wants to take care of you."

"I'm so badly organized," Kreg said.

Over Arthur Harris' shoulder, he saw Adam take a book from the woman's hand. Adam put the book back on a shelf without looking to see where it belonged and went on talking to her.

"It's unsettling," Arthur Harris said, "waiting for the move. I like to be dug in." His small dark neatness. He was much like Frank Roth but without Roth's edgy manner. Yes, Kreg said. It would be nice to have the move over with. Everyone would be happier when that was done.

"And they want to meet you. It's nice. All my people. All my people . . . there aren't that many of them. You hear they're only interested, that it's only the money they care about. I mean the kids. But that isn't so. A lot of respect for any real ability. Accomplishment." Harris half turned. He looked where Kreg was looking, toward Adam and the woman Adam was talking to. "You'll meet her," he said. "My wife. She'll come over in a minute."

"Adam," Kreg had to say. "My son, Adam." The woman had to be fifteen years younger than her husband. You would guess that Arthur Harris had a nice time of it with his young wife.

Harris faced away from those two. Not without willing himself to do it, Kreg thought. Then Harris was saying that he hadn't yet thanked Kreg for inscribing that copy of *The Climate of Constitutions.* Frank Roth had delivered it as promised.

"Nothing," Kreg said. "Pleasure to be asked."

"No," Arthur Harris said. "Not nothing."

"Just don't read the thing."

"Too late. I'm into it already. The fact is, again. I read it years ago."

Kreg said his book had been superseded. "New books with new material. That's what's supposed to happen."

"Not just the facts. I didn't mean only those."

Kreg considered but didn't make an argument that so many failures came precisely out of a lack of will to get at the facts. *Essential facts.* They were essential. That's what facts were. Essential. Basic. *The life of the law . . . has been experience. . . .* Everyone knew that. He said, "The new place. Where will that be?"

"You'll be happy with it. It's hardly a move at all. What we found was a larger space in the building you're in now. You'll have a longer elevator ride. Another eight floors up."

Which seemed tolerable. A big office, Arthur Harris had said. But Kreg had light from two sides where he was now. Would that change? Probably. Although he wouldn't ask about that. He'd said he wouldn't help with the move and if you disassociated yourself that way it wasn't fair to burden the workers with questions. Especially questions that might be taken as disguised requests. Nice that Frank Roth was looking after him. That Frank, to that extent, had put any resentment behind him.

"My young associates," Arthur Harris was saying. "You're going to enjoy them. Having them around. The hope of the world if that's not a dumb thing to say."

"Not dumb."

"But you dissent?"

"It's just that I don't know about the hope of the world."

They turned together when they heard the woman's voice.

She'd begun talking before they knew she was there. "We have to leave," she was saying. "I want to get out of here." A flush over her face. She wouldn't wait for Harris to introduce her. "Look," she said to both of them. "I can't. . . . Don't," she said to her husband. "Don't start anything. Please leave with me. Will you just leave now."

Fifteen yards across the store the young aficionado of new fiction was facing discreetly into a book with a green cover. Arthur Harris looked for only a moment in that direction. "Nice," he said. "That's some nice son you've got yourself." His hand was already on his wife's arm. He was already moving her, moving with her, away. Toward the exit. They would pass where Adam was standing but not close to him. They would be separated from him by half the width of the store.

"I think I fucked up a little," Adam said.

They were walking west on Fifty-seventh Street. They had stopped for a traffic light at Sixth Avenue. Adam kicked at a matchbook on the street.

"She'd be used to an ordinary light pass," Kreg said, remembering that Arthur Harris' wife was a pretty woman. "It wouldn't throw her into quite that state." *I can't,* she had said. She hadn't completed her thought. *Can't what?*

"I guess it wouldn't," Adam said after considering what Kreg had said.

"I guess not."

"Maybe a little raunchy," Adam said. "You don't want the details?"

"Exactly what you said? I don't need to know that, do I?"

"Not especially. I don't think you do." Adam bent and picked up the matchbook. Flipped it into a garbage can. "Keep our city clean," he said.

Green. Go.

When they were across from Carnegie Hall, Kreg said, "She probably told you that her husband was talking to me?"

"She might have."

"What you said to her, whatever you said, was it particularly strong because of that? *Raunchier* than your usual approach?"

"I'm having a little trouble. I don't actually follow your train of thought." Adam pulled at the lapels of his coat, adjusted the set of it on his shoulders. He said, "You would think there was some purpose to hurt you."

"I was asking you that."

"*Nevaire,*" Adam said. "*Jamais de la vie.*"

Kreg considered the image that then came into his mind. *Perfectly natural. Natural that I should think of that. The patient defeated humorous face of Adam's headmaster. The man agreeing to take Adam back into school. Knowing though, or rather certain in his mind, that Adam had done what he was accused of doing.*

You know, finally the headmaster had said (had surely felt he had to say), it isn't only that he doesn't believe in anything, ethically I mean, so much as that he refuses to. He won't. It's as if there's some associated excessive cost. Just too much to pay.

Our dear boy, Iris had said in the cab. He's not really a good one.

But there was the enduring strength of the tie. Ordained inexorably maybe by a fragile coded ribbon in the cells of his body. Some partisan genetic message that, at whatever point it might be, sparked a strong emotion to cherish. Although wouldn't there be a gene for survival that when necessary would countermand those other instructions? *Don't let him take you down.* Apparently, in his own case, that gene was weak.

What he'll do, the headmaster had said, once in a while he'll toss out, throw at us in a sense, some scrap to show us how much he knows and how much he doesn't care that he does.

I've heard him do that.

We get them sometimes. Very smart and self-destructive. . . . It's as if they know some essential secret that privileges them to act that way. Of course, there isn't any secret, and life catches up with them and they really don't do very well.

Unless they change.

I always try to believe that's possible, the headmaster said.

Adam wheeled and stopped. "Tell me," he said. "Can you remember numbers?" He explained about the attaché case with the combination lock. "I mean it would be awful wouldn't it if you met Van Atta for the big exchange and nobody could get the mother open? Have to borrow a chisel from the janitor. No dignity to that. So try to remember it: 9-8-1."

"But couldn't you write it down? Put it on a piece of paper when you give me the suitcase?"

"I never thought of that."

"Really not?"

"Only a joke," Adam said.

Kreg, not knowing (not able to know) how close Adam's story was to its end, but even so, with the action itself eventually to regret, struck out. Started, even with his hand in midair, to pull the blow, but couldn't totally check his motion. His open hand, at the completion of its short arc of strike, touched lightly against Adam's right cheek. . . . No provocation, not in anything that Adam had just then said. *Then why did I do it?*

Adam danced, feinted. Jabbed twice at nothing. He brought his right into the air six inches from Kreg's belly. "So watch it," he said. "Don't ever cross me, Black Bart. I lose control and use my killer fists." He stopped. "Listen," he said. "Fun, you know. Great evening. The chow, everything. All of it. But I have to go now. South into the obscure lanes of the Village." He saw a cab. "That one," he said. "Avram's cousin, I bet."

Cartons of books on the floor and next to them other books in stacks. The books in the other rooms had been put back on their shelves and except for what was here in front of him the apartment seemed more or less as it had been.

New paint on the walls and no doubt a fresher look. But where was the change if you hadn't noticed before that it was dingy? Although there was a change here. And it was significant although not apparent. It was a change at law, in legal relations. What Kreg had owned outright, he'd soon be holding under the terms of a mortgage loan. This place would be pledged and also his country home. He'd be twice a mortgagor.

Because Van Atta had imposed certain conditions that would cost.

Van Atta had been perfectly willing to talk on the telephone.

"I'm in touch with him," Kreg had said. He was too abrupt because he was unsure of the conventions here. How did you talk to people like this? about matters like this? Should there be easy chatter about beatings, maimings? And about whatever crookedness was behind those things?

Van Atta led him gently. "And he has it? He has the package?"

"He doesn't think he should keep it."

A moment then before Van Atta said, "When would he want to return the thing?"

"You could pick it up from me. I'd need a day, a half day."

That was good, Van Atta said. But not tomorrow. The day after, he'd fly in. Look over the stuff and they were done. Ten minutes. It was a good decision, he said, because that merchandise wasn't right for the fellow's life-style. "In my judgment he couldn't of afforded it. Not over any period of time."

Kreg said there was something more to this. There was the matter Van Atta had once raised about a penalty clause.

"What I can't tell you," Van Atta said. "I can't tell you that won't be. There's no way just to wipe out the past like it never happened."

But this was a condition, Kreg said. He was beginning to be more comfortable in this conversation. This was what was sometimes called a condition absolute. The penalty would have to be recalculated in dollars. That could be done, couldn't it? Almost always in his experience.

Van Atta said, "I don't think the guy has the dollars."

"He has a friend."

"It would be heavy. The amount, I mean."

"The friend assumed that."

"Then you take a percent of the value of the merchandise, one hundred percent," Van Atta said.

Kreg said, "If you could give me something realistic."

"You don't understand," Van Atta said. "It's like you told me about the condition absolute. Not to negotiate. There's no negotiating here, none at all."

"Then yes. All right." Kreg didn't even think about it.

"Maybe you should sleep on it," Van Atta said. "It's the custom, you wouldn't know about it. . . . You say yes and I take you up on that, then you owe. You're on the hook for all of it. He drops into some dark hole with the merchandise and you still have to come up with it. For the merchandise and the penalty both. So don't, maybe don't be so quick with yes."

"Yes," Kreg said.

"Then it's yes. Your call. I got to accept what you tell me. Also, you know, it's only cash. It's always a cash transaction."

Ridiculously, Kreg's mind was already calculating the tax he would owe on the sale of his securities. And how much for his prints? his porcelains? Bare walls if it came to that. Less clutter on the tables. He was looking at the oxblood vase Deane had touched. Mouse Kelly would write a check. Never ask what it was for or when he'd get it back. Mouse would write the check, *if asked.* But he wouldn't be asked. *Nevaire.* "The penalty," Kreg said. "That part can't be covered immediately."

No answer at first. Then, "Tell me about time. You need how much time?"

Kreg was using the phone in the living room. George Grosz on the wall across from him. A fat man eyeing a thin woman with a poodle. How much for a Grosz? Kreg's fingertips touched the table with the oxblood vase. How much? . . . Although it might not be necessary to sell these things. He thought of his cousin. Marvin, the former real-estate tycoon. The present bankrupt. By now they were both of them to have been rich. *Have to raise an unexpected million. Not a problem. Don't even think about it.* Four hundred, he said to Van Atta. Or close to it. A week from tomorrow.

"Three fifty sure?"

Kreg tried to remember the value of his account at his last statement. Over three eighty. Probably a little more. Three eighty-five he said to Van Atta would be a safe figure. He said that for the balance of the money he would be mortgaging his home . . . both homes. How long would that take? He couldn't give a date. Not long.

"Cash?" Van Atta said. "You're able to get cash?"

"Only from my bank."

"I thought. Well that's no good, is it? You don't want it that way and I don't want it that way. Start a lot of questions. So what if I introduce you to somebody? The guy'll process it for you. There's a service charge but he's reliable."

"The service charge?"

"That's two percent. I think I can say that. Usually, someone new like you, an outsider, it would be more than that. Three and a half, four. But the guy is a friend of a friend. He would want to accommodate me. So two."

"And not negotiable?"

"Sure it's negotiable. Up is the way he'd negotiate. Like I said, he would want to be helpful to me."

Why, though? Why would I impoverish myself for him? A man over thirty. I don't know him anymore. I know that he's dishonest, shifty. This also would have to be agreed, he said to Van Atta. Once the original item was returned, from that moment, the penalty clause was suspended. *Impoverished. That was self-pitying. Not really true. A million, though. I'll be paying him a million of mine in cash plus the other million from Adam.* Actually, more than that. Twenty thousand to Van Atta's money changer. And the four that Adam had spent.

Kreg thought about the prep school upstate. These days there were no telephone calls from his cousin. Eight units had sold in the first unit to be converted. That was before the project had foundered. You would imagine those tenant owners. Mostly retirees from New York. An enclave of them in a strange place. He thought also about the slow erosion of unseeded embankments and the gradual disappearance by theft or reclamation of whatever stacks of bricks, lumber, iron rod had given the place at least the illusion of hope associated with any functioning construction site. . . . There would be an ongoing storm of subpoenas and injunctions. *My eight hundred thousand. If I had that money, I'd have most of what I'll need for Van Atta.* About the penalty, he said. That would have to be canceled from the time of the original payment.

"Suspended," Van Atta said. "It could be suspended for a reasonable time. Then later, after the final payment, it's off for good. . . . You have to understand, I would rather not have to put on, invoke, that other kind of remedy. Do my business in the normal quiet way. Anyone would prefer that." The day after tomorrow, Van Atta said. In the evening. Was that good? Around nine?

"My apartment," Kreg said. He started to give Van Atta the address.

"I know where it is. Tell me something. Now it's a deal. There's no taking it back. But are you sure you should of done this for him? Committed yourself that much?"

Van Atta had given the impression of a genuine and regretful concern. What puzzled Kreg later, thinking about the man's comment, was his own impulse to respond. *I don't know. I can't tell you that.* Some such reply. But he'd checked himself and he hadn't. "Nine o'clock," he'd said again. "I'll be alone."

"Only the two of us," Van Atta had said. "That's the best way."

Kreg, in the lined chinos and flannel shirt that he wore in the winter, began to look through some of his books. He was in a low chair and whatever he wanted was always just out of reach. He puffed a little from the effort of stretching. There were books he'd had for thirty years. He moved to the floor and sprawled like an awkward child. *Maine's Ancient Law* there and *A History of Tammany Hall.* He wanted to read something. . . . He would be able to stop thinking about Van Atta. He was sure of that. But he knew also that he would not be able to stop thinking about Adam. He picked up a novel that he remembered nothing about, only the cover and where he'd read it.

He had been on a beach. That he did remember. The far eastern end of Fire Island and almost no houses there. None in sight. He was a young man. Alone. Hot summer sun but a dry day with a breeze and the perfect clear light and the bright reflections off the water. The breeze ruffled clumps of beach grass. Pale green blades with serrated edges. Everything spare, bone-spare. No human sign.

But two weeks later, after Adam's attaché case (with forty-one-hundred missing dollars replenished by Kreg) had been returned to Van Atta and after Kreg had sold his securities and paid over that money also, Adam was dead. He was killed in the wet snow outside Kreg's country house by the man whose head he'd smashed. Nate Hobart tried to help him and Nate and the black shepherd were killed. Nate killed Hans Kalb. So they were dead, all four of them.

Kreg drove north with Iris and Etkind Rossoff. At the prosecutor's office he told a detective and the young district attorney only that Adam had lived away from New York for some years and had recently returned. He said that Adam had never mentioned Hans Kalb or discussed any connections to Latin America. He said he'd never heard of a man named Isidore Frankel. He didn't say anything about an attaché case with the combination set for 9-8-1. He was asked about it but said he'd never seen it or hadn't noticed it.

A sandy-haired man who stayed in the back of the room asked about Karl Van Atta. Kreg caught the trace of a Southern accent; he said he'd talked with Van Atta several times when Adam had taken an apparently unauthorized vacation but nothing after that. He really said only that Adam had appeared troubled and uncertain of his plans . . . and uncommunicative about his recent past.

Everyone was solicitous of his feelings and after a short time he was excused with apologies for having troubled him . . . for having had to. Iris and Rossoff were outside in a waiting room and weren't asked about anything.

Then there was the fifteen-minute drive to Kreg's house. He drove with Iris sitting next to him and Etkind Rossoff in the back. Iris looked out of the window on her side. Kreg saw, in the rearview mirror, Rossoff looking down at his hands. Nobody talked. Kreg took a back road that ran first on a diagonal off the direct route and then parallel to it. A sudden curve that he should have remembered but hadn't. He horsed the big Chevrolet into the turn. *That's what I have, he'd told Nate Hobart, a U.S.-made station wagon. That's what I told my neighbor, who was involved in this by me and is now dead because of that . . . as Iris or Rossoff might have been killed helping me.*

After a while they were on a ridge and Kreg could look ahead and to one side over the countryside. Now in the winter, with no leaves on the trees, the system of roads that linked one place to another (places he knew) was a completely apparent structure. Nothing to impede his view. And sound would carry. *Gunshots. The sounds, first of Kalb's .38, and then of Nate's shotgun. Wouldn't those sounds have carried? Then, after you had heard them and decided where they were from, how long before you made a call? How long before someone was there? How long had it actually been? Long enough of course.*

There was another sharp turn and then a long meadow. First Nate Hobart's place and then Kreg's. The cars were still in his driveway, the rented car that Adam had used and a tan Mercedes. The owner of the general store at the crossroads that comprised the town had described a man like Kalb. A man with an accent who had driven up in a car like that, parked carelessly, throwing wet dirt in his sudden stop, half blocked the driveway and pushed ahead of a customer in his rush to get directions for Kreg's house.

The house was at a bend in the road and as you came up to it there was a good oblique view that took in its front and near side and most of the yard back out to the barn. It was a white building with black shutters, just pre-Civil War but still in the Federal style. And the barn was red. All classic colors. Common.

Kreg pulled up behind the other cars. He got out and walked in the slushy snow that stayed on the ground all winter. He walked around to the back of the house. Adam had fallen here. This was where they'd found his body. Kreg knew as much about that as the police did. He'd forced the information from them.

That's only details, the detective said. What do you need that for?

Tell me, Kreg said.

The detective, almost Kreg's own age, said to put all this out of his mind. Some things, it's better not to know them.

Just tell me.

So he knew where Adam had died and he knew that Nate Hobart and Nate's black shepherd and a man named Hans Kalb had been found close to each other, almost in a heap, around the far side of the house. Kalb. *My customer, Van Atta had said.*

The whole area was scuffed. There were the footprints of the dead and the police. And surely the curious who had followed after them. But in one place the snow was completely gone. This seemed to be an area of convergence. Exactly here, Kreg guessed. Facedown in a fetal crouch. Hands to the chest and stomach. Face unmarked, only becoming pale from the cold and the loss of the blood that drained down toward the ruined middle.

Kreg looked back toward his car. Rossoff had gotten out and was standing next to the front door on the passenger side, not exactly watching him. Iris was still inside.

A maple between the house and barn with a wagon wheel bolted to the tree. Kreg walked to that. The wheel had been an early toy, something for the boy to spin. But there was always rust and it never did move freely. Kreg touched his hand to the iron rim, feeling the place where the pitted metal met the wood it bound. There were still traces of yellow-brown paint, the original color of the wheel.

The headmaster's hand had moved over a thin religious cheek. Heavy blue shadow of his scraped beard over the fine bones. Yes, he's clever, the headmaster said. Sometimes he'll come up with something he can hold in front of the others . . . original enough to let them know that, whatever he might have said, they couldn't have thought of it. Hunting prints on the walls. The hand stopped. Long fingers splayed now over the back of the man's neck. Early gray hair. It's always done, he said, in a way to let them know he doesn't value his own thought. He'd just as soon throw it away. . . . It's as if he's outraged by his own mind, the headmaster said.

Kreg kicked against a splitting wedge. Triangular piece of iron. Leave it out all winter, that didn't matter, but what was it doing here? He had two or three of them. He picked up the wedge and carried it to the barn. Pulled open the big door that was never locked and tossed the wedge on the dirt floor near a stacked row of firewood. Of course he was remembering back to Adam's fall against such a wedge, this one or another. And the blood-covered toddler's face. Adam wasn't even trying to wipe the blood from his eyes. There was only the child's frightened angry bawl straight up toward the orange sun.

Wet now, coming in through his shoes. He went into the barn and looked around, although with no focus to his mind. Nothing in particular that he wanted or wanted to see. A scythe, his mower, shovels, the beams and rafters themselves. Those things were all neutral in his imagination. "Brandt," he said. "You started this." No foreknowledge that those words were coming. No knowledge why he'd said them.

When he went out and pulled the door shut behind him, the iron pulley wheels and track that guided them screamed against each other in the gray cold.

On the other side of the house, pale morning sun started to warm him. He wasn't moving and there was no wind to draw off the accumulating heat. He made a picture in his mind. Nate would have fallen *here* and Hans Kalb *there.* Nate's black shepherd next to his enemy, so also there. Kreg turned his face to the sun. Then he looked toward Nate Hobart's house. What was it the old man had heard? A pistol shot or maybe some scream from Adam. He'd have gone immediately for the shotgun. Take a moment to check it, find shells. Cursing his half-crippled fingers and his lousy eyes. Then he was telling the dog to *Come on. Stay with me, goddammit.*

Rossoff and Iris came around the corner of the house and stood next to him. Iris had waterproof boots but Rossoff's city shoes, like Kreg's, were already soaked. The leather took on a dull matte look when it was wet through that way. Iris asked if he wanted to go into the house. But why would he? Nothing had happened there. When Kreg didn't answer her, she took his arm. She began to move him.

He stopped again at the place where he imagined Adam to have died. He was certain it had happened exactly here. *He fell here and in this position.* Some small tight heavy thing in his stomach began to expand up through his body. He went absolutely still. He refused to conceive of himself as a big disheveled middle-aged man crying.

"Maybe," Iris said "maybe I'll drive back."

"I'll drive."

"No," she said. "I know you can. You're capable, but I want to drive."

Etkind Rossoff looked from one to the other of them. Not willing, at this unrepublican moment, to vote. Also puzzled, it might be, by the ultimate diseconomy of any opinion he could offer . . . its blank deadengine inefficiency as a means of moving events (this event) even the smallest further distance.

There was the sound of a motor. The special sound of an uncertain driver simultaneously racing the machine and holding it back. One foot on the accelerator and one on the brake.

Kreg went around to that side of the house.

His station wagon blocked the driveway so the blue car that was moving slowly toward him was mostly on the lawn, the wheels on one side chewing into the wet grass there.

The car stopped and he went to the driver's side. It was a thin-faced man of eighty with his wife next to him. A local. Probably, Kreg thought, from one of the farming families of the area. A face he knew. He'd seen it from time to time at the general store or at the lumberyard. Here and there.

The man had stopped the engine.

Kreg imagined his actions now.

He walked to the car. Leaned against it. Did you want to come in? he said.

The old man cleared his throat. He had a little pipe and he chewed convulsively on that. He made some unintelligible sound and looked quickly at his wife who stared in front of her.

No, Kreg said. Come in. Look over the scene. You can see where it happened. It's too cold for a picnic but you could walk around a little. He peered into the car, looked down. You have those warm boots. Not Mrs. though. We don't want her catching cold.

I'm sorry. . . . Barely uttered by the old man in his angry embarrassment.

Don't be sorry. Kreg swept into a mannered gesture of eighteenth-century welcome. He bent at the right knee with the left foot extended. He extended his left hand, palm up, the right crooked behind him. Avanti.

Of course not. Not actually. He didn't say or do those things. There was only his thick awkward and humorless elephantine self. Blinking into the old man's car, not willing to give away even so much as the sense of his outrage at this piddling intrusion. Showing nothing. Not that it would have mattered. He was certain there was no significance to any of his actions. . . . Nothing. Only himself staring down at the old man.

The old man who finally turned the key. And nothing happened because he'd left the car in gear. He wasn't looking at Kreg but he wasn't concentrating on what he was doing either. He kept turning the key and hitting the gas. When he finally did get started he backed out too quickly without looking behind him. After the car was in the road the woman turned her head and began to speak to him.

Only when the squarish sedan was some distance down the road would Kreg, if he had ever assumed that courtly bent-kneed posture, have straightened from it. *Although I could put out a chair. Now that my yard has become a public space, I could sit impassively and wait for the curious to show. Sell my recollections like Sitting Bull in his later years.*

The car receded and then was out of view. What began to surprise him was his sense of how quickly the final shape of his life had begun to reveal itself . . . like a sculpture accelerating its own shaped progress out of stone. Almost certainly he was going to wind up with little and would have to guard particularly against self-pity. The outburst against Brandt a few moments ago in the barn, that had been a weak man's way at a time of stress to put a claim on the strongest person he'd known.

There was certainly some surge toward form . . . and a sense of speed.

The last scene of this drama that had ended with the death of his son . . . when had that actually begun? Pick a start point. Maybe it had been when he'd called Van Atta. And they made their arrangements and Van Atta came to his apartment.

"Man to see you," the doorman said. "He says you expect him." The voice came over the old intercom in Kreg's building, distorted by an accompanying medley of echoes, crepitations, sputterings.

When Van Atta came out of the elevator he held the door for a moment and turned to say good night to some passenger still inside. Kreg heard the response, the cracked dry voice, not totally in control of its own breath, of a fairly old woman. And the whiny yelps of the spoiled tiny dogs. It was the fat lady with the yorkies.

Van Atta in his cashmere coat might have been a successful salesman of retirement condos arrived to close on a two-bedroom unit with a good view of the sixteenth hole.

"Very nice," he said when he came into the apartment.

Kreg hadn't considered in advance his obligation in these circumstances. He hadn't thought of himself as host here. He was somewhat surprised to hear his voice suggesting maybe a whisky. Something else? Whatever Van Atta would like.

"Yes," Van Atta said. He had the appearance of a man who always knew how things should be done and took care to see they were right. "Bourbon," he said. "Do you have bourbon?"

Kreg made the drink and a scotch for himself. His hands shook a little when he poured the drinks. *I have this man, he was thinking, in my apartment and I am acting the host for him.* He went inside and came back with the attaché case. He fumbled, thickfingered, at the scored brass wheel of the lock. 9-8-1. He told Van Atta to make a note of the combination. He had the case on a small table that also held a Canton ginger jar, shells, a geode and minuscule pre-Columbian heads and fragments. Also a Tiffany frame with a photograph of his parents.

They both, Kreg and Van Atta, looked at the banded stacks of bills.

"There's no room here," Kreg said. "I'll move this so you can count the bills."

"I'll assume," Van Atta said. "I'll assume it's all there."

"You mean you'll stipulate. So if there's blank paper under the top bills, it still counts as a million?"

"I would take the chance if you tell me it's all there."

"You'd lose," Kreg said. He took an envelope from his inside jacket pocket. "This isn't there. It's forty-one hundred dollars. Also I'd rather count."

"If you say."

Kreg took the open case into the dining room and put it down on the big table he so rarely used. He gave the envelope to Van Atta. "That first," he said. "Then we can do the attaché case."

It took some time to count one million dollars.

From time to time, Van Atta sipped courteously at his drink. Before he left he gave Kreg a typed list. Names with amounts next to them. "The money from the securities," he said. "When you get that, you run it through your account and you make out the checks the way it says here. It's six of them and it adds to three eighty-five. Three eighty-five, that's what you said you were getting?"

"Yes," Kreg said. "Three eighty-five." He read the list of payees. The first item was for seventy-four thousand two hundred forty-six dollars and eighteen cents. There was one for over one hundred eight thousand and one of only nineteen-odd. He asked, what was the Charleston Recreational Transport Company?

"I don't know," Van Atta said. "Why would we care? . . . Those new bills," he said. "I don't like handling them. That flat chalky feel they have."

A week later Kreg's broker wired funds to his bank and Kreg wrote the six checks. For the first time in thirty years he owned no securities. He felt briefly as if he were floating away from something.

He had to see someone on Park Avenue and then he went to meet Van Atta.

Through a fine dust that wasn't quite snow he walked (with his mind not particularly at that moment on burdens) past the bronze Atlas of Rockefeller Center and west on Fiftieth Street into the RCA building. Van Atta was looking up at the murals. Workers of the thirties with caps and rolled sleeves. The strong shapes behind them of industrial buildings, smokestacks, heavy machines. "Interesting," he said. "As I understand it, the old man, John D., didn't know what he was buying."

"No," Kreg said. "There were other murals here before these. He found out about the artist's politics and he replaced them with what you're looking at." Kreg wondered, how did a man like Van Atta come to know, even inaccurately, the history of the murals Diego Rivera had made for John D. Rockefeller? But he reminded himself that he was in the presence of the enemy. He touched his breast pocket on the left side. He could give the checks to Van Atta now, he said. There was really no reason for him to go along for the exchange.

Van Atta considered this. "I can see your point," he said. "But that's not the way you do it."

He took Kreg, through the flurry, to a building on West Forty-eighth Street. It was mostly diamond and jewelry merchants there but the sign outside the office they went to read ATTORNEY-AT-LAW. No name, though. Under that in smaller letters it read *Tax Planning* and then *Consultant.*

The man in the office was only fairly heavy but you got a sense of the actual fat under the skin, the yellow fat itself. He had black hair as coarse as an Indian's. "You wouldn't remember," the man said to Van Atta, "but years ago we met once before in person. With the guy from Rochester."

"Oh, I remember," Van Atta said.

"Anyway I'm glad I can help you. Friend of his."

"It was good of him to set it up," Van Atta said. "I appreciate it." He said now if Kreg had those checks . . .

The heavy man examined the envelope Kreg gave him and then took another envelope from his desk. He met Kreg's eyes for a moment and gave that to him.

"Do we count it?" Kreg said.

"No," Van Atta said. "Not from the banker." He smiled politely at the man.

"Then three eighty-five," Kreg said when he passed the money to Van Atta.

"Less two percent," Van Atta said.

"That's seventy-seven hundred," the lawyer said. He saw them to the door and shook hands with Van Atta.

"Not always the nicest people," Van Atta said when they were on the street.

Kreg reminded him that from now on Adam was to be free. He'd be able to move around and he wouldn't be molested. Kreg would call Van Atta when the mortgages closed. *Free, he thought. Not exactly.*

"Like we agreed," Van Atta said. This time he was the one who tapped his breast pocket. "I tell you though. It was me, I don't know I'd of done it. I don't think I would."

The year turned. Adam came uptown for a talk. He was thinking more and more that Boston might be the place. That was an idea he couldn't get out of his head. Of course he would need a stake, they both knew that, and he didn't want to be making a series of small touches. Ten thousand they agreed and Kreg got the money in a few days. He could still manage on that scale.

Adam didn't want to move back into the apartment on West End Avenue. He liked it in the Village and Etkind Rossoff didn't mind him staying there. So why not? It wouldn't anyway be for very long.

Kreg had an early dinner with Rossoff at a delicatessen restaurant on West Seventy-second Street. He began to speak to Rossoff, not about Rossoff's hospitality to Adam of today but about the refuge he'd provided in the recent past . . . about risk willingly assumed.

Rossoff began to listen to him. Then he held up his hand. "No," he said. "No, no, no." He called a waiter and ordered for them. Matzo-ball soup for both of them and then for him, Rossoff said, a corned-beef sandwich. Brisket for the other gentleman. "Not so quick with the sandwiches," he said. "Wait till we finish the soup. . . . Your son," he said to Kreg. "He thinks he's having a good time. He goes out. He sleeps late."

"He says you don't mind him there."

"No trouble to me. But he acts like a rich boy. Is that so good for him?"

Kreg asked about Boston. Had Adam said anything about going up there?

"Why should he leave? It's nice for him where he is." What seemed odd, Rossoff said, was that Adam had made no move to communicate with California. He had a girl there and his apartment and his things. Wouldn't there be some feeling that you should get back to your own place?

Maybe, Kreg said, Adam had been in touch. Maybe Rossoff didn't know about it.

"Possible but I don't think so. I bet you not."

The waiter came with their soup. Rossoff rubbed the bowl of his spoon with his napkin. He examined the spoon and then began to eat. "Hot," he said. "I always want my soup so hot."

Kreg was thinking that Rossoff was probably right. Most likely Adam just didn't think anymore about his California connections . . . as if he'd never had them. Adam had always been able to walk away from any tie that didn't, right at the time, suit his needs. Nothing allowed to rub, chafe or pull. Abandonment was a technique that would always allow him to maintain some essential lightness of tread.

I do that too. Except I don't leave. I push people away. The result's no different. . . . We really have something of a family history in that regard. Which you don't know about. We leave, abandon, reject.

At eight or nine years old, for example. Kreg's father had been stuck with him that Sunday afternoon. Kreg remembered it being a raw day in the fall or winter. They waited on the corner and then a car came for them. There was just room for his father to squeeze into the back. Kreg was half on his father's knees, half standing. He knew some of the men in the car. One of them asked his father if Philip was old enough to gamble.

They drove across the Queensboro Bridge. The steel grid of the road made the car vibrate when you rode over it. You could feel the vibrations up through your body (or was that the remembered surface of some other bridge? Some other ride?). Almost no traffic in those days on a winter Sunday.

And then the Piranesi spaces of Queens Plaza where they parked. Tracks of the el overhead, stairways leading to the tracks. All shadows and wind. An empty place with sometimes a sheet of newspaper blown from here to there. Maybe yesterday's *Sun* or *Journal-American* or *World-Telegram.*

One of the men owned a building there. He had the keys to a restaurant or cafeteria that was out of business or closed for the day. The men went inside for their card game. They were pinochle players. Kreg's father said for him to play outside. Or he could sit in the car if he wanted.

It was as if the space of the plaza were expanded infinitely because there was no one in it. Streets led out into a wastescape of unpopulated structures that were only structures. No other imaginable function, no notion or possibility of habitation or use. And some open lots with thin tufts of yellow grass where the paving was cracked.

On the far side of the plaza there had been a billboard of a young woman in a red dress. The dress was whipped against her body by wind. She had one hand raised to hold her hair in place. Her legs were together, knees bent a little. A leash was wound around her legs. A white puppy with black spots was running in circles around her.

Kreg didn't now remember what it was that the billboard had advertised. And didn't say anything to Rossoff about abandonment. He did say that Adam fairly soon would no doubt make a move.

Rossoff shook pepper into his soup. "Why?" he said. He tilted his head a little, partly closed his eyes. Beginnings of a smile that could turn into a Viennese kid's grin (an expression out of a tradition of punning and weak empires). "Why would he do that?"

"He seems to want to make a start."

"Seems," Rossoff said. "You want that. You want him to want it. Maybe he doesn't want it." He put down the pepper shaker. "He thinks you do it with mirrors," he said. "He wants to start at the top." Rossoff's head went to the side again. "I told you, he thinks he's a rich man's son."

"That's possible," Kreg said. But there was no blame he was thinking because now it was as if it had been Adam there in Queens Plaza almost fifty years ago. And that seemed a total mitigation of whatever lies and evasions and petty selfishnesses followed.

He'd had no book with him or even a ball to bounce against the side of a building. By late afternoon it was already getting dark. Once in a while a train, a series of purple (and later purple-black) boxes, would come into the station. Rectangles of light in the chain of boxes but no sense that actual persons were in them or came in and out of them.

Sometimes after a train had left the station a figure would come down one of the stairways. But those figures were always dark and seen only in outline. None of them came toward him. They always turned into one of the streets leading away from the plaza. A few times he went into the restaurant and watched from a distance the table where the men were playing cards. There was a bottle of whisky on the table. And glasses and packs of cigarettes. After a while his father would say it was too smoky in there. Wouldn't he want to go outside and breathe some decent air. Once he ignored the hint and stayed and one of the other men, a big man with a belly, the one who had been driving the car, turned in his chair to stare at him and then he went outside. He was wearing corduroy knickers. That time of year the insides of his thighs were always chafed from the cheap coarse fabric. The material was standard for those pants, a dark brown with flecks of black.

Fairly late on, after it was solidly dark, there was someone real outside. Philip had moved away from the restaurant toward the corner, which was as far as he dared to go. There was nothing that he heard behind him or was aware that he heard. But he did turn suddenly. And the figure was there. The man was coming in his direction. He was heavy, bent. He had a crooked leg. He was carrying some kind of bundle. He was coming, not down one of the streets leading into the plaza, but along the perimeter of the plaza itself. He would go past the restaurant and then to the corner where Philip was standing. *And the man might have been closer to the restaurant than Philip was. The man might have gotten there first and cut him off from safety.* Philip knew he would not be able to get back. There was some drain at his knees and through the bones of his lower legs. *He would not be able to move his legs.* Then he began to run.

This time when he was inside his father didn't tell him to go out. He looked at his watch and told Philip where the men's room was. He also said there was a water tap behind the counter and there were water glasses there.

Maybe Adam was not in some essential way able to move his legs, as it were. Kreg didn't say that. Rossoff finished his soup and ate slices of rye bread and pumpernickel with butter. He finished his cole slaw before the sandwiches were brought. Kreg said, "You don't mind him there? He says you don't."

"Once in a while," Rossoff said, "it's not so bad to have somebody around."

"Family meals. Talk around the table."

"Not so much. He's out. He comes and goes. The meals were before he could go out. That was when Iris was coming down to take the messages."

Kreg didn't want to seem to be asking for information. He finally said he'd assumed she still went down to Jane Street.

"No," Rossoff said. "Not since he's able to go on the streets."

"It was a useful arrangement."

"Why would she keep coming down there?" Rossoff said. They had their sandwiches now and he began to eat. Rapid precise bites. He didn't speak while he was eating. Usually they talked all through the meal. Rossoff was normally a talker in what Kreg thought of as the manner of the traditional European café or coffee-house intellectual. It was true they had never discussed how it was with the diminutive chain-smoker and women. How would it be? Rossoff worked almost through the night and drank cheap brandy. And had an aphorist's taste for controversy. But also a logger's big hands, long broad-tipped fingers. Possibly there was some corresponding largeness of the sexual organ or appetite. Kreg had seen a horror clip of a naked Jew in the camps. No meat left on the frame. This had been frontal and there was only bone and the absurd thick dangling flesh of the cock and what it represented that would surely be the first part of the body to come fully alive if the body lived. Rossoff had not been in a camp. He had gotten out before the final sweeps. On the other hand, there had never been any mention of family.

So then what message from the instrument to the imagination during those weeks when Iris was at his apartment every evening? The long legs and the easy pelvic swing. A woman who could smoke with him or let it be. Always some hard or humorous challenge in her manner. Rossoff must have speculated about the possibility of converting challenge to invitation . . . and then considered the mirrored image he sometimes saw. Also of course there was the question of Iris' relations with his friend Philip Kreg, a question of appropriateness or even loyalty.

And some weeks later, after that delicatessen dinner, after the death of his son, Kreg, with no afterview in his mind of the aged intruders' incongruously baby-blue automobile, watched down the curved length of the totally empty road along which their car had gone. Now he was really looking at nothing.

He walked out onto the road and looked both ways. There was nothing he was looking at.

Then an urgent fullness in his groin and he started back up the driveway. Iris and Etkind Rossoff were already in the car. Iris had not set herself in the driver's seat.

Kreg went behind the barn where it was totally isolated. Even so he faced the barn wall to piss. He hadn't wanted to go in the house and anyway couldn't have used it for this because there was no water. The pipes had been drained for the winter. Nate Hobart had arranged that for him. The snow was deeper here. Kreg got a small load of it over the top of one shoe. He shook himself and zipped up. Something about a free leak over his own land. Of course that land was (already in his mind and soon to be in law) less absolutely his than it had been. His ownership was going to be encumbered by a mortgage that would have no purpose at all except to create the burden of its own repayment because the loan it evidenced no longer had a purpose. The money would go to Van Atta. He didn't question that. He knew what he would say and he knew Van Atta's response. Trained mind of the lawyer.

The agreement was that he would not be harmed. You covenanted that.

My people. Not me. Not anybody under my control. Your words. You said it. This guy went out of control. But he wasn't mine.

Van Atta would make his points reasonably and regretfully. That he was no insurer against injustice. And that he wasn't collecting a windfall here. Kreg would certainly understand that Hans Kalb had *associates.* And they weren't going to walk away from the money. They considered themselves entitled. *Latins,* he might say as if that meant something.

But this conversation would not take place. Because Kreg was not going to initiate it. He was not going to claim or bargain. Just pay. What he found extraordinary was the realization that he actually wanted to pay. He wanted to divest himself, to give over the money. He wanted most specifically to pay it to Van Atta . . . who was the *claimant* here. Kreg leaned forward. He extended his arms and pressed his hands with their splayed fingers against the wall of the barn. Thin wash of red paint almost faded into the siding. He turned his head to the right and pressed his left cheek against the old wood. After a while his body stopped shaking.

He began to walk back to the car. He stepped around his compost heap and decided not to come back here. He would sell the place and take whatever equity was left. Somebody else could clear it out for him, auction off the contents and give away what didn't go. He'd offer real estate with a house. Not furnished.

And not to be replaced.

Kreg thought of himself as he had been moments ago with his arms out, pressed to the barn wall. Soaked wood and that flat wash paint against his face and hands.

He had put in apple trees along the downward slope of land behind the barn. No last looks. As things are real in the world, that view could remain real in his imagination. That would be fine. Whatever had actually happened was fine. Just no long looks back. A limit to *la nostalgie.* For example, he'd fixed a persistent leak in the downstairs toilet and then started to replace the rotten floorboards next to it. He probed the wood with a screwdriver. A soft crumble wherever he jabbed. Even the joists underneath were gone and the job became a project that needed the professional help he refused to call. Why shouldn't he remember that?

Before he got in the car he kicked mud off his shoes.

Ten minutes down the road he pulled in at a restaurant.

"Oh yes," Iris said when she knew where they were.

She knew the place. Everybody up here knew it. Family-owned. Pizzas, hamburgers, but also a steak if you wanted. A real menu and middle-aged waitresses, with sometimes a bandage over a varicosed calf, who took an interest and remembered their customers. They tried to make it nice for you.

"If we could get a drink," Iris said.

For a while when Adam was small this place had been a favorite. It was where they stopped on a Friday night going to the country. Adam always wanted pizza. They didn't sell it here by the slice so Kreg would order a whole one for the table. He and Adam would finish what they could. Susan would take one slice. She'd nibble at that and at some point would catch the waitress' eye. Maybe, she'd say. Maybe she'd have another martini. Kreg was never able, he knew, to keep a truly neutral expression. *Possibly, just this once, it isn't going to hit her. Possibly we will finish our meal and her speech will remain crisp. Unslurred.* Adam was alert as a faun to Susan's evasive withdrawal, Kreg's fury and despair. But later he might be sleepy. Sometimes Kreg had to carry him to the car.

After Susan left, Kreg and Adam would stop here alone. Once in a while, going back on a Sunday evening, they would rendezvous with Iris. When Adam was older they joked about the pizza but they always ordered it for him. That had become a ritual, a joke and a ritual.

Kreg now said he'd have a scotch. Bourbon for Iris and Rossoff said red wine. Chianti. Did they have Chianti?

"Does a goat eat tin cans?" the waitress said.

When they had their drinks, Kreg put his hand around his glass. He had the intolerable thought that some people on an occasion like this would gently clink glasses and toast the memory of the dear dead boy.

Rossoff cleared his throat. He noted that it was already late for lunch but you weren't looking at very many empty tables. And there was still a flow of orders coming out of the kitchen. "So they have a pretty good business here?"

"Yes," Kreg said. "They always have. . . . Haven't they?" he said to Iris.

"The place is a standby up here," she said.

"Good food," Rossoff said. "I guess it's always good?"

"Not really," Iris said. "I wouldn't say so."

"You said a standby?"

"Well there didn't used to be anyplace else around. Maybe people got used to coming here."

Kreg said, "I didn't ask when they'd release the body." They were in a high-backed wooden booth. He was next to Iris on one side with Rossoff across from him. The booths were wide with space for two people to sit comfortably apart from each other. He was glad of that. Right now he didn't want to be close to anybody. He said, "I want to have some kind of service for him."

Rossoff examined the salt shaker. "I can find out for you," he said. "I'll call up there in the morning." He put the salt shaker down and picked up a bottle of A.1. sauce. He was looking at the label. "But I think there's plenty of time," he said.

Iris said that was probably true. Yes, she said. Something in the way of a service. She was crying a little and made no effort to wipe the tears from her cheeks.

"I don't know who to ask," Kreg said. "That girl in California. I don't know if he kept up with anybody from school."

"His mother," Iris said.

"Of course," Kreg said. "But it won't be a crowd, will it?" He said to excuse him for a minute. In the men's room he washed his hands and face and then cupped more water in the palm of one hand and put that awkwardly to the back of his neck. When he came out he stopped at the bar and asked for a scotch. He didn't care about the drink that was waiting for him at the table. This was a separate room from the part of the restaurant where Iris and Rossoff were sitting.

"Peel?" the bartender said.

Kreg considered just how he wanted this drink to taste. No, he decided.

He drank standing, not at a stool. *All I want, he thought. Not to put it out of my mind. Not that at all. I don't want to do that. But if I could get some perspective on what happened. If I could achieve a view of it. Just some little measure of distance so it isn't all spin and aimless energy.* Perspective, though, would be something different, something related to detachment and a possibility of rest. So no need for any precise knowledge of the actual event, the actual taking place, as it had in fact happened, of that one of the possible versions of Adam's death.

In fact, or for instance . . . he (Kreg) had been in his office. Adam had gone back to the apartment on West End Avenue (he had begun to divide his time between Jane Street and his father's place). Kreg took Van Atta's call. *You have to get him out of there Van Atta said with nothing personal in his voice. I can't control him so get him to go someplace for a while. . . .* Or maybe no call at all. Maybe only Adam's sudden view around a corner or a glimpse out of the window of Rossoff's apartment. And then his heart starting to pound and the quick run for an alley or some back way out.

Kreg hunched over the bar.

"Fuck it. You had to bump me," the man next to him said.

Kreg said he was sorry for that.

"You're sorry," the man said. He rubbed his fingers over the wet outside of his shot glass. Then he rubbed them together. Square-faced, neat, with a starched collar and a tight knot to his tie. He was wearing the kind of black glasses you couldn't see through and looking at Kreg but not exactly head-on. "I'm talking to you," he said. "You look when someone's talkin to you. And look at where the fuck you're bumpin everybody."

"I'd better get you another," Kreg said.

"I don't want you buyin me any goddamn drinks," the man said. "Just why don't you keep the hell away, you can't control your goddamn elbows?" He was still facing slightly away from Kreg, his head angled just a bit toward the window at the end of the bar. Winter light coming in.

Then Kreg heard the growl and looked down and saw the dog. The bartender was starting to mop the spill. *Blind.* He mouthed the word at Kreg. "Kind of a little bit of a mess we got here," he said to the man. "I think this calls for a little replacement. We let the house take this one."

"You let any careless son-of-a-bitch get away with it," the man said, "you wind up, they walk all over you."

The bartender winked at Kreg, who remembered him as a teenager bussing tables. He belonged to the family who owned the place. He probably had some recollection of Kreg as a kind of regular. An old-timer here.

There was room at the other end of the bar and he motioned for Kreg to go there. "You got it, Mr. Havens," he said to the blind man. "I know what you mean."

Kreg moved. He only wanted a few minutes alone. He didn't want Iris and Rossoff to start wondering where he was.

He was thinking about Adam in flight. In flight again.

Adam rented a car. He was the only customer in the place. One of the Avis girls was on the phone and the other one went into the garage when he came into the office. The one on the phone was a tall blonde with high cheekbones and very clean hair. She was talking to Jonathan at the other end. Southern softness to her voice. But everything started so late on the weekends and she was going to be dead in the morning. Two syllables to dead. Day-ed. Me too, Adam thought. I'll be day-ed too. That big fucker with the cropped hair is going to bust in here with a .45 in his hand and start to bang away. Adam was sweating. He knew he didn't look his appealing best.

He was tapping his American Express card on the side of the counter and the girl sent disapproving rays in the direction of the offending plastic. Screw you, Adam thought. Your daddy runs the Aetna agency in Corinth, Mississippi, and you went to Ole Miss and got speared by guys who couldn't make the tennis team. . . . Hans Kalb was three blocks away, homing in on Avis. One hand in a bulging coat pocket. . . . Certainly.

Now, the girl said, when she was ready for Adam.

The full insurance, Adam said. And he was going out of state and he was the only driver.

The girl started. Did he want the full insurance? She took two short calls while she was completing the form. When she was finished, she looked suspiciously at the Amex card itself. . . . Hans Kalb was a half block away. Kalb was outside now. Waiting for him to come out the door or even just to turn.

Adam blasted out of the city with his collar up and his dark glasses on. Not aware or not caring that the house in the country was closed, cold, waterless, he headed there as if it were safe for him.

How closely, Kreg was thinking, had Hans Kalb really followed? How had he known or guessed that the country was where Adam would go?

Adam parked there, at the house. He found the key that was always behind a shutter on the back porch and went in that way. Into the kitchen with the farm table at which he'd eaten baby food and later sometimes done his homework. In his teens he'd had a great passion for BLTs and he made them there on that table. He looked at a circular burn mark in the wood. He didn't remember what it was they'd been arguing about, he and his father. But he remembered the argument itself. And the iron skillet in his hand. Two pot holders around the handle. Smell of the cooked bacon. He'd put the skillet down. He knew it would burn the wood. He'd walked out of the house with his father shouting after him to come back.

Kreg over the years would remind himself to sand out the burn mark but he never got around to doing that.

Adam went upstairs. His collection of college pennants still tacked to his bedroom walls. Eight or ten of them. Harvard, Iowa, UCLA. No theme to the assortment. Before he was into his teens he was already saying they were childish but he never took them down. His iron farm bed had cost possibly five dollars. Now they were selling them on Columbus Avenue. Also those patchwork quilts. Susan would have gotten the quilt. He'd had it as far back as he could remember. He always called his mother Susan, although never Philip to his father. Cold now. Adam crossed his arms, hands to the opposite elbows. He could see his breath in the room.

Nate Hobart gave him lunch, stew that he had left over and rye bread. He told Adam how you made the stew. Sear the beef in kidney fat before you cook it, that gave it a deeper flavor.

Shit, Nate said. You really did it. I mean you really got your young butt in a royal sling. The black shepherd stretched on the floor. Nate reached down and pulled at the fur behind the dog's ear.

Didn't I? Adam said.

Nate would tell you that you'd fucked up or how to raise the grain before the final sanding by wetting a piece of wood you were refinishing. When you were old enough, he showed you how to put a new edge on a chisel. But he didn't tell you you were good or bad. He just didn't talk that way.

Stay over, Nate said. Best place for you. He won't come here.

Maybe he will.

I don't think so, Nate said. And if he does, we'll kill his ass. He jerked a thumb toward the closet where he kept his guns. Adam knew where they were. Nate curled his lip over his teeth. Bust his ass, he said.

In the middle of the afternoon Adam borrowed a pair of boots. Too big for him but he was able to get around. He went back to the house but this time not inside. He walked to the road and admired the house from the front, the lovely white cube with the honey-colored wood of the front door, original fanlight over the door. Then he went into the barn and he walked behind it to the edge of the cleared property. Low ground there with a tangle of some kind of briar at the edge. He wasn't going to try to push through that. Every year a path had to be chopped out, once in the spring and then again at least a touch-up during the summer.

Although this wasn't nostalgia time.

But what else besides remember was he going to do with himself? He could be here for days. There would be Nate's library and Nate's whisky and little walks around the property. At night go into town to a movie. What the hell else was there?

"Get yourself outside of that," the bartender said. He put another scotch in front of Kreg. Kreg reached in his pocket and the man shook his head. "Catch you double next time," he said. Kreg swallowed what was in the other glass and the bartender took that away. He spoke to the blind man who made some answer that Kreg couldn't hear. Only the rasp of the voice itself. The man tilted his face again in Kreg's direction. Black circles of his glasses, deep etch of line from the nostrils to the corners of his mouth. Sniff out the enemy.

. . .

"Maybe you should go in there," Iris said.

"I think I should leave him alone. I'm sure he would prefer that."

"I don't know."

"Yes," Rosoff said. "We should probably let him be. That's the best."

Iris said all right about not going to check on Kreg. But not the best, she said. It wasn't the best.

Kreg faced into his drink. This one here and one waiting for him back at the table. That was nice. Maybe Iris would have to drive the rest of the way. She'd offered, hadn't she? He drank half his drink. He was trying to get it straight in his mind about Adam. How painful, how frightening had it been? Possibly not too bad. Only moments really of terror. The brief chase and then the heavy numbing thwack into the stomach of Kalb's shot. A long-barreled .38. Kalb had had that and he'd had a Magnum. But the Magnum wasn't used. He never fired it. At first, when you were shot that way, there was no sensation. The impact usually knocked you down. But you were *numbed.* So Kreg had read and that was the point on which to concentrate.

Go back.

Adam was in front of the house. He was looking west across the road and across a field. He was looking at the late sky and the heavy clouds and the complex articulation of trees, bushes, fences seen at that distance and that made the landscape in front of him. Black lines and masses under a weak light. A walker passed. Every once in a while a car.

Then the tan Mercedes was in the drive. The little two-seater, the convertible model. Adam had seen it and paid no attention. A car like that hadn't seemed a threat. What he'd been watching for was a sedan. Bigger, darker. This thing had loafed amiably along the road (only peripherally noted). Then the sudden accelerating turn into the driveway. Squeal of tires. Before that there hadn't been any noise.

The car was between Adam and the house.

Everything he felt was in his stomach and his legs. If he could move his legs. . . . He began to try to run. Hans Kalb was yelling and coming after him. Adam, he was yelling. Adam. I get you, little boy. Kalb shot at him. He had to get away but he couldn't get too far ahead. He had to know that Kalb was behind him. If Kalb stayed back and waited. . . . You could come around a corner and find him there. He was wearing Nate's boots and they were too big. They made him clumsy. . . . It was funny. Even in the stormeye of his panic, he knew it was funny. The clumsiness. An old home movie in black and white. A grainy print, streaky. Not real. Only a knee slapper. He was laughing and running. Because they were so funny, running around the funny house in the funny snow. These big boots he was wearing. Come on, Adam, Kalb called. I want you, Adam.

If you could see this scene from across the road, black shapes in the failing light. Adam began to hear other sounds, noises from around the house. Nate's dog. Shots.

Kreg didn't finish his drink. He saw that the television set at the end of the bar was tuned to a news show. Last night he had seen a full thirty-second spot of his own house and his barn and yard . . . and of the *site.* He didn't want anything more like that. He put down some money and started to move off. Waved one hand to the bartender. The blind man, Havens, certainly sensed him leaving. Some stiffening in the man's back when Kreg passed him.

Then it was quiet. Adam began to move slowly. Possibly he could get to his car. Now he was between the back of the house and the barn. No sound anymore. Nothing from Nate or the black dog. His own tracks here. His or Kalb's. He began to edge forward. . . . And then there was noise behind him. And it was Nate. Because that was who it had to be. And he turned and it was not Nate there.

Kreg turned the corner into the main room of the restaurant.

Leaving Kreg alone, Iris was saying, might be best in the circumstances. "But that's not the best at all. It's different. It's not the same thing." She saw Kreg coming into the room. Without her glasses it wasn't a good distance for her. But as he appeared, he might have been any kind of big purposeful man. Even a happy jolly one. "Ship under sail," she said.

"Still floating," Rossoff said. "Not sunk yet."

"Not for now," Iris said.

During the few days the story lived, Hans Kalb was described by the newspapers and on television as a Colombian businessman with interests, worldwide, in a range of industrial and financial enterprises. He was said to have been prominently connected with certain conservative groups and it was usually mentioned that he was of German descent (as Adam had conceived him to be). Adam's connection to Van Atta and Frankel was played up because he had worked for them and they had been named in several investigations of organized crime. Van Atta had never been charged, but years before, Frankel had been convicted twice in New Jersey on assault charges in connection with labor disputes in the meat business.

Kreg himself was treated sympathetically as the scholar-attorney father of a son gone wrong.

The detective from the district attorney's office in Connecticut called. He reviewed Kreg's statement. Was that all correct? Maybe there was something else that had come to mind? Or papers that had turned up or someone asking about Adam?

No, Kreg said. He asked about the man in the office with them that day. "He was with the government, I assume? Federal?"

"What's the point to that?" the detective said. "Forget him. He wasn't there." Then he said, "Tell me. You. How you gettin along? You makin it?"

"I'm sitting up," Kreg said. "Taking nourishment."

. . .

He relocated two blocks from his former office. He rented from a partnership of seven or eight men, about the size of the firm he'd left. He paid a fixed amount that included his secretary's salary, plus something over for his long-distance calls and any unusual expenses. His office was half the size of the one he'd had. He was able to make do but never lost the feeling of being cramped for space.

He stayed busy. There was the work of the Foundation. And now the need to invest the funds it had got for its Brandt Systems stock. Soon after Marcu consolidated his acquisition of Brandt he did send for Kreg. Not a surprise but what Kreg had not expected was that Marcu would seem embarrassed by what he so evidently wanted to do.

Kreg had almost no other corporate work but his appellate practice began to expand. This was on a referral basis, briefs and motions. He had always liked the research that went into appellate briefs and also enjoyed being on his feet to argue them. He thought that usually he huffed and puffed to some pretty fair advantage. The small practitioners who referred the work to him knew they weren't qualified to handle it. "Hey," one lawyer said. "I do contracts and I get you out of jail or I sue you. Get you a divorce, you're no longer compatible. Meat and potatoes, you know. A *theoretical* issue, though, that's not home cooking anymore." But the work he did came easily enough to Kreg. He was using only some small portion of his energies . . . and knowing that was in some way satisfying to him, comforting. He wasn't sure why this was so but he did on occasion recall that he'd had a feeling almost of relief at his last meeting with Marcu.

Once he met Frank Roth on the street and they had a pleasant-enough five minutes together. Roth of course had attended Adam's funeral.

He spent less time in the office than he'd used to. Especially in the evenings. He didn't like being alone in a small place and the library wasn't what he was accustomed to. Later he worked at the Bar Association or at home. At the apartment, he had taken from a drawer a framed picture of Adam as a small boy and set that on his bureau. *Why shouldn't I? he thought. If I didn't, I would only be pretending I don't feel as I do.* He thought about Adam and also quite a bit about Nate Hobart. Sometimes he was a bit drunk when he went to bed. He thought about that too, but not as a tendency that would have to be watched or contained.

In late April there was the closing of the sale of his house in Connecticut and he paid the balance that was owed to Van Atta.

He had dinner with Etkind Rossoff. Rossoff had a sabbatical coming up and said there was a chance of a guest professorship in Siena.

"Do you speak Italian?" Kreg said.

"On my mother's side, they were from Venice."

"You never mentioned that."

Rossoff lifted his shoulders as if he was embarrassed. "No reason," he said. "There was never any reason to talk about it." Maybe now they should order, he said. The roast duck, he thought. Every so often he had a strong desire for roast duck.

"Yes," Kreg said. "The duck and draft pilsner with it." There would have to be someone, he said, to take Rossoff's job at the Foundation for the year he was away. "Maybe a professor from Siena?"

Rossoff said he'd been thinking about that. And he had a few names to suggest. He asked, not giving the question any particular weight, about Iris. How was she doing?

Fine, Kreg said. Fine so far as he knew. "Although really it's been a while." Every few weeks, he called or she called. Twice he had seen her. Once for a concert and once they'd gone to the theater. They were careful together, tentative. Kreg didn't particularly understand why that was so except that it had to do with Adam's death. He was thinking about the sense of shame that could burden a survivor . . . which was something Etkind Rossoff would know about. . . . He wasn't careful or tentative talking to Rossoff. He recalled his thought of some months back that there might again develop some close connection between himself and Iris.

Rossoff said, "You will say hello for me?"

Kreg began to think that the three of them might not meet again. Why would they? What would be the occasion? Rossoff when he was with Kreg would always ask about Iris and send his regards to her. And Iris, if she and Kreg continued to see each other, might once in a while think to mention the little professor. "Yes," he said. "Of course I'll say hello."

Some months went by and it got well into the summer. Kreg had thought several times about calling Iris and each time decided against it, although not by way of rejection. Adjournment, postponement, deferral were terms that might have come to a lawyer's mind.

Then Iris called him. "I'm taking a week off," she said.

"You'll go to Connecticut?" Kreg began to recall the shapes and contours of the countryside there . . . and to consider that he himself had not been out of the city this summer.

"Actually not," Iris said. It seemed she had the use of a house in East Hampton, near the beach on Georgica Lane. The place belonged to a colleague from the office, a bachelor vice-president who was off to London to do a job for their affiliate there. She mentioned a name and Kreg recalled a tall humorous man whom he'd met several times at her house.

It was a matter of noxious stuff, Iris was saying, in an age of concern for the environment. The client was a chemical company and even Liverpool wasn't welcoming its new plant. Possibly American techniques of persuasion would be effective. Iris doubted they would. . . . But the point was the man would be away and he'd offered her his house. . . . Shingles, roses, near the beach . . . a tiny place. And she hadn't been out there for how many years. So why not? This once? A change. She could close Connecticut for a couple of weeks. Or Kreg could use it if he liked.

A change. Kreg had thought of a change. He'd considered briefly cruises, resorts. But there was really no impetus toward either. He'd imagined conversations with trim alert widows in shorts, himself in linen pants and a shirt with epaulets.

"Or maybe," Iris went on, "you'd rather be at the shore?"

He made some foolish remark about the two of them cooped up in a small place.

"It's not *that* small," she said. "Two bedrooms, if that's on your mind. . . . What I'm saying is, maybe you'd like to come out there for a couple of days."

A Thursday afternoon in August. Kreg was seen by Sam Marion and John Tamamura who were looking for a toy store on Main Street in East Hampton. Tamamura had promised his youngest niece a present from the East Coast. He thought he might find something here.

In June Marcu had bid fifty-six for GT Industries. He still thought of it as Grissom-Talbot which was the name on most of the reports he read. He got the company for sixty-three in July and began to integrate this new operation with what he already had. He arranged a few days at Gurney's for a dozen of the senior people . . . so these men could get to know each other. No meetings and no agenda. He himself stayed at the house in Southampton. It was an easy drive back and forth and he was more comfortable there. On the last day he would have them all to his place for a buffet luncheon and an afternoon on the lawn . . . where he was now with Claire. She said the arrangements for his party had been taken care of and it would all be very nice, a lovely afternoon for the people from his company.

Sam Marion arranged guest privileges at Maidstone and he'd played today with Tamamura. They were both golfers and each of them had spotted the other as a comer, maybe a future contender for some top position. Someone to get to know.

They were talking about the four-hundred-yard, par-four ninth hole. Beautiful, the way it doglegged past the brush-covered dunes. View of the water. Sam Marion had bogeyed the hole and Tamamura had made it in par.

"Nice, though, isn't it?" Sam Marion was saying.

"Kind of great," John Tamamura said. "That's all. . . . But I tell you," he said. "I want you to come out some time. In the spring. You drive down to the desert and play La Quinta. You get the light and that time of year flowers all over the place."

"Terrific course?"

"The best," Tamamura said. "Where is this store?"

"We're going to find a store. Someplace where you can buy a doll."

"Not anything. This is special. It's a rock and roll Barbie." Tamamura looked into a pocket notebook. "Barbie and Rocker," he said. . . . And he had something else on his mind. Marcu, he said to Sam Marion. What was it like working with Marcu?

"It's only a few months. All right, I think."

"Because the way he aced out Bronheim. They were close, as I understand it. I know he expected to stay on the Board. And then the deal was closed and it's bye-bye and thank you for your resignation. It makes you wonder about him a little."

"I think that was different," Marion said. "I think it was personal." He looked into the doorway of a big stationer's that might have a toy department in back. "Here," he said. "We can try this place."

John Tamamura was thinking about Julie. He would be working out of New York now and it was tempting to consider bringing her East with him. But he knew he wasn't going to do that. Julie was somebody else who would be aced out. "Or they can tell us where else to get it," he said.

Sam Marion looked for a moment across the street and that was when he saw Kreg. Kreg was wearing a long-billed cap and khakis and a washed-out blue polo shirt. No tan. He was with a woman and was carrying a bag of groceries. Marion recalled a scene from the television news of some months back. Kreg, at the time of his son's death, pushing through a cluster of reporters. A woman in a raincoat with him, perhaps this woman. . . . Marion had the impression now of a warship . . . overgunned and awkward to handle, not effective against the new class of opponent. The woman did have a tan. As best Marion could tell at that distance, she was attractive. Attractive for her age, he thought, although somewhat too thin.

He didn't say anything to John Tamamura who had not followed his gaze or noticed the big-bellied man and who now turned into the store. "I'll bet they have it," Sam Marion said. "Your lucky day."

. . .

Marcu in the late afternoon used twenty free minutes to work over a draft of his quarterly report.

> The addition of Brandt Systems, including its Kyber division, and GT Industries to our family of companies will strengthen our existing capabilities and will also propel us into exciting new areas of technology.

He read through and initialed at the end. Approved. He ticked off in his mind the assets under his control, the actual manufacturing facilities, equipment, real estate, patents and the dollar symbols for each of them. He considered his grip on them. . . . It was going to be the kind of cool evening you sometimes get after mid-August, probably too cool to drive comfortably in an open car. He had looked forward to the run from Southampton to Gurney's, through the flat rich landscape of the area, with the sense and sometimes a view of the ocean to his right and the heat of the late sun on his head and on his shoulders and arms.

After dinner Kreg sat with Iris in the screened porch to the side of the house. He was in a swing chair for two, suspended by chains from the ceiling. Iris in a wicker armchair faced him kitty-corner from the end of the porch. They looked quietly into the small neat yard with its hydrangea bushes and small trees. Russian olives and Korean pine were at the perimeter, placed so this house was effectively isolated from its near neighbor. You couldn't see or hear the ocean but you could smell it.

It was about nine-thirty. Even with a sweater, Kreg occasionally shivered. He'd been in the sun during the day and his skin was sensitive to the change in temperature . . . a minor admonition from a regulatory system of the body.

Iris was wearing an Irish fisherman's knit cardigan that he remembered from years back and had her arms crossed in a self-hug over her chest. Now she made a brrr sound and said why didn't they go for a short stroll and then pack it in so far as the outdoors was concerned. Kreg was pleased at the *expectedness* of this. In the country she always took a walk at night.

There were the cozy lights from inside the houses of this relatively populated area so you didn't get the almost absolute blackness of the rural Connecticut night. Kreg twisted his neck to see the Big Dipper and the North Star. That he didn't really know the stars except for those had always seemed to him a deficiency to be corrected. After they'd been walking for a few minutes he stopped shivering. "Listen," Iris said before they turned back. He did and now could hear the sound of the sea. For a few minutes they stayed there hearing the beat and fall of waves against the shore. Kreg looked up again. He was remembering a telescope he'd bought when Adam for a few weeks wanted to be an astronomer. The telescope had been kept in the country house and of course had gone with the other things there.

Then they walked back.

Inside there was most of the last bottle of a white burgundy they'd had with the fish stew Iris had made. A faint pleasing aftertaste of the meal was still in his mouth.

Iris held back a yawn. "We could make a fire," she said, "except we might not last to see it."

"I don't think we would." If ever again, he was thinking, he were to look for a weekend place, it might be one like this. Near the ocean, where there were more people and where it was more contained, easier, it seemed to him. Then he had a moment of weightlessness, no plan or will, as if held in a long period of fatigue and lassitude. He didn't know if, as he was, he was his real self or not.

Iris, seven or eight feet across this tidy small room from him, caught his eye. She drank some wine. "Do you like it here?" she said.

Kreg realized he'd have to begin thinking more in terms of what he liked and what he wanted. "Of course," he said. "Of course I do."

"I mean, really," she said. "Do you? Do you really?"